THE

❋❋❋❋❋❋❋❋

Alka Seltzer sex . . . love with the improper stranger . . . sex toys hiding in the medicine cabinet . . . women wrestling in the sand . . . erogenous zones where you least expect them. When a taboo kept consenting adults from indulging their pleasure, *Penthouse* was there to shatter it—and the party never stopped. These are the letters and the moments that started it all, still as sexy and surprising as *Penthouse* readers can make it.

OTHER BOOKS IN THE SERIES

Erotica from Penthouse
More Erotica from Penthouse
Erotica from Penthouse III
Letters to Penthouse I
Letters to Penthouse II
Letters to Penthouse III
Letters to Penthouse IV
Letters to Penthouse V
Letters to Penthouse VI
Letters to Penthouse VII
Letters to Penthouse VIII
Letters to Penthouse IX
Letters to Penthouse X
Letters to Penthouse XI
Letters to Penthouse XII
26 Nights: A Sexual Adventure
Penthouse Uncensored

ATTENTION: SCHOOLS AND CORPORATIONS
WARNER books are available at quantity discounts with bulk purchase for educational, business, or sales promotional use. For information, please write to: SPECIAL SALES DEPARTMENT, WARNER BOOKS, 1271 AVENUE OF THE AMERICAS, NEW YORK, NY 10020

LETTERS TO PENTHOUSE I

THERE'S NOTHING LIKE THE FIRST TIME...

EDITED BY EDWARD SPRINGER

WARNER BOOKS

A Time Warner Company

If you purchase this book without a cover you should be aware that this book may have been stolen property and reported as "unsold and destroyed" to the publisher. In such case neither the author nor the publisher has received any payment for this "stripped book."

WARNER BOOKS EDITION

Copyright © 1976 by Penthouse Press, Ltd.
All rights reserved. No part of this publication may be reproduced, stored in a retrieval system, or transmitted, by any form or by any means, electronic, mechanical, photocopying, recording or otherwise, without prior written permission of the publisher.

This Warner Books Edition is published by arrangement with
Penthouse Press, Ltd.

Warner Books, Inc.
1271 Avenue of the Americas
New York, N.Y. 10020

Visit our Web site at
www.warnerbooks.com

 A Time Warner Company

Printed in the United States of America

First Warner Books Printing: July, 1977

Reissued: February, 1980

Contents

	Introduction	7
1.	Marriage Beds	13
2.	Penis Size	69
3.	Breast Size	85
4.	Incest	91
5.	Fighting Females	99
6.	Enemas	107
7.	Masturbation	147
8.	Circumcision, Male & Female	152
9.	Aesthetics of the Vagina	159
10.	Spanking	167
11.	Navels	207
12.	Shaving Pubic Hair	211
13.	The World of Amputee Sex	222
14.	Autofellatio	285
15.	Potpourri	287

Introduction

Perhaps the greatest shift in awareness in our time has been the movement away from blind acceptance of authority. This reaction against self-appointed experts and leaders has almost invariably taken the form of violent revolution in the past but, occasionally, as with the Quietist approach in ancient China, large numbers of people have simply, without fanfare, turned their backs on the political, economic, psychological, religious and educational hierarchies. In America, especially since the beatniks began their much publicized technique of dropping-out and with the amplification of that idea by the hippies of the sixties, greater and greater pressure to disengage has been felt. The traditional organizations, the government, the church, the state educational systems, have all lost their power to mesmerize and compel people to follow their dictates.

Of course, nature abhors a vacuum, and a legion of new forces have rushed forward to fill the void. The central struggle in our time is in the hearts and minds of the people themselves. Will we take this chance to throw off the shackles of authoritarian thought as it is manifested in our social institutions, or will we succumb to the next historical wave of new groups promising salvation, replacing Christianity with Scientology, Capitalism with Socialism, the Pope with the Guru, and the politician with the therapist?

This question is as pointed in the area of eroticism as in any other. At the beginning of the century, if one wanted to know what was "normal" one went to the marriage manuals. There, some self-annointed expert translated his (it was always a man) personal prejudices into objective-sounding language, bolstered his viewpoint with carefully selected case histories, threw in a smattering of two-bit scientific jargon, and came to conclusions which augmented his private inclinations and basic assumptions.

Perhaps the single strongest breakthrough in overthrowing that kind of thinking was the publication of the Kinsey Report. Here, for the first time, we learned what people actually did, and not what someone thought they should be doing. Moreover, these were not bizarre examples from the psychiatrist's office, but instances of everyday, average people who came from all walks of life. The Report, in a quiet way, told us that what we knew all along was indeed true . . . that we did indulge in homosexuality, masturbation, adultery, mate swapping, and a host of practices which the "authorities" assured us were perverse. A great many people began to ask the unsettling question: If millions upon millions of us are involved in a certain practice and are enjoying it, why should we be concerned about the condemnation of a few stuffy men who write thick, dull books promulgating their prejudices?

The Report, however, did have several drawbacks, most of them linked to the fact that it was a pioneer effort coming out at a time when even to talk openly about sexual practices was considered extraordinarily risque. As a social scientist, and a good one for his time, Kinsey went to great lengths to avoid value judgments, good or bad. He wanted only to report the facts as he saw them. The unfortunate result, however, was to cast a dim pall over the entire Survey, giving it the feel of exposing our dirty laundry, showing us something we ought to be ashamed of. In the context in which it appeared, its dry neutrality paradoxically suggested a form of prurience.

The thrust toward erotic liberty gathered momentum until, in the late sixties, the doors were blown off most of the closets in the nation. At that point, millions and millions of people were willing and anxious to state that their practices were not only existent but actually sources of pride and joy. They were willing to speak not only to men doing a survey in which their identities would remain masked, but to newspapers and on television and to their friends and neighbors. They were no longer willing to accept the cultural straitjacket which labeled everything outside a narrow arc of behavior as sick. Homosexuals, sadomasochists, transvestites, orgiasts, swingers, bisexuals all begin to march and demonstrate, demanding that they be recognized in their full humanity.

This was the point at which we hung in a fine balance. Were we indeed going to go forth as a people, secure enough to allow ourselves the widest range of possible erotic behavior, no one condemning the person next door, with the only criterion being mutual consent between adults? Or would we allow ourselves to slide into a new form of control? Those who would assume command of the revolution wasted no time in showing themselves. The old morality having been overthrown, there was a scramble to define the new. Into the breech jumped the "sexperts", the exact same people as their nineteenth century counterparts, but now preaching compulsory liberation the way their forebears had promulgated strict observance of puritanical standards.

In the midst of all this, a very few voices were raised to remind us to maintain a basic sanity, not to cling to dead cultural modes nor to blindly embrace the latest fads, but rather to look within ourselves and know who we are and what we want, and then to live that out, neither defending our positions nor attacking those of others. And in the forefront of this relatively tiny contingent of sensible voices was *Penthouse* Magazine.

Through its philosophy of enlightened *laissez-faire*, *Penthouse* projected an aura of erotic liberty which was based on self-knowledge and responsibility. It published scores of articles in which every possible variation on the sex act was gone into, and presented from the inside, that is, experientially and not judgementally. It was as though the editors were saying, "Here's what's available, here's what's possible, here are some of the pluses and some of the minuses, now go ahead and decide for yourself."

A major vehicle for the development of this approach was *Penthouse* Forum, the letters section, the most salient of which are presented in this volume. Here, *Penthouse* arrived at the ultimate in pure reflection on what people are actually doing and how they feel about it. This is the final development away from the dogmatic tomes of the eighteen hundreds, and that which provides the crucial element missing even from the liberating impact of the Kinsey Report—the element of individual response to his or her behavior.

All previous surveys have at best given some idea of what people are doing, but have left out all indications of what they are deriving from their actions. Whether something is pleasurable or painful, whether it creates difficulties in life or opens up new lifestyles, whether it produces guilt or jealousy, and how one came to it and whether one is happy with it, are crucial questions. Since people get into different erotic scenes in a search for pleasure or fulfillment or meaning, leaving out that aspect of sexual activity seems a mammoth failure of reportage.

But in these letters, people not only tell what they do, but why, and what the results are. The advantage of this is stupendous for the reader. In the same way that millions of Americans breathed a sigh of relief upon reading the statistics of Kinsey's report, learning that they were not alone in some practices they might have been ashamed of, here millions can give a shout of joy that almost everything is out of the closet. Not only that a lot of us do things that we have traditionally been told are unnatural, but that we can enjoy them, grow more wise and healthy through them, and have more fruitful relationships because of them.

In this collection, for example, something is gone into that had previously been the source of bad jokes and intense shame: sex among and with amputees. Here, this entire area of human drama surfaces not as an aberration or embarrassment, but as a rich and marvelous example of the power of the human spirit to transcend the limitations of the body. To think that tens of thousands of people had been condemning themselves to loveless lives because they had lost a limb or even two, and have found a path to erotic fulfillment through reading about others like themselves who have discovered a way to discount their physical condition, is itself enough to give these letters inestimable worth.

Among other practices that are rarely spoken about, even in much of the erotic literature, but which, judging by these letters, are very widespread, are spanking, enemas and shaving pubic hair. In this collection, people come out and speak plainly about their desires, feelings and practices. Worries about penis size, breast size, and the pros and cons of circumcision, both for men and women, all make their appearance.

Have you ever been turned on to the navel as an erogenous zone? Don't be surprised. Some of the letters deal with that subject. Have you ever wondered about shaving your pubic hair? Don't be ashamed. It's practically a fad. Are you married and involved in things that you have been taught married couples just don't do? Well, more than 15% of the letters are from husbands and wives who do just about everything, from classic monogamy to huge orgies. The subject of incest also comes to light, and most of the reports state that sex between brothers and sisters, and even between mother and son, doesn't have to be traumatic or horrible, that it can be a beautiful human experience.

Again, in no way is any specific practice put forth or touted or condemned. These letters are simply a mirror, a way for us to look at ourselves in as comprehensive a manner as possible.

As editor, of course, I had my own prejudices and

thought that certain categories should be represented which don't show up here, or was negative toward some of the material that did. But I realized two things: first, this volume of letters is meant to represent the erotic activity of the people at large, and not the predilections of just one person. And second, I found my own erotic horizons expanding because I was forced to explore areas of experience that I might ordinarily have dismissed as not being important or interesting. Editing these letters was an education, and like any true education, it was also entertaining, moving and challenging.

This book may be the most liberating erotic experience you may have ever received. It truly represents the sexual state of the nation.

Edward Springer

1

Marriage Beds

Many years ago I found I was playing second fiddle to a real live, beautiful and buxom neighbor in the important wifely function of building my man's hard-ons. Our marriage had started much like most. We met at a college dance back in the days when you danced cheek to cheek and belly to belly, holding your partner close as your legs slid in and out together to romantic music in a dimly-lit hall. He had a terrific erection that was soon boring against my girlish vulva. For once, I didn't pull away or pretend to ignore it, but decided to grind back as lewdly as I knew how at that age, just 19, and I whispered in his ear that he felt "just marvelous and so big". Naturally, he asked me for a date the next night. I gave him my address and also told him I hoped he would bring "his big friend". He did just that, and though we went to a movie, we were soon petting intensely, left early and drove to a lover's lane where we had our first sex with each other, almost as soon as we arrived and turned the lights out. When we "came up for air," we sat smoking and drinking whiskey, and I began to giggle at my boldness of the night before. My wandering hands began petting him again until he had another hard, and then we had even better sex. This was a definite change from my usual pattern of behavior. I was not a virgin, several times over, but I had never taken such overt actions.

We married 2½ months later. Our honeymoon was sex, sex, sex day and night. I would greet him at the door with a French kiss and unzip his fly before he let me down, so I could stroke his penis and feel it jump to life in my fingers, even if we didn't fall into bed immediately. This idyllic period lasted a year and a half till he graduated. Then we moved to another city and our sex relations were heavenly whenever we had them, but the frequency was far less. We rarely did it two nights in a row, and sometimes would go almost a week without finding the time or the inclination.

Two things happened to open my eyes. First, my sister and I overheard our husbands talking together when they didn't know we were around. The men were on our apartment balcony when our neighbor came out in a sunsuit. She was a really stunning gal, a few years older than me, a redhead (dyed, but a good job), with a pair of at least 40 inch honeydews straining her thin cotton halter almost to splitting, as well as practically spilling out of the deep-cut neckline. I heard my husband tell my brother-in-law this neighbor was always giving him a hard-on and my sister's husband replied he was a "tit man" too. He asked my guy if he ever got a "piece of that" and my guy said no, but he would like to. He grumbled I almost never gave him a hard-on any more and my brother-in-law said my sister was "getting too settled down" and was always "acting like a wife." Were we girls surprised and mad! We sneaked out of the house and went for a long ride to talk things over.

While thinking about how I had failed to remain sexy, I began to realize that we were doing so many things for the community and the church, we weren't leaving time for a decent sex life. I knew the next move was up to me. I dispensed with girdles, which I hadn't really needed and began to buy sexy French undies from mail order houses. I got dozens of naughty panties, wicked bras with holes for my nipples to poke through and tiny ribbony garter belts and I would give him a show at least once a week. My nighties were for wear around the house or all day at weekends and not for in bed, of course. I might wear just a sheer slip to cook dinner in or any other "costume" I could get into, to keep his interest up and his penis, too.

Also, I began to insist we go to bed earlier. We had been staying up till nearly 12 o'clock, but I began leading him into the bedroom at 9 pm, before we were too tired to play. Which we did with the lights on, as in our first year of marriage. This has been our pattern ever since and there are darned few nights when we don't have sex, even though we're now 44 and 46. We gave up the idea of having children because we thought our sex pleasure was more important. I am positive my husband has never had relations with another woman since the day I overheard him talking about the redhead.

I am careful to tell my man if another guy gets hard looking at me and this always pleases, and stiffens, him. I also smooch him shamelessly at movies, cocktail parties, even back in lover's lanes once in a while and don't give a damn who knows it or thinks I am making a fool of myself. I like what he has in his pants and *that's* what I am a fool about. I have even taken hula and bellydance lessons so I can keep him erect. I have bought him girlie magazines and sent away for nude photo sets and porny films. *I* introduced *him* to Penthouse. I watch for sexy things to call to his attention. If I see a well-stacked type coming along, I nudge him and point out the jiggling yummies with a man-type ribald comment.

I have made a career of building my husband's hardons. I am sure we have missed some things other people value because of our concentration on sex, but this has been right for us. When we explain to friends why we seem antisocial or disinterested in sports or the theater and tell them "Our hobby is sex" in a half-kidding tone, we usually get a laugh, if nothing more. Some think I must be a nymphomaniac, others feel I am a little vulgar in flaunting my curves so obviously or otherwise offending their ideas of propriety. I have even been accused of trying to outdo today's college-age kids, which is a laugh since my interest is just one penis, not any convenient or available one. A few friends have dropped us when the wife thought I was deliberately turning on her husband. But many women tell me they envy my sex life and wish they could "get away" with my lack of inhibitions, enthusiastic emphasis on bed activity and determination to monopolize my husband erotically. I tell them to let themselves go and I am quite sure some have done so, even after years of lukewarm married sex.

One question I am always proud to answer is whether I can still give him a hard-on night after night. Of course the answer is yes. We may have slowed down a bit from 20 years ago, but neither of us has thoughts of sex with others. Unlike pornography, the real thing never gets old and dull for us. When you have sex so often, there never is any problem about lack of staying power, premature ejaculation or an "unready" wife, believe me. It's the daily habit that counts. We think it's my job as the wife to give him hard-ons, but we both have the fun of working them off. So, I say, women of America and England, here's to the greatest of God's gifts, the husbandly hard-on.—*Mrs. G.T.C. (name and address withheld), Glen Burnie, Md.*

* * *

While vacationing in California last summer, my husband and I became curious about the many ads in tabloid newspapers for nude models and decided to answer one just to satisfy our curiosity. We phoned one of the numbers given and were told to report as a couple to the studio. We arrived and were greeted by a receptionist and told to wait in the tiny and rather dingy lobby. Then she ushered us into the studio, which consisted of some cameras, lights and a large bed with a purple spread. The photographer looked us over, asked us if we had done any modeling before, told us the fee and said we could get started at once. He instructed me to sit on the bed and said he would begin taking the pictures as I took my clothes off. He took several shots each time I removed an article of clothing. When I was totally nude, he told me how to pose, and I assumed different positions that emphasized different areas of my body.

After this had gone on for some time, he told my husband to disrobe and join me on the bed. Watching me pose in the nude had given my husband an erection, but the photographer said he wanted the photographs while my husband's penis was relaxed so we took a break, during which we were offered coffee by the receptionist. Still nude, my husband and I chatted with the receptionist for several minutes, during which time my husband achieved the desired appearance.

We resumed the session with the two of us on the bed and were given a variety of poses to strike, most of them being some sort of sexual foreplay. Finally I was instructed to simulate fellatio on my husband, which I did while finding it difficult to hold myself back from making it the real thing. By the time the photo taking was over, both my husband and I were in such a state of arousal that we had to force ourselves to put our clothes on. We accepted our pay (which we were later told by others was below the standard rate) and hurried back to our motel room, where we spent most of the day. We have since obtained a copy of the magazine with our photos in it and needless to say we find leafing through it a very arousing experience, which is usually followed by intense lovemaking.—*Mrs. J.N. (name withheld), Racine, Wis.*

* * *

My husband and I have been readers of Penthouse for the last year. We find it candid and refreshing, especially the Forum letters pertaining to the sexual exploits of married couples. Our marriage has lasted 20 years; I married at 18 and am still considered by both sexes an attractive woman. About ten years ago, I found that I preferred fellatio to all other forms of sex. I received no argument from my husband on this score. However, with three children in the house, ages 13 to 18, we find it difficult to get together when the urge strikes us. I service him nightly and sometimes in the a.m., but it's difficult with breakfast, school lunches and bus schedules, etc. Saturdays are often a waste with the kids running in and out.

We have taken to driving into the country on Sundays where I perform fellatio while he drives slowly down a deserted road. We have both found this to be exciting and stimulating. Because of the distance, we have recently used the huge parking lots that surround supermarkets. A few weeks ago we were parked not five feet from the sidewalk. All any passersby could see was a lone man sitting behind the steering wheel, presumably awaiting his wife in the store. If they only knew! On the Saturday mornings my husband is required to work, I visit him in the office where he is alone. He locks the office door and drops his trousers while sitting in a swivel chair and I kneel in front of him, take head and go on with my marketing.

Last year I visited relatives on the coast where I had the opportunity to meet four men and orally milk them. A few days after my arrival home I divulged this fact to my husband who became so sexually aroused on hearing of my exploits that I had to blow him twice in 15 minutes! We discussed my proclivity and agreed that twice a month we would go hunting. Telling the children we were going out dancing, we would hit various cocktail lounges and bars. I would strike a conversation with a likely looking prospect and, if he agreed, we would go to the car and while my husband drove, I would go down on my subject in the back seat. Then he would drive while I serviced my husband. It became easier as time went by, first just two men a month; then I found this so exciting we started picking up two men a night twice a month. I give head to my husband while we drive to the hunting area, then again after I finish the first man.

My husband, being a salesman, comes in contact with many men. I asked him to procure some married men as they are clean and won't raise any fuss. We stagger the times when to meet them on given nights. As I always assume a false name, they have no idea we are married.

On these assignations I wear a blouse or sweater and skirt without any underclothes. Once a man finds I'm completely naked underneath he readily becomes rock hard and eager for release.

Last month was a banner one for us. One evening I was feeling horny as hell and contacted three men within two hours. I serviced two of them and my husband twice each. We then drove to a bowling alley where we met one of my husband's clients. He must have stored up for two weeks! I finished him in about ten seconds and he then asked for a 69. I removed my skirt and accommodated him, though I don't care for distractions when I give head. Later, at a bar, my husband met a man he had booked two days earlier. By the time I blew this guy twice, my neck and jaw muscles were getting tired. My husband and I stopped and had a drink together and on the way home I gave him a finale.

During fellatio I come about five times and at the end of that evening I was completely drained. I had received a total of 12 ejaculations and was really spent.
—*Mrs. E.H. (name and address withheld), Milwaukee, Wisc.*

* * *

I have read the letters about bondage and tying up with a great deal of interest, since my wife has developed what I think may be a unique method of keeping me in "check." She used to be in the Woman's Royal Naval Service before I met her, and she had some elementary training in radio and electrical circuitry, but she got the idea from my brother-in-law, who is something of a technical wizard, and owns his own television repair business. Last Christmas, when he came round to visit us, he brought what is sometimes known as a "joy buzzer"— a battery-operated electric-shock machine. He gave us a couple of mild shocks with it, and left it with us, but I thought no more of it until one morning I was woken by a hollow, stinging feeling in my penis. I discovered that my wife had pulled back the blankets as I lay naked in bed, and had wired up my penis in such a way that whenever she touched the wires with a battery which she held in her hand, I got a mild electric "twinge."

The shock was not at all pleasant, but despite myself I got the most tremendous hard-on which only subsided when she took the battery away. My wife, who is a very dominant character, then decided that I would have to wear the wiring device when I was out with her, with a connection on my trousers-belt. Whenever she felt like it, she could then touch the battery against the wires on my belt, complete the circuit, and give me a painful little shock on my penis. If erection resulted, the punishment was increased, since one does not always want to have a huge hard-on in the middle of shopping, or in the car.

I suppose the answer would be to surreptitiously remove the wires, and let her think I am being hurt, but I don't think I would have stood for this kind of treatment in the first place if it hadn't been for my personality, which is the kind which naturally enjoys some degree of humiliation and discipline. My wife on the other hand is something of a disciplinarian. She is now threatening to use even more powerful "shockers", which I am looking forward to with a mixture of dread and anticipation.— *W.K. (name and address withheld), Swindon, Wiltshire, England.*

* * *

I believe that something that happened to me recently, and my response to it, might interest your Forum readers. As background let me point out that I am a student and can usually work only part-time at most. My wife works, but her job does not pay very well. Thus financially we have had it pretty rough. Needless to say I was very pleased when, earlier this year, my wife began to have opportunities to work overtime and earn some more money.

One evening I decided to go to pick her up early so that I could wait in her office and be with her while she finished her work. When I got to the building the front door was locked, but I knew the back entrance would still be open, so I went in that way. When I got to my wife's office she was not there, but I thought I heard something down the hall. The sound was coming from her boss's office and the door was about an inch ajar so I peeked in. I could hardly believe what I saw. Across the room my wife's boss was standing there with his pants and underpants down round his ankles. Kneeling in front of him was my wife, wearing only her tiny bikini panties. She was "servicing" him with her mouth. Almost transfixed, I watched quietly, until in a minute or two I saw him finish in her mouth. Fearing an angry or embarrassing scene, I quickly returned to my car. In about ten minutes my wife came out, acting as if she had just finished a normal day's work.

When we got home, I told her what I had seen. She started crying and then, through her tears, she tried to explain. She said that we had needed the money so much that she had decided this was the only way to get it. Her boss, who is only 38 and divorced, knew of our financial plight and she said he had hinted to her about doing this. She had ignored him until the time came when we were really unable to pay our bills and then she did it, she said, because she felt we had to get the money.

She then told me all the details. She said that, after everyone else had left, he would lock the front door and then they would go to his office. Usually he would first have her do a striptease for him and then, when she was naked or nearly naked, he would play around with her in various ways. When he was ready she would kneel down, pull down his pants, and finish him with her mouth. She said he rarely wanted to have regular intercourse because he could not hold back for more than a very few seconds. Besides, she said, he was built very small down there and he could not use it very well.

When I heard her story, I felt more sorry for my wife than angry with her. I thought of all she had had to endure just because she thought we needed the money, and I was angry with myself for putting her in this position where she felt she had no other choice. What I had done to her was far worse than anything she had done. So now I am taking fewer courses and have gotten a steady job so that she will never have to work "overtime" again. Things will be better in the future but I will never be able to forget the sight of her, nearly naked, on her knees in front of another man.—*J.R.S. (name and address withheld), Washington, D.C.*

* * *

Having read Mrs. S.L.'s letter from Pasadena in your September issue, I am prompted to comment that if there were more married women with her outlook on sex, there would be less divorce, cheating and philandering in this country. My wife also pleasures me in every way but her favorite form of sex is fellatio. We have been married 22 years; she went down on me on our wedding night and literally hasn't come up since. Night and day, asleep or awake, she will not be denied. We have had this form of sex in every room in the house including the attic and basement and on virtually every piece of furniture including the television and washing machine. We are both highly sexed persons, my wife especially so, and it is not uncommon for her to fellate me four or five times within a 24-hour period.

Several years ago on a vacation we were driving through a desolate part of the western states when I noticed her fingering herself beneath her upraised skirt. I asked if she were enjoying herself and "how about me?" Without a word she leaned over, unzipping my fly, pulled out my erect penis and finished me off as we drove down the deserted road. On arriving at the motel we changed into bathing attire for a swim, but not before she had had me again. After dinner we returned to the motel and I laid down on the bed nude and, having an erection, she promptly took it into her mouth. Being tired from eight hours of driving I immediately fell asleep. When I awoke about an hour later Terri was sitting in a chair entirely naked and smoking a cigarette. She smiled and inquired if I had a good rest. I asked why. She said: "I blew you while you were sleeping." For some reason this excited me sexually and my penis began to rise. I asked if she would like to do it again. She said, "You know it," and, stubbing out her cigarette, suited the action to the words. On awakening in the morning my wife repeated the performance and to my surprise informed me she had raped me three times during the night!

During our 22 years of marriage we have only been separated once and that was during my year in Vietnam. On my return, my wife confessed she had had sex relations with other men. I was neither surprised nor angered by this information as I understood her intense sex drive. My wife had two steady boyfriends whom she serviced twice weekly each. Neither knew of the other of course. To say my wife is oversexed is a vast understatement. She knows and practices over 18 ways of masturbation, not including the common finger-in-the-vagina technique. If she liked regular sex as much as fellatio no ordinary man could keep up with her.

She has often told me of her desires to perform her favorite act on various men we have known. Though we have never cheated on each other while together, an occasion did arise about five years ago when I agreed to her suggestion. It happened this way. A bachelor friend of ours used to visit us several times a month for dinner and drinks. He was good looking, and extremely well endowed. I happened to mention this to my wife one night, and she said she would like to vacuum him. About a week later Bill visited for the weekend. We had all been drinking heavily throughout the evening, and on retiring my wife immediately took me into her mouth. When she finished she stated she would like to do the same to Bill. I was excited by this idea and told her, O.K. go ahead. She seemed surprised but also pleased with my attitude. However I made one stipulation: I had to watch. She agreed and we crept silently into the living room where Bill was sleeping on the sofa. He was covered only with a sheet and was snoring loudly. As I watched from the doorway my wife bent over our house guest and very slowly and quietly uncovered him. I was in the greatest state of sexual excitement I had ever known. Here was my wife about to ravish a man right before my eyes! A quarter moon gave enough light to see everything clearly. Bill lay sleeping on his back, clad only in shorts and a T-shirt. My wife knelt down at the side of the couch and carefully put her hand into the open fly of his shorts extracting his penis. Bending over, she applied her mouth to the head and it went into an immediate erection. As I watched fascinated the thick shaft gave three or four spasmodic jerks. Terri gently covered the sleeping figure and we rushed to bed together and she repeated the performance on me.

My wife is 42 years old and has neither a line in her throat nor a wrinkle in her neck. Apparently daily sexercise has a therapeutic value!—*David S. (name and address withheld), Phoenix, Arizona.*

* * *

I enjoyed reading both Mrs. S. J.'s and R. A.'s letters in the December edition about third-party sex. I have had fantasies about having sex with another man as well as my husband for years. It was only after attending a party at which I consumed more than my fair share that I let slip my "dream." Much to my surprise, my husband confessed that he too had so fantasized. Not too much later, I arranged to invite a handsome man to our home. After getting through the preliminaries (and a nice dinner of beef and wine), we all three ended up in our king-sized bed.

Not only does my husband derive extreme erotic pleasure from watching another man have sexual intercourse with me, but on occasion he will hold me down and let the other man really "give it to me!" Sometimes we will all three take part, with me receiving the male organ at both ends at once. This is *extremely* enjoyable for me . . . especially when both men are able to bring themselves to orgasm simultaneously!

My husband tells me that the thing which really turns him on is seeing the pleasure I derive (I am quite vocal during intercourse) from being made love to by another man. My only advice for others is, if you haven't tried it . . . don't knock it!—*Mrs. R. R. (name and address withheld), Newport, Rhode Island.*

* * *

Last night my wife and I celebrated our first wedding anniversary by inviting some friends over, and one of my friends stayed over after everyone left. He began by joking that since he missed kissing the bride on the wedding night he should make it up on the anniversary.

He began playing around with my wife and each time I didn't protest they gradually grew bolder and each time escalated. I sensed they were both becoming aroused and were approaching the point of no return. Then he managed to slip my wife's panties down and they had sexual intercourse on the couch right in front of me. When they'd finished both apologized, saying they got carried away and didn't intend to go that far.

The thing that puzzles me is my own reaction. Instead of being angry I was aroused and experienced orgasm. Until that night I was very jealous. I'm beginning to wonder whether this is normal or whether I'm turning queer or something.—*R. A. (name and address withheld), Baltimore, Md.*

* * *

I married in 1959, shortly after I came to New York to study medicine. My husband was 25, I was 18. After four years of deep affection but some intimate discrepancies, we began swinging with an experienced middle-aged couple, who helped my husband in changing my medieval mind. Since they went back to Europe, we have had separate affairs, my husband less frequently than I because he is a busy physician and, above all, because he has made me the source and center of our sexual happiness.

He adores to hear my confidences just after I am with boyfriends. He asks for a detailed description of their physical peculiarities and preferences and an itemized report on our exchanges. In fact, he soon knows their anatomies and likings better than I do, even when he has not seen them. Before our dates, he advises me how to make them happy, according to their characteristics, and he ardently awaits my coming back with the results of his suggestions. He asks me to offer them the more warm and lurking places of my body and the best secrets of my skill; he regrets when I confess I did not want to indulge in all their capricious desires; he shares my joy when I am going to spend my evening with one of my preferred sweethearts and he welcomes my enjoyment at my return with our best champagne.

Last year I met a strong and passionate young man who often left me exhausted and with traces of his pushes and bites. My husband healed them and pampered me like a child. The slightest masculine odor I may bring home makes him instantly powerful and he penetrates and sucks me wherever we are. Then, after bathing me tenderly, we go to bed and the tales of my love happenings precipitate his spasms, so I have to stop at the most striking revelations, graduating them little by little.

I am happy to give him such enchantment, but I am beginning to dislike the unceasing conversation about my lovers and our bed behavior. I thought he might be a repressed homosexual, so I invited a handsome youngster to dinner and at the proper moment I encouraged them while I went out with a companion. My husband answered, with a laugh, that it would be wonderful to enjoy such an attractive boy, but he had never liked man-to-man intercourse. Later, he insisted it was not his preference, any more than lesbianism was mine. His libido—which brings him in a second to a sort of rapture—comes from knowing I am going to surrender every corner of my body to a man I like, to see me fully satisfied after an evening of total sexual abandonment, to hear they admire my beauty and expertise.

When I have told him this is a form of prostitution, he denies it because we have never received money or valuable gifts from anybody. If he is unable to spend our yearly vacation with me, he generously tells me to invite the boyfriend of my choice, and he pays our expenses. He has never imposed a love affair on me, and I break them at my will. I love him in every sense, yet I fear this is a dangerous happiness. Perhaps some of your readers can offer me advice?—*Mrs. S. S. S. (name and address withheld), New York, N.Y.*

* * *

Would that the proximity was such that my wife and I could become acquainted with Mrs. E. H. of Milwaukee and her husband (July) for, like them, we have a definite preference for oral sex. Before writing to you, we tried to recall when we last indulged in intercourse. It was well over three years, we decided. Our fellatio/cunnilingus indulgence is almost daily and, though we are not forced by a family to seek deserted side roads or supermarket parking places, we have gratified each other on several occasions in the back seat of the car during a drive-in movie as well as on the floor of my carpeted private office, which locks. Though we don't risk the promiscuity enjoyed by Mr. & Mrs. E. H., we do have a small circle of playmates whose sexual partialities are identical to ours: my brother- and sister-in-law, a slightly younger married couple, two married men and a bachelor who commits fellatio while delighting to my wife's propensities. I, too, get voyeuristic stimulation from observing my wife's performances and she, in turn, becomes inordinately excited from watching my gluttony. All in all, our rumpus room is the scene of unrestrained epicurism six nights out of seven!—*J. L. B. (name and address withheld), Denver, Colo.*

* * *

For the shoe and foot fetishist, my husband has an erotic fantasy which involves me. It's the sexiest foreplay I've ever known. He ties me up on the floor, stretching me out. I'm nude, except for red, three-inch, spike-heeled shoes. After teasing my clitoris with his tongue for a few minutes, he removes my shoes. Then, with his fingers or with some soft feathers, he tickles my feet (a little sadistically), especially on my soles and in between my toes, for up to half an hour. My feet are highly ticklish, but this is a pleasurable punishment to endure. It drives me crazy, but nothing gets me hotter. I'm 33, so is my husband.—*B. W.*

* * *

Although many of your readers have written about their enjoyment of enemas, I am surprised that none have related the pleasures of another anal delight—anal intercourse. My husband and I first experienced the pleasures of anal intercourse several years ago, after reading about it in one of the sex manuals that became popular in paperback editions then.

As both of us are quite adventuresome sexually, we were eager to try a new form of sex, but I was somewhat apprehensive about the possibility of pain involved. Our experiment began after the usual amount of sexual foreplay, which was intensified by the anticipation of something different. My husband paused to apply a liberal amount of lubricant to his penis. I lay on my stomach and spread my legs far apart to make his entry into my anus easier. When his penis touched my opening, I found that I was too eager to wait for his efforts alone, and I began to push against him to speed things up. He entered me much more easily than I had ever believed possible, and the pleasurable sensations caused by the movement of our bodies produced orgasms for both of us in a very short period of time.

We enjoy anal lovemaking, but have not substituted it for the more convenient forms. We have found that it can be very enjoyable for couples like us, who desire more than one orgasm per lovemaking session. We enjoy anal sex as our second act of love, not only because it adds variety, but because the anus is tighter than the vagina just after intercourse.

We have also found that anal intercourse allows my husband to stimulate my clitoris with his hand—I lift my hips while he reaches underneath me. The first time that he did this, I couldn't believe the extreme excitement that I received from having both my anus and my clitoris the objects of simultaneous stimulation. If my husband prefers to apply his hands elsewhere, I am able to use my fingers on myself.—*Mrs. A.C., Milwaukee, Wis.*

* * *

The letter *A taste for drives* (July) reminded my wife and me of some of our own exploits. We'd been married five years when we spent a vacation at a well-known Gulf Coast resort. In the room next to us were a couple from Iowa, Paul and Ella, who were about our age, full of fun and quite open in their sex talk. We went out with them a lot.

One evening, after we'd returned from a nightclub, Marge told me that Paul had knocked against her in a dark part of the dance floor and had pressed his hand between her legs. Then, while they slowly danced, he put one hand between her legs and rubbed her almost to climax. When Marge warned him Ella and I might notice something, he suggested perhaps we were doing the same.

The next evening, we visited the nightclub again and I gave Ella the kind of touch-up I knew Paul was giving my wife. During the floor show, we were masturbating them. When it was over, we agreed that we should all come back to our room. But when the girls were undressed and had showered, Paul backed out, saying he couldn't watch someone have sex with his wife. Next morning they checked out of the hotel.

About six years later, we bought a house in a new town and were moving furniture there. I looked up and saw a short, good-looking guy. He said his name was Billy, he was 19, and he was known as "Mr. Fix-it" in the neighborhood. Billy asked me if he could be of help, so for the next two months, while we were decorating, he worked for me almost full-time.

I noticed he was simply overcome when Marge was around. He would get an erection that was difficult to hide. Realizing that Marge was aware of this, I kidded her that I would have to watch Billy as he might rape her. She replied that he might not have much trouble.

One afternoon Billy and I had just finished some

planting when a flash flood hit. I invited him to join us for dinner. Marge had on her normal house clothes, a see-through pair of white shorts with bikini panties and a sheer blouse with no bra. During the meal, Billy never took his eyes off her and when the time came to leave the table, I noticed he had an uncontrollable erection.

I laughed at him and said that after 11 years Marge still had the same effect on me. Billy commented that Marge was the sexiest woman he had ever seen. I laughed, and asked if he could bear to see everything.

Billy almost went wild when Marge let her shortie pants drop to the floor and pulled off her blouse. I suggested that he and I pull off our clothes, and he lost no time. We were surprised at the size of his tool. I said to Marge: "He is all yours." Without a word, Marge pulled Billy down to her. She pushed his face between her legs, and as he made contact, she explained what he was to do. He learned fast—her climax was like an explosion. Marge then pulled him to his feet and bent over and milked him. That night, we asked Billy to spend his vacation with us. We had sun, sand and sex for ten days.—*D. R. W. (name and address withheld), Winston-Salem, N. Carolina.*

* * *

Penthouse has been responsible for a fantastic change in my sex life. My wife and I had a merely adequate relationship, but now I can just about get in the door at night before my wife is going down on me.

She greets me in one of the exotic outfits she has recently started to purchase from a California specialty shop, hands me a drink, and starts to tear at my clothes before I can even put down my briefcase. We immediately head for the boudoir where various issues of Penthouse are spread out on the satin sheets of our king-size bed. While I gaze at the girls, my wife rests her head between my legs and licks my cock and balls till I'm wild with passion. She then gets up to seductively remove her transparent black nylon gown. Clad only in crotchless black nylon briefs, she snuggles next to me and masturbates to an orgasm while she looks at the nude Pets and I suck on her nipples. Finally she climbs on top of me and with a gentle rocking motion brings me to climax.

Not only do we have sex more often (frequently two or three times a night) but each orgasm is much more intense. My wife and I both thank you for the privilege of reading your great magazine, which has proved to be the catalyst in our sexual transformation.—*K.W.P. (name and address withheld), Garden City, New York.*

* * *

I am a housewife in my early 30s. My husband and I, though happily married, have always been conscientious devotees of new forms of sexual stimuli, such as those advocated in Penthouse. Because of a few successful endeavors, suggested by the pages of Penthouse, I feel almost an obligation to share our "secret" with other readers.

A few years ago it seemed that my insatiable appetite for sex might devour us both. It was then that Edgar, whose hobby is electronics, made his titillating discovery. Using a small transformer, Edgar attaches a tiny electrode to each of my breasts, approximately ½ inch below the nipple. He then "turns me on," simultaneously performing cunnilingus. Needless to say, the effect is that I experience intense orgasms and a pleasure previously believed unattainable. It is after this ritual that Edgar and I perform sexual union and achieve a mutual satisfaction, surpassing even our wildest hopes. But perhaps many couples may hesitate to use artificial stimuli?—*Mrs. A.R. (name and address withheld), Lewisburg, Pa.*

* * *

Mrs. E.H.'s disclosure (July) about the way fellating other men aroused her husband has prompted me to write of my experiences. I have been married less than a year and my husband's sex activity is limited to cunnilingus. I get very turned on in bed and, though I tried telling him that I needed deep penetration, I just couldn't get this from him. So I began to have outside relations and, feeling a great deal of guilt, I finally confessed this to him. To my surprise, this excited him and he actually encouraged me to attract men to our home.

We now have a ritual which we go through about two or three times a month. Either my husband or I brings a man home. We have a few drinks during which I sit in such a position that the man can see my panties—I wear the shortest of miniskirts. After a while, my husband suddenly remembers an errand he forgot and takes the car. By this time, our guest is turned on and after a few preliminaries we retire to the bedroom.

During our sexual intercourse, my husband usually sneaks back into the house and secretes himself in a strategic position. After the man has his orgasm I immediately make some pretext that I hear my husband coming and hurry him out of the house. Remaining in bed, I await my husband who immediately mounts me and gives me the greatest cunnilingus job ever! Though it is only in this manner that he is able to have orgasm, he is extremely pleased just to see the degree of sexual satisfaction I receive from really getting it the way he knows that I need it. Married couples should tell each other of their desires and fantasies more often—perhaps they are both thinking about the same thing!—*Mrs. Marilyn T. (name and address withheld), Little Neck, N.Y.*

* * *

When I married a little over three years ago, I knew very little about sex. I had never even seen a naked boy or man, except in paintings and statues. On our wedding night I did not think that there was anything unusual about the size of my husband's penis. Erect, it was almost as long as my middle finger. I was so uninformed about sex that I was afraid it had increased in size so much that it would cause me pain when my husband entered me for the first time. Fortunately, that did not happen because, when he was ready, we had trouble finding a position in which he could achieve entry, and he was able only to get the top of his penis into me before he reached orgasm.

This became the pattern for all of our sex sessions. For over half the time that I have been married, I did not think there was anything unusual about our sexual intercourse. At the same time, I thought it was far less enjoyable than I had expected, and my husband shared my feelings. Because of our growing dissatisfaction, we had sexual intercourse less and less, not even once a month and my husband returned to masturbation as his main sexual outlet. When we began to read publications which dealt with sex, we learned that our pattern of sexual intercourse was far from normal, and how much smaller than average my husband's penis was.

Then one day, much to my surprise, my husband bought an artificial penis (dildo). Shaped like a normal erect penis, it is exactly six inches in length. It fits over my husband's penis and is held in the normal upright position by a strap, which goes around my husband's hips. I agreed to let him use it once, but made him promise that he would not try it again if I did not like it. That night, when we went to bed, we kissed and caressed each other for a short time, as we normally do and, when I was ready for him to enter me, he strapped on the artificial penis and put some lubricant on it.

At first, I felt some discomfort but, as he began to move it back and forth inside me, I gradually started to experience feelings of pleasure that I had not had before. As my excitement grew, I encouraged my husband to increase the size and speed of the movements he was making with the artificial penis. It felt so good that I achieved a state of sexual arousal that I had never reached before. On other occasions, I had attained orgasm when my husband masturbated me during our foreplay, but this time, I was so excited that I lost control of myself. I did things that I had never done before. I moved my own hips wildly to increase the movements of the artificial penis within me. I moved my hands rapidly over my body and my husband's body, and I even caressed my own breasts and nipples. I brought my husband's head down and made him kiss my breasts and suck my nipples. My husband tells me that I called out sexual words and phrases that I would not ordinarily say out loud, and he tells me that, when I reached my orgasm I cried out so loud that he is sure the people in the apartments around us must have heard. Afterwards, I was exhausted, but made sure that my husband had a chance to take off the artificial penis and achieve his orgasm in the way that he used to.

Of course, this was not the only time that we have used the artificial penis. Now my enjoyment of sexual intercourse is even greater than the first time we used it. We have sex more often now too, sometimes once a week. That may not sound much for a young couple (I am 25, my husband is 24) but, since our frequency of sexual intercourse had almost fallen to zero at one point, this new rate is a great improvement.—*Mrs. J.S. (name and address withheld), Arlington, Va.*

* * *

Unlike Mrs. E. H. (July) who enjoyed fellatio while taking a drive in the car, I find that this practice just warms me. Unfortunately it finishes my husband for a while when I am just getting started. The obvious answer to my problem was to make it with more than one male at a time. On vacation, I found out how.

I was walking along the beach one day in a brief bikini and three young men, playing volleyball, asked me to join in. In no time at all, it was evident they were on the make—and I was, too, though they didn't know it yet. Volleyball on a hot day in the sand is hard work so we went off to the walled swimming pool. After about three margaritas, the conversation got around to skinny dipping. By then, I had my courage up and went right in *sans* suit. Believe me, a shaved pussy at that moment was like an aphrodisiac to those fellows!

After horseplay and suggestive conversation, we went into the pool house to towel off. Within moments, right there in front of me were three good-sized hard-ons. I threw caution to the winds and went down on the one nearest me. By the time I had finished off the third, the others had regained their desire and erections. I was in a state of frenzy. I couldn't get enough and I wanted to screw like never before. Each of them was terrific, they didn't come too soon and it was like a constant orgasm for me. Never in my life had sex been so complete! In a period of about an hour, I had more than 20 orgasms. It was fantastic!

The very next day the whole scene was repeated, but the fact that they were not complete strangers now made it a little less exciting. I debated about telling my husband but finally did. His reaction was something else. He got so excited that I blew him right then and there. Afterwards, he wanted the whole story over again with all the details and he became hard almost right away. This time we balled with great satisfaction for both of us. Next morning he wanted to hear it again and again I went down on him.

Ever since then, once or twice a month we rent a room in a convention resort hotel. At these places there are always plenty of good-looking loose men hanging round the bar in the evenings. It is no trouble at all to end up with two or three in our room for drinks, and they have an evening beyond their wildest dreams.

I have found that, if I go down on them first, they recover and make a much better lay and it starts me off on cloud nine. My husband always goes with me and takes delight in participating as if I had just met him also. We never hint that we are married; rather he just met me like the others. Our sex life for the last five years has been perfect. We get along better than ever, sex between us at home is better and I have the variety that I needed.—*Mrs. Joy G. (name and address withheld), Oceanside, Calif.*

* * *

Last winter, my wife prevailed on me to take into our apartment her "dear old friend, Doris" who, by a chain of misfortunes, had lost her only sister and her fiancé within a month. Expecting a wan distraught female, I was surprised to meet an attractive dark-haired lady with animated poise, a somewhat distant air, but seemingly eager to adapt to our ways. Within a few days she was helping with cleaning and shopping and a few times I thought she exceeded my wife's performance in the kitchen. It became positively exhilarating to have her around.

We are a very physical couple. My wife and I do daily yoga exercises, we go swimming and we consider ourselves casual and without pompous get-ups. In a way, Doris cramped our life-style, because she was very prim and proper. Our *ménage à trois* was pleasant enough, and I thought, with a little modification on Doris' part, it could be perfect. When she started to hint she might be wearing out her welcome, I suggested she let her hair down a notch or two. The way Doris complied and my wife's exuberance in accepting her partnership left me strangely puzzled. There was hardly a thing we did not share in. The girls, being almost the same size, shared clothes, sometimes even pajamas, so that one of them came down to breakfast topless. We had communal baths and showers, doors were left unclosed and Doris didn't mind me seeing her climb into bed in the living room in sheer stuff. Only our bedroom door was still sacrosanct at night.

One evening, my wife heard a slight tapping on the door just when I sorely needed a rest after our jousting. Doris complained of an intolerable headache and my wife consoled her with aspirin and a stiff drink. But the headache persisted and it was suggested that a good body massage would do the trick, for which job I was appointed. I applied my hands to Doris' totally naked form and she responded most gratefully, offering herself to my kneading motions with abandon. Her occasional moans and the suppleness of that prostrate body made me delirious. When, after a thorough massage, her body looked faintly rosy in the dim light, she asked in a high girlish voice if she could cuddle up with us. My wife did not refuse. I was already afflicted with an oversize erection that became impossible to hide. I was told to position myself between the two of them in our oversized bed, and my wife began to strip me. It was a sort of unveiling exercise, because to my feeble efforts to obscure the evidence of my excitement, my wife responded in anger, displaying my erection to Doris in all its glory. The way she showed me off as if I were hardly attached to my penis. She demonstrated its length and width to our new bed companion, as if I were some curious tourist sight, devoid of human traits. The young stranger then compared my physical characteristics to those of her former boyfriend, explaining the differences in great detail to my wife. Then she began bugging my wife if she could "use me a little bit."

The way the two of them went about me was a delirium the like of which has never occurred to me before or since. I must have finally lost my composure, because the memory left only feelings of unrelieved passions.

The three of us are now deep into it. Thanks to the sensibilities of my two women our relationship continues, though slightly abated, for Doris is now planning to leave once she has found a more lasting male relationship. And I am still surviving. —*F.D. (name and address withheld), E. Orange, N.J.*

* * *

One night several weeks ago I left my husband and a friend in our basement family room while I made sandwiches and coffee upstairs. Upon returning to the basement I came upon a scene that was deeply shocking. My husband was committing fellatio with such concentration he failed to hear or sense my reappearance. Our friend, however, saw me.

The seriousness of the situation and my husband's compromising indiscretion should have been the forerunner of a family quarrel. Instead of feeling angry, I was amazed, for our friend was displaying a truly prodigious piece of virility. My husband leaped to his feet and sheepishly made apologetic noises but all I had eyes for was our friend's beautiful, unspent erection. For the first time in my life I appreciated the permissiveness we hear so much about. Shameless as it sounds, I wanted that large penis!

Our friend was visibly mortified and was awkwardly attempting to restore himself. It was sheer impulse—I blurted out, "No, don't," and spontaneously stayed his attempt at concealment.

The rest is a shameful acknowledgement of weakness and adultery. No one suggested undressing. It was automatic. The three of us simply began to disrobe and in the nude our friend was even more overwhelming. I sought no condonation for my compulsion and sprawled brazenly on the floor in unmistakable surrender. He fulfilled my expectations. My ecstatic outcries aroused my husband beyond anything I ever saw. When it was over he all but raped me.

What followed was embarrassment and misgivings. Neither of them would permit me to indulge in self-reproach and persuaded me to yield to more adulterous intercourse which I thoroughly enjoyed. The feeling of guilt disappeared with my second deliberate indiscretion and sometime later I watched my husband and our friend indulge in fellatio. I was fascinated.

Since that unforgettable occasion I have indulged in a whole new behavior pattern with little or no self-censure. The intimacies with my husband and friend are orgiastic now—cunnilingus, intercourse and homosexuality unrestrained! I no longer think about the unconventionality of the arrangement.—*B.W. (name withheld), Denver.*

* * *

The letter about love in threesomes from Mrs. S. J. (December) prompted me to write you of another three-way love affair involving my sister that actually served as therapy to help the poor girl overcome a tragic personal problem. It happened about six years ago, to my twin sister.

My sister had been married only a year when she and her husband were in a private plane crash. He was killed and she lost her right leg. My husband and I invited her to come live with us, but no matter how we tried to lift her morale and help her adjust to her tragedy, she brooded about her poor husband and was especially despondent about her amputated leg. Because she was left with a very short stump she found it painful and cumbersome on an artificial leg, so she resigned herself to just limping around on her one leg and crutches. She was ashamed to go out in public with a missing leg and just moped around the house, doing a little bookkeeping at home because she was too self-conscious to work in an office. Nothing we could do seemed to cheer her up.

Then, one morning after she had been living with us about eight months, I walked into her bedroom and found my sister lying nude on her bed with her one leg drawn up and stroking herself vigorously in her genital area. I was shocked when I realized she was stimulating her own orgasm. When she finished she tearfully explained and I then understood her problem. She had been without any sex for the eight months since her husband died. It was especially frustrating for a girl who had been married only a year and had led a very fulfilling sex life with her husband. She sobbed on my shoulder: "What else can I do? I'm a one-legged cripple and no man will ever want to make love to me." I tried to convince her that her life was not over yet, but she was totally depressed and I feared she might attempt suicide.

I discussed my sister's problem with my husband and we decided that, as an experiment, I would share my husband with my widowed sister. We laid out ground rules that he could spend an hour or so in her bedroom with her once or twice a week, but no overnight sleeping with her. And only while I was at home. It was to be a confidential experiment within the family, since she was my own flesh and blood. My husband and I had been married only three years at the time, had one child, and had a normal sex life of our own. But I consented so long as no love affair developed. It was strictly an adult arrangement and we all understood the rules. And I would give them total privacy while together.

Our experiment was a success and I soon began to see my sister smiling again for the first time since the tragic accident. When my husband made love to me the first time after he had made love to my sister I naturally wanted to know how we compared. He told how the poor girl had to struggle at first with only one leg there but finally learned to compensate for the missing leg and had proven herself a capable sex partner. But I had no reason to be jealous, for my husband's own relations with me seemed even more affectionate than before. Once, after our arrangement had been working successfully for a few weeks and my husband was making love to me in our bed, I suddenly wrapped just my left leg around him and held my right leg away from him. "Guess which twin?" I asked, trying to imitate my sister's one-legged position. He instantly responded "The two-legged one, honey, and there's no comparison so don't get worried. But your sister still does okay with that one leg of hers, and she'll have no trouble keeping a guy happy in bed when she finds the right guy."

My sister soon began going out in public on her crutches, and her whole mood brightened following our experiment. She began to dress smartly and got herself a good job in a local office. She eventually met a nice fellow and is now happily married, with two children of her own. Before her wedding we told her husband-to-be of our experiment and he understood why I had allowed my husband to satisfy my sister's needs temporarily. My husband and I are back together as a twosome, and I have no plans to share him with anyone else. But I have no regrets about having helped my sister overcome her tragic situation.—*Mrs. L.W.E. (name and address withheld), Cambridge, Mass.*

* * *

The letter from Mrs. S.R.F. of England (September) re curing a husband of wearing women's clothing suggests you might appreciate my wife's attack on my rubber fetish.

We have long had our sex on a large rubber sheet

(from Macy's) with my wife wearing a rubber bathing cap since the feel and smell of the rubber stimulated me to greater activity. My wife apparently tired of this for one morning after the kids were off to school, she invited me to bed for a surprise session. We stripped, but this time she told *me* to put on the rubber bathing cap. As I did, she produced a pair of rubber gloves which I put on with great expectations. My dear wife then tied my hands behind my back, wrists to elbows, and pushed me face down on to the rubber sheet. Pushing me diagonally across the bed, she strapped my ankles together with a leather book strap. She tied my strapped ankles to one corner of the bed and, with another cord, tied my forearms to the top of the bed. At this point, she slipped a second rubber cap over my chin and face, fastening it tightly behind my head. There was a slit in the cap at my mouth and here she inserted a 2″ piece of large diameter rubber hose into my mouth. I was so excited at this point I couldn't open my mouth quickly enough. A string which had been inserted through the hose was tied firmly at the back of my neck. She next wrapped the rubber sheet around me and taped it as tight as she could with adhesive tape. With a comment that I had plenty of rubber now, she smacked my buttocks gently and left the room saying she'd return in an hour or so.

It was over an hour and a half before she came back and I was getting pretty stiff when she began gently rubbing me from head to toe. Her comment that "Now *I* have fun" didn't register for a moment, as she put several belts round my thighs, waist and upper arms and drew them just as tight as she possibly could. The next thing I knew she was spanking me with all her energy with one of my loafers—she told me later she planned 30 wacks for each buttock. Being helpless in all that rubber with the stimulation of the beating, I came after about 20 smacks and the rest was real torture. After a remark that *that* should cure me, my sweet, kind, loving wife left me to do her chores. An hour or so later, she let me up and asked if I was cured of "that rubber business." I couldn't help but smile as I agreed—but added that bondage was even better.—*T.G. (name and address withheld), Bronx, New York.*

* * *

Your magazine has been instrumental in solving a problem which my husband and I have had for the past six years of our eight-year marriage. Your article on troilism (August) and C.F.'s letter in your September issue describing a sexual encounter with an oralistic woman hitchhiker, combined to evoke our solution. Perhaps its disclosure will be of interest to others.

I married my husband when I was quite young and a virgin. The marriage caused me to cut short my college after barely beginning. Within two years, I began to resent this marriage, because it had come too soon. It had denied me the sexual experimentation which I had always believed to be an intrinsic part of college education. This resentment culminated in an arrangement to have a motel owner send me lovers during a weekend my husband was away. I sexually satisfied over a dozen men, but strong feelings of guilt prevented me from reaching any sexual orgasm. Your troilism article caused me to realize that, while I desired sex with other men, I could not gain any satisfaction without my husband's participation.

After disclosing the motel affair to my sympathetic and intelligent husband, I have, for the past few months, enjoyed sexual threesomes with hitchhikers. Our method, clumsy and self-conscious at first, is really quite simple and very exciting. We have an automobile which sits three in the front and limits the amount of rear-seat window space. A US Marine training base some distance from our home provides an abundance of young, handsome and clean hitchhikers. My wardrobe is one of several conservative, short-skirted dresses, with front buttons from throat to hem. A touch on my husband's leg signals my approval of the hitchhiker and the start of our mutual seduction.

It is not difficult to get a young Marine involved in a chat about sex. We encourage this by telling of our own experiences and never fail to mention an affair of troilism. The conversation is deftly directed to my legs, and my husband raises my skirt to demonstrate his point. Then, illuminated either by daylight or a large lamp in our radio, our young friend is treated to a view of sexy panties, a neatly trimmed pubic region, or, more recently, the very smooth mounds of a shaven pubis. The dialog of sex increases, as do my passions.

My husband then starts to masturbate me, in partial view of our new friend. Paradoxically, this is not enough to encourage assistance from my right. It takes a whispered "Play with me, too" which almost always results in the man starting to fondle my breasts. There seems to be a universal aversion to one man touching another, even while both are being satisfied by the same woman. When I feel our hitchhiker to be aroused we usually stop and the two of us have intercourse on the back seat, while my husband drives and listens. Several times I have found the man to be so exciting that we spend the evening in a motel, during which the only limit is our joint imaginations.

Our threesomes are lessening in frequency, from two or three an evening to about once a month. I feel that I have made up for my lost time, and now it is just another sexual variation to us—important, but not our prime outlet.—*Cindy, (name and address withheld), Orange County, California.*

* * *

On pages 28 and 29 of July's *Penthouse* I felt that I had—or rather we had—come home. The lady describes her encounter with anal intercourse so beautifully that I just had to write to you. I hope to find more letters on this much-maligned way of sharing of the innermost secrets of womanhood.

My wife and I have been devotees of this way of love for thirty years, and the years have only added to the enjoyment of using her anus and rectum. We do not neglect vaginal intercourse, but there is no way for me to approximate the sheer pleasure I experience when her anal ring clutches my penis when I have penetrated her deep enough.

Fellatio and cunnilingus are also in our range, and give much mutual pleasure, but nothing like an anal insertion of the penis. True, a couple needs mutual trust and consideration.

Since we have a mess of kids, it is obviously not a method of birth control for us: Also, for those who never tried it, there is nothing in the rectum until a few seconds before evacuation of the bowels, so they should not be squeamish. Until a man has spent several minutes slowly and lovingly inserting his finger into his love's behind to lubricate and relax it, he hasn't lived.

We wish you success with your magazine—and hope to see this and other letters on this subject in print.— *(Name and address withheld)*

* * *

I am a regular reader of your magazine when I can obtain the copies, not allowed in Spain. I want to tell you of a custom which could be classed as "human bondage" but very light and innocent. However, it is quite satisfactory for moderate feelings such as ours. I have a long belt made of very rough vegetable fibre with two rings in one side. When my wife and I go to bed, I extend the belt across with the rings close to my wife's hip. After the required arousing games and when I am already over my wife, with everything in its place, I pass the belt over my buttocks, close the loop through the rings and tighten it. In this position we remain, moving our bodies but without any possibility of being separated for a long time. We have reached up to four orgasms in one hour of rolling all over the bed.

I name the system "Mate-n-lock" but I cannot patent it since it is a trade mark for electrical connectors. However, I think it is not a bad name for this innocent game. —*A.A. (name and address withheld), Barcelona 17, Spain.*

* * *

The recent letters in Penthouse regarding spanking, etc. have really turned me on. I appreciate the frankness with which you are willing to treat such taboo subjects, and this gives me confidence that you will see fit to publish material in another unusual area.

To me, the most erotic thing possible is the knowledge that another man has seen my wife partially or completely naked. We are faithful to one another, and have an excellent relationship, but I must confess that I am delighted whenever there is an occasion for any man to see her body. Of course the most frequent such occurrence is her visit to the doctor. Though there are some women doctors in town, I insist that she go to a male physician, preferably a young one. The night after a doctor's appointment, we invariably have unusually good lovemaking, with her telling me about the examination in minute detail during intercourse.

My wife is young and quite beautiful; thus the sight and feel of her body should be a treat for any man! Typically, though, the doctor does not see her completely disrobed. Ordinarily, he examines her breasts while exposing her body to the waist, but the rest of the examination is more sedate. On one or two occasions, however, she has been almost completely naked while being examined, and holding a conversation with the doctor. This is intensely erotic to me, and has at times been so to her also. She is usually neutral, but on rare occasions has come home aroused from a particularly good examination.—*A.C. (name and address withheld), Laramie, Wyo. 82070.*

* * *

I am a man of 40, happily married to a girl 10 years younger than myself, with two nice children and a very good job in an international company here in Brussels. Until a few months ago, my sexual life was quite normal but nothing unusual happened.

For years, a cousin of my wife has been visiting us one Saturday each month. She is a nice girl of 26, still single but very modern; her name is Monique. One evening three months ago we were all sitting in the living room after a good dinner. Some of your magazines were lying on the table. My wife took one of them and with Monique started to read. They were very surprised to learn from your readers' letters that some males take pleasure in being dominated by females. Monique mentioned that one of her secret daydreams was to be a slave in a harem, and my wife said that she has always been very excited by that idea—so I told them that if this was their secret wish, I could be their sultan for one night.

Monique and my wife burst out laughing but I noticed that they were anyway very aroused by my idea. I started to pinch and caress my wife's legs, and she didn't stop me, although it was in front of Monique. I then decided to do the same to my wife's cousin. Soon I had undressed the two females completely. When they were naked, I told them that they were from that moment my slaves, and ordered them to kneel. Life being a mixture of pain and pleasure for a harem slave, I decided to submit them to my desires. I took my belt and started to whip them both. They didn't ask me to stop; on the contrary, I realized they were becoming more and more aroused.

Then I decided to sit on the sofa and asked them to do a belly dance, after putting on an appropriate record. They were so excited they began to dance immediately, one trying to surpass the other in erotic poses, and the spectacle was so fantastic I only ordered them to stop after more than a quarter of an hour.

When the dance was over I told my slaves to join me on the sofa. Monique said she did not want sexual intercourse but she said she was ready for anything else, so I did "all the rest" to Monique and had intercourse with my wife. Afterwards, we agreed that none of us before had such satisfaction in our sex lives. Since that memorable day, one Saturday each month we have had the same session. The two females like so much this new game they have improved the décor. We have a special "harem room" in our apartment and they wear (at the beginning at least) very exciting harem pajamas. For my birthday, I even received a whip. Once a month now we can forget we are civilized people of the 20th century and realize our most secret desires.—*T.F.P. (name and address withheld), St. Giles, Brussels, Belgium.*

* * *

When my husband and I had been married for two years I found he was a transvestite, and my first impulse was to leave him. Instead I went to see my friend Gladys, who owns a ladies' outfitters, and asked her advice. She said: "It's funny you should bring up your problem. I've been reading letters on the subject in Forum, and the way writers dealt with transvestites. One school of thought favored the cane or whip and the other the 'Petticoat Treatment.' The Petticoat Treatment is not as degrading as the whip, and if we both put our heads together it could be more fun. The main thing is to *make* him wear women's clothes *all* the time, not just when he feels like it."

We drafted a form setting out what Fred had to wear, and for how long, and a clause specifying punishment by me for failing to wear them. On arrival home, I confronted Fred with his sins, made him sign the form and told him that from tomorrow the only male garments he would wear to work would be a shirt, his suit and socks and shoes. His undies would all be feminine, nylon slip, bra, frilly panties, nylons and a corset. Fred agreed readily but I shook him by adding that each month he would have to wear a sanitary belt towel and sanitary panties.

Each night when he came home from the office he had to change either into a frock or blouse and skirt. In the past he had liked to go out for a drink now and again, but now he was too embarrassed to go in his new finery.

As summer came Fred's enthusiasm for being corsetted waned, and I mentioned this to Gladys. She asked his waist size, and showed me a formidable back-lacing corset some two inches smaller. A few days later I called in and saw the finished product. Not only had she sewn in extra boning, but she had put in larger sized eyelets at the top and bottom of the lacing, so that two small padlocks could be fitted and the wearer locked in. Gladys also sold me a pair of all-rubber panties which I had ordered, and gave me a pair of handcuffs. She gave me a suitcase to take them away, and when I got home I put the case in the wardrobe in our spare bedroom.

The following Saturday when Fred arrived home I soon spotted that he was uncorsetted. So I went to see Gladys, who said that somehow we would have to entice him into the spare room, where we could both deal with him. Back at the house, Fred still hadn't changed and was sitting in an armchair reading the paper. I told him that I had something special to show him in the spare room, and to my surprise he went upstairs without question. Once inside, I locked the door, brought out the suitcase and emptied the contents. Then we both pounced on the frightened male and undressed him, after which Gladys handcuffed his hands behind his back.

Fred lost his temper and called us some filthy names, so I gagged him with a fresh sanitary towel, after which we really went to town on him. We fitted a sanitary belt and towel on him, then pushed a rubber dick up his bottom and adjusted the towel so that it held the dick firmly. Next we put on his rubber panties and imprisoned him in the tightly laced corsets by fitting small padlocks through the laceholes. There was a bra among the things I had emptied from the case, but I hadn't taken much notice of it until Gladys said she had modified that too and would like to fit it on Fred. I discovered that sewn inside, at the point of each cup, was a small springloaded clip.

Gladys tied Fred's ankles to the bedposts, then, while I masturbated him through his rubber pants, she put the bra on him with sadistic glee, clamping his nipples into the spring clips. I wondered if things weren't getting a bit out of hand.

Finally we put a cloth bag over Fred's head and pulled

the drawstring tight, and watched him wriggling futilely as he became more and more sexually excited. Foolishly I agreed to Gladys's suggestion that we leave him all night to stew in his own juice.

Her next move was to invite me to the flat above her shop for a cup of tea and a chat. As we talked, it became clear that Gladys hated men, and was proud of the way we had humiliated Fred. I wanted to leave to see how he was, but she made tea and as time passed she brought up the question of my staying the night. I told her I hadn't brought anything with me, but she pressed me and finally I agreed. After we were both in bed my suspicions about Gladys were confirmed. She was a lesbian, and if I had had any sense I would have returned home there and then. But she began working on me, and once I was roused she strapped on a dildo and clung to me while she ravished me. When it was over I was sickened and revolted by the whole affair, and as soon as I was able next morning I left her flat and hurried home. Fred was still trussed up, but apart from being stiff and sore he was all right. He said he never wanted to wear anything feminine again. Gladys and I are barely on speaking terms now, but I don't mind, for of the two I prefer Fred.—*Mrs. S.R.F. (name and address withheld), Radcliffe, Manchester, England.*

* * *

Your readers may be interested to know what it is that a woman really enjoys when she is making love. It turns me on for my husband to strip himself naked, and then to undress me in front of a long mirror so I can watch him removing my clothing while erect to the fullest extent.

When I too am naked, he turns me around and enters me from behind, holding my breasts in his hands. We continue like this until he bends me forwards so that my breasts can be stimulated even more firmly, then we go down on the floor in front of the mirror and he acts like a bull with a cow. After several deep lunges, he gets off and lies flat on the floor so that I can straddle his body.

After we have moved to the bed, we still keep the mirrors of our dressing table at such an angle that we can both see our bodies writhing together. I do not like my husband to be gentle, and much prefer him to lunge into me with fierce thrusts. Sometimes we rope our bodies together just to obtain the feeling of satisfaction when we move around and the ropes tighten on our flesh.

At the time of the month when we cannot have ordinary intercourse, I gain great pleasure from dealing with my husband either with my hands, mouth or anus; for I realize that an intensely sexual man must be rid of his urges at regular intervals, and I have no wish to deprive him of his pleasure just because I cannot have mine. We have been married for 12 years, and hardly a week goes by that we do not have intercourse at least 10 times.—*Mrs. S. L. (name and address withheld.) Pasadena, Calif.*

* * *

I am 38 years old and my wife is 35. She has a very good figure and is quite attractive, so naturally I am proud of her and like to show her off—but not in the normal way! I find I get a great deal of sexual excitement from taking photos of her, not in the nude, but in the seminude. She wears a sweater with the buttons undone to the waist, so her breasts are exposed, a miniskirt, stockings, black suspender belt and high-heeled black shoes.

She has shaved her pubic hair leaving only a small V-shaped section in front, cut very short, so that her vagina is fully visible. This means that in certain positions I am able to get photos showing all the details of her charms. I don't mean by this that she is posing with her legs wide open, making a spectacle of her vagina. This type of photo is too vulgar, and there is nothing crude about my wife.

My work as a salesman provides me with a golden opportunity of showing the photos to different customers.

She likes to be told the remarks that were made about her while we are having intercourse. It excites her. A number of customers have asked me who the model is. I tell them, "It's my wife," but I know they don't believe me. About three years ago, though, one guy took me at my word and asked if she would model the pictures to his instructions. She was thrilled by the idea, and she now phones him about once a month, when he gives her instructions on how he wants them taken. He also talks dirty over the phone. I think she must lead him on, because he has told me he comes off while talking to her. She has done very well out of him. He buys her some lovely presents, and gives her money as well, although they have never met.—*R. W. (name and address withheld), Baltimore, Md.*

* * *

The letter from Mrs. V.P. of Brentwood, England (Forum, July), appears to me to be somewhat self-contradictory. She claims a failing, which I agree is common to many women, of being unable to tie knots in an expert way. Yet the method she describes of restraining her husband must depend for its success on the secure knotting of the cord of thin rope. Properly carried out, the result can be very effective, but certainly uncomfortable for the victim over a lengthy period of time.

Mrs. V.P. says she does not know where to obtain straps or handcuffs. The former can easily be purchased from any saddler's shop, of which there must be several in Brentwood. All that is necessary to begin with is a number of such leather straps about 21 inches long and half an inch wide. If these cannot be bought, then dog collars of a similar size can be used instead.

Using straps or collars is simple. One should be put loosely round one of her husband's wrists, and the other passed under the strap and round the other wrist. Both can be tightened to the desired degree, forming efficient handcuffs. Other straps of varying lengths can be bought or specially made, depending on how they are to be used.

For several years my wife and I have been ardent bondage enthusiasts, and used the foregoing in the early stages. Since then we have acquired much more sophisticated equipment, allowing us to indulge in an intimate variety of methods of restraint. Mrs. V.P.'s purpose appears to be to dominate her husband and to indulge in a certain amount of sadism. Whether or not she does it in order to provide increased sexual pleasure to both her husband and herself is not clear. Does she change roles with him? My wife and I do this always, and the sexual delights which follow while in bondage are completely satisfying.

We have never indulged in flagellation, much preferring pleasure to pain. We find that oral love play, together with the use of vibrators and at times a dildo, provide us with everything we could wish for. We do not disdain blindfolds and gags, both of which are useful additions to our repertoire.—*A.L. (name and address withheld), Glasgow, Scotland.*

* * *

Your article on troilism prompts me to write to you about an experience that started my husband and I off on threesomes.

About a year ago my sister Karen, who is 25 and three years younger than my husband and I, came to spend several months with us following the finalization of her divorce. During the course of our conversations about her new life with no man in it, she commented that she was in desperate need of sexual expression, but the thought of going to bed with "just anyone" revolted her.

To keep her mind off her loneliness, my husband, Steve, took Karen everywhere with us. One night after watching a movie with several very explicit love scenes, Karen joked that I had better watch out or she would be making a play for Steve. I carried the joke along and suggested that she sit next to him on the way home.

Suddenly I was intrigued by the idea of my husband and sister making love together, and I decided to see what I could do to keep things rolling. I told her that since we were sisters, it would be all in the family and that she could go ahead. As Steve was mixing cocktails in our kitchen, I whispered to him that Karen probably needed a man's touch and suggested that he go into the living room and sit next to her on the couch while I finished making the cocktails. I gave them several minutes alone before bringing in the drinks and mixed several more rounds—each time giving them lengthy periods of privacy.

We were all getting a little high and on an impulse I suggested that we play strip poker. They quickly agreed, and soon we all were nude. As soon as Steve had removed his final item of clothing I could tell Karen was getting desperate, so I said "He's all yours for the night, Sis, I'll just watch."

They didn't have to be told twice. Within minutes, they were engaged in heated lovemaking, while I sipped a drink and watched with fascination. After their climax, I left them alone and went to bed, terribly excited by what I had watched, and eager for Steve to join me. He came in about half an hour later and we made love like we never had before; with the excitement of such an unusual experience still fresh in our minds.

The three of us repeated the scene several times, and on some occasions Karen asked to watch while Steve and I made love. In the 10 months or so since Karen moved to another city, Steve and I have had similar experiences with two other girls and our regular lovemaking alone has reached new heights of passion. Our sex life has taken on a new dimension which we both thoroughly enjoy.—*Mrs. S.J. (name and address withheld), Milwaukee, Wis.*

* * *

I feel compelled to tell you and your readers of some recent experiences that have brought my wife and I closer together. We had been living a "normal" life: a 9-to-5 job for each, TV, going out to dinner, etc. One night, while out to dinner, my wife confessed to a one-night affair with an old schoolmate she had not seen for years.

After my initial shock I found myself with an erection, in a highly excited state. I asked my wife to go to the ladies' room, remove her bra, and show herself off to the men in the bar on the way back. She did me one better by removing all her underclothing. The sight of her beautiful breasts and nipples moving under her sheer, clinging dress almost drove me to an orgasm just watching.

Several of the men at the bar were visibly affected. One of them started to talk to her, but she said she was "busy," handed him her panties and then joined me. We made love for three hours that night—the longest since we were married four years ago. Since then my wife has had several affairs with men at my encouragement. Later, she repeats what happened for me. Sometimes while making love she will tell me about an incident which excites me highly. Other times she might give an "instant replay" by wearing the same clothes and doing the same thing she did with the other man.

Last year when the company I worked for went out of business my wife started to work the bars one night a week, and brought home $100 or more for only two "jobs." Sometimes she would find someone she really liked and invite him to our apartment for a "doubleheader." It didn't take her long to learn how excited I get watching her having cunnilingus performed on her while she fellates her partner.

My wife and I have begun to enjoy each other much more since we began this diversion from the "norm." It is not a steady diet of this life, but an occasional fling that keeps us happy. My wife is now a more experienced lover, as I am, and we now have a deeper understanding of so-called swingers. My wife's occasional prostitution gave us enough money to buy a new boat for cash, and my more relaxed manner helped me move into a nice $38,000-a-year job. We're both under 30 and beginning to enjoy life.—*R.A. (name and address withheld), Atlanta, Ga.*

* * *

I find that your *Forum* gets more interesting every month. In the June issue, I enjoyed the two readers' discussion of the word "fuck." Although both were wrong, you set them straight on the fact that the word is older than either of them suggest. I find the word a great turn-on in bed when the wife and I use it in regard to our relations. It really turns me on for her to use it when we are pumping away late at night.

The letter from one reader was interesting, about a ribbon tied at the neck of his penis in an attempt to get a bigger penis. This is true, I believe. A condom also makes an extended erection. I still use condoms after fifteen years and after all these years, my wife still says to me, "You've got a big hard-on tonight, honey." I'm only five and three quarter inches hard if I measure the upper side, but if I measure underneath the penis, I'd be seven inches. But believe the upper-side measurement is correct.

That is sufficient for any woman—or almost any. My own spouse and I have, for a good many years, often screwed standing with me behind and her in a half-crouched position over a chair. If she is really horny and in need of more penetration, I can really make the five-and-three-quarter-inch erection work to the equivalent of maybe seven inches, or even eight inches, particularly if I raise high into her vestibule.

I would like to see other readers' letters in regard to the standing "dog-fashion" posture, and am wondering if perhaps there are other men who have discovered the benefits of the high movements inside the vagina, combined with what I call a "jackknife" and a number of "tailspins." It really gives me, as well as the spouse, a lot of added stimulation.—*C.L. (name withheld), Lexington, Ky.*

* * *

I am writing this not only to share the personal joy I feel in being able to once again experience the pleasure of a happy sex life, but to possibly be of some help to those who may have the same problem I once had.

For the past few months, due to business and other problems, I have been unable to experience an erection and my marriage was in danger. As time went on the problem became so complex that I was convinced that I had become totally inadequate. My wife and I tried everything from sex manuals to hard-core pornography, all to no avail. Then one day while working with a tuning fork, I accidentally dropped it in my lap and had a feeling of such sexual delight that I could hardly control myself.

Later that night, while my wife was sleeping, I used the tuning fork on myself and achieved such an erection that I woke my wife and she couldn't believe her eyes. We were able to have intercourse and achieve mutual orgasm for the first time in months.

Now, prior to intercourse, my wife takes the tuning fork and moves it along my penis until I reach an erection. This also excites my wife tremendously and we both enjoy intercourse more now than ever. Our marriage is back to normal and I find myself more able to cope with my business and other problems as well.—*(name withheld), Baltimore, Md.*

* * *

I'm writing this letter to you with my husband's knowledge. It's about an event that took place a little less than a year ago. My roommate from college asked my husband and me to spend a weekend at her new home in upstate New York. We arrived in time for drinks. To our surprise we found another couple, plus our host's sister and her girl friend—three men and five women in all. Dinner was early since the evening was warm and we all wanted to go into the pool as early as possible. By this time the drinks were putting everyone in a happy mood and there was a little horseplay. My roommate said she was going to take my husband on a tour of the house to show him the work her husband had done on a number of rooms; so that left me at the pool with two men and three other women. At the pool our host's sister said she and her girl friend didn't have their suits with them and the men said who needs suits? With that the girls took their things off and into the pool they went, followed by the men. The other wife and I stood there and then decided to join them—which was a lot of fun. Everyone was having a good time and we girls decided to give the men something special. Our host's sister and I made love at the side of the pool, which drove the men crazy and we were followed by the other two girls. By this time my husband and my roommate arrived from the tour of the house and I was surprised to see both of them nude. It seems they saw our actions from one of the windows and had a little lovemaking in the house, but when they arrived at the poolside my husband still had a hard-on. As the night went on, the air became cool so we all decided to go into the house and our host showed stag movies. I had never been so hot in my life and most of all when I saw my husband having intercourse with one of the other girls while I was having it with another man.

Since that time we have spent a number of weekends with this couple, alone or with their friends present, and each time it became better. Now all I have to say to my husband is let's go, and he's at the door. By the way, we don't bother to wear any underclothes now since it's a waste of time.—*(name and address withheld)*

* * *

When my husband recently brought a copy of *Penthouse* home for the first time I thought it was just another men's magazine. However, a few days ago I happened to pick it up and read it and was pleased to find that it was delightfully frank in helping people with sexual problems.

When my husband came home from work we discussed the philosophy of *Penthouse* and in doing so discovered that both of us had been too inhibited in our demands for sexual satisfaction. My husband is thirty-one while I am only twenty-two, and perhaps this gap has prevented us from being completely free and open with each other.

We have been married for two years and already the physical pleasures have begun to wane, although I never mentioned this to my husband for fear of hurting him. However, on the night we had been talking about *Penthouse* we experimented for hours with new positions for making love, asking for and doing things which before then had been unmentionable. In particular, we discovered that both of us had sexual fantasies and soon we invented a little play which gave us both great sexual satisfaction.

In the play my husband acts the part of a brutal prison camp officer and I a woman spy who has just been brought to him for interrogation. We both wear suitable garments for this. He acquired an old army uniform and boots and I wear a dirty, torn dress. First my husband threatens me and shouts at me while I refuse to talk. He then ties my hands behind my back and begins to fondle me, at the same time sneering and laughing at me in the approved theatrical manner. This may go on for several minutes until he hauls me to my feet and rips my dress down to my ankles, revealing that I only had silk stockings and old-fashioned shoes underneath. He then ravages me, kissing and biting my breasts, and then forces me to fellate him, sometimes to orgasm, during which time I climax at least two or three times.—*Name withheld, Northern Territory, Australia*

* * *

My husband and I are avid readers of your magazine and we thought we might contribute this suggestion for bringing variety into the average sex life. We are a happy married couple in our early thirties.

The first few years of our marriage were exciting since I had no premarital sexual experience. But as in most marriages, the "newness" wore off and we found ourselves a little bored sexually. This came to a crisis point when my husband brought home a "swingers" magazine and suggested we give it a try. At first I was hurt and angry. But eventually we were able to discuss it openly. My strict Catholic upbringing just wouldn't let me accept the idea of a "swap." We tried improving our erotic stimuli to each other. When we went out, I wouldn't wear anything under my dress, we made love in the car and at motels, etc., but while these things were all fun there was still something lacking.

Quite by accident I stumbled upon an answer. I'm a member of a health club, and part of the exercise schedule calls for a massage at the close of the workout. I always enjoyed the massage, found it relaxing, and enjoyed chatting with the masseuse. But I had never considered it an erotic experience since I have no bisexual interests. One afternoon I was drowsing on the table after a particularly hard workout when I suddenly realized that I was reacting to the rhythmic stroking massage of my thighs. My hips were rotating and, although I was very apprehensive, I couldn't stop! Though no words were spoken, the young girl gradually localized the massage, gently stroking my pubic area and finally massaging my clitoris. My orgasm lifted my hips from the table and afterward I was truly relaxed. The masseuse was so casual and businesslike that I felt no guilt and from a later discussion I found that she provides this same massage to many of her patrons and does not consider herself or the act bisexual—just a friendly physical experience. When I told my husband of it that evening he was fantastically aroused. We made love for hours. We tried the massage at a local "parlor" with both of us present and watching. Although he really enjoys this, and I enjoy turning him on, I find his presence inhibiting. However, I have continued the massages at the health spa, and never fail to achieve fantastic orgasms and to turn him on by telling him about them. This has provided a necessary outside stimulus without the frightening commitment of "swinging." We have not limited our outside stimuli to this, having developed a non-swapping relationship with a couple with whom we can discuss our fantasies. We have found the massage to be an exciting, relaxing, and totally gratifying experience.—*Name and address withheld*

* * *

My wife and I have been married for some time, enjoying a very happy life devoted mainly to raising a big family. Sexually, we have always been very compatible. We started out shyly but became better lovers as time went by. We have managed to keep in good shape, and she is actually still a very good-looking gal.

The main point of this letter is to tell you that I think some of the features in your magazine are a real help to people. Like all couples, we have our favorite erotic fancies. Sometimes, as it must be in all marriages, it is a little embarrassing to reveal desires. I have had pleasure in seeing women in chains, and the first time I revealed this to my wife and she consented to let me chain her wrists, I experienced an enormous orgasm. I was surprised to find that she did not mind and indeed had a good one herself. As time went on, of course, we would occasionally escalate. Eventually, I purchased a pair of handcuffs for her, and made up some leg chains. The point I am trying to make is that both of us felt a little queer about the use of chains occasionally. We never really abused one another, but we were a little uncertain about it. Then she read a recent column by Xaviera Hollander and it convinced her that we were not that odd.

The last time I had to go to Detroit on business she came along. We had looked forward to a little fun, but it proved to be a strenuous trip and I was unable to show much interest in sex. So she insisted on spending an extra day. We loafed most of it away and that night we had a pleasant dinner. Evidently she had planned on a little more activity than I realized, because after we returned to our room she started to take charge.

First, she asked me to shave her crotch, I did so, leaving all the hair in front, just cleaning off the lips. By this time I was beginning to regain my interest in sex. She went to her suitcase and removed a pair of handcuffs, which she put on behind my back. I was really surprised to discover how uncomfortable it had been for her so many times. Standing in front of me now, she took out a pair of lace bikinis which she put on my legs and drew up. I could see myself in the mirror and I felt like a perfect fool with her black panties on. They had a slight hole in front and my cock slipped out the hole. She laughed at me and said that she was going to teach me a lesson for exposing myself in front of a lady. So she painted the tip of my cock with lipstick. Then she really surprised me; I had a box of French ticklers at home which we seldom used, but she had one in her purse and she put it on me, saying that it would serve to protect her modesty, as she did not like to see a naked prick. I felt like a damn fool, handcuffed, wearing a tickler which was particularly fancy—so she had me walk around the room a bit while she lay on the bed.

Then she got up and put on stockings, garter belt, and an open bra and pushed my face into her breasts. I sucked her and kissed her until she told me to get down on my knees, and she said I better start eating if I wanted to be relieved of my enormous hard-on. Well, I gave her the best I could and she had a terrific orgasm. I begged her to let me come too, and she said she would take off the cuffs, since I had been so dutiful. After she did this, she inserted me and the tickler and we had a tremendous screw.

I asked her later on where on earth she got so many ideas and she said it was from the article by Miss Hollander, which she had improved a bit for us. I really think we owe Miss Hollander our thanks. We had a wonderful time, and we both came home feeling relaxed and happy. Now that I know she is capable of turning the tables on me this way I am, of course, looking forward to the next time. At this point I'm uncertain whether I prefer to have her for my slave or to be her slave. I know one thing: whenever she wants me, she can have anything she wants.—*(Name and address withheld)*

* * *

For the first five years of our marriage, our sex relations were conventional (i.e., including fellatio and cunnilingus). However, after reading letters to *Penthouse* and

Forum Magazine we decided to try some kinky things to spice things up!

One technique which we find mind-blowing combines the wild release of masturbation with the erotic kicks of urination! When we indulge in this sex play, we both refrain from urinating all evening. My wife sets up a small folding bed (rubber-covered mattress of course) in the bathroom beside the tub. We both strip naked (my wife has shaved off all her pubic hair so the sensations are more intense) and engage in about half an hour of heavy love play. Then my wife puts on a very tight sanitary belt with a regular Kotex sanitary pad. She lays on her back, parts her vaginal lips and presses the Kotex pad tightly against the moist labia, then she closes her legs and I stimulate her breasts, nipples, and areolaes. She particularly likes me to squeeze, pull, pinch, twist, suck, and bite. While I do this she slowly urinates till the Kotex is absolutely sopping wet. The feeling of the wet Kotex rubbing against her vaginal lips and erect clitoris gives her an unbelievably intense orgasm—usually followed by two weaker ones!

Then she unrolls a rubber safe and puts it on my rock-hard penis. When my erection subsides, I *strongly* urinate till the safe is one big bag of hot urine which she holds. Then she manually and orally stimulates my balls and anus. While she moves the large rubber bag of urine around, she massages my prostate gland till I experience a phenomenal ejaculation—thick clumps of my white semen floating in the warm yellow urine. In the tub she removes the safe so that the bag of urine streams over our genitals bathing us in the warm liquid that we both enjoy so much.

After a warm shower and bath, we towel each other off and have wildly exciting intercourse in our bed. Such an evening leaves us so sexually sated that we do not desire sex for another week or so. Although we have tried other kinky things (e.g., inserting a tampon in my rectum) we like the above sex technique best and use it about once a month. Needless to say, our sex life is incredibly satisfying!—*Name and address withheld*

* * *

The article in your July issue about men who like to wear women's undergarments brought back memories of what I experienced five years ago. I was thirty-eight at the time and my sex life and marriage were on the rocks. If we had relations every other week my wife and I were lucky.

One night we were going to a masquerade party, and my wife decided I would go as a vamp. I had just showered and shaved my legs to the knees, and I was standing naked in the bedroom. My wife handed me an old satin half-slip she wore when we were first married. Without realizing it, I put it on inside out and started to adjust it on my waist when I got a hell of an erection. I felt like I was on fire. I grabbed my wife and started to kiss her neck and breasts, which just made me see red. I suddenly sat on the floor and performed cunnilingus for the first time with my wife. She quickly climaxed, but she wanted more. So I had her lay on the bed and I inserted my finger and played with her until she was again ready to climax. Then I pulled the slip up and got on top of her. She was hopping all over the bed and begging me to come. When we climaxed it was the greatest act we ever had. We just lay there completely exhausted.

At the party my penis kept on slipping out of my shorts and rubbing against the satin side of the slip which kept it half erect most of the night. About eleven my wife went upstairs to the hostess's master bathroom. I followed her up and we made love again on the bathroom floor. About one-thirty she asked me if I could fuck her again—which was a word she could not stand to hear or use before. We left the party and went home.

We started to strip but she told me to leave the half-slip on. She started to rub up against me and asked me to make love to her the way I did before we went to the party. All the time we were going at it what amazed me was I could do it three times in one night. I felt like I was twenty years old again.

She begged me to keep the satin half-slip on, and if I

woke up in the morning with an erection to wake her up. I did and we did!

When I got home from work that night I found my wife had gotten rid of the kids. She took me up to the bedroom and had me put the half-slip on again, satin side in. She started to kiss me and at the same time massage my penis with the slip. It is impossible to describe the pleasurable feeling that gave me. I started to kiss her and suck her rock-hard nipples. She begged me to sit on the floor and kiss her until we were both ready to come. My penis was throbbing from the satin slip massage and the lovemaking, but I hopped on top of her and I thought the bed would break.

She told me to put my pants on over the slip and we went downstairs and had dinner. Over dinner she told me how much she loved me, and how hot she had been all day just waiting for me to come home from the office. In fact she had never enjoyed sex so much and couldn't get enough. For the first time in her life she felt like a whole woman. We made love twice more that night.

Since that time she has ordered satin sheets, more satin half-slips, and some full length satin nightgowns. When we rub against one another it gives us a soft smooth feeling and drives me up the wall.

Over the past five years we have made love four to five times a week. With kids around the house sex is hard at times, but my resourceful wife finds a way. We both feel like we have been reborn and liberated. All I know is satin has added that spice to our life.—*Name and address withheld*

* * *

Recently my husband took me on one of his business trips to an east coast city. I went sightseeing, while I imagined he was attending a meeting. But that evening he told me his associates had, after lunch, taken him to a massage parlor. I was furious. Next day, I was considering whether to go back home when the idea occurred to me—why not try it myself? After all, I consider myself a liberated woman. If he could get a massage, so could

I. It took visits to three massage parlors before I found one that had a male masseur. Since my husband had been given the full treatment by a masseuse, I also wanted to ensure that I got what was right for me. What an exuberant feeling to have my body kneaded by the strong hands of a masseur! I also asked for a local massage, as I knew my husband had had one. The masseur was absolutely great and I had a climax like I never had before.

That evening at dinner, I told my husband. At first he looked hurt, then jealous. After a few minutes, he accepted that if he could do it, it was only fair to let me do it, too. We forgave each other, discussed our experiences and went on to show each other by practical demonstration what skilled hands had done to each of us. We had a delightful night, and then decided to visit a massage parlor together to pick up as many sensuous strokes as we could. Afterwards, we realized that there was no cause to be jealous as we didn't have any sexual intercourse or personal involvement with the other person.

The next night my husband suggested that we both get a massage in the same room at the same time, so that we could share our experience visually. Since most parlors are set up to accommodate only one customer to a room, we had a difficult time finding one that would make adjustments for us. But we were lucky, and it was the most fantastic night yet. Back home, we decided that massage parlors were the ideal half-way house between sexual monotony and wife-swapping. We'd talked about swinging before with some of our friends, but never got round to it because of the risks. But, since most men are voyeuristic and most women are exhibitionists, a husband and wife can satisfy their desires by getting their massages in the same room.

Cautiously, we approached our friends with this idea, at first without telling them about our experiences. Most of them agreed that it was a satisfactory substitute for swinging. Though there are several massage parlors in town, none seems prepared to offer a dual service. One masseuse hung up on my husband when he told what we wanted—I guess she thought he was making an obscene phone call. Regrettably, some cities seem to be closing their massage parlors.—*Shirley H. (name and address withheld), Rockville, Md.*

* * *

I have never seen the controversial movie *Deep Throat*, but my husband endearingly refers to me as his "little Linda Lovelace" because of my irresistible penchant for fellatio.

I am twenty-four years old and we have been married for seven months. I readily accepted my introduction to fellatio, and although I thoroughly enjoy coitus, I discovered I *preferred* fellatio. It is intimate, exciting, and stimulating. An aphrodisiac! I actually have an orgasm as a result of my husband's emission. He is delighted because of this uncontrollable attraction for him, and my craving has grown into an obsession during seven months of marriage. It now includes my brother-in-law and two close friends of my husband's. He excitedly watches the performances. More recently it also had included a telephone repairman and a bachelor neighbor. My husband is not aware of these two latter indiscretions. I don't want to wreck my marriage with this intense desire and want to know if some of your distaff readers have the same problem.—*C.H. (name and address withheld)*

* * *

I guess I have a television fetish. When I was a little girl I spent most of my time in front of the set, and now I spend all my time there. This works out just great since my husband likes to play cards every night.

Sometimes, though, he will come home early and I will get him to make it with me on top of our set. Sometimes he even reads TV Guide as we're doing this.

It's my opinion that this variation adds much strength and vigor to our sex life. My husband agrees. Have you heard from others who have had similar experiences? —*E.G., Saugus, Calif.*

* * *

In the short time I have been acquainted with your magazine, I have found myself fascinated by the natural poses and fantastic forms your models take on. My wife especially enjoys your letters column, for it has given her (and me) new sexual courage and insight.

I am quite impressed by the number of readers who enjoy cunnilingus and fellatio. For several years now, my wife and I would engage in these activities with great secrecy. Usually, as much as our privacy would permit, my wife would wrap my penis in a sugar-honey mixture which would increase my erection by at least two inches. She would then wrap a towel filled with ice cubes around my penis, freezing this delightfully tasty dish. At the same time I would prepare a tiny pizza-like creation in the oven which I would insert into her vagina before bedtime.

I cannot begin to tell you how this mutual culinary creativity has helped our sex lives. Not only does it satisfy our late-night hunger for food and sex, but it also allows our imagination to run completely wild. My ability to command an erection, which I had not mastered, has increased at least 500%. My wife also enjoys a new sexual asset from our sexual feasts. Previously, she had found it uncomfortable to practice fellatio, a custom I began to enjoy immensely overseas, and would only take two or three inches into her mouth. Now, it is all I can do to keep her satisfied with seven.

In closing, I should mention there is one tiny drawback to our practice: since we began this midnight feasting, both my wife and I have gained over 10 lbs, but we think it is well worth it.—*R.K.S. (name and address withheld), Milwaukee, Wis.*

* * *

When my wife and I are in the mood for sex we both

get undressed, then we stimulate each other until we are both aroused, then we make love until we are both satisfied. After reading your letter columns I couldn't help wondering—is there something wrong with us?—*Tom Fields, Austin, Texas.*

2

Penis Size

I have recently been divorced after seven years of a somewhat less than blissful marriage. I loved my wife, and think I still do, but through most of the years we were married she ran around with other men. Needless to say, I am not so naive as to believe that I am perfect, but I did at least think that I was a good lover. But my wife's running around with other men led her to discover that not all men are equally endowed, and I must admit that at most I am just average.

We have been divorced for seven months now, but it wasn't until just last week that my fantasy of being the best lover she had ever had came to an end. She finally told me that it wasn't anything about the way I made love to her, but that I just wasn't large enough to fully satisfy her sexual needs. After hearing this straight out and cold I just came apart. I am writing this in the hope that you or one of your readers will be able to give me some information on enlargement of the penis.—*M.R. (name and address withheld), Lancaster, Ohio 43130.*

* * *

After reading you magazine, I feel compelled to write on the subject of size. It seems that too great an importance has been placed on the size of female or male genital areas, or breasts, in the woman's case.

I have had an affair with an average-sized man who has completely restored my belief in sex. His lovemaking leaves nothing to be desired; it is beautiful and open and manly. Our sessions leave us breathless and our mutual orgasms are numerous.

I have experienced anal intercourse with him, and due to his size found it stimulating and sexy. I doubt if I would have tried this with a "hung like a horse" guy.

I think the importance of size should only be measured in the size of your heart and the size of your needs and how you get them satisfied. Your magazine offers many wonderful ideas and your articles are very stimulating. It definitely isn't the "same old thing," like the competition every month.—*Name and address withheld.*

* * *

You still label yourself a magazine for men, and I feel you're wrong. One of the main topics of conversation with women is sex, and all my friends read and quote you. I think that soon Penthouse will be a family magazine. The teenagers, both male and female, who visit my apartment read Penthouse so avidly that they won't let me throw away the old copies.

Another thing I wish you would debunk is the contention by experts that the size of the penis makes no difference. They're crazy. The most thrilling experience is a tight fit, and every extra inch of length adds to its intensity. I wish further that you would show more of your nude models. While I am not a lesbian, I enjoy seeing the female figure with pubic hair. You should also show some beautiful males—front view and all. Almost all great art shows the male figure in its entirety—why not Penthouse?—*Miss O.N. (name and address withheld), Lincoln, Neb.*

* * *

Your letters discussing penis size have been interesting, but this one will try to give you a woman's view on the subject. I have had many lovers and fortunately of all races and colors. Only one, an Irishman, had a bigger than average penis, and he was an average lover, nothing special at all. My best and most enjoyable lover was a Portuguese, with an average-size penis. The difference was that he made me feel like the most desirable woman in the world. In addition, he was secure in the fact that he was making me happy, and the farthest thing from his mind was the size of his penis.—*Dolores Robertson (address withheld), Los Altos, Calif.*

* * *

I have read your magazine for several months now, and there is one subject that I have wanted to see discussed in the Penthouse Forum. Many doctors and writers have said that the size of a man's penis makes no difference in sexual intercourse. Instead of these "experts," I would like to hear what your readers think. I knew a number of young men intimately before I was married and their penis sizes ranged from one that, when erect, was only as long as my middle finger, to the size of my husband's, which I once measured and found to be 8½" long and slightly over 2" thick. On the whole I found that, while the men with the bigger penises were not always the greatest lovers, they did seem to have fewer problems with sex than did the ones with smaller penises.

Many of the men with smaller penises worried more about their own enjoyment than they did about mine; and several of them suffered from premature ejaculation or occasional impotence. On the other hand, I have found that a large penis like my husband's fills me up so much that the extra friction causes me to reach orgasm more quickly and more often. In addition, a large penis seems to make possible more variations of sexual intercourse. My experience has shown me, at least, that big penises are better than small ones.

I know that some girls must feel this way, too. I like to take Polaroid pictures of my husband when he is nude and has an erection. Then I like to leave these pictures in places where my girlfriends will "accidentally" find them when they visit me. Over half of them have told me how much they envy me, and one of them even offered to pay me if I would let her have intercourse with my husband just once. I am keeping him all to myself, though, and I keep him so satisfied that he does not have the energy left to even think about another girl. —Mrs. L.S. (name and address withheld), Washington, D.C.

* * *

I read every so often in Penthouse of readers' inquiries on how to enlarge the penis, and no one seems to come up with the answer. Perhaps my experience in Thailand as a Japanese PoW can help solve their problem.

When passing near the Japanese sleeping quarters I often noticed round flatstones, of varying diameters, with a hole in the center. These stones intrigued me for some time until one day I saw how they were used.

Relaxing on the edge of his bed, naked, a Japanese soldier pulled his flaccid penis through the center hole, and an erection ensured that the stone wouldn't come over the knob. He then sat for as long as he could, letting the weight of the stone dangle from his erect penis. This must have been a painful process but it seemed to be quite successful judging by the number of dangling penises I saw, and their length.—*H.T. (name and address withheld), Ruislip, Middlesex, England.*

* * *

I noticed in your August issue that Mr. L.M.C.'s wife thought his penis was "small" at 5¼ ins. long and 4-15/16 round. If I'm not mistaken, Masters and Johnson call 5¾-6¼ ins. long the average for the male.

Mine measures 5½ long by 5¼ and I have never had any complaints from the opposite sex. True, a 9 in. or 12 in. penis would be much more impressive, but where would you find a woman who could actually accommodate such an organ and enjoy it? My wife, after three children, still says I have all she can handle comfortably. I believe it's not how big a penis is but how it's handled by the woman so she can receive fullest enjoyment from it that matters.

If Mrs. L.M.C. is unhappy with her husband's size maybe she should have checked the fit before, or perhaps she has stretched her vagina through use, age and children. If she still believes the fit is too loose, a good doctor can apply a couple of stitches and her husband would seem huge.—*R.H. (name withheld), N.A.F. Selfridge A.F.B., Mt. Clemens, Mich.*

* * *

It has been with an avid interest that I have followed your Forum column; it is refreshing to find a reputable magazine where one may openly voice one's opinion on most intimate subjects. It is also pleasing to note that there is active reader participation in this column—especially in the discussion concerning the size of the male penis. Until your magazine, such a subject would have been taboo.

This subject is of particular concern to me. Your contributors have stated that penis size is not really important to the woman. Perhaps, however, some of your readers are overlooking the feelings of the male. I, for one, am extremely self-conscious about my small erection, and no amount of assurances that women don't mind will cure me of my inhibitions. Your writers on one occasion noted that penis size is proportionate to overall body size. I have been thinking that since exercise may substantially alter one's physique (e.g. Charles Atlas, et al), is there not some recognized form of exercise that can increase the length and width of an erect penis? Since I am sure this is a subject of interest to many of your readers, and that many will know the answer to this question, I implore any who have any suggestions to please respond to this column. After all, guys, we are all in this together!—*Al C. Davis, Pensacola, Florida.*

* * *

Mr. L.M.C. of Indianapolis stated in your May Forum that his penis at full erection measures 5¼ inches long by 4-15/16 inches in diameter. Either Mr. L.M.C. or Penthouse has made a very big mistake. According to his measurement, his penis is about as long as a 12 oz. beer can and as round as a stick of bologna. Can you picture that as "insufficient equipment?"

I can't help believing that Mr. L.M.C. meant circumference, not diameter. If there was no mistake, then he should see a physician about his deformity.—*A.C. Bryant, Cleveland Avenue S.W., Atlanta, Georgia 30315.*

* * *

From time to time, I have read letters in *Penthouse* from women who place great emphasis on large penises. I would like to comment on the average and smaller-than-average-sized male.

I am single, in my late twenties, and have had many beautiful sexual experiences with some wonderful men, both black and white. These have included men with penis sizes ranging from small to "hung like a horse," and I feel that penis size does not necessarily make a difference in performance or enjoyment. I have what I consider a capable, average-sized vagina, and have handled large men. However, my most enjoyable and memorable sexual experiences have been with men who are small to average.

I have multiple orgasms and for me to thoroughly enjoy myself (my partner permitting and able), I like to go for long periods of time; I usually climax at least four to six times. I can remember occasions, after having sexual romps with men possessing seven to nine-and-a-half-inchers, where I have become raw and sore as a boil; sitting becomes very uncomfortable, and the slightest pressure is very painful. This discomfort can last anywhere from three to ten days, and definitely puts me out of action. However, when I have sex with a smaller-sized man, I am able to feel his every move as he goes in and out, from top to bottom, side to side; I can climax many times, and I am ready and able to have more the next day or on the next occasion.

Also, I have noticed that men with smaller penises seem more anxious to please and that many of them view sex as an art; and like any other art, they put in a lot of work and effort to achieve perfection. So, to the women who feel that the larger the better, I say it's not how much you've got, but how you use what you do have.

The intent of this letter is not to argue that smaller is better than larger (this is a matter of personal choice), but to give due credit to the smaller-sized men. They may not be the biggest, but like Avis, I think they try harder —and there's nothing wrong with that.

I enjoy your magazine. I think Forum is the greatest example of freedom of expression I've seen. Thanks.—
(Name and address withheld)

* * *

I am an au pair with a French family and their son René, aged 16, buys and reads your magazine. His parents don't know this, but I found some copies when cleaning out his room, and the son begged me not to tell on him. I promised, but I am sure his father knows anyway. He is a proper Frenchman—he takes every opportunity of touching or rubbing against me or his wife or René's girlfriend.

In two of your magazines I read about the size of the penis—large and larger! I am 20 and I have been in Paris for three years and have seen six boys and had sexual intercourse with two of them. None of them had a penis longer than 5 ins. I know because from the tip of my finger to my wrist is exactly 5½ ins. so in fondling the boys I can judge their size. I have also asked my girlfriends about it and they say the same, though we hear that black boys are bigger—is this true? Please tell me the correct size of the penis and, more important, the thickness.

Before I made love I used to try putting my finger in but I couldn't and the first time a boy did it I was sore for days afterwards. The two boys I have had were gentle, but they both stretched me to the limit. I am worried that I could not take a penis of the dimensions you quote, first because of entry pains, and second because of what would happen inside if the boy was 7 or 9 ins long—surely such a penis would injure me? I was so worried about this I tested myself by inserting a thin candle as far as it would go, and under unpleasant pressure it penetrated to 6 ins, but I hate to think what would happen with a boy so equipped thrusting in as far as possible. Both my boys satisfy me and I enjoy intercourse with them five or six times a month but I am always sore for at least the next day. Am I abnormally small?—*Cathie (name and address withheld), Paris Xleme, France.*

* * *

I have been married three times. My first two husbands had average-length penises—5½ to 6½ ins when erect. However, my third mate, he is of average build (5ft 11ins and 175 lbs), has an organ slightly less than 7½ ins long in the flaccid state, and it erects to 10½ ins long and 7 ins in circumference. While I doubt that my husband is any world-record holder, we have both wondered how his length compares with some of the largest penises on record.

Incidentally, aside from the fact that a much larger organ is more enjoyable for oral sex, I have not noticed any significant difference among the lovemaking abilities of my three spouses. I have also had no problem in accommodating my present husband quite comfortably.—*L.St.P. (name and address withheld), Auburn, Maine.*

* * *

Perhaps those of your readers who are not generously proportioned will be interested in how I developed an organ of respectable size. Three years ago, when I was in Vietnam and aged 23, I measured three inches in the flaccid state and 5½ ins in the erect condition. Today, in the flaccid state my penis measures 5 ins and it erects to 7¼ ins. And its diameter has been increased proportionately.

I credit this penis enlargement to a device I bought in Tokyo a few weeks before I returned to the United States to obtain my discharge from the Army. It is called a linga pendulum. A synthetic rubber hourglass fits behind the head of the penis and a sizing clamp, attached to the hourglass, can be adjusted for a precise fit. Two interlocking pendulums fasten to the clamp. These are rubber and have loops at the bottom to hold locks which in turn are used to suspend weights of various amounts. One can add a number of these small weights to give the desired downward force.

The weights gently stretch the penis and at the same time help to develop and strengthen the vital erectile muscles of the organ. Immediately on awakening in the morning, I put on the equipment and wear it while showering and eating breakfast. About 45 minutes a day has done the trick for me. After three years' experience and training, my genital muscles are toned up to the point that my erections are rock hard and at 90 degrees to my body. Perhaps the linga pendulum won't do the development job for everyone, but for me the results have been most gratifying.—*George Jones (address withheld), New York City.*

* * *

After reading the letters about penis size in the December issue, I began to wonder if the male sex organ could be increased in dimension by forcible stretching. My apparatus for the job was a ribbon from my girlfriend's hair, tied in a sailor's knot around the neck of my penis. This ribbon was then attached to a sweatband that dangled loosely around my leg below the knee. The contraption caused me no discomfort, so I decided to wear it around the college campus as it was completely invisible.

The simple act of walking now takes on a new dimension for me. My penis receives a gentle tug with each consecutive stride. Apart from the obvious physical stimulation, I am convinced that the wearer of such a device also receives highly beneficial psychological assistance in living in this all too sexually oppressed society. It enables the wearer to be reminded of his masculinity in whatever situation he finds himself and is a most effective form of reassurance, however basic it may appear. When in a crowd I feel distinctly male-animalish, where in the past I felt only anonymity. My girlfriend says I smile more, too.—*C.M. (name and address withheld), Stillwater, Okla.*

* * *

I have some advice which may help the husband of Joan, who complained in a letter to Xaviera Hollander (December) that her husband's penis is too small. My wife also used to be dissatisfied with the size of my penis, even though I was able to bring her to orgasm several times during one session. After each successive orgasm she needed more cock.

Nine months ago I began stretching my penis while it is in the flaccid state by grasping it close to the base and pulling downwards, as if one were milking a cow. Before I started the stretching exercises my cock measured 6½ ins by 1¾ ins when erect. Today it is 8½ ins by 2⅛ ins when erect. I'm able to satisfy my wife even more as well as gain greater enjoyment myself knowing that I am pleasing her so well.—*J.P.W. (name and address withheld), New York, N.Y.*

* * *

George Jones' letter (December) prompted me to relate my own experiences in the cause of penis enlargement. I was playing my tenor saxophone one evening for my wife. The tune happened to contain many low notes, so the bell of my saxophone was pressed against my genitals and every time I hit a low note, a surge of excitement flashed through my loins. Before the song was over, I had attained an erection. As I was wearing only boxer shorts, my wife commented on this. After she had gone down on me, she suggested that she blow low notes on the instrument while I dropped my testicles into the bell of the horn. Once again, my penis developed a huge erection. Seeing this, my wife substituted my penis for the mouthpiece of the saxophone and milked me dry. I was sure I'd had it, but my wife insisted that we repeat the procedure and much to my surprise I was able to climax in a matter of minutes.

My saxophone has become a third party in our sex life and just the sight of it makes my wife go nuts. After about a month of this routine, I was able to ejaculate five times in an hour and, even more amazing, my erect penis had grown almost an inch.—*N.Y. (name and address withheld), Edmonton, Alberta, Canada.*

* * *

There seems little doubt that psychiatrists and others who have alleged that penile dimensions are meaningless in terms of sexual satisfaction of females have been attempting to ameliorate the feelings of inadequacy often expressed by patients with small-organ complexes. I am quite convinced that Mrs. B. A.'s assessment (May) is not only subjectively, but objectively, valid.

As a male with greater than average endowment, I am in a position to judge. I have been told repeatedly by women that they had never before experienced such profound gratification. With few exceptions, this was their first encounter with an extraordinarily large organ, and while there may have been some initial fear, it was overcome by a strong sense of curiosity concerning the validity of the so-called "myth" about large phalluses. The real myth is the claim there is no difference.

Since I am not gifted with unusual ability to delay orgasm, nor am I an inexhaustible sexual athlete I can only attribute the reaction of these partners to the size of the penis. Strangely enough, though I have never found a partner capable of accepting the entire length, all of them were certain that they had succeeded in doing just that.

Men not gifted with large organs can surely make the most of what they have, however. It is far better to have an average or even a small organ, intelligently used, than a large one applied with no finesse, tenderness or technique. Heifetz can make music on any old fiddle, but the finest Stradivarius will sound like the squealing of a tomcat in the hands of a clumsy, unfeeling lout.—*D.M. (name and address withheld), New Jersey.*

* * *

I have a small, or I should say, large problem that I want to get off my mind. I'm falling in love with a rather petite coed here at college, whom I have been dating for several months. My problem is the size of my penis. It is about 5 ins long when limp and 7 or 8 ins when hard, but it becomes as thick as my wrist. I am a 21-year-old virgin male!

Whenever I try to make it with a chick, she may be willing until she gets a good look at me. I have tried to solve the problem of erections in embarrassing situations by frequent masturbation, but this just seems to make me hornier. I don't want to scare off the girl I want to marry; so far I haven't had the courage to mention it to her— or even to discuss sex for fear that the subject might come up. But I do believe that a good, healthy sex life before marriage is important. Do you have any suggestions? My roommates say they would give anything to have my problem, but it's not worth the trouble, believe me.— *T.C. (name and address withheld), Lawrence, Kans.*

* * *

I'd like to disagree with Mrs. B.A. (May) in her preference for large penises; however, I cannot. I equate the stigma of a small penis in a man with the painful and infuriating stigma of small breasts (like mine) in a woman. But large penises have always been more pleasurable for me; perhaps I've been spoiled. My ex-boyfriend had a wonderful length and a definite advantage in circumference. I loved this and since I've split from him (no pun intended) I have met many nice and intelligent men, but most of them have not been large. I don't find small ones so exciting physically, voyeuristically or psychologically.

As for Mrs. B.A.'s love of enormous members, when I was 18, I had a lover from Nassau. He admired the size of his penis more than anyone else and loved swinging it around in front of a mirror. My roommate saw it one day and said it was matched in size only by a baseball bat. When we had intercourse, he had an interesting way of bouncing me and the mattress up to meet him, rather than moving his body toward mine. I enjoyed sex with him, though unfortunately I bled a little after each encounter. I was in good health, but I felt he was just too much for me, despite the theory that a woman can accommodate any size or length.

I've since known many girls who also experienced being bounced by my Bahamian friend. They all said they couldn't walk or sit comfortably for days afterwards.
—*J.L. (name and address withheld), New York City.*

* * *

I am a student at a large university in the eastern United States. My academic capabilities are such that I have more than enough time to indulge in certain "extracurricular" activities. However, I find that my equipment is not adequate to provide the satisfaction which I feel I should be getting and giving. This deficiency is a great source of anguish and torment to me.

I have tried every device and technique available, including the flat stone with the hole in the middle mentioned in your October issue, but I have been less than successful. What I would like to know is, do you or any of your readers know of any operation or therapy which would improve my dimensions?—*A.H. (name and address withheld), University Park, Pa.*

* * *

In answer to Mrs. L.S.'s request (January) for opinions on the size of penises, I must cast my vote in favor of the large variety. Certainly in my case, the small ones have never managed to give me the least degree of pleasure.

Now take a large penis. It is a thrill to touch one. The sight of a really large penis in full erection is just about the most arousing thing in the world . . . at least for me. I get absolutely in a lather just imagining it, never mind really seeing one. The difference between the feeling one has when a large penis is in one's vagina and when a small one is "in there" is so great, I simply can't fathom how these experts can say "the size makes no difference." To them it may not, but to me it most assuredly does.

A large penis that I merely heard about in college has come back to haunt my fantasies over the years. It seems the proud owner had to hold it in both hands when he urinated as otherwise it would have draggled in the water of the toilet bowl. This particularly huge penis was further described as unusually thick; so thick, in fact, that it would fill the loosely cupped palm and fingers of an average sized woman's hand. Would that be about 3 ins, or is that utterly impossible? The proud owner of this mammoth organ was certainly in demand among the coeds who attended the University of California at this particular time some 30 years ago. He got rave notices from those girls who had the guts to go all the way with him. In those days before the Pill, it took considerable courage to let oneself go since the fear of pregnancy was always lurking and skulking about on the fringes of one's sensibilities.

I recently noticed that this same individual has a real

estate office in a town near where I live. You wouldn't believe the thoughts I have had about going there under the pretense of looking for a house and then by some hook or crook finding out for myself if all those stories of long ago were really true!

My own husband of 32 years has a really wonderful penis which certainly pleases me in every way and I have never had any problem having an orgasm when we have intercourse. But I must confess I would love to see what an even bigger penis would achieve with me, pleasurewise. Are you surprised that a normal 55-year-old woman, mother of four sons, would feel this way? Mrs. L.S. can put me down in favor of large or should I say . . . ENORMOUS?—*Mrs. B.A. (name and address withheld), Piedmont, Ca.*

* * *

I would like to comment on the letter (December) of Miss O.N. of Lincoln, Nebraska. She makes it quite clear that she prefers a large penis, both in length and circumference. I would appreciate it if she (or any woman who prefers a large penis) would answer several questions:

1. At what point does she differentiate between a large penis and a small penis? 2. Does she require prospective males to reveal their vital statistics in order to gain her company in bed? 3. Assuming the answer to the previous question is no, suppose she discovers her male friend has a small penis—does she mock him, laugh hysterically, and terminate things right there, or does she proceed regardless and why? 4. After intercourse (assuming a small penis to be acceptable), does she state her displeasure, act indifferently, or compliment him so as not to damage his ego? 5. Has a man with a small penis ever satisfied her? 6. In her experience does a large penis mean a good lover? 7. How many women does she know who prefer a large penis?

I am one of those males who is not well hung. My penis is a classical stubby (no dangle in the flaccid state and a small increase in length when erect). I don't suppose Miss O.N. could understand how so little can provide so much pleasure for so many.—*R.B. (name and address withheld), Newington, Conn.*

* * *

3

Breast Size

I am increasingly angry at my fellow males' infantile fascination with large breasts. To many of them the rule of thumb is the bigger the better. Personally, I find an over-endowed female with large hips and breasts sickening and the sight almost turns me off altogether. I find a thin woman with firm yet small breasts to be far sexier than her plump counterpart. Females such as Ali McGraw are far more sexy. Also, small-breasted women are generally in better physical condition and are more responsive in bed.

The fascination with large breasts seem to directly relate with the "large penis and missionary-position syndrome." These men are totally ignorant sexually and I feel sorry for them. They don't know what they are missing. Right on with small breasts!—*D.W., Irvington, N.J.*

* * *

Although I'm not a regular reader I have looked through several issues of *Penthouse* and feel it is superior to other magazines of its kind in all respects but one. Your magazine tends to be more artistic and less degrading to women. It is your obsession with models having large breasts that annoys me. Certainly you should appeal to all tastes, and many men are more attracted to women with large breasts than small breasts, just as many women are more attracted to men with large muscles than small. But certainly all men and all women don't feel the same way.

I happen to be one of those women with sexy green eyes, long blond hair, long slender legs, and smaller-than-average breasts. I have seen no women of this type in *Penthouse*.

It is an American, egotistical fetish to be so entranced with breast size, and I resent it. I once had hang-ups about it; I was afraid to go to bed with a man and have him find out my long legs are on the same body as small tits. I've found that liberated men and men who are not self-centered are not so concerned with this and consider me very sexually attractive. I've gotten over it; unfortunately some men haven't. What about you?—*Nancy N. (address withheld)*

* * *

After reading about the flat-chested housewife in your February Forum, I had to write and tell her to be informed before rejecting an idea!

Give up your barbells, lady, and go see a good plastic surgeon. The initial consultation costs peanuts, but it can change your life—it did mine!

My bra used to fit on backwards. My scant 32A was the subject of much ridicule and jest among all of our friends. I joked, too, because I was so self-conscious about my lack of tits. Inwardly, I would resent it, and look to my husband for reassurance. He was wonderful, but he couldn't help gaping at the other braless foxes as they bounced by.

Finally, at age twenty-one, I found out about the

Cronin Sylastic implant by Dow Corning. I went to see the most reputable plastic surgeon available in the Palm Beach area. With much opposition from friends, and to the horror of my family and in-laws (how dare I tamper with what nature gave me!), I had mammaplasty surgery.

I was in the hospital only three days. An incision was made where the fold of my breast was supposed to be. The implant was placed under my mammary glands and my own skin was stretched over the whole works. I am still able to nurse my babies without difficulty.

If it had cost $5,000, instead of only $1,500, I'd do it again! I am the proud owner of a pair of round, firm, full 32C's! I look like a woman now, instead of a fourteen-year-old boy. My husband is overjoyed, my family is relieved, and my friends tell me I look great. My clothes fit beautifully. My swimsuit clings instead of caving in, and my husband's mouth waters when I take off my shirt.

No woman deserves to feel as depressed as I am and that pathetic woman in your February issue. Lady, do you have enough moxie to stand up for what you want, regardless of opposition, or do you want your husband to keep sighing over *Penthouse* Pets' jugs and not yours?—*Mrs. M.B., West Palm Beach, Fla.*

* * *

My husband is a regular reader of *Penthouse* and I also enjoy reading your magazine. Though many magazines claim to be "liberated," yours is one of the few that can say this in all honesty.

However, my main object in writing to you concerns the attitude of many men who prefer small-breasted women to those of us who are more generously endowed. Though they are apparently few and far between, it is my opinion that these men have some stupid notion that women with large breasts have less feeling in them than those with smaller breasts. I have discussed this with a lot of men I know, and you'd be surprised how many of them actually believe this fallacy! Have I got news for all you guys who believe that crap! I wear a 36C bra and I get just as much (or more) excitement and sexual stimulation from having my boobs fondled and caressed as anyone else. I know for a fact that women with big tits have just as much sensitivity in their nipples and breasts as the chicks with little tits! Thanks for letting me sound off.—*B.M., Warrensburg, Mo.*

* * *

I am small-breasted, and barely start to fill a 34-A cup. I am twenty-four and have two children who I have successfully nursed, each for twelve and a half months.

I was always able to cope with my breast size by developing my sexual abilities and an optimistic attitude. But lately I am extremely depressed about my figure.

My husband looks at *Penthouse* and compares the breasts of the photographed girls to mine. He sighs loud enough to be sure I will hear, and then he tells me how great they look. He continually calls me "flat-chested," and gapes at girls on the street.

In desperation, I ask him, "What can I do? I am what I am."

I have done exercises faithfully for ten years and I don't want to mess up my body with hormones, creams, surgery, etc., in case I want to conceive and nurse again. What's the solution? Why are some men so hung-up on breasts?—*Name and address withheld*

* * *

I very much enjoy reading the articles and stories in *Penthouse* looking at the lovely girls. I would like to respond to some of your letters praising large-breasted women and the ability of large breasts to be more stimulating. I don't agree with this.

After the breasts grow over a certain size, they aren't as shapely and have a tendency to sag more. I am aroused by a lovely pair of breasts no matter what size they are. Small breasts can be quite appealing. The most important thing to me is whether it pleases the woman to have her breasts caressed and kissed. Sensitivity is the key. To use an old cliché, "More than a mouthful is wasted anyway."

Take heart, small-breasted women! There are some men who really admire small breasts. It is the woman behind them that gives them their appeal.—*Name withheld, Placerville, Calif.*

* * *

I would like to reply to the woman who wrote in the February *Penthouse* Forum asking for an answer for her husband's complaints about her being flat-chested. I would like to suggest one answer that works.

I was a 32A and bothered immensely about it. I never felt sexy around other women even though I have a pretty face and nice legs. There were a lot of clothes I couldn't wear, and forget about finding a bathing suit with a thirty-two inch top and a thirty-five inch bottom. I finally decided to seek help through my doctor. He recommended a fantastic plastic surgeon who gave me all the facts.

The operation is called mammaplasty augmentation. It is a fairly simple operation. A silicone filled bag is implanted into the breast, thereby enlarging it. The silicone bag never becomes hard, nor will it get lumpy. Approximately one month after the operation it becomes softer, until it feels and looks real. After about two months no one can tell the difference. The scars are about one and a half inches long and are under the fold of the breast. They are almost invisible.

There are no big risks with this surgery that I have experienced or heard of. It is a little inconvenient for the first month. I couldn't lift my arms over my head or lift anything too heavy. I had to wear a bra for three to four weeks. Bathing was also difficult.

I highly recommend this operation to any woman who is serious in her desire for larger breasts. The cost runs from about $1,200 to $1,800, which is high, but I believe the operation would be well worth it to any woman whose feelings about herself will be heightened for the rest of her life.—*Name and address withheld*

4

Incest

From your recent issues it appears that sibling sex might be more commonplace than is generally assumed. I might also venture to say that the publication in your magazine of letters on the subject helps to promote more understanding.

In my own case, Sis and I experimented with each other when she was thirteen and I was fifteen, over twenty-five years ago, but had not touched each other since. That is, up until two weeks ago when I stayed overnight at her home in Illinois while on a business trip there. At about two o'clock I awakened with her shaking me and telling me that I was snoring too loudly and that she could hear me in her room downstairs. (Her husband works at night.) I started to whisper my apologies and turn over when I noticed through her gaping robe as she bent over that she was naked except for stockings. I asked if she didn't wear pajamas and she countered by asking if I really minded. At that point we started to fondle one another and had an absolutely great lovemaking session. On my return trip two days later it was absolutely delightful. I firmly believe that my future trips to that area will be a lot more fun than before.

I must point out that she still has a trim and attractive figure, and I want to add my voice to the chorus of those requesting pictures of some of these mature and handsome women. Mr. Guccioine has amply demonstrated his ability to photograph women invitingly and attractively. I am sure he could do an even better job with older ladies who will have a great deal of sensitivity and understanding.—*Name and address withheld*

* * *

Last summer I was with my girl friend in the woods near my house. We were both completely naked and screwing our hearts out. My mother and my teacher are very good friends and nuts about birdwatching. About ten minutes after we had started, my teacher saw us through her binoculars and told my mother. They walked over and started to stare at us. We were very embarrassed and all I could say was, "Well." (My father had died years before.) After a few more minutes my mother asked if they could join us. They were undressed in seconds. After a few minutes we were all screwing. Since that day (as I'm an only child) I sleep with my mother every night. We sometimes have my chick and teacher share our king-sized bed with us. We have sex for a full weekend. Now, the thought of another girl never enters my mind except for my chick, my mother, and my teacher. —*(Name and address withheld)*

* * *

In regard to the letter in your August Forum concerning the sibling lovers, I, too, have experienced sex with my sister and it has been the best I've had.

When we were growing up, our bedrooms were joined by a door that was permanently locked. I made a small hole in this door so that I could view my sister while she was undressing. At the age of thirteen, my sister being sixteen, I became totally aroused while watching her undress and decided to confront her. I barged into her room wearing only jockey shorts and there she stood, totally nude. We both just stood there for about thirty seconds, our eyes in constant motion, not missing an inch of one another's body. Without a word said, I walked over to her and began kissing her, pressing her warm, firm body to mine. She was offering no resistance so I eased her down on the bed and at the same time removed my shorts. I began sucking and kissing her breast until she was moaning with pleasure. I deflowered my sister that night and we have enjoyed sex together to this day. I am now twenty-six, single, and enjoy sex with other women. My sister is married and the mother of a two-year-old girl, but we continue to enjoy our "special relationship" whenever possible. The reason she did not resist me that first night was that she had wanted me as much as I wanted her. She told me afterward that she had been trying to think up an indirect way for it to happen. Neither of us feels it is wrong. Our sexual relationship is beautiful!—*(Name withheld), Santa Ana, Calif.*

* * *

In reference to the letter written by E.R. from Chicago in your August issue revealing the affair with his sister, I have a similar situation. I am twenty years old, brought up in a normal middle-class household, and considered attractive. I am currently having an affair with my older sister.

It all started a year and a half ago during Christmas vacation in 1971. I was sitting listening to my stereo one night, when Mary, three years older than I, walked in my room with nothing but a bra and panties on. I was quite surprised since she never before left her room unless she was fully clothed.

When I lowered the volume, Mary stuttered and hesitated. Finally, she asked apprehensively, "Have you wanted to make love to your sister?" I confided that, yes, I had many times, and confessed that it was a shame that she was my sister. "You feel the same way I do, don't you?" she asked. I nodded affirmatively. I went to give her a kiss on the cheek and she flung her arms around me and kissed me hotly on the lips. We slowly undressed each other and we made love. I almost had forgotten that she was my sister. She has to be one of the best I've ever had. We still make love every chance we get.—*(Name and address withheld)*

* * *

I was really turned on by E.R.'s letter (August) describing his incestuous relationship with his sister.

I, too, enjoyed my older sister's body for over a year. We couldn't keep our hands off each other. We sexed it up all over the house whenever the opportunity presented itself. Sometimes we couldn't wait and risked getting caught.

One time our stepmother almost caught us when I was standing Sis up against the wall of her room. We heard Mom coming up the stairs, so we went into a walk-in closet without missing a stroke. The excitement of possible discovery increased our pleasure immensely. Although she never said anything, we felt Mom knew what we were up to and we were very careful after that.

A few months later my sister, who was twenty-one and four years older, met her future husband and our relationship tapered off. She married some months later and moved away.

In the eight years since her marriage my sister and I have seen one another some four or five times without any thought of sex.

Then E.R. in your August issue did two things—brought back exciting memories and gave me a hard-on for my sister.

I lost no time in visiting her and took *Penthouse* with me. The evening of my arrival, my sister, her husband, and I sat around talking and I steered the conversation to *Penthouse*, pointing out various articles for each to read. She, of course, was given the E.R. letter. I watched her closely for her response as she read the item. A slow blush spread over her and I detected labored breathing. I could see that it was having an effect on her. In fact, her husband asked her if she was feeling ill, but she laughed it off.

She gave me a penetrating look, which told me that she knew what I had in mind. For the remainder of the evening she was somewhat cold, and I figured that I had struck out. I went to bed certain that I had made the long trip for nothing.

Next morning, I was rudely shaken awake from a deep sleep to find my naked sister abusing me orally. "You lousy, horny bastard," she cried, shaking me violently. "Why did you come here?"

My response was immediate. In a matter of minutes, she was in bed with me and we had resumed our relationship. Her husband was at work and we screwed all day long. By the time my brother-in-law returned from work I was worn to a frazzle. This went on for about a week.

I returned home shortly thereafter. Spoke to Dad the other day and he told me that my sister thought she was pregnant. Is it possible that after eight childless years of marriage my brother-in-law finally hit the jackpot? I wonder.—*(Name and address withheld)*

* * *

I am writing in response to E.R.'s letter in the August *Forum*. I'm a woman who started reading *Penthouse* when I found out about Xaviera Hollander's column in it. My experiences were with my brother, and they started when I was twelve. (I am now nineteen.) He is seven years older than me and was nineteen when we started messing around. As I recall, I was in his room and wanted to know something, but he wouldn't tell me. Finally he said he would tell me if I pulled down my pants. This was the first time he had ever acted like this and I was shocked. But I really wanted to know, so I showed him. He messed around with his fingers, and then tried to put his penis in. He got it in about halfway, but he was too much for my twelve-year-old frame.

We messed around on and off until I was sixteen. I felt rather guilty about it, and was scared I would get pregnant. He kept getting more and more insistent, so I went out and got some rubbers. We started having sex regularly, and with the fear of pregnancy gone, I really got into it. After my parents and grandmother would go to bed at night, I would sneak over to his room or he would sneak over to mine. The thing I liked about it was that it was so convenient. I could get all the sex I wanted and never even had to leave the house! When he moved into an apartment, I would go over and see him. No one ever thought anything about going over to see my own brother.

The reason our relationship finally stopped was because I went to college over twelve hundred miles away from home. During this past summer I wasn't limited to just my brother for a partner. I had three other friends who would be up and ready anytime I wanted. I had a great thing going and I'm really sorry I had to leave it. Now I am so frustrated sex-wise I can hardly stand it. I have embarrassing sex dreams almost every night. Many times they are about my brother and me, and this is strange, since I haven't done anything with him since last July, and I've had other partners more recently than him. I guess that goes to show that subconsciously I still place my brother ahead of my other lovers. I guess maybe you never get your siblings out of your system once you have had the type of relationship I have had with my brother, but I don't feel guilty about it, and don't regret having it.—*(Name and address withheld)*

* * *

Although I never thought that I would write to a magazine, I have undergone an experience that I feel needs relating, and *Penthouse* seems the only place to do so.

I have just ended an eight-month affair with my sister. The entire situation has affected me to such a degree that I fear I will be unsatisfied with anything but an incestuous encounter.

My sister, twenty-nine, is an attractive, dark-haired

widow. She returned to our home immediately after her husband was killed in an auto accident. She went into mourning but never came out of it. She did not date, and as she had no children, led a rather empty life. I was twenty-one at the time of our first intimacy, at home for summer vacation. My parents had gone out for the evening and I had just come home from a very frustrating date. In the privacy of my bedroom, I stripped and began to masturbate my frustration away. To my astonishment, my sister barged into my room. I was terribly embarrassed and expected her to say something nasty. Instead she smiled and said, "Do you need sex that badly?" I nodded. She closed the door behind her and began to take off her night clothes.

I was speechless. As she stripped, it was as though I was seeing my sister for the first time. Her breasts were firm and well shaped and her dark pubic mound made my erection swell. I finally blurted out that what she was doing was wrong, from a religious (we are lapsed Catholics) and moral point of view. Her reply was, "Nothing is wrong if it makes us happy."

She got on the bed and began to suck me, her entire body moving with the rhythm of her mouth. My mind was totally messed up by what was going on, but it did not prevent me from coming in her mouth with complete abandon. After she had swallowed my load, she pulled me down and I proceeded to give her as complete a workout as she had given me. Her climax was unbelievable and she kept calling out her dead husband's name with each spasm.

That wasn't to be all for that evening. After a short rest, we made total love, from every conceivable position. As I sucked her breasts and kissed her, I began to overcome my enormous guilt, but only slightly. I enjoyed her immensely but I knew deep down that it was all wrong.

For that entire summer we made love every opportunity we had. We reached the stage where we would both pretend to go out for the evening and then go to the apartment of a friend of hers, where we would fuck the night away. Our home life continued with the normal spats between siblings. However, no matter how severe an argument we had at home, it never interfered with our sexual relationship.

When it came time for me to leave home for graduate school, I thought that our relationship would come to an end, but I was wrong. My sister came to visit me on weekends and we made love as before. It was affecting me so strongly that I gradually came to love my sister in a totally new way. I could no longer relate to any other girl. I wanted only to make love to my beautiful but forbidden-by-society sibling.

On my last school vacation, a few weeks ago, my sister revealed to me that she had met a guy and that she would no longer visit me. On the pretext of finding me a bandage, she took me into the bathroom and sucked me off for old time's sake. It seems that as far as she is concerned, everything is all right now. Perhaps that is so for her. But all I can do at night is lie in my bed and dream of her glorious breasts and cunt. I'm getting sick over the guilt and the longing. I've considered seeking professional help, but I'm simply too ashamed to discuss this with anyone. I would be interested in knowing whether any of your other readers have had similar experiences and whether they've shaken the need for incestuous love.—E.R., Chicago, Ill.

* * *

5

Fighting Females

I am a normal, red-blooded, American male, who gets very excited watching two lovely young ladies engage in a knock-down, drag-out, hair-pulling fight. Is this normal? I have read other letters in your magazine by men with the same feelings as mine. As far back as I can remember, I have been extremely turned-on seeing two girls fight, wrestle, or box. Ever since the sixth or seventh grade, I was always among the first to arrive at a girl-fight.

I often have fantasies about two beautiful young ladies fully dressed getting into a fight and literally tearing each other's clothes completely off. Then they continue to fight and wrestle until one completely surrenders. The more I read *Penthouse* and other magazines, the more I see other letters like mine. Could you have a pictorial in a future issue featuring a sexy, wild girl-fight? It would certainly give great pleasure to us female violence freaks.—*H.C., Omaha, Neb.*

* * *

I recently had the opportunity to watch two lovely girls battle it out for real on the beach here in southern California. Both girls were arguing over a man they were dating. One girl was a willowy brunette in a black bikini and the other was an Amazon-like blond in a flower-print bikini. The blond was at least six feet tall and very well built. The brunette was a foot shorter and many pounds lighter.

When both girls started to fight I thought that the blond would win for sure. First she punched the brunette in the jaw and sent her reeling backwards. The brunette landed a few timid punches on the blond's breasts and face but didn't really cause any damage. But then she must have seen the blond's sunbronzed belly staring back at her. The brunette quickly sank her fist into the blond's belly. The blond blew out an agonizing gasp and doubled over with both hands on her belly. The crowd cheered. The brunette kicked her in the chest as she doubled over —lifted the blond's hands away from protecting her belly—and punched her in the breadbasket again. The blond doubled over again, gasping for breath and crying. The brunette slapped her in the face and the blond toppled over backwards, moaning on the sand. The brunette gave her a savage kick between the legs and the blond passed out.

Watching this spectacle, I had an orgasm in my swimtrunks. My girl friend could barely wait to get away from the beach to have sex with me. We made passionate love well into the morning and talked about the experience we both had enjoyed.—*J.M., Los Angeles, Calif.*

* * *

I am a young housewife twenty years of age who enjoys your magazine. My mother and mother-in-law are also regular readers. We particularly enjoy the letters from your readers—but we do wish you would have a pictorial on older women as both my mother and mother-in-law are living proof of older women being beautiful. My mother is forty-one years old and measures 38-26-

37. My mother-in-law is thirty-nine years old and measures 37-26-36—and both have long sexy looking legs. I am at half their age and I measure 36-24-35 and would be hard pressed to top them in a beauty contest. I mention statistics only to point out that magazines like your own do not really give older women their fair share of praise.

Recently we have noticed a growing interest in your readers on the subject of women wrestling. My mother-in-law and I decided to try it out and see what we thought of it, if anything—and this is what happened. It was a spur-of-the-moment decision and we were both clad in what probably would turn on most men—short skirts, sheer panty hose and halter-tops. Since neither of us had done any wrestling in the past we agreed to wrestle at five-minute intervals with one-minute rest periods. We knew very little about holds, etc. so we agreed to wrestle free-style—anything goes, but no elements of cat-fighting allowed. We lasted only fifteen minutes before we were both exhausted. We managed some awkward but effective holds during our match, including headlocks and leg scissors, but we mostly just rolled around my rug exchanging the upper hand. The only real damage was the loss of two pairs of panty hose which would catch, snag, and finally run when we engaged in some stiff leg wrestling. Actually, this leg wrestling proved to be my undoing. Towards the end of our match we were both tired but my mother-in-law managed to trap both my legs with hers, and although I tried with all my strength, I could not break my legs loose from hers. Our legs must have resembled pretzels as they were locked so tightly together. I finally conceded to her because I could not dislodge her from the top position.

We both enjoyed our match and my mother-in-law felt a sense of accomplishment in beating me. I did not like losing but I feel I gave my best and it was a good experience. I plan to beat her in the future anyhow as we may wrestle each other weekly for the exercise and competition. She and my mother wrestled this past week in bikinis and I was the referee and timekeeper. They wrestled to a twenty-minute draw and really showed me a thing or two as they went all out and found themselves equal in strength and stamina. They engaged in a mutual bear hug contest for a full three minutes and although I thought they would both faint, neither would submit to the other. My mother-in-law tried her leg-hold trick towards the end of their match but met her equal as my mother managed to trap one of my mother-in-law's legs with her own and kept her to a stalemate. My mother and I are going at it next week. Keep up the good work but please do not write off older women—take it from me they can hold their own against us younger women if they keep in shape. Many thanks from three liberated women.—*Name and address withheld*

* * *

I have been reading *Penthouse* for nearly a year now and I would like to comment regarding "wrestling contests" engaged in by women which seemed to turn-on some of your male readers.

I am thirty years old, 5 feet 7 inches tall and have been told by men as long as I can remember how attractive I am. Unfortunately, I am one of those unlucky women who is literally flat-chested although I can say I do take pride in the rest of my body. I am happily married, or at least I was until a few weeks ago, and I have a sixteen year old stepdaughter from my husband's former marriage. At sixteen, she is built like you wouldn't believe: 36C-25-35 and 5 feet 4 inches tall. Besides all of that going for her, she is a real beauty who swims a few miles every day during the summer and skis constantly during the winter months.

Five years ago I lost my temper and gave my stepdaughter a mild spanking for failing to come home from school when she was supposed to. At that time, I am sure she consented half-willingly due to my mother image plus a definite height advantage. Recently, my stepdaughter and I had been arguing about whether she should be allowed to stay out as late as she wants on a date. Naturally, I said no. At the time our differences of opinion were becoming more emotional we were vacationing at my husband's fishing cottage which is located in a fairly deserted beach area in New England. He was out fishing somewhere and my stepdaughter and I were alone on a small beach area concealed by high grass and trees.

When I told her that she deserved a good, sound spanking, she told me that if I thought I could do it I should try—and she said it in such a way that I had no choice. That was my mistake. As soon as she had spoken, I reached for her and accidentally caught her bikini bra-strap and it ripped off. I couldn't believe the size and firmness of her breasts! It was the first time I had ever seen her partially nude. Then she said something about teaching me a lesson that I would never forget.

We were both standing facing each other by this time. She grabbed my long hair and pulled down hard and suddenly my legs just buckled and I went down on my knees. While on my knees I tried to wrap my arms around her legs in order to get her down but just as quickly as I had been forced to the ground she lifted me to my feet by lightly grasping my shoulders. She repeated this about a half dozen times; then she allowed me to get my arms around her waist while I was still on my knees and she was standing over me. She just stood there with her hands on her hips and sort of laughed as I squeezed my arms around her waist with all my might in order to get her to the ground. Looking up at her, I couldn't even see her face because of her monstrous breasts just above my head. She then very coolly reached down and grabbed my left arm and pulled it up behind my back. I was totally powerless and knew that I had no chance. With her other hand she unclipped my bikini top, let it fall, and gave my tiny nipples each a pinch. I felt like a weak, little child. Still holding my left arm behind my back she sat down and lifted me up and across her lap facing her. With her right hand she yanked off my panties. Never had my body been so useless and powerless!

After that she stood up, leaving me nude and lying flat on my back and, as I looked up at her, I can't tell you how much I envied her youth, power, physical stature and beauty! Then she bent down on one knee, turned me over and lifted me face down across her knee and spanked me until I cried. When she stopped I turned to her and begged her not to humiliate me anymore. Still crying, I buried my face into her huge, firm, beautiful breasts. She held me closely, now aware of my humiliation, and as she did so, I reached orgasm like never before—with my husband or any man!

I ask you: how can the consequences of such a "contest" turn any man on? I continue to read *Penthouse*, and I would like to see how your male readers (or female) react to my humiliating experience.—*Name and address withheld*

* * *

In the recent issue of *Penthouse*, I read a letter from a man who said that since childhood he has been sexually aroused by seeing girls fight or wrestle. I, too, have always been turned on by girls wrestling. As a teen-ager, I had an ejaculation watching a movie of women wrestling, and I always get excited watching females wrestle on TV or in the flesh. Most of the girl wrestlers are very sexy, shapely and good looking, with beautiful, strong legs and thighs and well-formed bodies. I am sure many men and women, as well as the wrestlers themselves, must become extremely aroused by two scantily clad Amazons pitting their strength against each other.

Recently my wife and I had the good fortune to meet two attractive girls who were good at wrestling. They came to our house, and after dinner and conversation, suggested pairing off for wrestling. First, the two girls put on a match. Then each of them paired off against my wife and against me. Everyone wrestled in the nude. I was brought to climax several times during the evening, once while the girl wrapped her powerful bare thighs around my head and squeezed me until I thought my head would burst like a grapefruit; and again when one of them got the same head scissors on my wife; and again when my wife got the same hold on her.—*R. H., Concord, N.H.*

* * *

One of the most exciting experiences in my life happened last summer. My girl and I rented a holiday cottage in New Jersey and she had a girlfriend staying down also with her boyfriend. My girl Phyllis is 20, blonde, 5ft. 6in. and weighs about 123 lbs. Her girlfriend is 17, 5ft. 3in., and she weighs 108 lbs. Both of these girls are beautiful and they would always wear the smallest bikinis on the beach.

One day when we got back from swimming we were sitting around eating sandwiches when Jean (the young one) poked her finger in Phyllis's belly and asked her when she was going to lose all that fat. It's true she has a little pot belly, but it's kind of cute. I could see my girl trying to think of a comeback line but Jean has a perfect body so she just got up from her chair and said: "I may be fatter than you but I can still beat you in wrestling any day, teeny-bopper." My girl jumped on her to try and pin her down but Jean slipped away and managed to trip Phyllis and put her on her behind. She straddled Phyllis and pinned her shoulders down with her knees. I never saw my girl embarrassed like that before. She tried her best to get up but that young chick was too much this time. She finally let her up and said: "Nice try but you lost. Any time you want a return match let me know." God, did I love that!

Later in the week I kept asking my girl if she would ever wrestle Jean again. I finally got them together on my bed one evening about 11 pm. Both had on bikini panties and bras. Finally my girl said: "Let's do something exciting, Jean, and wrestle." She jumped on her and they were at it again. I should say by now that I was sexually aroused. I watched intently and could hear nothing but grunts and groans and could see nothing but arms, legs, feet, beautiful behinds, breasts, etc. Positions changed quickly but to be honest about it my girl was getting beat. That young chick was in too good shape for her and she knew it. Jean was really just toying with Phyllis. Like one time she was on top and Phyllis was on her belly and she just unhooked her bra and gave it to me. She finally rolled Phyllis on her back and easily pinned her down, bare tits and all.

That has to be the most exciting thing a guy can watch! Please run an article on women wrestling—not the big fat ones, but young beautiful girls.—*John Myers, Newark State College, Union, New Jersey.*

* * *

6

Enemas

I've just finished your July issue and took particular notice of another of the continuing letters about the pleasures of the enema. Although I had wanted to write in the past but did not, I now have the courage to share my pleasures with your other readers.

My youngest recollection of anal stimulation is at about the age of seven. In normal child homosexual contact, we would undress and imitate our parents taking our temperatures substituting for a thermometer our fingers, pens, swizzle sticks, and occasionally wax crayons (although they tended to break). I enjoyed this tremendously. Growing into my teens, I continued it privately.

At age fifteen I was dating an eighteen-year-old college freshman. Because enemas had by that time become one of my favorite stimuli, upon visiting his apartment I was quick to notice his enema bag hanging on his shower nozzle. We had explored each other sexually and I wasn't too shy to inquire about it and even suggested that he use it on me. He used an enema only to cleanse his bowels and was shocked at my suggestion, but only at first. After my confession, he admitted that he too received sexual arousement from an enema. He subsequently agreed to experiment. It was at this time that I experienced my first full orgasm, although our experimentation was limited to the conventional "fillers;" water with soap and seltzer.

It's been five years, and many experiences since have refined my tastes to the optimum that I wish to share with your readers. I suggest a two-way enema to be followed by analingus. My two favorite fillers are two parts milk to one part cocoa (preferably luke-warm) and tomato juice (bottled *not* canned) with a dash of lemon juice at room temperature.—*B.J. (name withheld), Huntingdon Valley, Pa.*

* * *

In your July issue, a reader from Detroit describes his humiliation at being given enemas by his mother while lying on his back. He states that this is the wrong position to receive an enema.

Not so, particularly for an infant or a child. Almost any book on child-rearing or child-nursing, written between 1900 and 1930 recommends this position for children. Indeed, the many illustrations show the child lying on its back, with the legs extended upward by the nurse's left hand, and the tube being inserted with her right hand. In about half of the pictures, the child is receiving the enema on a padded table, in the others the child is on the nurse's lap.

I received my enemas lying face down across my mother's knees. I suspect that the reason for this was that she used a squeeze bulb syringe, and it was necessary, in her thinking, to refill it four or five times during the procedure. Certainly this was much more convenient for her if I was face down.

I remember being called into the bathroom. On the bench, next to my mother, would be a white basin full of soapy water, with a bar of Ivory Soap floating in it. She would be stirring it with the enema syringe. Across her lap was a bath towel. She would lift me across her knees, and hold me down with her left elbow. With her left hand she would pry my buttocks apart. Her right hand held the syringe. There was seldom any big deal about the operation, and no delay. The tube went in, squeeze, out again and refill. This went on until I yelled "enough!" or the juvenile equivalent. No tears, no fuss, no discussion. I know I cooperated with her because I rather enjoyed the attention.

All that was, alas, many years ago. But although I have had many enemas since then, and enjoyed every one of them, I would love to meet the woman who would take me face down over her lap and do it that way. It would probably be a grotesque sight, but would be a pleasant variation from the left-side, knee-chest, or lie-on-the-back positions that are routine today.—*E.M. (name withheld), Portland, Oreg.*

* * *

My rather dominant girl friend and I discovered a most exciting and pleasurable new routine, concerning the pleasures of an enema.

On the occasions that she wishes to give me an enema, I am ordered to get the equipment and bring it to her. We proceed to the bathroom where I strip while she fills the bag with warm, soapy water. I assume whatever position she decides is preferable (the most frequent positions are the knee-chest position with my bottom high in the air, or lying flat on my back with my legs spread apart and flexed) and she inserts the tube, which has a large douche nozzle instead of a smaller enema tip. After the full bag of soapy water has run into my bowels, I retain it until I have performed cunnilingus on my girl friend. After she is satisfied, I am allowed to expel the enema. After I finish, we have intercourse, and we have found the whole routine to be totally enjoyable, and an excellent addition to our lovemaking repertoire.

Occasionally, the enema is used in a different fashion, as a punishment for some misbehavior on my part. When this is the case, a very different procedure is followed. I am stripped and tied face-down in a spread-eagle position. The filled enema bag is emptied rapidly into my bowels and frequently an additional quantity will be injected to increase the discomfort. I have to retain the enema until I am released to expel it on penalty of the procedure being repeated. If she has decided that an extra severe punishment is in order, the tube will be removed after the regular enema has been injected and the business end of a large feminine hygiene bulb syringe will be inserted in my rectum. The bulb will then be forcefully squeezed and slowly released at irregular intervals without warning. This pumping action, involving as it does the sudden injection of over half a pint of water into an already uncomfortably full bowel is a very effective addition to the punishment. This treatment is one that I avoid as much as possible, unlike the regular enemas, which I enjoy very much.—*Name and address withheld.*

* * *

As a child of 12, a nurse gave me an enema when I was sick. This caused me to have an erection and for reasons unknown at the time, great excitement in anticipation of this treatment. It was the first sexual experience in my life, though it was done for more lofty reasons, and ever since then I have sought women to give me enemas.

My experiences have not always been too successful, because most people—even those in the massage business—take it as an insult and think that there must be something strangely wrong with having anal desires. I'm convinced that the real reason behind this problem is the soothing, decongesting effect on the prostate and relief of sexual tension. However, I have met only one woman completely honest about her anal eroticism—and this includes the people I've met in various clinics—*B.W. (name withheld), APO San Francisco, Calif.*

* * *

As long as I can remember up to age fourteen, my

parents gave me enemas for no reason. Most of the time only my mother gave them to me, but I can remember on two occasions over the years when my father gave them to me. For either of them, the procedure was the same. I would take off all my clothes and get down on my hands and knees facing the bathtub. My elbows would be over the rim of the tub and they would insert the black nozzle, not the regular short one, but the slightly curved one with the four sides coming to a rounded point with holes in each side.

As I got older I would give myself enemas and would be unable to understand why there was pain all the way through the procedure (not knowing that I had the bag hung too high). When I was thirteen I let my brother give me two enemas and they also were too painful to hold and even complete, and I still didn't know why. Then, when I was fourteen my parents gave me the last enema that they would ever give me. This one was different for two reasons—both parents were present, and second, the bag was not used. In its place was a sink full of warm soapy water and a squeeze bulb with a pipe on it similar to the one normally used, but longer. I was in the same position—on knees facing the tub, elbows resting on the inside rim—and the bulb was filled by squeezing it and letting it go while the nozzle was in the mixture. It was then inserted into me and squeezed several times. As a result, I received a terrific erection and felt very bashful and red in the face; my parents did not say anything and I was glad of that.

When I was about fourteen or fifteen years old, I experimented with enemas on myself. One time I weighed myself on the bathroom scales and wrote the weight on a piece of paper. I gave myself an enema and reweighed. I found that I had gained five pounds. After this weight, I emptied my bowels and decided to weigh myself for the third time. I was back to my original weight. I do not know how much I weighed at the time, but I do remember the five-pound gain after receiving the enema and before expelling it.

Over the years, I found that by trying various positions and by draining the tube and nozzle to expel air, an enema can feel good if given properly.—*Name and address withheld*

* * *

I would like to thank you for printing C. M. Bateman's letter (September Forum) on the use of the soapstick suppository. As a child my mother gave me soapsticks frequently and I have been using them as a sexual stimulant ever since. Until your recent publication I thought I was alone in this predilection. I have tried using enemas but I still prefer the soapstick.—*Alan F. (name and address withheld), Buffalo, New York.*

* * *

I was certainly delighted to read your recent Forum correspondence on "Special Preference." Enemas are well established as part of the sex routine of sophisticated Americans. Mutual enemas while enjoying *soixante neuf* is an old game—and an excellent one too!

Massage salons in the Washington area (which are really places where sex liaisons are either arranged or completed) are used to being called several times a day by people who want enemas—and they seek them for sexual gratification, not therapy.—*Franklin Roth, Friendship Station, Washington, D.C.*

* * *

I was very pleased to see your magazine take the initiative on the subject of the good ol' enema. It needed to be taken out of the Victorian closets (as referred to by one of your readers). Enemas were much a part of my boyhood and teen years, living in the 50s on a farm in Northern Ontario. Except for aspirins, Mother's only remedy for us four boys was the enema, and we all got more of them than aspirins. Mother had a big red rubber bag and tubing, to which was attached a white ivory nozzle and, though we always got the enema for anything from headaches to sprained ankles, they were also given to all of us at special times. These occasions were the weekend before we went back to school, in the spring (to get us "spring cleaned") and after we got back from camp. All four boys, separated only by one year in between, had to remain in bed on these special occasions, usually on Saturdays. Mother would give the eldest boy the enema first, in front of us all. As we had no Dad, the eldest then helped in giving enemas to the others, so not only did we learn not to be ashamed of our bodies but to give and take enemas without shame or guilt in later years.

It was only in my later teens that I began to get erections when the warm soap and water flowed in, and I began to think about giving enemas to other people, especially girls. At 17 I had to go to a clinic for a minor operation and it was there a young girl gave me an unexpected enema. While the operation involved the lancing of a boil on my knee from a football injury the night before, the doctor insisted that I get a good cleaning out so I could rest in bed afterwards without having to go too often to the bathroom. This was indeed the sexiest enema I had up to this time! The young brunette nurse aide showed me into the treatment room. Once inside, she told me I was to receive an enema. I had still not got into my pajamas and was wearing bell bottoms and a sports shirt. She left me alone for about five minutes sitting up on the treatment table. There was a huge glass jar affixed to the wall above the table and from it was connected a very large rubber hose and a rectal nozzle three times as big as the one my mother used at home. I began to get an erection in anticipation of the treatment ahead of me and started to masturbate to be surprised by the brunette's return. Without any embarrassment she came over and started to remove my shoes. Next she unbuttoned my shirt and then, seeming to ignore my projecting penis, pulled down my pants. Once again, I felt like my mother was doing this, but there was nothing to beat it for a sexually arousing activity. She asked me to lie on my left side and proceeded to fill the glass jug with warm soapy water.

This enema didn't finish like all previous enemas.

When I had taken all the soapy water, she told me to hold it for a few minutes and proceeded to rub my stomach. It was then our eyes really met in earnest and she spoke for the first time. She said she would love an enema and I told her I had learned how to give them at home. She went over, bolted the door and then she undressed. Instead of giving her an enema first, we had the most lovely sex after which she then got the enema. As it was after 10 p.m. there was no one else waiting for treatment, so it was enema/sex/enema/sex till 2 in the morning, and we were both cleaned out front and back!!!

I am now married to the same girl and the enema bag is on our bathroom door for all to see. Not all our sex sessions include enemas, but most of them do and they add great excitement. The enema has greatly helped our sex life.—*B.H., (name and address withheld), Toronto, Canada.*

* * *

Through the pages of your fine magazine I learned of the relaxing value of a good enema, but I scoffed at its sexual powers. After a hard day of studying, I needed something to relax me, so I tried it. I was no more than a pint full when my domineering girlfriend barged in unexpectedly. *She* immediately recognized the sexual implications of the act, and was angered that I should start without her. She forced me to pump myself with painful quantities of water, whipping me all the while with the lovely cane that is always by her side. Normally whipping and other aspects of exciting bondage cause me to reach orgasm without intercourse; with the enema the effect was doubled. Within minutes, my mistress had thrashed me into such a frenzy that I exploded violently. She, seeing me the happy prisoner in this most happy state, immediately changed places with me. Her reactions were even more intense. Later that evening, we discovered the joys of oral contact in areas we'd once found repugnant.

We should all be grateful that we live in an age when mature people have a forum such as your magazine in which to share their discoveries in the boundless world of pleasure.—*Michael N. (name and address withheld), Meadville, Pa.*

* * *

After reading letters in your columns on the subject of enemas, I am prompted to write of my experiences. I had an aunt who was a nurse and I believe this woman would recommend an enema as the proper treatment for any illness that befell any member of our family. It seems that hardly a month went my without my older sister or I receiving an enema at the hands of our aunt.

If my sister and I got into a spat, mother would contend that we were cross probably because we were constipated and would call our aunt to come over and give one or both of us her special treatment. The procedure was almost always the same. We were given a full warm soapy enema and made to hold it for a few minutes so that it would give us a thorough cleaning. My sister seemed to have more trouble holding the water than I and my aunt would frequently insert a finger in her anus to make her hold the water. She did this to me once and I liked it so after that I would usually release a little water so that she would insert her finger into me.

When I was about 11 my aunt decided that we were too old to watch each other receive our treatment and I was greatly disappointed because I had come to enjoy watching my sister receive her enema almost as much as I enjoyed receiving mine. I am sure that my sister never got any pleasure from her enemas and at about 15 mother stopped requesting them for us. I tried once to get my sister to give me one but she would have no part of it. After that I started to visit my aunt and on these visits I would suggest that I might be constipated and she would always oblige me by giving me the enema that I sought. I think she really thought she was doing me a service.

My aunt died while I was at college and I had to resort to giving myself enemas, but there was very little gratification when they were self-administered. There is no doubt in my mind that these childhood enemas are the cause of my desires now.—*M.W. Hampton, San Angelo, Texas.*

* * *

Some years ago I had to give up premedical work for financial reasons so I enrolled for nursing training—the only male in a class of 14 girls. Four girls and I formed a small social group which met occasionally in the apartment of two of them, and before long the nursing arts we were learning in class were extended to after hours to practice our newly learned skills. In my case, this included being catheterized by the group of giggling girls, and being subjected to an enema known as 3-H (nurses' parlance for high, hot, and a helluva lot—administered in the knee-chest position with a hospital-type rectal tube). I had my chance to reciprocate, however: the catchword around the apartment was "Whose turn is it tonight?"

The finale came when I got my draft notice and on my last night before induction, the girls and I had a swinging party with a gallon of rotgut wine. One of the girls mentioned how much some patients objected to enemas, and that launched a bleary discussion on how to give one with a minimum of discomfort. We ruled out anesthesia and then concluded that only a major distraction would do. The evil little minds, of course, would only focus on one thing—intercourse. Carol—a petite brunette—volunteered, and as I was the only male I had no choice. The girls soon scrounged up an enema bag, a glass Y, and two rectal tubes, plus large pitchers of hot soapsuds. One tube I inserted in Carol and taped it to her inner thigh, and I assumed the missionary position and the girls inserted the second rectal tube in me. Needless to say, I was in a high state of sexual excitement and Carol and I went at it. Then the girls released the water, which we were getting simultaneously through the glass Y. The result was the wildest turn-on Carol and I had ever experienced; in the process, each of us took more than two quarts of soapsuds but could not have cared less. In retrospect, Carol and I decided that the enema was secondary to intercourse but actually enhanced it—the hot water and the increasing intestinal pressure heightened the pleasure.—*W.B. (name and address withheld), Philadelphia, Pa.*

* * *

Just recently I picked up a copy of Penthouse in Montreal for the first time and I can tell you I was glad I did. I really enjoyed your fresh and intelligent approach to sex in all its forms. A letter on "special preference" was of special interest to me. For years now I have been fascinated with enemas as a pleasant and safe companion to sex. As the child of a doctor in England, the administration of enemas in the home was commonplace. Any time we were sick the syringe was brought out by my mother, who swore by it as a natural therapy for nearly every ailment from slight fever to stomachache. We had no girls in our family; so when I or any of my five brothers were enema-ed there was little secrecy or embarrassment. Many a time my brothers or myself received an enema in the shared bedroom and this continued until we were nearly all in our mid-teens.

I came to Canada and married over 14 years ago a lovely Canadian girl. She was amazed at first when I told her about the open use of the enema in our English country home. Though she had enemas as a child in her farm in mid-Western Canada, she told me they were very private affairs, and when it came to anal intercourse early in our marriage, she nearly had a nervous breakdown. It was only after months of discussions with our local doctor that her frightened attitude to enemas and anal invasion was brought to light. Our doctor's advice was that I should play enemas with her once or twice a week at the beginning. I was to be her "mother" and she the little girl again. It was slow going at first but soon she saw the enema as a good friend in sex play and we now have anal intercourse with great pleasure, and no guilt on her part. It is a great way to practice birth control and the enema as a preliminary greatly enhances and facilitates it.

The enema is now coming out of its Victorian closet, as attested by the letters to your Forum and the number of enema and colonic parlors which I saw advertised in the London (England) daily newspapers during my recent visit to that country.—*P.S. (name and address withheld), Montreal, Quebec, Canada.*

* * *

Your Forum correspondence on the use of enemas somehow fascinated me to the point where I had to write! I can remember when I was 10 or 11 lying on my stomach on the bathroom tile floor with nothing on and getting an enema from my aunt. This usually happened when I had a cold or when my aunt "felt" that I was somehow constipated. I suppose that at that time I was mostly embarrassed to be lying there completely naked in front of an older woman, not counting the odd sensation of the enema, the syringe, and her hands on my behind. I assumed that it was all for my own good!

She spanked me in a similar fashion too. There was a small but sturdy clothes hamper in the bathroom, and whenever I misbehaved she would take me there, take all my clothes off and give me a spanking. She sat on the hamper and draped me over her lap, but she always gave me the spanking with an open hand and I can still feel it!

However, what fascinates me now is what B.W. wrote about in your November issue. Every once in a while I get the "urge," let's say, to have it done again! Unfortunately, I have never been lucky enough to meet a woman who is completely honest about anal eroticism. —*J.W.H. (name and address withheld), Englewood, New Jersey.*

* * *

I have read with increasing interest many letters in your columns relating to special preferences and I would like to tell you my experiences.

I give myself enemas because I haven't been able to find anyone that can do it as well as I can. I usually end up taking two to three quarts of warm soapy water and the sensation is great. I do this about once a week and after my enema it is about three days before I have another bowel movement.

I am concerned that I might be doing myself bodily harm, but I have not gotten the nerve to discuss it with a doctor. If any of your readers are doctors I would really appreciate their comments.—*D. S. Davidson, Oklahoma City, Okla.*

* * *

I have read Penthouse for almost two years and Forum is my favorite column. I am—as I believe many of the writers and readers of the "Special Preference" letters are—"anal erotic." Many parents are afflicted in this manner; it may be mutual between mother and father towards their children, in that they administer unnecessary enemas to them; it may be just the mother or father who administers them to male or female children or it may be a favorite (and successful) form of punishment meted out to a disobedient child.

In the past year I have researched the history of enemas, and in many case histories it has been found that the male parent has been the leader in this field, giving enemas to children from five to, in one case, a 17-year-old girl. The unnecessary administration of enemas can cause a child a serious psychological trauma that may be carried on throughout life and into the next generation. In my research, I did not discover any sexual urges for the enema, though it was admitted that enemas were sometimes sexually exciting for some people. I read medical and home nursing books and periodicals, where the proper use of enemas was described in detail, sometimes with illustrations. I could write at least a page about the equipment used, solutions, frequency, etc. I myself take an enema or series of them every two or three months and have experimented with my findings. I recommend readers to procure a copy of a book on yogic enemas.—*M.G.R. (name and address withheld), Halifax, Nova Scotia, Canada.*

* * *

I am one of the (I am certain) statistically significant part of your readership who thumbs through Penthouse at the newsstand and only buys it if there is a "special preference" letter. I don't mean to sound vindictive in saying this; it just so happens that in pursuit of literature regarding my own preference there is a need to be selective, and publications which mention the subject of enemas are rare indeed. One thing I have noticed is that if a magazine or book makes any reference to enemas it is almost immediately sold out whereas other publications might hang around for months. It is remarkable to me that publishers employ such unsophisticated market research techniques that they have not discovered the potential market for the subject.

My enthusiasm for the enema goes back to dimly recalled childhood. I am lying over my mother's lap and she is injecting many syringefuls of soapy water to cure me of fever, upset stomach, laziness, etc. As other of your writers have pointed out in their own experience, my mother thought the enema was the cure for everything. In a large family the special attention lent a definite emphasis to the circumstance. After I was seven or eight, Epsom salts replaced enemas, and except for efforts at self-administration I led an arid existence until after the war. Whilst visiting a girl at her family's house in another city I was feeling somewhat out of sorts and the girl first suggested, and then insisted, that she give me an enema. She produced her own equipment, a combination syringe, and somewhat clumsily performed the operation. Naturally I told her it hadn't worked, so the operation had to be repeated, twice. Your readers will readily understand that I married her, and why.

There have been times when my wife would give me daily enemas, if only to get me out of bed in the morning. However, her stern New England upbringing forbids the use of them for any but therapeutic purposes. I have only given her about 50 enemas in the 25 years that we have been married; she will only tolerate them when she is *in extremis*. On one notable occasion, however, I gave her three punitive enemas in one afternoon.

You can well imagine that I am quite frustrated in seeking outlets for my special preference. I estimate that at least 10% of the population is interested in enemas. A carefully dropped reference to enemas during a late dinner party just last Saturday night (it can be done, and tastefully) brought an immediate and defensive response from the two girls I was talking to. "And what's wrong with that?" said one. If ten million adults are interested, why can't at least some of them get together for discussions, histories or even demonstrations? How do people with such inclinations meet and let down the barriers of reserve?

Through a limited correspondence with private individuals I have been trying to start an informal association called the Society of the Sacred Ibis. Any true student will recognize the ibis as the bird who first demonstrated enema techniques to the ancient Egyptians. They experimented on themselves and as a result elevated the ibis to sacred status. If the SSI could be formed, or at least recognized, local chapter meetings could be advertised in the local press without offense to the uninitiated. Or direct questions could be asked of other people. A mutual acknowledgment of recognition by two parties in a conversation would clear away many problems.

My own special preference, as yet a dream, is to be given an enema whilst lying over the lap of a woman. Other than that, I recognize the enema for therapeutic, friendship and punitive purposes. An enema taken first thing in the morning is a splendid way to start a productive day. Three or four enemas after ten hours drinking, and before retiring, will clear the head and body, and allow me, for one, to wake the next morning after four hours sleep ready for anything that has to be done. Friendship enemas I can only speculate about. Punitive enemas I have given and been given, and they are effective.—*E.M. (name and address withheld), Fairfield, Conn.*

* * *

Your magazine is showing women the way to freedom of expression in the press and, more importantly, within the home and marital life. Many couples would be happier if they could speak freely to one another of their deep passions. I am a 34-year old divorcee, who enjoys your magazine immensely. I look for the "Special preference" letters as I love being given enemas, but I could never bring myself to ask my ex-spouse to give them to me, thinking this must be a morbid taste.

After much soul-searching, I find it is no crime to be anally erotic. The crime is making it a problem, being unable to face the fact that one is human, full of feelings and desires. I wish my desires could be fulfilled and controlled within a couple's loving relationship, instead of in secret, extra-marital affairs.

No one objects to getting pleasure from taking a bath. Yet, when we bathe our internal organs, using an enema, it is frowned on by everyone from medical men to preachers. Probably, high pressure enemas are harmful and should be rejected on medical grounds, but many sluggish, inactive persons would feel better and probably live longer if they used a slow-filling warm water enema to bathe their colons more often.

I prefer being given enemas to taking them myself because I am exhibitionistic and wanted most of all for my husband to take a personal interest in my body and its beauty. I like the warm flow of water and the erotic feelings of receiving the injection. It's better to live your erotic life at home than in bars or massage parlors. Women still lose their husbands and men their wives, because we have never become used to speaking our innermost sexual thoughts except to a cheap whore or otherwise liberated person of low morals. Putting labels on behavior is wrong in itself and does not solve any of the human problems.—*Mrs. E.J. (name and address withheld), Boulder, Colo.*

* * *

After reading with great interest the letters in your *Special Preference* column, I thought I would relate my experiences and would like to know if anyone else has had a background similar to mine.

As a small boy of four to seven I can remember my mother often giving me enemas at various times. The type of equipment used was a red hot-water bottle inverted with a red hose and black plastic rectal tube. The position she had me in to receive this humiliating treatment was on my back, face up, while the tube was inserted between my legs underneath my genitals. I know this is not the proper position, as was explained in previous letters to this column. Nevertheless, this is the way I received them, and because of this, the way I preferred to give them later on. It was never explained to me why I had to have them; I don't recall ever being sick when I received them. I remember one summer day when I was out in the yard playing with my playmates and I was called into the house to find out that I was about to get one. I quickly ran upstairs and closed the bathroom window so the children outside wouldn't be able to hear any commotion, as I used to raise a fuss each time I had one. My fear was that my playmates would be curious why I had to come into the house and ask the reason why the next day. Luckily no one ever asked.

The real damage this caused was to my emotions. Often I would go to bed at night and masturbate. The fantasy I had in my mind while masturbating was giving an enema to someone I either knew or had met. Mentally I would be giving them the same way I had received them. My imaginary patients could be either male or female, usually children of all ages and in some cases even adults. I knew nothing of sexual intercourse nor had any sex education at all at that young age. Not all children appealed to me. It depended on their build and personality. It was their legs that excited me. Boys in their shorts and girls in their short dresses. Often I would daydream and picture myself as some type of specialist whose job it was to go to the home of a certain child after having received a call from his parents and administer an enema. Later on, when I learned about sexual intercourse, the thought of that didn't seem as exciting as giving an enema. I never received any enemas after the age of seven. When I reached my early teens, my fancy turned to mostly younger boys and would have to be described as homosexual. However, I would like to emphasize at this point that it was not the receiving of enemas as a younger child nor the masturbating that caused this perversion. Neither had I ever been approached by a homosexual. My drive toward young boys was caused entirely by other circumstances, which are too lengthy to explain at this time. Remember that at one time girls as well as boys could excite me, at an earlier age.

The dream came true—during World War II there was a shortage of help in the hospitals, and at the age of fifteen I went to work as an orderly. I was surprised to find out that enema-giving was to be part of my job. Of course, working in the men's ward most of my patients were adults, which I didn't enjoy at all. But once in a while during those war years, with overcrowded conditions, a young boy would be admitted to the men's ward, and when I was lucky enough to get one on my list I would be in my seventh heaven.

I can remember just about every young boy I gave the treatment to. One time there was a twelve-year-old boy out of my own neighborhood who knew me and who became my patient. After he recovered from his appendectomy and went home, he told everybody he knew what I did to him. Something I never would have done had I been in his place. What surprised me most was that these young boys never seemed to resent me for giving them their enemas, even though for the most part they hated them. It was a rewarding experience, especially when I would later on meet one on the street and he would recognize me. I would always get a warm greeting from them. I worked in the hospital for two years. My hours were after school and weekends, and full time in the summertime. When I was seventeen, I left the hospital, but my desire to give enemas never ceased, and in later years I had to find other means of giving them. I still have this desire today. I never married, as my sexual desires deviated from the norm.

My advice to parents is to never give a full enema (one with complete apparatus) to a child younger than the age of eight at the least, and then only for a purpose which he understands. Never give them for punishment. That is not what they are for. Make it a rare treatment. I do believe every child should have at least one in his childhood; I found out in the hospital that the children who were most fearful of them were for the most part those who had never had one before. I don't go along with this idea the Canadian mother had who gave her three sons enemas on certain days of the season every year. I sometimes wonder if these mothers aren't a little perverted, too. Maybe some of you out there know.— *(name withheld), Detroit, Mich.*

* * *

Reading the letter from J.A. of Nutley, N.J. (November) brought to mind what happened to me several years ago, when I was 16, and dating a girl who had an older sister, a graduate nurse. I visited my girl's home frequently and often stayed overnight in their guest room. One weekend, Nancy's parents were away but Karen was home from her hospital job, to supervise us really. I woke up on the Saturday morning with a stomach ache and told Nancy, who called her sister.

Karen insisted that she take my temperature, and fetched a white thermometer case and a jar of Vaseline. Only when she smeared the thermometer with Vaseline did I realize what she was going to do. I felt like leaping out of bed and hiding, but was too embarrassed to move. I hardly felt a thing except the gentle probing of the thermometer as she pushed it in, but she put her hand over my buttocks to hold the thermometer in place and that really caused me to have an erection, covered by my pajama shirt, thank goodness.

Since I had a slight fever and stomach cramps, Karen suggested a mild enema would pep me up. When I said I'd rather not, she only laughed and said it wouldn't hurt. She told me to lie still and relax. A minute or two later,

Karen was back with her small feminine hygiene kit, and was attaching a small enema tip to the rubber hose. I guess she gave me the enema very slowly because I felt no discomfort at all. A few moments later I went to the bathroom and, sure enough, I felt much better during breakfast. Nancy didn't even mention the incident during the day and neither did Karen, much to my relief.

That evening before bed, Karen came into Nancy's room where we were listening to records and announced it was temperature time again. My face was as red as a beet but Nancy went off to the bathroom while Karen took me to her room where again it was bare bottoms up for her thermometer!

Four years ago I married Nancy after she graduated from nursing school. She's a great wife but when sickness comes along out comes the old rectal thermometer and it's bottoms up again. I really don't mind rectal temps and I take hers that way, too. The only thing I don't like is that Nancy will leave the thermometer and Vaseline out when I'm sick and just about everyone knows what it's for.—*R.W. (name and address withheld), Waterloo, Iowa.*

* * *

Since I am not a doctor, I cannot offer a professional opinion on whether D. S. Davidson (August) is doing himself harm by taking enemas. But from 30 years of taking and giving enemas, I would suggest he has probably benefited from them. As long as the quantity of fluid injected is comfortable, the equipment he uses is immaculately clean and the flow is gentle (about 24 ins), while he lies on his left side or in a knee-on-chest position, I can't see what possible harm he could suffer. Recently I read a newspaper article in which the indomitable Mae West attributed her good health and body tone to daily enemas, which she was said to have taken for years.

My own history started when I was five and very constipated. I never realized the sexual implications of my enjoyment of enemas till I was about 11. One Saturday morning, I was across the alley, visiting my friend Jimmy. I went into his bathroom and saw his mother who had his 10-year-old sister Patty with pink bare bottom across her lap, just starting to give her an enema. I quickly stepped back into the hall and watched her instruct Patty, "Tell me when you've had enough and it hurts." I guess the infant bulb held 3 or 4 oz, but Patty didn't say, "That's enough" till her mother had deftly injected eight to 10 bulbs full. Watching this process from the hall was a very pleasant experience and I found my little penis standing stiff as a flag pole. The whole enema picture took on new significance for me after that.

Later I questioned Patty and she said she liked the enemas every Saturday morning, while Jimmy got his enema every Saturday night from his father. For the next couple of years, we often got together when their parents went out and played "Doctor." She sneaked her enema bulb from the bathroom and I moved it gently in and out of her anus. She wouldn't let me inject water into her, but liked the feel of the syringe being inserted. She then insisted on doing the same to me, which always gave me a stiff erection. We never explored her body or mine any further, as we still didn't realize the sexual aspect of what we were doing.

During my teens and in college, I took enemas occasionally for the sensation of well-being I got from them. For years now, my wife has administered enemas to me every five to seven days: I give them only occasionally as she prefers anal massage from a vibrator. I'm a hotel executive and often travel away from home. Most larger hotels have a registered nurse on call for illnesses, emergencies or temporary care of older guests. These girls are always ready to administer the "treatment" for the regular hourly fee, plus expenses. Recently at a hotel, I called the special duty nurse to administer an enema but she explained that hotel rules were that no female hotel employee was permitted to stay in a man's room unless he was ill, elderly or in need of care. She suggested we needed to get someone else to stay with her. I agreed, so the nurse called the housekeeper for a floor maid to help her take care of a sick person.

The floor maid was young and black and pretty. The nurse mixed the solution from pre-measured enema soap (which I carry, along with travel syringe) and asked the girl to hold the bag about 2ft over me while she administered the enema. It was the first time she had ever seen one, and she asked what was in it. The nurse told her it was a cure for toxic bowel condition and the girl said she would like to take one some time, if the nurse would show her how. As a result, the nurse asked my permission to give the girl an enema as soon as my treatment was completed. This I readily gave.

While I was in the bathroom the nurse cleaned the equipment with alcohol and mixed another bag of fluid. I then held the water bag while she gave the girl the enema, which she seemed to enjoy. By this time, I was extremely aroused sexually and casually asked the nurse if she would accept additional money for extra services. She said she wouldn't dare because the hotel might blacklist her if she were caught. My only recourse (which I rarely do) was to relieve myself after the nurse and maid had left. Incidentally, I paid both of them well for their time.

Most nurses I have talked with, whether young or middle-aged, married or single, seem to accept that enemas are quite normal. Their attitude seems to be that this is simply another nursing service and nothing more.— *J.C.S. (name and address withheld), Minneapolis, Minn.*

* * *

I had my first experience of an enema at a hospital while undergoing tests at the age of 19. A young nurse's aide arrived one morning to flush me before barium X-rays. While she was delivering a massive three quarters or so of pure soapsuds, I had an erection that would not quit. Finding me fully aroused, the girl locked the door and quickly removed her clothes. At this point she prepared an enema for herself and following evacuation of the soapsuds, she then administered my barium. After applying the barium paste, she inserted a rectal plug and demanded that I service her with the other soapsuds solution. After delivering this to her and then inserting a plug, we engaged in reckless sex till we reached a rousing climax.

A few years ago, my wife had some gastric trouble and bought a large fountain syringe. It was only then I discovered that she had had enemas from early childhood. Her mother used to give massive five- to six-quart enemas for disobedience when my wife was a teenager, and she started to find them sexually exciting. Since then, the enema has become a daily late evening routine for both of us. After one quart to act as a flush, we follow with three or four quarts and insert rectal plugs before sex, always enjoying the most violent climaxes.

Based on 20 years of experimentation. I have found that dishwashing liquid detergent—one cap per bag—plus two tablespoons of bicarbonate of soda are a soothing solution. The douche nozzle, when fully inserted into the rectum, delivers the enema with maximum sensation and no cramps. Lukewarm water is best and it is advisable to wait at least six hours after intake of food. Alternatively, castor oil or Epsom salts may be used as a purgative. At first, use no more than two quarts for the solution until with experience one learns one's limits. The enema should be delivered slowly with the syringe no higher than three feet above the stomach. For a series of enemas or irrigations, use plain water and soda.—*G.S.W. (name and address withheld), Cleveland, Ohio.*

* * *

Through my work as a hospital orderly and through self-experimentation, I have learned about successful methods of giving and receiving an enema. Basically the enema is a colonic stimulant that results in a strong peristaltic action. In the male particularly, this action stimulates the prostate gland, thereby heightening the sexual urge, often resulting in a more satisfying ejaculation. For success, the enema must be given slowly and gently. The desired position is lying on the left side with the upper thigh and knee flexed (Sims position). Most adults can take from 1 to 1½ quarts of solution, which can be simply hot water about 105 degrees F. However, the conventional soapsuds solution is very effective and provides additional stimulation.

If soap is used, it should be mild. One hospital supplier has a special liquid enema soap in premeasured, disposable units that affords a convenient-to-use uniform dosage. Either the conventional enema bag or a soft rubber rectal tube connected to an irrigating can may be employed. After a full enema has been taken, the solution should be held in for a few minutes until a strong urge to evacuate results.

Sexual partners often enjoy giving each other enemas prior to intercourse. I used to believe that the enema was an uncomfortable and embarrassing treatment when one was sick, but now I regularly use it, both as a relaxant and as a stimulating preliminary to the sexual encounter.—*J.S.B. (name and address withheld), Hanover, N.H.*

* * *

As a teenager, I was sent to an institution for delinquent and hard-to-manage girls. The treatment was tough, and by the time I had spent 40 months there I regretted ever having skipped so much school. One part of our life there might interest you: the enema routine. Every Saturday evening, the 15 girls in our dorm were made to strip and form two lines before two toilets. Then the head girl administered enemas. No one was allowed to speak, except the head girl, but we could all watch.

The girls receiving enemas would bend over and touch their toes. If the head girl didn't like you, she would jam the nozzle in forcefully and deeply, without greasing it. Sometimes extra hot water was forced up a girl's behind, which made her scream. After an enema had been taken, the girl would go to the back of the line and hold it till everyone else had been given enemas. Each girl had to put her finger in the behind of the girl ahead of her to keep her water from trickling to the floor. If anyone screamed, cried or complained, we would all have to hold our enemas 10 minutes longer.

There were always a few girls who couldn't hold their enemas, and it was our job to clean up after them. Then we formed a gauntlet, and the girls responsible for the mess would crawl between our legs very slowly while we slapped their bare behinds.

Matron was strict, and all girls were up by 5 a.m. every day. After an hour of calisthenics (done naked, to the embarrassment of new girls), we had to take cold showers. Matron would beat girls who weren't doing their exercises properly. Discipline took the form of a leather strap across the bare legs, thighs and buttocks. If too many girls were not doing their sit-ups and push-ups fast enough, we would all be forced to lie down with our buttocks high in the air and our shoulders, arms and knees on the floor. Once, we were leathered 16 times. Our behinds were swollen for days, and it didn't help to have to sit in class five hours a day!—*C.W.T. (name and address withheld), Binghamton, N.Y.*

* * *

I have taken a special affection to Penthouse. It is so honest in all its presentations and the articles about enemas are terrific. Since I can remember, I have had enemas but never felt I should enjoy taking them till I read your letters. My wife and I now take enemas together. Thanks to Penthouse, we are learning to enjoy them with our sex life.

For years, we secretly took them, but never in each other's presence. My wife regularly gave enemas to our three teenage boys for nearly every ailment and, as they grew up, she began to feel slightly guilty when she discovered two of them were getting erections during the procedure. Now she knows we all have this sensual feeling and there is nothing wrong in giving them this healthy intimacy with their natural cravings, but we would not give our boys enemas unless we felt they were needed for a health situation.—*B.W. (name and address withheld), Quebec, Montreal, Canada.*

* * *

I was amused by C.W.T.'s letter (November) concerning bizarre activities at an institution for delinquent girls. Her story reminded me of the punitive enemas my aunt used to give her two teenage daughters. One day I arrived at my aunt's house just as one of my cousins was about to undergo correction for having deliberately torn her sister's dress in a fit of envy. The culprit tried to rectify the situation by apologizing, but undauntedly my aunt was gathering the enema equipment. I was too fascinated to make a polite exit, till my cousin blushingly asked her mother to send me home. To my surprise, my aunt decided I could stay, as an additional embarrassment for the malfeasant.

In honor of my presence, she was permitted to retain her bra and panties. But I was not disappointed. I have always considered her attractive, and seeing her in a tight pair of silk panties gave me quite a thrill. The recalcitrant was ceremoniously ushered into a bedroom and reluctantly laid face down on some towels spread over the bed. She whimpered as my aunt lowered her panties in front of me and her giggling sister. The silken undergarment was arranged as a useless decoration below her knees, leaving her shapely buttocks and thighs fully exposed. Then, while my curiosity rose, my aunt attached a rubber rose to the enema bag and inserted a nozzle at the loose end. I noticed that she used a larger hygienic nozzle rather than the regular device provided for enema usage. She carefully greased this threatening plastic tube as its intending victim stared in horror. Ignoring her entreaties, my aunt prised apart the unhappy girl's fleshy cheeks and the glistening black nozzle was slowly pushed into her rectum until it nearly disappeared inside the forced opening. Having checked that the hose was properly secured, my aunt instructed her whining daughter not to move and then went to the kitchen to prepare the special enema solution.

During my aunt's 15-minute absence, my cousin, doing as she was told, maintained her awkward position, looking absurd with the red enema hose stretched like a strange clothes-line from her quivering behind to the limp bag hanging on a bed post. Her sister was beside herself from enjoyment and our continual taunting and banter aggravated her ordeal. Unsupervised for so long, we took advantage of the opportunity afforded by the slightly protruding nozzle. To our amusement, we discovered that, by merely manipulating the implanted object, we could obtain splendid reactions from its unwilling possessor. We were like children mischievously torturing a captured dog by playfully twisting the outraged creature's tail. Much like a helpless animal, my cousin was at our mercy. The muffling noise of a radio rendered her screams for help useless, while a great fear of my aunt's wrath prevented her from freeing herself. So, submitting to the inevitable, she meekly held her pose while her sister and I each took turns in experimenting with the nozzle. We were treated to an exciting show of squirming, fanny wriggling and childish complaints.

Just when we heard my aunt returning, my partner-in-mischief suddenly jerked the enema hose from its moorings in her alarmed sister's mid-posterior. I was at first mystified by this unexpected maneuver, but its purpose was to become apparent. As my aunt came back into the room, she found her errant daughter frantically attempting to restore the nozzle and immediately misinterpreted her intentions. Wrongly identifying the prankster and ignoring the victim's self-vindicating accusations, my aunt swiftly reinserted the nozzle and carefully filled the enema bag with the pitcher of solution she had prepared. She told us the dreadful-looking milky concoction contained a mixture of hot water, soapsuds, baking soda, salt and mineral oil. With all in readiness, she opened the stopcock, starting the flow into the pseudo-patient. My aunt skilfully released the liquid in intermittent spurts by pinching the hose. First, she would let it gush, causing the recipient to writhe in distress as the pressure quickly mounted. Then she would stop it momentarily, allowing the pressure to subside to a tolerable level. In all, well over a quart must have been emptied out of the enema bag.

My cousin believed that the completed enema concluded her degrading public exhibition, but my aunt insisted on scrubbing her heretofore private areas with a wash cloth and toilet paper in much the same way as one might clean an infant for a diaper change. Even after that, my aunt made her wait at the bathroom door and stand facing the wall only steps from the physical relief she craved.—*N.P. (name and address withheld), Tolland, Conn.*

* * *

It is a pity, but Dorothy Smith seems to have missed the boat entirely on enemas, as evidenced by her letter appearing in the July issue. I do not doubt that a "forced enema of over three quarts of really hot soapy water" would be most unpleasant. But who would expect this to be titillating, especially when given by persons of the same sex as part of an initiation ordeal?

If given correctly—slowly and gently so as to preclude any semblance of discomfort—a warm saline enema can be an erotic experience which heightens the arousal of both partners. Neither my wife nor I have sado-masochistic tendencies; we use enemas in the boudoir solely because it provides an extra source of pleasure during foreplay.—*D.H. (name and address withheld), Dallas, Tex.*

* * *

I have been a registered nurse for two years. Your special preference letter induced me to write this nurse's point of view on the enema.

The enema can be a very pleasurable experience, as I found out during my first week of nursing school. After I complained to one of the doctors of stomach cramps, he told me to report at his office that evening for a full checkup.

I arrived just as the last patient was leaving. The doctor instructed me to remove my clothing except for my panties and to don one of those backless hospital gowns. The examination proceeded; after a short time he said he would give me a barium enema.

The procedure requires several preliminary cleansing enemas and I was told to roll over on my stomach. Both ends of the table were lowered until my bottom was three feet higher than my head and feet. The doctor removed my panties and placed my legs at the sides of the table, revealing my thighs and behind. A rectal thermometer was placed in my anus. I felt quite apprehensive and embarrassed. I had never had an enema before.

By looking at a large mirror I noticed the doctor assembling his equipment. He had decided on the largest rubber rectal tube he had—an inch wide and three feet long. To my surprise, the thought of this huge object being forced into my rectum excited me considerably. After lubricating the tube and removing the thermometer, he slowly inserted the rectal tube into my bottom for a good ten inches. The tube was left hanging as a solution of warm water and soap was mixed in a metal can. The can was attached to the waiting tube and the warm solution filled my rectum. To my pleasure, the procedure was repeated five times before I was ready for the barium enema.

As I was returning to the table, no longer embarrassed and looking forward to the barium enema, the doctor entered the room, accompanied by an X-ray technician at the nursing school. He explained that the technician would assist him with the barium enema.

After assuming my position on the table, minus my gown, the new arrival fitted a rubber glove on his hand and lubricated it. To my great surprise, he slipped his finger into my waiting anus and proceeded to thoroughly lubricate it until I began to quiver from the exquisite sensation.

The tube used for the barium enema was three feet long and one inch wide. On the tip was a massive soft rubber bulb, to prevent premature expulsion of the barium. The bulb was lubricated. The doctor parted my buttocks and the aggressive technician pressed the glistening bulb against my parting anus until it slowly disappeared into my rear. The end of the tube was connected to a can containing four quarts of the barium solution. The solution flowed as my stomach slowly expanded to twice its normal size. The tube was clamped and removed from the enema can, the other end remained in my bottom. The table was then lowered and I rolled over on my back, placing my feet in metal stirrups. X-rays were taken. They then led me naked to a bathroom, the enema tube still dangling between my legs. After I assumed a position directly over the toilet, the doctor reached between my legs and gently pulled the tube from its moorings. I fell to the seat, expelling the massive amount of fluid.

Since this first experience with the enema, I take great pleasure in both giving and receiving them. Using a No. 32 rubber rectal tube (available in all drugstores) and a three-quart enema can, I have the male patient remove his clothing and assume a knee-chest position on the bed. This position puts the subject's backside high in the air and his legs wide apart. I explain to him that I often use enemas myself and find them soothing and pleasurable. I lubricate his anus inside and out, using a rubber glove. Then ten inches of tubing is inserted slowly and three quarts of warm soapy water injected. As the fluid is running in, the patient's stomach is massaged to relax the stomach muscles. The tube is clamped and he is placed on a bedpan. Again massaging the patient's stomach, I slowly remove the tube.

My patients tell me they have had enemas before, but admit they prefer my method. Most nurses enjoy giving enemas to young male patients who are not seriously ill. Nurses frequently use them to cleanse or relax themselves simply because the enema, properly given, is a very pleasurable experience.—*Registered Nurse, Dover, N.J.*

* * *

I'm delighted to read the enema letters in *Penthouse*. My sexual interest in enemas started at age eight, when I was given one in a hospital by a pretty nurse's aide. My next one was at age twelve, when my parents toured Europe for the summer and I lived with my Aunt Joan for ten weeks. Aunt Joan kept a red enema bag and a bulb syringe in the bathroom. Two days after I arrived, I saw the damp enema bag drying on the towel rack and I visualized Aunt Joan giving herself an enema. I wished that she would insert that black nozzle in my backside.

I withheld my bowel movements for the next three days and innocently told her I didn't feel well. She diagnosed the problem as simple constipation. About a half-hour later she took me into her bedroom. On the night table were a bowl of warm soapy water, petroleum jelly, the rectal syringe and paper towels. She removed my pants and shorts, seated herself on the side of the bed, raised her dress above her stocking tops to avoid wrinkling and put me face down across her lap.

The warmth of her thighs, the lubrication of my anus by her vaseline-coated finger, the gentle insertions and withdrawals of the syringe nozzle, the warm enema flowing into my bowels, the sight of her pretty calves and thighs, produced the most pleasurable sexual feelings. After she had injected all of the solution, she kept me across her lap for five additional minutes to allow the enema more time to work. Then she wrapped a towel around my hips and I ran to the bathroom.

During the rest of my ten-week stay, she continually inquired about my bowel movements. If I admitted to not having had one for more than forty-eight hours, she would give me an enema.

My interest in the sexual aspects of enemas has never waned and I enjoy giving and receiving them as well as reading about them.—*Frank T., Braintree, Mass.*

* * *

Because you have been open-minded enough to publish letters from readers who have what you call "special preferences," my wife and I are indebted to you for having provided an additive to our sex life. As a consequence of reading letters in your magazine, my wife announced one evening that she was going to give me an enema. I soon found myself across her lap as she sat on a chair in the bathroom where she had prepared a half-filled enema bag. When she applied the petroleum jelly to my rectum I realized that she had uncovered an erogenous area I had not earlier known about. Administering the enema obviously stimulated her because when it was completed we engaged in torrid sex. Several weeks later when we reversed the process and I administered an enema to my wife, she discovered that she has a far more satisfactory climax when her colon has been cleansed. We surely do not overdo the enema as part of foreplay, but when we do use it occasionally, we surely enjoy the sex which follows. Thanks.—*(Name withheld), Washington, D.C.*

* * *

A couple of years ago I was driving on Route 80 through northern Pennsylvania. Up ahead, I noticed a VW going off to the side of the road. I pulled up to offer aid. The young lady in distress had run out of gas. I suggested siphoning gas from my car to hers, since the service stations were off the road and few and far between. The only thing to do the trick was syringe tubing and I asked Debra if she had a douche bag. She was, as could be expected, rather taken aback but rummaged through her luggage.

I've liked enemas since childhood, and when I unfolded the travel syringe, I found an enema tip rather than the curved douche pipe. I also noticed that the tip and some of the tubing were smeared with vaseline. For any enema buff this is a dead giveaway. I siphoned the gas into the VW. Have you ever seen a VW getting an enema?

I suggested to Debra that she go to the next gas station and that I'd follow to make sure she got there. The town was fairly large and I invited her to dinner. During the meal, I asked her about enemas and found that she was as fixated as I was. I suggested that we share a room for the evening. She refused but indicated we might discuss enemas at greater length in *her* room. At the dinner table she described an enema and held up an imaginary bag; looking through the imaginary hanging hole at the top of the bag, she winked at me. I invited her to town, where I bought her a new enema bag. I also bought a colon tube; Debra had never seen one. Almost all hospitals use them rather than the hard plastic tips because they are made of flexible rubber and are less likely to do internal harm. The colon tube is about a half-foot long and can be used for deep insertion.

In her motel room, Debra showed much anticipation when I attached the gizmos and filled the bag with warm water. But simply holding and admiring a filled enema bag is only a still life. Trying out the new toy was a mutual desire. Debra was most willing to undergo the anal douche, but on one condition—no sex. "I'm still a virgin," she said. She assumed the knee-chest position and I inserted the vaseline-coated colon tube to the hilt as the waters flowed in. Actually, sex could not have matched the pleasures Debra derived from that enema. She moaned and groaned and, I'm sure, climaxed to the music of the gurgle of the solution.

We exchanged only enemas that evening, but Debra did relieve my highly charged state through means other than vaginal. We never did see each other again. She left in the morning before I did, leaving only a lasting enema memory.—*R. L., Detroit, Mich.*

* * *

In your July and October issues, C.A. of Georgia and W.M.V. of Fort Worth refer to their use of enemas as preliminary stimulants to other sexual activities. I have also, for a number of years now, used enemas as a prelude to masturbation when normal sexual activities were curtailed for one reason or another—usually between relationships, when I have broken off with one girl and am not yet sleeping with another. I have never been able to broach the subject of using enemas prior to intercourse but would like to very much and will when I feel the time is right.

When taking enemas, I have always used soapy water, as warm as the fingertips can stand, and at least one full quart of this solution at a time. I have also found that using the female vaginal douche pipe, instead of the regular small enema tip supplied with the syringe, is extra stimulating, in that it tends to remain inserted in the rectum without being held in place by hand. However, I too would like to know the proper procedure for giving or taking an enema if Penthouse or C.A. of Georgia would care to comment on this. Also, just how much of what solution should be used and at what temperature?—*B.M. (name and address withheld), Arlington, Texas 76011.*

* * *

The letter in your July Forum concerning enemas as a sexual stimulant came as a surprise to me, and many other readers I am sure. In discussing (with great enthusiasm) your magazine with others, a majority of people mentioned this letter and related similar anal experiences.

In the October issue you carried a letter from W.M. Wilson. Congratulations to him for inquiring and you for printing his letter. It is a known fact that anal sex is now the "in" thing. Perhaps the function of an enema in a man's case would be to simulate the orgasm of a man into a woman via anal sex.

Thank you for all the service you give—the intelligence to discuss issues and let people know there are others in the world with similar interests!—*Mrs. M.H. (name and address withheld), Lanhan, Ind.*

* * *

I am a nurse employed in a city hospital. I have been following your Forum and in particular the letters on "Special Preference" for some time. I would like to contribute the following information. Enemas should consist of approximately 1-2 quarts of warm water, and baking soda or soap may be added. The person should lie on his left side with knees drawn to the chest. The bag should be suspended two feet above the body. They may also be given in a sitting position on the toilet.

After years of work in hospital I must agree that enemas can give great sexual excitement and/or satisfaction to the patient or administrator. For those of your readers interested in using enemas as sexual stimulants, may I suggest the premeasured Fleet enemas available in drug stores. These are less uncomfortable and easier to administer. Research on this subject, through various manuals, suggests that enemas are used by lesbians to give anal gratification.—*S. Kaufman (address withheld), Wash. D.C. 20001*

* * *

I would like to take this opportunity to thank you for printing the letters in Forum on the use of enemas as sexual stimulants. For 20 years I thought I was alone in the use of enemas, but thanks to you I see I am not alone. Perhaps I can contribute a little something of my own: for some time now I have also used the soap suppository or "soap stick." This may be slightly uncomfortable to some, but the effect is the same as an enema and extremely stimulating.—*C.M. Bateman, Parsons, Kansas.*

* * *

For many months I have read your magazine and thoroughly enjoyed most of the material that you publish. One of my favorite sections is letters by readers concerning their sexual experiences. Recent issues have contained a number of letters explaining the pleasures of enemas.

I have recently been discharged from the hospital. After having taken a test requiring the administration of nine enemas during one day, I can only conclude that people who gain sexual gratification from such an ordeal are not playing the game with a full deck. Far from producing an erotic feeling, an enema is nothing but a pain in the ass.—*E.H. (Address Withheld)*

* * *

After reading the letters to the *Penthouse* Forum of the last several issues, I am not surprised to see that the pleasure of the enema is a controversial subject. Most of the letters indicated that the colonic stimulation leads to a different realm of sexual enjoyment, and a few considered it insipid and undesirable.

A few years ago in the question-and-answer section of a medical periodical, the journal answered a woman who had asked why her husband enjoyed enemas by stating, "Well, don't you know that in various steps of sexual development there is such a stage as anality and anal pleasures, which precedes genital and phallic stages, and a person who enjoys anal stimulation is somewhat fixated in his sexual activities in a pregenital period. . . ." This explanation, though acceptable, is not plausible to many sexologists.

I have a different explanation for the pleasurable enema. My theory is based upon a proposed sexual typology of men and women. Men and women, according to their modality of sexual enjoyment, are divided into two groups—clitoro-penile and semino-vaginal. Penile man and clitoral woman are characterized by displaying direct, ostensible, and overt pleasure-seeking. They are prompt in learning how to satisfy their sex drives. Their most sensitive erotic areas are fully accessible to them and their partners. That is why they are called clitoral and penile. Their orgasmic experiences are clear-cut, memorizable, and faithfully repeatable. The seminal man and vaginal woman are characterized by showing a tangential, camouflaged, and subtle approach in their sexual behavior. For them, the prerequisite for satisfactory sexual enjoyment is an amalgam of conscious and semiconscious elements. Their erotically sensitive areas are located partially inward and are not totally accessible without the aid of instrumentation. Their sensation of sexual pleasures is scattered and vaguely demarcated. It has to be mentioned that, like any broad categorization, only a few people are totally semino-vaginal or clitoro-penile; and the rest are predominantly or slightly typified.

Now, what does this have to do with the pleasures of enema? The individuals who have discovered the enjoyment of colonic stimulation are seminal men and vaginal women. For them the cerebral representation of sexual sensuality does not focus upon the glans-foreskin combination or vagina-labia minor combination, but rather upon larger and more scattered anatomical entities such as: colon, prostate, seminal sac, uterus, vagina, and other visceral organs. The concept of sexual typology does not claim that the semino-vaginal type cannot enjoy clitoro-penile stimulation and vice versa. The types are not inborn, they are developmental; effective experiences during the crucial periods of the individual's life determine the predominance of either semino-vaginal or clitoro-penile sensitivity.

Is either of the two types superior to the other? No. Each type has its own merits. The advantage of the clitoro-penile is that in this type the sensual touch is precisely outlined. It is close to awareness. It is relatively free from emotional vagueness, and it does not require many auxiliary attributes to reach its high peak of climax. In the semino-vaginal the sensuality has a wider horizon. It has many allies and attributes. The intensity of the climax is longer, though it has a blunt or a plateau summit. The pleasure of the enema is one of the attributes of this type. Possibly there are some semino-vaginal individuals who would enjoy colonic stimulation but have not initiated the experience.

It has been said that a penile man and a clitoral woman have the blessing of being in a satisfactory sensual accord. Nothing has been said about seminal man and vaginal woman. But it is understandable that seminal man with clitoral woman or penile man with vaginal woman might have sexual discord. Should they seek different partners? Not necessarily. By becoming aware of their own inclinations and those of their partner, a greater mutual collaboration and attainment of fuller sexual enjoyment is not out of their reach.

Clitoro-penile and semino-vaginal modalities are a baseline of sensuality. Sexual drive is in a constant state of flux, but it returns to its baseline. An enema lover does not employ the colonic stimulation as a solo device for sexual satisfaction. As a matter of fact, an enema lover, being a semino-vaginal, could dream of many ingenious devices to stimulate deeply situated visceral organs. Though the colonic stimulation brings some to orgasm, in the majority the enema is a prelude to the orgasmic finale attained by the direct involvement of genital organs.

The concept of sexual typology does not elucidate all the puzzling shadows of the pleasures of the enema and other sexual derivatives. There are other theories and implications, and all of them have some shortcomings. One should be cautious of overgeneralization. I believe that one good medium of enlightenment is sharing experiences, as in Forum. I hope that I am contributing some by the explaining of the why's.—*A.H. Hemmat, M.D. (Psychiatrist), Fayetteville, N.Y.*

* * *

When I first discovered your special preference letters last summer, they struck an immediate cord of response. I have been a devotee of enemas since the age of six, when I first remember being sexually aroused by one.

When I was twelve, a friend told me his version of the facts of life. This fellow believed that anal intercourse was the primal sex act and that it satisfied the most basic human instincts. I was quite aroused, and from that day on, I took a great interest in female buttocks. This portion of the anatomy is still my biggest turn-on. It is a completely heterosexual fetish; male asses turn me off entirely.

At about this same time (age twelve), I began to experiment with self-administered enemas when my parents were away from home. This practice continued until I graduated from high school and went away to college, when having a dormitory roommate made it impractical.

While a freshman at college, however, I met and began dating a girl whose hindquarters I regarded as sheer perfection. Imagine my delight when I learned (my finger strayed there—half on purpose) of her anal eroticism. Before long, our petting sessions included mutual masturbation with our fingers busily digging into each other's backside. But it wasn't until we finally rented a motel room one night that I sampled the pleasures of an enema.

When we had registered and locked ourselves into our room, she undressed and watched as I unpacked the enema bag and its attachments. Her cheeks were flushed and she was in an obviously aroused state. She lay face down on the bed, with a large motel towel under her pelvic region. Trembling and sporting an incredible erection, I inserted the nozzle between her perfect buttocks and heard her sigh with pleasure. As the water flowed into her rectum, she moaned and moved her buttocks from side to side, repeatedly saying how marvelously good it felt. "Stop," she finally said. "I'm full."

Later, she administered an enema to me. I am not ashamed to say that I came spontaneously—with no penile stimulation whatever. We were married about a year later, and we continue to satisfy each other with enemas, etc. I regard myself as a perfectly adjusted man. Neither of us feels that any of this is "dirty" or immoral. We now have two children, and continue to have straight intercourse as well as our special preference sessions.—
Name and address withheld

* * *

About six months ago, I stayed home from work to dry out after overindulging at a wedding reception I had attended the previous evening. Around midmorning, I went into the backyard for some fresh air. My next-door neighbor saw me and asked why I wasn't at work. She is a fairly attractive widow, about fifty, and has a shy manner. I have helped her several times with odd jobs and became fairly friendly with her. When I told her about my hangover, she seemed to blush and became slightly excited. Pretending to be angry, she scolded me and started leading me by the arm to her house.

In her kitchen, I watched while she mixed several spoonfuls of baking soda in a pitcher of warm water. I told her that drinking soda water wouldn't help me, but she only laughed. When she began to swish a bar of soap in the solution, I became alarmed and said there was no way I would drink that stuff. She laughed again and said, "Of course not, silly. I'm going to give you an enema." I thought she was kidding until she fetched an enema bag and poured the mixture into it. When I tried to protest, she continued her mock severity and said, "No arguments, young man," and marched me into the bathroom.

She started unbuttoning my shirt and I became embarrassed and told her I would just lower my trousers. But she insisted on removing every stitch I was wearing. When I was naked, she instructed me to kneel on a towel with my head low and buttocks high. She knelt next to me and inserted the enema nozzle, telling me to let her know when it started to hurt. Soon I felt quite full and told her. She removed the nozzle from my rectum and I thought the treatment was completed. Instead she massaged my belly for a minute, reinserted the nozzle, and continued the enema.

Later that day, I felt better and went over to thank her for helping me. She told me she found enemas very stimulating, but that giving herself an enema was too awkward to perform as often as she would like. I jokingly said I would give her one anytime she wanted me to. To my astonishment she asked me to give her one right then and there. I asked her how she wanted me to give it to her, and she said to just do what she had done for me. As I stripped her, I got a terrific erection. Seeing her naked, I couldn't keep my hands off her, and we had intercourse right there on the floor. Since that day, we have given each other several enemas with sex afterward. I have found that they are very pleasant sex stimulants.
—*Name and address withheld*

* * *

7

Masturbation

I have a favorite way of masturbating that I use quite frequently and I want to share it with your readers. I love to masturbate into the vacuum cleaner by putting the hose over my bare penis. What I do is turn the cleaner on, have the hose connected to the suction end with the other end directly on my penis, sit back on the cleaner, and enjoy drifting from orgasm to orgasm as the hose milks my penis. And believe me, it leaves me totally satisfied and relaxed.

In all the times I have done this, I have experienced no harm or injury.—*Name and address withheld*

* * *

Since I know this is a problem shared by many women, I thought your readers might be interested to hear about how I overcame my hang-up on orgasm. Like many women, I had masturbated almost from the time I could remember and I was able to bring myself to orgasm in this manner. But when I got married (I was a virgin till then) I found to my surprise that I could not obtain an orgasm during sexual intercourse.

After a while, I overcame my shyness and, thanks to an understanding husband, masturbated myself after normal intercourse. At my husband's suggestion I then tried rubbing my clitoris and upper areas of my vagina *during* intercourse and found that I could have an orgasm at the same time as my husband in this way. Not only is this extremely gratifying for both of us but I find that just the thought of my masturbating turns me *and* my husband on.

I enjoy sex a great deal but I still also like to masturbate. On numerous occasions my husband has asked me to masturbate for him. He has even bought me a vibrating rubber penis and gets a thrill out of seeing me stimulated by "someone else." Many times we masturbate each other in preference to vaginal intercourse. We have tried all types of variations in lovemaking and find them all gratifying. The main point is that we don't have any secrets from each other. If either of us have anything we want to try out, we *tell* each other about it. Consequently, we have a very happy sexual married life.—*Mrs. R.R. (name and address withheld), Newport, Rhode Island.*

* * *

My wife and I are both twenty-nine years old, and avid readers of *Penthouse*. We especially enjoy the *Penthouse* Forum, which contains what we think to be some fantastic reading, knowledge, and ideas. Lately, we have been reading quite a lot about mutual masturbation. Although we have never tried it, and never thought we would, it sounds exciting.

Recently, during one of our frequent sexual bouts, I had just finished bringing my wife "off" orally for the eighth or ninth time, and had gotten up to go to the bathroom. When I returned I was quite surprised to find my lovely wife lying on the bed, breasts heaving, legs spread wide, the fingers of one hand holding open her lovely quim while the fingers of the other hand were gently massaging her clitoris. Just from reading the articles I knew that watching a female in the act of masturbation would turn me on, but seeing my wife lying there working on herself was simply wild! I stood there speechless until she brought herself to orgasm. In ecstasy she arched her back, let out a little cry, and came! I thought I'd pop right then and there.

After seeing a sight like this, I was unable to keep myself from her, and immediately went down on her again and brought her to yet another orgasm. As I came up for air she asked me if I would stand at the foot of the bed and masturbate so she could watch. With a bit of embarrassment I consented, got up, and began hammering away only inches from her face. It was plain to see that she was enjoying every minute of it. Suddenly she laid back down, opened her legs and her honeypot once again, and started to give her clitoris still another workout. Watching her masturbate, while I was doing the same, was fantastic.

I stopped just short of orgasm, sat on the bed next to her, and helped her out by holding her furry patch open for her while she teased her throbbing clit with her fingertips. Within moments she reached what she says was the strongest climax of her life. Afterwards we united, and had the most glorious fuck ever.

Later that night we discussed what had taken place. We both admitted that we had dreamt of masturbation, and that we had kept our fantasies hidden because of embarrassment. We were in complete agreement that it was a fantastic experience, and promised each other that we would definitely repeat it often.

I myself find now, after this experience, I want sex with my wife more than ever. I often find myself sitting at work daydreaming about her at home, on the bed, legs spread wide, masturbating alone, awaiting my return. At times like this I find myself with the most fantastic hard-on, which takes all my self-control to keep from hammering away at.

Long live masturbation! It has definitely brought joy into our lives, and has brought my wife and me even closer together than ever before.—*Name and address withheld*

* * *

I am a woman who has tried a variety of masturbation aids myself, except artificial male organs, which I would rather not have in the house. I have yet to find something that can beat my present sex aid, which has given me many hours of writhing enjoyment. I refer to the good old-fashioned cucumber. Before anyone starts laughing I can assure you that with a kitchen knife and a little patience, a large cucumber can be shaped into a very lifelike penis. It is not quite as hard, but nevertheless it is almost as good. I usually treat myself to two large ones a week and use them to make two models. I use one for masturbation and one for simulated fellatio.—*A.L., Billericay, Essex, England*

* * *

Having read many interesting letters in your Forum, I thought that I would write and describe some of my experiences with masturbation—truly one of the most widely practiced sexual practices in today's world.

Having lived with my girl friend for three years here at the University of Virginia, I have found many ways to work masturbation in as an integral part of our sex lives. One of the most gratifying ways my girl friend has found to alleviate sexual tensions is to gently massage the insides of my thighs, and then turn my stereo up to maximum level and place the headphones, one cup each, around my testicles. The vibration drives my penis to a rigid erection. At the same time, my girl friend sits across the speakers and the vibration, particularly during bass notes, gives her extreme sensual pleasure.

Sometimes, after servicing my testicles with the headphones, she pours natural honey on my erect penis and then proceeds to lick it off. The sensuous pressure of her tongue, particularly around the head of my penis, drives me to almost unbearable ecstasy.

While these practices may sound unusual, they have

had an amazing effect on our sex life. And, truly, the measure of a mutual practice in the art of sex is not how conventional it is, but rather how much it is enjoyed by those who practice it.—*Name withheld, Charlottesville, Va.*

* * *

8

Circumcision, Male & Female

Sexindex is an excellent feature which I look forward to reading in each issue of Penthouse. However, I should like to point out some omissions in the June installment. In Victorian times and until about 1930 many medical advisers advocated the use of specially designed chastity belts not merely to enforce chastity but to prevent masturbation, which was thought to be dangerous. They were prescribed for children, young people and lunatics, both male and female. There was a special type of chastity belt, which had a one-way trap mechanism to prevent intercourse *per anum*, while permitting the back passage to be used for its normal function. While on the subject of chastity belts, how about a full-page color picture of one of your delightful models wearing one: the censors could hardly object for anything more moral is hardly imaginable.

Under clitoridectomy, you mention the two simplest forms of female circumcision, removal of the clitoral prepuce and the slicing off of the tip or glans of the clitoris, but more complicated forms are practiced in many parts of the world. These include removal of the whole clitoris including the shaft, removal of the labia minora (possibly you will have an entry on labiotomy) and the slicing off of the inner surfaces of the labia majora. These last two operations are often followed by the closing of the vaginal orifice, usually known as infibulation. This may be done either by tying the girl's legs together until the wound has healed over, or by stitching the two surfaces together with a needle and thread. You say that the operation is ofen performed when the girl is sitting with her legs held apart, but many tribes expect the victim to sit still and show no sign of pain. If she cries out, she will be ostracized by her friends and relations.

Female circumcision, clitoridectomy and labiotomy have all been advanced as cures for masturbation, as has cauterization of the genital area. Similarly, males have been infibulated, circumcised to discourage masturbation or had their glans or urethra cauterized. These rather weird attitudes to masturbation were prevalent in the 19th century and survived into our own.

Most of my criticisms of Sexindex derive from the fact that you do not have the space to include all the necessary information about each of the subjects. What is needed is a full-sized article about each topic.—*J. G. McCulloch, Easter Rigghead, Avonbridge, Falkirk, Stirlingshire, Scotland.*

* * *

The foreskin is an ugly and wrinkled surplus scrap of tissue which conceals the beauty of the penis. The circumcised cock, with its head permanently and proudly exposed, and the ring of scar tissue far back on the penis where the skin and mucous membrane are joined, really turns me on.

I love to shower with my boyfriend and pull on his penis and tug on the remaining skin and feel the smooth throbbing head without having to roll back any surplus covering in order to remove the debris underneath. After our shower he likes me to dry his penis with a rough towel and then apply a few drops of oil and gently massage and pull him.

Talk about loss of sensitivity is nonsense. My boyfriend was circumcised when he was fifteen and he says it is as sensitive now (age twenty-five) as it was then. Prior to circumcision, his foreskin extended an inch beyond the tip. It was like having a finger hanging between his legs. The result of his circumcision was to clip off the foreskin an inch behind the rim. Now, the sensitive pink head gently bobs to and fro and brushes against his clothing as he walks. During erection the skin is stretched tight and in intercourse it is massaged by the in-and-out action.

It is not really possible to keep the foreskin pushed back permanently without having it permanently removed. I say, men, have your precious foreskins removed and join the clipped generation!—*R.M. (name and address withheld)*

* * *

After reading the January *Penthouse* Forum, I was quite annoyed with this letter by some cocksucker who goes by the initials R.M. I am twenty years old and have been going out with a handsome, intelligent man who is twenty-four. We've been messing around for a month now. He hasn't got a circumcised cock, and I am fond of this fact. Nothing feels better than sticking your tongue in and separating the foreskin until you reach the head of the penis. R.M.'s letter was *bullshit*. I have spoken to many girls who definitely believe nothing beats what nature creates.—*A.B. (address withheld)*

* * *

I am writing in regard to the letter on circumcision in October's *Penthouse*. I have not had extensive sexual experience, but enough to compare the sensations between circumcised sex partners and uncircumcised sex partners.

In my opinion the difference is substantial. The uncircumcised penis is the most exciting sight I suppose I will ever view. In sexual foreplay and oral sex, the feel of the foreskin against my fingers, thighs, lips, tongue, eyelids (really, the whole body) is an unforgettable experience. During intercourse, the penis with foreskin is by far more stimulating than one without it.

In articles I have read, it is sometimes stated that the foreskin protects the glans and, therefore, the glans being more sensitive, the climax in the uncircumcised male will be much quicker. Of course this depends on the individual, but I find this to be totally false. In fact, in my personal experience, my uncircumcised partner lasts longer than any circumcised partner I have had intercourse with.

I do think it is a shame that obstetricians feel compelled to perform circumcision on every male baby. It seems to be taken for granted that it is the thing to do. The mother is, therefore, influenced by the doctor's attitude when she should at least consider leaving the baby uncircumcised.—*Name and address withheld*

* * *

I have just read the July issue of your magazine and found letters both in the Forum and to Xaviera Hollander dealing with the subject of circumcision. Having recently undergone the operation after thirty-two years of misery, fear, and embarrassment, my relief and satisfaction with circumcision is hard to express.

While Miss Hollander advocates her preference for the circumcised penis, her comment that the operation is painful for adults is not only inaccurate but a significant misunderstanding that is shared by many. In my own case this led to many years of sexual frustration. Once having resigned myself to the operation, because it was a necessity due to constant minor infection and the inability to retract the foreskin for cleaning, I finally got the nerve to visit a urologist for an examination. From that point on it could not have been simpler, less painful, or handled in a more dignified manner.

A quick examination by the urologist and an explanation of what was to follow put my mind at ease. The actual hospital stay was only two nights and one day with the circumcision done with a local anesthetic, taking only twenty minutes. Exactly two weeks after the operation was performed, the stitches were gone and a whole new life of sexual pleasure opened up. For those who suffered as I did with the fear and embarrassment of having circumcision performed, it is too simple to wait any longer.

The letter from the lady in Detroit in Forum is hard for me to accept, now that I have the experience to compare the circumcised with the uncircumcised penis from the male viewpoint, as she did from the female viewpoint. My wife and I have literally started a new and exciting sexual life since the operation. After eleven years of marriage, we are now closer than ever, and enjoy the full act. Many times my wife will, with complete surprise to me, take out my penis while I'm watching television or reading, and fondle it or perform fellatio. I too become very excited seeing the erect "head," previously unknown to me. It may be imaginary, but the penis without the foreskin appears much larger.

From one who has experienced both ways, I cannot advocate strongly enough that men be circumcised.—
D.B. (name and address withheld)

* * *

I could not resist making a reply to Mr. Thomas's letter regarding circumcision in the October Forum.

I agree wholeheartedly that a male should be allowed to decide for himself whether or not he wants to be circumcised, and only after he has had the experience of being uncircumcised. However, when the time to make the decision arises, I would recommend that the man dismiss any thoughts of parting with his foreskin.

After two years of marriage, with a most satisfactory sex life, I had to have an appendectomy. As I had not been circumcised, I asked my surgeon to take care of this while removing my appendix. He immediately agreed to comply with my request, although there was no physical necessity. It was a spur-of-the-moment gesture on my part, and one which I shall regret all of my life.

My foreskin was not tight or long and retracted very easily. In my late teens, I developed a habit of leaving it pulled back whenever I was nude. The glans would become dry after a while, but still remained sensitive. When I married, at age twenty-two, I realized that sex was a little better if I kept my glans covered except when bathing, urinating, masturbating, or during intercourse. Of course, during an erection the glans was always fully exposed.

It gave me a feeling of super masculinity to pull the skin back while bathing my penis and replace it after drying. My wife likes oral sex, and daily bathing kept my penis odor-free and tasteless.

After the circumcision, my glans quickly began to toughen and became less and less sensitive. At my present age of twenty-six, I have almost no feeling in the glans. After prolonged intercourse, I am frequently sore around the rim from the friction against the dry head and from the unnatural tugging on the overly taut skin of the shaft. Naturally, when my pleasure in sex diminishes, so does that of my wife.

In summary, I cannot stress enough that those who have parted with their foreskins can never know the full pleasures of sexual stimulation as nature intended.—*Name and address withheld*

* * *

I have read several letters in your magazine from people who claim to derive pleasure from pain, but my experience was rather different. I was faced with the situation that either I undergo some pain or my girlfriend would stop giving me pleasure. My girlfriend Cathy is a receptionist for a lady doctor specializing in gynecology. The doctor is a staunch believer that all men should be circumcised. Cathy started putting pressure on me to undergo surgery. I managed to stall her off until she gave me an ultimatum that either I would be circumcised or no more sex. Since we had been enjoying a fantastic relationship I gritted my teeth and agreed.

The lady doctor agreed to do the surgery and set up an appointment for me on a Friday afternoon in her office. Cathy wanted to watch the surgery and assist the doctor. With two women in the room and me lying naked on a table, I began to get the uneasy feeling that something uncontrollable was going to happen. It did, after the doctor had shaved off my genital hair and started pulling back my foreskin to clean underneath it. I got a strong erection and just couldn't make it go down. The lady doctor was unperturbed by this, but said that she couldn't perform the circumcision if I had an erection. My efforts at detumescence failed, so the doctor took a pair of scissors and made a small snip in the end of the foreskin. I must have jumped an inch off the table, but the erection wilted very fast. In order to prevent further uncontrolled events the doctor gave me a very light anesthetic which took the edge off the pain but still left me with a sharp stinging sensation. With Cathy holding my shoulders to prevent my squirming, the doctor finished the surgery rather rapidly. After stitches had been taken and the wound bandaged, I was sitting on the edge of the table and saw that rather large strip of flesh that had been cut off and I wondered if I would ever be able to enjoy sex again.

Cathy helped me get dressed and drove me to her apartment. I healed rather slowly due to the fact that I got carried away and imagined myself to be in better shape than I really was! Well, all that pain is over now and I have a large scar where my foreskin was, but at least I can have all the pleasure I want.—*G.H. (name and address withheld), Los Angeles, Calif.*

* * *

9

Aesthetics of the Vagina

J.D., (February) tries to convince women that an important part of their bodies is naturally repugnant, disgusting and odious, and should be spruced up by shaving, cleaning and inserting chocolate into the vagina. Perhaps he is suffering from a psychological fear of being swallowed up by women and is terrified of the sight of a mature healthy vagina, while a shaved vagina, resembling a child's, alleviates his anxieties. Maybe he perceives women as below him and uses their differences (the functions of a vagina as opposed to those of a penis) to support his feelings of disgust, hatred and fear.

We know our bodies don't stink just because they produce an odor unlike a man's. That smell is normal and healthy in a woman because our bodies have an obviously different function in sex. Any man who can't appreciate it and prefers flavored douches or crunch bars is not really a man. If you want a fake plastic woman, get yourself a Barbie doll!—*Linda and Barbra, (names and address withheld), Middletown, Conn.*

* * *

I am 25 years old, a college graduate, and have always considered myself the All-American boy. However, lately, I have begun to think that there is something seriously wrong with me since I would much rather perform cunnilingus on a young lady than have normal intercourse. Friends tell me that there is nothing like the real thing and any fellow who prefers cunnilingus to straight screwing is abnormal.

Frankly, I just love to eat pussy (or chocha as we call it here in Puerto Rico). I have found that most girls are turned on more by being eaten than by my penis. My goal is to please my mate and therefore I have no qualms at all about chowing down on her.

My favorite trick and the one thing that seems to win me more girls than any other single act is this: I place my girl in a rocking chair and she tilts her body back slightly as I begin tasting her forbidden fruit. After a few minutes, when she is beginning to turn on, I place one or two green olives into her vagina and then open a can of beer (my favorite drink). I pour the beer onto her stomach just below her navel and it then drains down into my open mouth. By now the girl is usually so turned on she is speaking a language no one has ever heard. Now I pluck the olives out of her vagina and drive her to ecstasy. More often than not I am able to eat a complete jar of olives in one sitting. I just can't think of a better way to get drunk and turn your girl on at the same time.

I've only performed this act with half a dozen girls in the last year or so. However each of these chicks has been after me day and night ever since. One said she would follow me around the world until my dying day. Everything was going great until my friends started giving me second thoughts. I don't consider myself a superman or a sexual acrobatic, just a young guy who tries to please his woman. What amazes me is that the friends who condemn me most are the super-macho types. Who is wrong?—*Mack Williams, (address supplied), Sabana Seca, Puerto Rico.*

* * *

My boyfriend and I have just finished reading your November issue—it's super! The beef that I have concerns mass advertisements for feminine hygiene products. Everywhere I go I see these ads—on television, in the newspaper, in magazines. When I first learned about them, I tried them. I had no problem with vaginal odors, but it was a new thing to do. But it didn't seem to do anything for me. All that happened was that my pubic region smelt like a rosebush. Next, flavored hygiene sprays came out—peppermint, strawberry and lemon. Again, they were novelties, so I tried them. But my boyfriend hated them. He told me eventually: "If I want to taste lemon, I'll buy a lemon. If I want to smell roses, I'll buy a rose." Then it hit me. He liked to have oral sex with a girl and not a sweet candy bar. He then told me that the smell of a clean, healthy girl's vagina is the most exciting odor he knows, especially during sex. The manufactured sprays just cover up the natural scents. So I'm now thoroughly against these sprays as a mechanism for male attraction.
—*Debbie Janz, Brock Ave, Toronto, Ontario, Canada*

* * *

My husband and I have experimented in almost all ways of reaching orgasm. By discussing this subject with friends we have learned many different techniques, my favorite of which is having my husband perform oral intercourse on me. In talking to some of my female friends, they feel that this is disgusting and dirty; however, they think nothing of blowing their husbands.

I would like to tell them that there is nothing at all dirty about the fluids that are secreted from the pussy during orgasm. There is something very erotic about a man's tongue exploring around my pubic hairs and in my vagina. I would rather be eaten out than have intercourse any day.—*Mrs. Betty Jenkins, (address withheld), Md.*

* * *

Well, as I suspected, that letter captioned *A matter of taste* opened a can of worms, or should I say a can of sardines?

To the "islander" (July Forum) I say a fishy pussy is a sick pussy, and if God had wanted us to eat that thing, he would have put a toothpick and a napkin down there.

I do not mean to say that all "boxes" smell like a carton of dried bait, but I do say that those who dote on this sort of thing really are showing a distinct proclivity towards the perverse. Sex is a reflexive instinct that we humans misuse as badly as we do booze. Any animal has more sense than we do—and you don't find any "muff-divers" among them.

From my own limited sexual experience, I'd say that 90 percent of women go down on men but only 45 percent of men go down on women. As you might have guessed, I tried it once and didn't like it—it was not finger-lickin' good. I am a plain old-fashioned top-fucker and that's good enough for me.—*R.T., Los Angeles, Calif.*

* * *

Just a comment on the letter, "A matter of taste," in the April 1974 issue.

I would like to point out the difference between oral sex and oral love. My differentiation is based on the basic principle of any relations between persons who love each other.

When you love somebody you are concerned with giving, not receiving. This may sound funny coming from a Latin-Spanish, male-chauvinist macho. I make oral love to give pleasure and satisfaction to the one I love. If by offering oral love I could not give my loved one any satisfaction, I would just quit right there and try something else, and this would not hurt at all my macho status. After all, what is better than having a woman respond to your every caress and command, including with your tongue?

On the other hand there is oral sex, which is performed

by the very selfish person, just for personal gratification. I'm not saying that this is always wrong. It would be if it's the only source of pleasure for a person, and then I would have to agree that "perhaps it's similar in structure to coprophilia" (I leave this to the consideration of Freud fans).

As for the aesthetic value of the open vulva, I would compare it to (and I consider myself an artist) the aesthetic value of an open mouth (ask your dentist about it). Still, nobody is opposed to the display of an open mouth that is part of the total composition of a photograph. (This is the difference between pornography and art.) To find titillation in either of the above cases we would not need Penthouse. A trip to the nearest medical library would suffice, they stock plenty of anatomy books.

I must insist that the female body (the best creation so far) as displayed in your magazine is as real as womanhood itself or your models wouldn't be real (and I cannot believe that).

I was asked once by a girl how could I stand her "fishy" odor. My answer was that "as any good islander, I love seafood." We laughed about it and she overcame her aversion to her own scent.—*Name and address withheld*

* * *

I am writing to respond directly to the letter in the April *Penthouse* that was published under the heading, "A matter of taste."

The writer spoke of the unaesthetic looks of a woman's pubic area and of its loathsome smell. This to me pitifully indicates that he is neither animal nor aesthete, for animals love its smell and artists are inspired by its looks.

But mainly I think he is sorrowfully wrong and sadly backward, for his body and soul have not learned that most gourmet tastes are acquired (how many people, at first try, loved oysters, escargots, caviar, frog legs?). Man and woman transcend the scientific when they fall in love —the looks, sounds, touch, taste, and smell of the beloved then become the very elixir of life. The "loathsome smell" of a woman's vagina is so missed by men at war that I understand many women have mailed dirty underwear to their soldiers on the battlefront.—*Name and address withheld*

* * *

After a not inconsiderable amount of sexual experience, I have come to the conclusion that a woman's randiness is definitely indicated by the size of her *mons veneris*—the mound of Venus.

Girls I have known with a flat and bony *mons* have generally been virginally-inclined, cool and stand-offish. But girls with a plump and cushiony *mons* have been hot in the pants, and usually raring to go. I would be interested to hear others' experience.—*A.P.K. (name and address withheld), Pinner Green, Pinner, England.*

* * *

Reading the July Forum, I decided that the letters concerning the virtues of vaginal odors just did not praise these delicious aromas enough.

I would like to offer this in response to the reader who wrote: "The 'loathsome smell' of a woman's vagina is so missed by men at war that I understand many women have mailed dirty underwear to their soldiers on the battlefront." I'm not familiar with army life, war, or soldiers, but I do know about prison life, and about men separated from women for long periods of time. For many years, the odor of a woman's vagina stayed with me, locked behind my sinuses, a gentle scent dusting across my lonely brain, stored within the chambers of my mind, a prized possession of my memory, as familiar as my motorcycle, softer than hot bubble gum it rolled around behind my eyeballs as I recalled a night in Baton Rouge. Turning the pages of a tattered *Reader's Digest*, the smiling face of a woman eating a slice of toast brings down a veil of happiness as the remembered odor clouds my vision.

But about two months ago, locked-up in the "hole," I

forgot that wonderful odor. It faded from my memory. It left me and I can't bring it back. I can't just run down to the local red-light district and refurbish the faded memory. I never thought it could happen, never dreamed I could forget—but I did, and I find myself empty—uptight. Sniffing the breezes, I smell only stone walls, captivity, loneliness and frustration. In desperation, I snorted an ounce of tuna fish . . . I'll never again laugh at any jokes comparing a woman's vaginal odor to fish. But alas, it too is sadly wrong! My heart feels the grip of claustrophobia. I can't get enough air and breathing no longer satisfies me. What is the smell of roses without the odor of a woman's vagina? Ha! Only roses —stinking roses! Since my memory has failed me I exchanged opinions on this subject with fellow convicts and found the majority agree that the odor of a vagina is not only sexually arousing, but equivalent to a soft, warm body on a cold night, a refreshing drink after a hot trip, a trusting pair of thighs wrapped securely around your ears while hearing the roaring sound of the sea and tasting the night salt air. It's the blue in her twinkling eyes as she dares you to go down there under the covers after an extended and excessively heavy humping. It's the damp mist that wraps around your laughter as you take her up on that dare. All this is gone.

I must wait and suffer years more before rediscovering the bliss and ecstasy that hovers tantalizingly beyond my reach. And the man who calls a vagina unaesthetic, with a "loathsome" odor, if he reads this he had better take warning—for if I ever meet him, I'll rub his dainty nose in a pile of . . . .—*B.A., address withheld*

* * *

The photographs in your magazine have left competition far behind. You have discovered a way of almost coming upon a girl by surprise, discovering her in some intimate act which crosses over the borderline into the world of an autoerotic sex fantasy.

The female genitalia you display are ones of fantasy— idealized and not at all like the reality. Like any ideal, they don't exist. But here the camera is lying and the enthusiasms of the reader for the illusion express themselves in terms of oral eroticism and anal activity.

The open vulva as an aesthetic object cannot survive a strong light or a truly disinterested look such as gynecologists might frequently get. The color, labia, skin textures, sebaceous cysts, and other assorted blemishes hardly make it an object to which one would feel compelled to apply his or her mouth—or use the mouth as a sex organ. The practitioner of oral sex on the vulva, clitoris, and vagina must overcome a sense of loathing to find titillation.

Adding to this, there are extremely unpleasant odors—the proverbial "fishiness" and other bacterial fermentations, yeasts, trichomonas, and odorous discharges often (but not invariably) associated with the vagina, supporting my suspicion that these devotees, as they reveal themselves in letters to your magazine, are indeed exhibiting a psychopathology that is perhaps similar in its substructure to coprophilia.—*Name and address withheld*

* * *

10

Spanking

I am writing this letter because I am horny and frustrated. My problem is trying to find a partner who shares my idiosyncrasies.

Several years ago when I was a horny but unsophisticated teenager, I chanced on one of the first issues of *Penthouse*. In the Forum there was a letter that dealt with the practice of spanking as a sexual stimulus. That letter turned me on as nothing in my life ever had. I became fuzzy-headed, throbbing and flushed with heat. I was, not to coin a phrase, "in heat," and "burning with desire," phrases which I had not appreciated in the past. I was going to screw, by God, right then and there. And I didn't give a damn who saw what. My boyfriend's cooler head prevailed, and we adjourned to the garage since he felt that balling in his family's living room in full view of his parents was indiscreet.

Unfortunately he would not cater to my demands. Screw me he would—but spank me he would not (although he had no objections to any methods of arousal *I* wanted to use on myself). I could never understand his refusal to spank me since I was obviously panting for it, and we split soon after that. I have continued to look for a man with whom I could share my enthusiasm for spanking.

In the past years since then I've had every kind of sexual/emotional relationship, even getting laid for a grade in college with a lecherous professor. It was only in this last affair that I was spanked. Dr. X was obviously hot for my body and I knew it. In a burst of honesty, he admitted that the only way I was going to get the grade I deserved (an A) was to have a late night conference with him. I agreed and we met in his office one weekend when the building was deserted. I was expecting a quick fuck or a blow job but this was not what happened.

He had me kneel in front of him, take his cock out of his pants and suck him off. This was only the warm-up. He undressed me and examined me thoroughly, kissing me here and there. Then he had me get on the floor on my knees with my head on the floor and my ass high in the air. After explaining that trying to avoid the blows would only make the spanking last longer, he started to slap my ass. I was in heaven! I was finally getting what I had wanted for years. He spanked me slowly and carefully with each slap getting slightly harder than the last. In a few minutes my ass was really hurting. I twisted away and told him I was thoroughly aroused and ready to screw all night. I had not counted on his reaction, which was to laugh and say that he'd hardly begun. He grabbed me, pulled me across his lap and held me firmly in place with his left arm across my back and his right leg pinning my legs tightly between his. Then he spanked me in earnest with the flat of his palm slapping my cheeks as hard as he could. I was crying and begging him to stop but that only made him slap me harder.

After an eternity he paused for a moment and I could feel his cock pressing hard up against my stomach. What amazed me even more was that I wanted him to keep on spanking. I think he knew what had happened because he laughed a bit, and continued with a final dozen slaps, each long, hard, and lingering. With each final slap, my cunt was getting hotter and hotter until I thought I was on fire. My thighs were tingling and my nipples were crinkled so tight that they ached. He released me and I stood up to feel the juice running down my legs. His erection was enormous and he was as turned-on as I was. Out of consideration for my still-stinging ass, he let me get on top and we balled wildly. As I was pumping madly away, half out of my mind with lust, he slapped me across the ass. That put me over the top and I had orgasm after orgasm as he slapped my smarting ass.

Somewhere out there are men who love to spank women as much as I love being spanked. Maybe I'll find one someday. Until then I content myself with the few pornographic novels that deal with spanking but don't go into whips and chains. And I remain both horny and frustrated.—*Name withheld, Tallahassee, Fla.*

* * *

Being an avid reader of *Penthouse*, I have followed Forum, and wish to relate some of my experiences on corporal punishment. At the present time, I am eighteen years old and a freshman in college and I have a brother three years younger than myself. I was brought up in a strict household, and my parents believed in corporal punishment for any aged child because of its embarrassing aspects. Recently, while at home on vacation, I became involved in a typical sibling argument with my brother and one of his friends. Before it was over, he had hit me and I had retaliated with an egg thrown in his face and some rather vulgar language which my father overheard. My father came in and ordered me to remove all of my clothes right there in front of my brother and his friend, and then took me over his knee and gave me a severe walloping with a paddle. I could not sit comfortably for three days and endured comments from my brother and his friends for days afterward. Needless to say, my language was much cleaner thereafter. This was not an isolated case—this type of punishment was common, and I'm grateful to my father for this type of upbringing. Dad's rules were simple—you knew that if you did something wrong, your clothes would come off and you'd be paddled, regardless of those present.—*M.U.* *(name and address withheld)*

* * *

I am an avid reader of the *Penthouse* Forum and am particularly interested in the letters about spanking. I think your readers will find my experiences interesting.

I am a teaching assistant at a large midwestern university. About a month ago I left some books in my office and had to return late at night to get them. When I got there I found two of my female students there copying a test. After surprising them I told them that either I would have to report them or arrive at some other form of punishment. They didn't want to be expelled, so they agreed to accept whatever punishment I prescribed. I decided on spanking. At first they protested, but they eventually accepted my terms. The terms were that they would be spanked in three installments on weekends when the office building was empty. Linda decided to go first, leaving Susan with a whole week of anticipation.

I got to the office early that Saturday and Linda was waiting for me. She seemed too much at ease for someone in her position; I couldn't figure it out. I got the hairbrush (which I procured just for the occasion) from my desk. She was all smiles as she crawled over my knees. Then I found out why she was so confident. I could see the faint outline of a magazine under her jeans! I pulled her off my lap and she immediately knew I was on to her. I told her that for such a trick she would receive all her spankings on the bare behind. She pleaded with me not to, but eventually submitted. She blushed from head to toe as she removed her panties. She was very careful not to expose anything as she once again crawled over my knees. I lectured her for five minutes on the evils of cheating, the whole time enjoying the view of her plump behind. Then I began spanking. I took my time, leaving four to five seconds between each swat. She maintained her composure for the first ten swats, then she broke down, lost all modesty and began kicking and crying wildly. Each time the paddle landed, her behind jiggled and she let out a loud yelp. As she wiggled and squirmed to try to avoid the blows, I saw everything she had tried so hard to conceal. When I finished the forty strokes her rear was a deep crimson. I stood her in a corner until she stopped crying. As she was dressing she said that she was sorry and deserved everything she got.

Next week Susan showed up fifteen minutes late. I used her tardiness as an excuse to spank her on the bare bottom too. When I told her to take off her dress I found that she didn't have on a bra. Susan was even more embarrassed than Linda as she stood there completely naked. I had her fetch the paddle from the desk and then bend over my knees. Her behind really turned red fast, and she seemed to be suffering more than Linda, so I set the brush aside and finished with a hand spanking. The difference was phenomenal. The hand spanking was much more sensual. I could feel the warmth and the quivering in her behind as I landed each spank. When it was over I couldn't resist rubbing her bottom. I continued until she stopped crying. After she was dressed she kissed me passionately on the mouth and then ran out.

Since then I have spanked each girl again and they have once more to go. I begin with the paddle and then use my hand. I am looking for ways to get more of my students over my knee in the future. Overall, I think spanking is fairer than expulsion for first-time cheating.
—*Name and address withheld*

* * *

In the very early stages of our married life, my husband did some very childish things and I often told him so. Then, one day when he had been worse than usual, I told him in no uncertain terms that he should start to grow up. We were preparing for bed and he was naked and he asked what I would do if he were a little boy, I replied:

"No problem. I would put you across my knee." He then asked if we could pretend he was a small boy, and a very naughty one at that.

This really appealed to me and in no time at all he was across my lap. I gave him a sound spanking and then reached for my hairbrush and gave him some more.

Call me a sadist if you like, but I enjoyed it. It released all my tensions and I felt on top of the world. We made love that night and slept in each other's arms, and never have I enjoyed it so much.

Since then I have used a variety of corrective instruments to keep a firm hold on him. Usually he lies across my knee and I use a folded strap, or a hairbrush, or just my bare hand. For more serious things he lies on the bed and gets the cane on his bare bottom.

Quite honestly, I get a kick out of being the boss but I am not at all sure who gets the most fun out of it, however much pain is administered. After the first time I had spanked him, I asked him at breakfast the next day why he had submitted to it at the hands of a woman. He said that he had once witnessed a man spanking his naked wife across his knee which had caused him to have fantasies about being spanked.—*D.H., West Hartlepool, England*

* * *

I was disappointed that in the August Forum no letters were shared about the exciting turn-on of a spanking. For my husband (a superstrong construction man who can really deliver a strong wallop) and me, spankings have been an addition to our lovemaking for the four years of our marriage.

Most of the time they begin as a punishment for some very minor infraction or oversight. For example, last week he noticed a tiny dent on the family car. He ranted and raved about the value of a car and my lack of consideration. "Wait till I blister your ass," he said, "next time you'll remember to be careful." I knew what was to happen next, and although I was excited with anticipation, I became penitent and fearful. "I'm so sorry," I said, over and over.

He grabbed me, pulled me over his knee and removed my panties. He also removed his shoe. Holding the shoe by the toe part, he then began hitting my ass with the heel. After a few strong wallops, I was crying and honestly begging him to stop. I tried to wriggle out of the way of the next blow. However, the more I resisted the harder he hit. After forty or fifty thrashes on my ass —when the fight was literally beaten out of me and I was sobbing in resignation—he turned me over and fucked me.

Another time, because of some undone chores, he decided to punish me. He grabbed two coat hangers and let me choose—a wire type or a wooden one. The wire one appeared less substantial so I chose that one. He laid me on the bed and promised if I moved I would probably get it all over and not just my ass. He then delivered the longest, hardest beating I remember. The sting was unbelievable and I couldn't keep from moving trying to get out of its way. Because of that I received several hard ones on the backs of my thighs. I felt as though I were on fire. But the more my ass was burning with hurt, the more my clit was quivering and the more I came. The red welts that hanger raised lasted nearly a week.

Sometimes, when there is no excuse for a spanking, my husband will look at me and say, "You have the whitest ass! I'll have to put some color in it." We have a little paddle—the kind you see at vacation gift shops—hanging in the den as a joke. But in our house it gets used—no joke. He puts me over his knee, pulls down my panties, keeps one hand feeling my cunt, the other slamming the paddle on my ass. No matter how long or hard I get it like that I love every second. One time he got so involved watching the bruises he didn't stop for nearly fifteen minutes. Although I came three times, I was reminded of that paddling every time I sat down for two days.—*(Name and address withheld)*

* * *

Spanking is something out of this world. A fire on my backside sets one up front. One day I saw this girl who was hitchhiking and I told her I would give her a ride if she met the following condition: either she had to spank me, or else I'd spank her. She agreed and decided she'd spank me. We drove off to a wooded area, got into the backseat, and I pulled my pants down and laid across her knee. She raised her hand and gave me a good hard slap. Then another and another. Twenty-four in all, twelve on each cheek. I could tell she liked it too, so I asked her if she wanted to be spanked. She said she would so I told her to lay across my knee, pulled down her panties, and gave her bottom a good solid spanking to match mine. She cried a little but I could see she enjoyed it as much as I did.

We went to a motel that morning and had sex like never before. Then I made her my wife. True enough! Now, although we've been married for quite a while, I still spank her bare bottom before sex. She still cries (just like my five-year-old who gets spanked for naughtiness), but really loves every minute. And the sex that follows is unbelievable.

Sometimes she pretends that she's a naughty girl and I, as her make-believe daddy, lecture her and then put her bare bottom over my knee and give her a good spanking with my hand or a shaving strap. Spanking is an important part of our sex lives and a part we really enjoy.—*J.T., address withheld*

* * *

Your letters about spanking really turn me on. I wish you'd run a lot more of them.

I must have been born a masochist. I can remember when I was seven and eight years old becoming wildly excited whenever my daddy would lay me across his lap, yank down my panties, and spank me hard enough so I couldn't sit down for a little while.

When I was in tenth grade, I did everything I could to force the principal to spank me. He took me into this office, made me take my panties down, bent me across his knee, and whacked me with a ruler until I could hardly cry anymore. This happened twice. There is something about a spanking that is sexual and intimate at the same time. When we passed each other in the hall after that, he'd look at me in a certain way and I'd look back the same way. He knew I loved every minute of it in spite of how it hurt.

I am twenty-three now and have been married for three and a half years, and I make my husband spank me as often as I can. Luckily, spanking my bare behind turns him on as much as it does me. I can't sit for hours after he's finished, but that doesn't stop us from balling like crazy. Lighting a fire on my behind seems to light one around in front as well. And though I am usually crying very hard when we go to bed together, I wouldn't change it for the world.

Every month I can't wait for *Penthouse* to come out. The only thing that would make it better, as far as I am concerned, is more and more mail about spanking, and even a few good pictures, if that is possible. Keep up the good work.—*Name withheld, Los Angeles, Calif.*

* * *

Let me second the comments of the anonymous writer who congratulated *Penthouse* (April 1974) on its exposure of that most exciting portion of a woman's anatomy—*le derrière*. With a little imagination I can easily picture that precious bottom stretched across my lap awaiting the tingle from a moderate spanking.

As per the request from the woman from Los Angeles for more letters relating spanking experiences, let me submit the following from my personal history.

I first spanked a bottom of the opposite sex when I was fifteen-years-old. The reluctant, but not completely uncooperative, owner of the bottom was my fourteen-year-old sister.

It all began one Saturday morning when we were alone in the house. It was getting late, and I walked into her room to get her out of bed. She refused, so I warned her that I would spank her bottom if she didn't get up.

She said I wouldn't dare. That did it! I playfully wrestled with her while I untied the drawstrings to her old-fashioned cotton pajama bottoms. Pulling the pajamas off her legs, I next wrestled her to a face-down position across my lap. Her panty-clad bottom was in perfect position for a few easy spanks. I then slipped my fingers under the top elastic band of her panties and lowered them first over one hip and then the other. She started struggling as I slipped her panties down her legs and then off completely. Her struggles continued as I alternately spanked one rounded cheek and then the other. In a short while, she got out of bed.

Thus began our Saturday morning ritual. My sister helped the game along by wearing several pairs of panties to bed on Friday nights. The next morning I would administer spanks to each layer of protection until none remained. Afterwards, I would retire to the bathroom for a hand job while she redressed for the day.

This was my first, but certainly not my last, experience with the pleasure of turning a girl's bare bottom pink.
—*Name withheld, Dallas, Texas*

* * *

I am trying to figure out how to get my husband to spank me. I am not kidding and I am not crazy. I occasionally (especially before my period) would love my husband to pull me across his lap and spank my bare bottom with his hand. I hesitated to ask him to do it, until my husband brought your June magazine home. I read those letters and I imagined myself being spanked and began to get excited. Maybe I won't like it after the first time but I need to know. I have hinted but to no avail. Pretty soon, I'll give up and start spanking myself.—*Name and address withheld*

* * *

I am writing to let D.H. of West Hartlepool, England (May 1974) know that she is not alone. I, too, spank my husband, and I have been doing so for most of the five years we have been married. Like D.H., I began spanking my husband in response to some very childish things that he had been doing. One day after he had done some especially bad things, I told him that I was so displeased with his misbehavior that I really would like to punish him. He asked me what kind of punishment I had in mind, and I told him I thought he deserved a good, hard spanking. To my surprise, he told me that, if it would make me feel better, I should go ahead and spank him. So I did. I sat down, and I made him take down his pants and undershorts. Then I made him bend over my lap, and I spanked his bare bottom as hard as I could. That night he had to sleep on his stomach because his bottom still hurt so much.

Like D.H., I enjoyed it. It rid me of all my anger, and gave me, instead, a feeling of excitement. After I had finished spanking my husband, I made him get down between my legs and do cunnilingus to me. As further punishment for him, I did nothing to satisfy his own sexual desire.

Since then I have continued to spank my husband whenever I think he has misbehaved. That means that he usually gets a spanking three or four times a week, but some weeks he gets a spanking every day.

Now when I spank him, I not only make him take down his pants and undershorts, but I insist he take off all his clothes. Then, as always, I make him bend over across my lap, and I spank his bare bottom. I start out spanking him with my bare hand, and, when my hand gets sore, I use the back of my hairbrush. When I have finished spanking him, my husband must get down on his knees between my legs and do cunnilingus to me until he has satisfied the sexual excitement that has built up inside me while I was spanking him. That sometimes takes half an hour or more. Afterwards, he must remain completely naked until I tell him he can put his clothes back on. If the spanking occurs in the evening, I often will not let him put his clothes back on until the next morning. Whenever my husband receives a spanking, he may not receive any satisfaction for his own sexual desires, and I watch him to make sure that he does not masturbate. As you can see, when my husband misbehaves, he is really punished.

Finally, like D.H., I must admit that I enjoy spanking my husband and punishing him in the ways I have described. It gives me a feeling of power that I like very much, and, sexually, spanking my husband's bare bottom excites me tremendously. In general, the sight of a man's bare bottom arouses me sexually, and the thought of spanking a man on his bare bottom and punishing him in other ways arouses me more than any other kind of sexual thoughts. As long as the man is willing, as my husband is, I see nothing wrong with spanking him and punishing him in other ways he deserves.—*Name and address withheld*

* * *

Would you or one of your readers please explain to my dear husband just why it is that a spanking hurts more on a wet bottom? I discovered this painful fact of life many years ago when my mother first hauled me out of a tub and applied her palm to my moist little posterior. I've consulted with friends and they all agree. *Everybody* knows it. But not my George! He says it can't be. He says water cools things off, even spanked behinds. He says I'm getting kinky.

I suggested an experiment. Let him wet one buttock, leave the other dry, and apply a paddle to both. (Or better yet, let *me* apply the paddle. That'd learn him!) He said I was turning into a real freak. He suggested I read Krafft-Ebing or the letters to *Penthouse*.

Now it happens that I am not a kink, kook, or fetishist. I just happen to believe that a good sound spanking sometimes does a child a world of good. And within reason, the sounder the better. And one day a few months ago when my darling daughter had gone to extraordinary lengths to provoke a paddling, I went to the bathroom and got a large bath towel and a wet washrag. I placed the former over my lap, and after my daughter had done likewise with her person, I sponged her rear with the latter. I then proceeded to dry off the wetness with vigorous strokes of the board. Her reaction was emphatic. So much so that I have used the same procedure on all occasions when discipline was required.

My daughter does not like my new method. She says it makes her feel all "icky." I suggest that the proper word is "sore." But George just thinks it's kinky. He says it *can't* hurt as much. Is there a doctor in the house who can tell why it does?—*M.N. (name and address withheld)*

* * *

I'd like to relate some experiences I had two years ago. My sister asked if I'd fill in a hand in her weekly card game, which I did. We got very involved in the game and didn't notice the time. About 6:30 P.M., my sister's husband came home to discover that supper hadn't been prepared. Without saying a word he left, but returned shortly with the other three husbands. He announced that the women were to be taught a lesson and would be spanked. I didn't struggle as I expected only a few playful slaps on my woolen slacks. Imagine my surprise when my husband lowered my slacks to my knees, and my further surprise when my panties followed. From the corner of my eye I could see the others were being bared in a like manner. Next I felt the sting of a good hard slap, followed by about a dozen more. My eyes and ears told me the others were getting the same treatment. A burning sensation told me my bottom was getting as red as theirs, if not more so.

We were then asked if we were ready to agree to have supper ready on time. My sister and another weren't, so my sister's husband said, "We must show them that we're in this together." We were then passed around to each husband, who gave us a dozen smacks. Finally we reached our own husbands, where we got a dozen more to remind us to whom we belonged. At this point we were all beet red and ready to promise anything. We were released with the warning that the same thing would take place should supper be late again. So far it hasn't.

At cards a few weeks later eight of us were discussing

the spanking when one girl was caught cheating. Another girl laughingly suggested that she be spanked for her errant ways. Our hostess promptly brought her hairbrush and the three girls at the cheater's table took down her pants and gave her bare rump a good workout of about a dozen slaps each. She was very red and how she kept from crying, I'll never know. We then decided that each week the low scorer would get a bare-bottomed spanking from the other three at her table. My sister and a few of the others admitted that they were no strangers to the hairbrush or the strap, being on the receiving end from their husbands. One girl swore that she had never been caned by her husband. As luck would have it, a couple of weeks later she was low scorer. As her bottom was bared for the spanking, the girl over whose knees she lay let out a cry of surprise. We all looked and noticed that Susan's bottom was a bright crimson. She then admitted that she was a frequent victim of her husband's hairbrush, and he had in fact administered a severe session the night before.

One girl suggested that she be paddled by all seven for her lying, but that was voted down as it was pointed out that her bottom was quite sore.

My husband tells me that as long as I act like a child, he'll be obliged to punish me like a child and continue the spankings. It's certainly no fun and I wind up with my head down and bared bottom up over his knee at least twice a month.

I'd like to hear from others who've had similar experiences.—*Name and address withheld*

* * *

I was a twenty-two-year-old bride, and was a very sloppy housekeeper, a nagger, and a chunk of ice in the bedroom.

My husband stood me as long as he could before he took action. One night he came home from the midnight shift at the factory, and after crawling into bed he tried to make love to me, but I resisted his efforts.

Seething with anger, my husband hopped out of bed,

grabbed a wooden hairbrush on the dressing table, and flung me over his knee.

For the next several minutes my backside felt the full impact of the hairbrush. As the strokes connected, I felt a sensational pain in my posterior and at the same time I felt a strong desire to have sex.

Falling back on the bed, I spread my legs and my husband mounted me. For the first time, we had wonderful sex which we both enjoyed. The spanking is responsible for this.

Now, whenever I feel like having sex, my husband obliges, but first we have a session with the hairbrush. A happier sex life has made me a better housekeeper, mother, and wife.—*Name and address withheld*

* * *

Hurray for Forum! My friend (married three years) has always hated the missionary position, but his wife refused him entry from the rear so he had to go to a professional house to enjoy it. *No more.* He read a letter in Penthouse which suggested using a paddle to give painful punishment. When his wife refused as usual to be coaxed, he let her have it on her bare behind with a hairbrush. As he found the brush too thick, he changed to a paddle. Because he was very angry, in spite of her sobbing and pleading, he gave her such a severe spanking that for two days she had to sit down very carefully. They didn't have sex that night but later that week, he began entry from the rear. He didn't penetrate her completely, but at least he tried. Now, if she hesitates too long or tries to avoid getting into position, he picks up the paddle and that is all he needs to do.

He started out to punish her, but now he says it increases his erotic desires to see her lying across his knee. She now knows him to be her complete master, even when he just gives her a few paddywhacks or just playfully strokes the cheeks of her buttocks.—*Charles N. (name and address withheld), Bronx, N.Y.*

* * *

I find your magazine very interesting, especially the Forum letters about spanking. I have had several experiences of this type. Some years ago, when I was working as a clerk for a firm on the outskirts of London, I had my own small office at the back of the building. It was rather lonely because nobody ever came down that way, except the occasional teaboy or messenger. Though my office contained an extra desk for a steno, I was far too junior to have my own secretary and so when I wanted a letter done I had to ring for a girl from the typing-pool.

One day rather an attractive young lady turned up with the letters she had typed for me. She was just 17 years old, I was 26, and I rather liked her but because of the age difference I didn't try to make any approaches. I went through the letters, checking and signing them, then came on one with three serious mistakes in it. For some reason, I was in a very bad mood that day so I spoke to the young lady rather sharply and asked her what she thought she was doing. She mumbled something which made my temper worse, so I then said, "What you need is a good spanking—come here." Rather to my surprise, she got up from her chair and walked over to me. As she stopped in front of me I caught hold of her and bent her over my knee. Again to my surprise she made no resistance.

She was wearing a tartan skirt (this was before the mini era) and I patted her bottom a few times then lifted the skirt up, under which she was wearing a white slip. I again gave her bottom a few pats then lifted the slip, revealing a thin black suspender belt and a pair of sheer white nylon bikini panties. I patted her bottom a few more times, then asked if she was ready for the spanking I had promised. She said "Yes." So I gave her six good hard smacks on the right buttock, during which she made a few little squeals, oh! and moans, but no objections. I followed with six slaps on the left buttock, with the same result. I then removed her suspender belt, gripping her more tightly round the waist with my left hand which was also holding her skirt and slip up, and proceeded to give her a further six. This caused a little more complaint and she started to struggle but I was holding her tight so she could only wriggle her bottom and wave her legs in the air. After six more, I rubbed her bottom and asked her how she felt. She was crying a little and replied that her bottom was sore and would I let her go, to which I said No.

I then started to remove her panties, at which she cried "Oh no, not on my bare bottom, please put my panties back." My reply was to bare her bottom completely (it was very red) and to rub it and give it a few pats, after which I asked if she was ready for me to continue the spanking. She said, "No, please, no more—that's enough" but I gave her another six, during which she struggled and moaned. Finally I rubbed her bottom for a bit, gave her a few more pats and pinched each buttock. I then let her get up, upon which she threw her arms round my neck and kissed me passionately. She rubbed her bottom, kissed me again, and remarked: "You really lay it on hard—I shan't be able to sit down for a week." She put her clothes back on, dried her eyes, touched up her makeup, then left the office to return a few moments later with a cushion which she placed on her chair. She then sat down, typed the letter correctly, gave it to me to sign, and left the office, taking her cushion with her. By the way, I was in a very good mood for the rest of the week: it certainly did *me* good, if not her!

About two weeks later the same girl came into my office with some letters she had typed. To my surprise I found among them either the original letter which had caused the spanking, or an exact copy, mistakes and all. When I drew her attention to it, she smiled and giggled a bit and said: "Yes I am a bad girl, give me a really sound spanking." Naturally I agreed, and after this the same letter would turn up on my desk approximately every two to three weeks, with the same result. This went on for about a year, until she left the company for another job.—*D.A. (name and address withheld), Rabaul, New Guinea.*

* * *

I've seen many letters in your excellent publication about "spanking games" between husband and wife, but I feel my experience is slightly different. A couple of years ago, my wife appeared at breakfast wearing only a flimsy negligee and became rather teasing. I threatened her with a spanking, and she dared me. So, putting her over my knee and wedging her shoulders under the table, I slapped her bare buttocks until she asked to be let up. No sooner had she got up than she said she wasn't at all sorry, so I repeated the treatment, this time with a long-handled pine clothes brush.

That evening our neighbor Joan looked in, as my wife had gone to the cinema. Joan is a smart, attractive blonde and behind her back she held a polished willow stick. She was very friendly and said teasingly that my wife had told her about the spanking after I'd gone to work, and showed her the damage! We had a sherry and I asked why she had brought the stick. She was doe-eyed and said she had always wanted a spanking but her husband would not oblige as he was very placid and more interested in marine biology than love.

We kissed on the sofa and started petting and she gradually worked herself face-down across my lap, then opened my flies and caressed my penis into a major erection. I slipped down her silk shorts and she opened her thighs so I entered along her lips, and she started pleading for a spanking. She was very moist and with each spank her vagina slipped up and down my penis. From a few gentle starting slaps I progressed to harder and harder blows which made her sob in ecstasy till we both came together. After another sherry, she knelt on the end of the sofa, bending over the arm, and asked, begged, for the cane. I gave her 12 quick medium cuts on the same spot and she writhed and sobbed "Harder, harder!" After six more as hard as I could apply them, she rose and kissed me all over and, taking the cane, gave me two dozen as hard as she possibly could. Then, with me on my back on the floor, she bestrode me and performed like a veritable Bathsheba. By 10 p.m. we were exhausted.

Pretty well every week after that for a year we had our little evenings. "Turn me over and turn me on" is Joan's motto.—*K.R. (name and address withheld), Sidmouth, Devon, England.*

* * *

I've read your articles and letters about bondage and spanking with a great deal of interest and pleasure, knowing that not everyone makes jokes at people who naturally enjoy humiliation and discipline.

I feel my experience may be of interest to your readers. A few years ago my girlfriend displayed to me a side of her that I had never seen. One weekend while we were away in the mountains, I had gone out to get some things for a party that night. When I returned, I almost fainted when I saw her standing there in black leather shorts and blouse to match, with black leather boots that went all the way up to her thighs. I dropped to my knees in subjection. Before I knew it, she had a large dog collar round my neck. She placed a small padlock through the metal tongue with a long chain which ended in her gloved hand and a pair of handcuffs around my wrists, bound behind me. It all happened so fast that I didn't even realize that she was dragging me to the bed, where she chained me to the bedpost. I watched her as she went to the dresser and removed an evil-looking cat-o'-nine-tails from a drawer. What happened that day was pure ecstasy for me, as for her, and ever since then it has become a part of my daily diet.—*M. J. G. (name and address withheld), Boulder, Colo.*

* * *

Though enemas have always been used in my house for the usual intestinal upsets, I can't remember ever getting one for disciplinary reasons. My daddy has a much better method. It's called spanking.

His rules are very simple. Everything I'm wearing,

and I mean everything, comes off first. Though I'm a junior in college and almost twenty-one years of age, this procedure is followed to the letter. The last time it happened was only three weeks ago.

He has a small paddle he made himself some years ago just for this purpose. The business side is ridged like a butter paddle, and it has a double line of small holes down the center. When I am completely naked, he sends me to get it. When I hand it to him, which I usually manage to do with a few crocodile tears, he sits down in a chair, orders me across his lap, and without saying a word, whacks me till my bottom is red, hot and blistered. By this time I am really crying, and there's nothing phony about it. Generally, after he finishes, I don't sit comfortably for the rest of the day.

My daddy is a wonderful guy. I love him and I wouldn't change places with any other girl in the whole world. And a lot of my girl friends have told me they wished their daddys cared that much about them. But when mine spanks, he really spanks.—*P.B. (address withheld).*

* * *

I have been very much interested in your readers' discussions about pain and pleasure. I, too, had thought that any activities involving pain or punishment in conjunction with the sex act were abnormal or deviant. But since I have had the opportunity to read your magazine and follow some of the letters, I feel better about my own experiences.

I am a young woman, twenty-four, and was brought up in a very "proper" home. Because I happened to have been blessed with a very pretty face and better than average physical endowments, and because my parents expected so very much of me, I must have had a somewhat unusual childhood. Because I was always "one of the prettiest" girls, many boys did not ask me out for dates. At the same time, my parents were teaching me the virtues of virginity and the sins of sex, and I spent much time reading and thinking about sexual things. I was also a perfectionist, I guess because so much was demanded and expected of me as a child.

My father did not believe in sparing the rod. I was not punished often, but when I was, it was usually severe. My mother would slap me in anger over my behavior, but for those "horrible" infractions my father was told. He would punish me by spanking, usually with a hairbrush, and after twenty or thirty whacks he would send me to bed without supper. One time, when I was out on a picnic with some of my girlfriends, we exchanged clothes in the woods. Naturally, I came home with different clothes, and my mother asked me about it. When I told her what I had done, she thought it was horrible, especially when she found that I was wearing someone else's underwear. I guess the idea of being naked outdoors was what bugged her. When my father came home, she told him, and he took me to my room. He made me remove my shorts and underpants and ordered me to hold my blouse up above my waist. When he removed his belt, I was sick to my stomach. Holding it doubled up, with the belt in his hand, he struck my rear quarters several times very hard. I thought I was going to faint and let go of my blouse and must have tried to protect myself. He made me remove all of my clothes, including my bra, and laid me face down across my bed. Then, holding the buckle in his hand but with the belt fully extended, he leathered me thoroughly from my waist to my knee joints. He hit me sixteen or eighteen times.

I had welts for several weeks after that and thought about my behavior and shame and the punishment and never could understand the rationale for it all.

I went away to college several years after that, and met many people who had had similar experiences. But a couple of years ago I met a man whom I love very much, and even discussed the whole thing with him (I had only discussed it with girls before). I often slept at his apartment, and we grew very close. One day, while lounging around his apartment, he saw me lying on the bed stroking myself. He watched, unnoticed, and I guess that my breathing quickened as I was arousing myself. He crept beside me and asked what I was thinking about, and it was then that I told him about the experience and that, after much thought, I agreed that corporal punishment was probably best in some circumstances. But it was the first time that I realized I was aroused by thoughts of being leathered by someone else.

Several months later we went to his family's summer cabin at a nearby lake. As we were walking along quietly outdoors, he kissed me. He began unbuttoning my blouse and held me close to him when it was undone (I don't wear any bra in the warmer months). He took it off and continued to kiss me there in the woods. When he tried to slide my shorts and panties off, I got very nervous, but he assured me that no one was around for miles. Very quickly I was completely naked, and he insisted that we keep walking. Leaving my clothes behind, we walked through the woods, he dressed and I completely nude. I had to admit that it was pretty arousing.

When we came to a tree that had some rope hanging from it, he reminded me of some of my fantasies about being beaten and asked if it was all right to tie me. I didn't know how to respond, and he took my hands and raised them high above my head, tying them together with the loose end of the rope. I was stretched, hands over head, completely naked. He kissed me several times, caressing me fondly, and I thought I was going to be delirious. He went to some shrubs nearby and broke off several thin branches and asked me which I liked best; I guess I had known all along what was going to happen, and I selected the one with small buds all along it. He stepped to the side and let it whistle onto my backside, and I screamed. He continued, mercilessly, with blow after blow, being careful to apply the lashes in different areas each time. He must have hit me fifty or sixty times, each time moving the lash a little so as not to repeat a spot. After a dozen or so, I was able to look over my shoulder and see the branch coming at me, and by straining I could see the damage being done to my buttocks and thighs. The whistle of the rod was what terrified me most, I think, but my backside was reduced to a quivering mass of red and purple welts despite my protests. He untied my hands and laid me on the ground, removed his clothes, and we made love right there in the woods, my flesh smarting from the whipping. It was pure ecstasy, at least for me.

Since then he has beaten me on several occasions, indoors and out, and always he undresses me and orders me into some position that exposes me completely. I always obey, and he beats me severely. One time, when his sister was visiting him for the weekend, he made me undress in front of her. She undressed as well and ordered me to bend over an ottoman. My boyfriend held my arms outstretched as I lay over the ottoman, and she whipped me with a cord from an iron. I was so humiliated that I cried from embarrassment, but when she was finished, I was ordered to whip her. I spared no mercy in applying the cord again and again to her unprotected flesh and evened the score as she begged for mercy. My boyfriend said I struck her seventy times. As she lay writhing and weeping, we made love on the floor next to her. That was the last time I ever saw her, though.

At any rate, I just thought your readers might be interested in some of my experiences and they should know, as I do, that whatever they do is fine if they are happy. My boyfriend and I couldn't care less what others think is normal.—*C.L. (address withheld).*

* * *

I would like to know if other women have similar experiences. Six years ago I married a kind, gentle professional man. I was a virgin and frigid.

For the first year I hated sex. I obliged passively since it was my duty. One evening, when my husband was about to mount me, he looked at me in disgust and left home. I was relieved.

He returned an hour later with a ping pong set. He removed a paddle and spanked my bare bottom until I was screeching. He then threw me on the floor and left the room. I chased after him and couldn't stop myself from seducing him. We did everything. I was transformed into a whore. Having never experienced orgasm before, I had three. We both stayed home from work the next day and had a glorious fucking session.

Six years later the paddle stays under our mattress as a reminder. I am frequently uncooperative in order to encourage spankings.

A spanking prior to sex relieves me of all my guilt feelings and allows my true sexual self to emerge. If anyone else enjoys a spanking before sex, please tell me that I'm not alone.—*C.M. (name withheld), East Meadow, N.Y.*

* * *

I had always read, with great amusement, your Forum letters on corporal punishment, but I'm not laughing any more! I am unmarried, 26, and accustomed to having my own way. My long-time (four years) fiance, John, is a loving gentle man who has given me a very long time to get all the hell out of my system before we wed. I guess I didn't realize it, but I took shameful advantage of this wonderfully patient guy.

On a hot July afternoon too much liquor and sun made me restless and base-tongued. I raged that any man who would take what he was taking from a 110 lb girl was less a man and I announced plans to take an apartment in New York. John said absolutely nothing, which infuriated me, so the next day I actually left my job and home and drove into the city.

It wasn't hard to find the kind of crowd I was looking for. The first time John visited me, he found me high on drugs and dressed in a see-through creation that showed every curve of my small frame. He wrapped me in a blanket, held me in his arms all that night until the effects of the drug (a bad, bad trip) wore off. When he left, I was more depressed and confused than before. He was a great guy and I loved him, but he didn't seem to have any spunk. How could I marry a man who would stand by and watch the girl he loved destroy herself?

I soon shook off my depression, by plunging into a series of sex, drugs, everything-goes parties. When John next called me, I was wrapped in the arms of a guy I'd just met, out of my mind on speed and music. Viciously I told him exactly what was going on. I was crying when I slammed the phone down, heartsick at what I was doing, but unable to stop myself. By 3.30 a.m. all my guests had gone and I'd just thrown myself across the bed exhausted. The door bell rang and I answered it to find a telegram and a box had been delivered. The telegram was from John and said simply "To Carol, with love." In the box, to my surprise, I found a large, lethal-looking hairbrush. Frightened, excited, and more than slightly confused, I got dressed and sat down with a drink, but I didn't have to wait long. Johnny arrived and held me, kissed me, then sat me down on the bed where he began a lecture punctuated by the words "spoiled," "wilful," "childlike," "in need of discipline," and ending: "And so, because I love you, I am going to punish you." Then he left the room to fetch the "gift" he had sent.

Thoroughly frightened by now, I made a desperate attempt to flee the apartment. But Johnny caught me and returned me to the bedroom. I guess I still had some fire left in me though, because I was spitting out words like "You wouldn't dare!" and "I'll never see you again." Johnny ignored me and I watched in terror while he positioned himself on the edge of the bed with two pillows placed over his right knee. He reached for me and I found the pillows rested just under my pelvis and raised my bottom up into a most humiliating position. He unbuttoned my outfit and let it fall to the floor. I lay there across his knees with my bottom stuck up in the air like some sacrifice to the pagan gods. My bikini pants didn't afford me much protection, but he still pulled them down and left me naked. He held me firmly across his knees and began recounting in detail all the bitchy things I would do no more. When he reached for the hairbrush I began to cry, knowing that four years of fury were to be released on to my bare bottom.

When the first stroke landed, I squirmed, screamed, pleaded and cried, but Johnny was spacing the strokes so that he could lecture in between and give me time to anticipate in horror the next stroke. In that regressed position, I looked at the floor and at my selfish self in a way that never could have been duplicated in any other circumstances. In between strokes Johnny (1) set a wedding date, (2) regulated my behavior, (3) sold my car (which I always drove too fast), (4) forbade the use of drugs, (5 modified my manner of dressing, and (6) told me I would quit my job. I agreed to everything. Still, the lecturing and punishment continued for over an hour and a half. When he released me, my bottom was disfigured with welts and bruises.

I am not proud that a 26-year-old woman had to be given an oldfashioned spanking to come to her senses. I am not proud of the fact that I provoked a gentle, kind man who loves me deeply. I am not proud of the fact that I am writing this letter standing, but I am thankful and grateful to God that I was spanked and thereby saved from what would have been my eventual ruin. I am to be married tonight to a man I love and respect.— *Carol M. (name and address withheld), New York, N.Y.*

* * *

I am a woman of 33 and have always enjoyed discipline, plus a normal sex life. I am divorced, but I hold a fairly prominent position at our local bank. Quite a few women I know enjoy this phase of sex; for this purpose I go 20 miles from the town where I live. For some years, I have had a relationship with a woman who has a clientèle of females who require "caning" or "spanking."

A certain ritual is observed: I arrive by appointment, generally in the afternoon, and I am ushered into her room. This woman is in her late 40s and her husband owns one of the larger hardware stores in town. I am dressed as if I were on a date, fully clad when she enters. She addresses me very harshly. I am told to undress, in no uncertain terms, and strip to the waist.

My hands are kept above my head at all times, and during this I am usually protesting. She removes my skirt and panties, and leaves me in my garter belt and stockings. A sofa is used for the beating or a small bench. I am told to lie across it with my posterior in the air.

She goes to a cabinet and selects a thin bamboo rod or birch branches. This is applied to my calves and buttocks 30 or 40 times. Once this begins, though I cry and protest, I receive intense orgasms, and to me it's wonderful. It lasts for four to six minutes.

I am not a lesbian by any standards; sex to me is what you make it. I have enjoyed "normal" sex, but to me a caning is a thing that many women need for release. I'm sure many do feel this way, but they're afraid to tell their husbands.—*Mrs. O.V.H. (name and address withheld), Urbana, Ill.*

* * *

I have been reading Penthouse for about a year and the readers' letters have encouraged me to write this. At one time I thought I was alone in my predilections. I have been married three years now (I am 31) to a woman four years my senior. She is the sexual aggressor and I find this extremely pleasurable. About a year ago I confided to her my most personal sexual desires. Since my boyhood I have always had thoughts and dreams of being spanked by an attractive woman. My wife wasn't overly surprised because during our courtship I had occasionally played some sort of spanking games with her. She gladly agreed to fulfill my desires.

Often now she takes me over her knee after taking down my pants and underwear and, as my penis gets extremely rigid, locks it helplessly between her thighs. While in this embarrassing position, she usually lectures or scolds me for being a naughty boy and repeatedly mentions that she is going to give me a good spanking. And let me tell you the tingling sensation of my bare behind in this vulnerable position is fantastic! She then proceeds to spank me lightly until I ejaculate. After ejaculation she keeps me over her lap and lightly rubs my bottom with her open hand in a circular motion which sends chills up and down my spine.

I am an executive and this little ritual relieves the

strains and tensions of a hectic day at the office and commuting in crowded trains more than any amount of alcohol could. Sometimes we will play a game: if I can prevent coming while getting spanked over her lap until she releases me, we can have sex. Occasionally, if I am extra tense or keyed up, she will give me both a spanking and then an enema with a rectal syringe, and during the course of one or the other I will ejaculate. The feeling of being taken over her knee and given a sound going-over is out of this world, coming from a responsive, attractive, big-busted woman.—*Charles E. (name and address withheld), Huntington, New York.*

* * *

Some time ago I was rummaging through a pile of magazines at a friend's house and came across three *Penthouses*, the first ones I had actually read (though I heard of them). In South Africa where I have lived for most of my life, and here in Rhodesia they are banned. What a winner you have, full of interesting reading, comments, and photography second to none.

I notice that in your Forum section you encourage discussion on personal topics and I would like to relate how my married life changed. The wife and I were continually at loggerheads. We started going our own ways, and as you can imagine, sexually we were a shambles. We seldom made love and if we did there was little feeling. About a year ago at home in Johannesburg, we were sitting reading, when out of the blue my wife asked to play cards. I said "OK, what shall it be—strip poker?" To my amazement she said yes, and what's more she named the stakes. If she won, two strokes across the bottom for every article of clothing that remained on her, and vice versa if I won, except it was to be one stroke. Not for one moment did I think she would keep to it, let alone beat me at cards, something she had never done. But not only did she win, she had five articles of clothing on at the end.

A bet is a bet and I always pay if I lose—I was marched up to the bedroom and laid out on the bed. The bamboo came down with plenty of "feeling," as she put it, at half-minute intervals, and I can assure you I landed up with ten stripes across my bottom. To relate what happened after that would be impossible, but our whole attitude towards each other changed. We had found something which probably we were too afraid to exploit before. Maybe not everyone is the same but as far as we are concerned, a little pain makes so much difference to lovemaking.—*John Kelly (address supplied), Salisbury, Rhodesia.*

* * *

I have just read a back issue of *Penthouse* and the letters on spanking really interested me. Some females may like to be spanked, but the vast majority do not. I base my knowledge on fourteen years of experience as an employee of a detention center for delinquent girls. During those fourteen years I witnessed many girls being spanked. Spankings were always administered by a senior matron on the spot that nature provided. The instrument of correction was an old-fashioned razor strap, referred to as "the persuader."

I have seen many girls, ranging in age from thirteen to eighteen, undergo a spanking. These girls turned snow-white in the face when the superintendent ordered them spanked. Some have tried to keep a stiff upper lip en route to the punishment room; others had to practically be carried or pulled down the hall to this special room in the basement. Without fail, all pleaded with the matrons to let them keep their underwear on, but rules stipulated that spanking must be on the bare posterior. After the third stroke of the persuader, the recipient would scream at the top of her voice and kick her legs frantically, but the spanking continued.

After an inmate had received the full measure of one dozen strokes, she was crying like a six-year-old and her backside was crimson. Upon being released from the spanking-table, the girl would invariably grab her bottom and dance up and down, sobbing loudly.

Never in my fourteen years at this center have I known

an inmate who had to be given a second spanking. Following their release or discharge from the center, several have written back thanking us for the spanking, saying they would always remember the lessons they were taught.

It has been a few years since I worked at this center, but I am confident that spanking is just as good a deterrent today as in those days. A good bare-bottom beating would remove the halo from our young people today.—*(Name and address withheld)*

* * *

I very much admire your magazine, especially its philosophy towards love and life, and of course its beautiful girls. Cassandra Harrington (February) is my favorite so far, and I agree wholeheartedly with Miss Harrington's social philosophy, that of peaceful and moderate revolution to effect positive changes in society. I read every letter in your Penthouse Forum, but until recently I didn't think much of the letters you printed extolling corporal punishment.

However, about a week ago I was visiting my 20-year-old girlfriend, a college sophomore, at her campus dormitory. It was her birthday, and she dared me to give her a birthday spanking. We had her room to ourselves, so I pulled her across my knees and gave her a few halfhearted slaps on the seat of her pants. After about the third slap, she jumped to her feet and asked me if that was the best I could do, and told me to let her feel it, and spank her "like a man." Taking my cue, I played up to her father-image and ordered her to bring me her hairbrush and then to take down her pants. She quickly did so, then meekly laid herself across my knees with her bare bottom at an extremely inviting angle. I became caught up in the spirit of the spanking and gave her 20 good hard whacks across her behind. Her hairbrush was wide and flat, and admirably suited to the job. After the spanking, she was very aroused, and so was I, and we enjoyed intercourse as we never had before.

That episode impressed me with the value of a little

pain where lovemaking is concerned, and I wanted to share it with your other readers. I have just one problem, in that my birthday is next month, and my girlfriend claims the right to give me what I gave her. I just hope that I enjoy a bare-assed spanking as much when I'm on the receiving end!—*Victor de Lyle, (address withheld), Potsdam, New York 13676.*

* * *

Would you allow three girls who share a flat, whose boyfriends all read Penthouse, and who all think it marvelous, to comment on your pain/pleasure controversy? We just can't understand men who want to be caned by their wives. None of us has found anything of the sort necessary to assist in lovemaking! But as we're all under 20 and away from home we've felt the need for some sort of discipline among ourselves, and since nine months ago, at the suggestion of our friend John, who's a teacher and lives upstairs, we've had a cane for this purpose.

John got it for us. He says it is the lightest available in the education service. It's 21 inches long, has a bent-over handle and is barely ¼" thick at the other end. But it has a terrifying swish and stings like hell. Those cuts from each of the others across briefs or pajamas—touching toes or bending over a chair—are not something any of us looks forward to, and usually keep the culprit on the straight and narrow for some time to come.

When one of us does anything really disgraceful—it's only happened once so far—our rules provide a much more severe penalty. Then we call in John to wield the cane; he has agreed to administer whatever punishment the other girls decide on. When I (Jennifer) got stewed just over a month ago and brought home and took to bed a perfectly horrible man, the girls applied this rule. They held a "court" and awarded "12 of the best" to be administered by John across my bare buttocks. John was more than willing when he heard the story—he told me I was disgusting, and believe me I felt disgusting.

John made me kneel on a dressing stool in my nightie

in front of the others and support myself on my palms on the floor. My nightie was pulled up above my waist. You could hardly imagine a more humiliating posture for a girl to be in, but I knew the humiliation was part of my punishment and that I richly deserved it, as I did the 12 agonizing cuts with the cane that followed. I very quickly found out that wielded by a muscular young man and applied with all his vigor, it hurt far worse than when used by the girls. I writhed and sobbed and ended by bawling like a two-year-old. But it has taught me a lesson! We all think our system is a good one. Let those who need a cane to titillate their sex lives carry one. We'll keep ours for its proper purpose.—*Jennifer, Pat & Suzanne (names and address withheld), London, England.*

* * *

I'm constantly amazed that your writers so often fail to distinguish between punishment and sex spankings. At our house the two are quite distinctly different. Position, dress, and implements may be the same, but results and mood surely aren't!

As an often-spanked wife of nine years, I think I've had enough of each kind to be at least a mini-expert. Using our experiences as a standard I simply can't see how the two can be spoken of as though they were the same thing.

For a sex-spanking, I turn into "Madame Tease." Attired in my crotchless panties and sexiest bra, I lie full length on my husband's naked body. After arousing him a bit, I begin to torment him, with almost-kisses, near-caresses, and soft touches. After I draw back from one of my promised, but not-delivered kisses, I'm warned, "The next one had better be real, or your rear is going to be warmed." Never one to turn down a dare, I again draw back just short of contact.

After a brief wrestle and a few almost escapes, I find myself head down, bottom up, over my lover's knees. I literally shiver with excitement as he slowly pulls my panties down and lets his hand wander over my bare butt.

The slaps are hard and stinging but they're given slowly, with frequent pauses for licks, kisses, and caresses of the afflicted area. These spankings are very thorough. When they're over I'm red, sore, and unbelievably horny. Most of the reason I love them is that I know that the ensuing lovemaking will be great.

For sex spankings both of us know we're only playing the game of the domineering man with the submissive wife. For punishment, though, there's no playing—only pain.

These start with my man grabbing me by any reachable area and throwing me over his lap. By the time I've caught my breath I'm bared. While I lie there I'm told precisely what I'm being punished for and lectured thoroughly. When the spanks begin they seem never-ending. These are twice as firm, three times as fast, and arrive without any loving pauses.

When I'm sobbing, bright red, and sometimes blistered, my husband considers the spanking over. But not the punishment—I'm then ordered to the corner, panties still down—and there I stay, facing the wall, for ten or fifteen minutes. Believe me, those fifteen minutes have involved no pleasure. There's absolutely nothing but pain —both in my burning ass and upper thighs as well as in my terribly humiliated emotions.

So I'm firmly convinced that spanking can fall either under the category of pain or pleasure. It depends chiefly on the mood of giver and recipient.—*Name and address withheld*

* * *

The first sexual experience I remember was quite unusual and has shaped my sex life since. My sixth grade teacher was a pretty blond twenty-three-year-old who believed that bottoms served one purpose on the body . . . and that was to be on the receiving end of a paddle. Somehow I had made it through the year without being the recipient of one of her scourges and was relieved that I had escaped them—but was also curious about what one of those spankings would have felt like. On the last day of school, after everyone had left for the summer, I approached the teacher and told her about my funny feelings wondering what a paddling was like.

She smiled sweetly and told me she had the same problem with one of her male teachers in junior high school. She took me to the back of the room, and told me to tell her all the naughty things I'd done that year and had not been punished for. After that, she pulled down my pants, turned me over her knee and really gave my bare seat quite a treatment. It was a good thing she had on a short skirt, for I came then and there!

About two years later, during the summer, my granny, whom I was visiting for a couple of weeks, asked our neighbor, a tall, stunning redhead, to look in on me. On a Tuesday afternoon, she knocked on the door and who was with her but my old teacher! Our neighbor had rented her a room in her house. We told our neighbor that she had been my teacher and then my old teacher added, grinning, that the last time she had seen me, my cheeks had been so, so red. I blushed, but then we all joked about it. Our neighbor said that granny had told her to use switch on me as a joke. We all agreed it might be fun, and the joke became real—for the rest of the summer I became their little slave boy.

Now, three years later, I'm seventeen, still baby-faced, and still receiving discipline from two lovely ladies with pretty legs and strong paddles. And I wouldn't trade my spankings for anything.—*Name and address withheld*

* * *

I am a French reader of Penthouse and I enjoy it very much. I noticed two or three times in the Forum that you mentioned the habit of French parents to punish their children by corporal punishment. I can tell you that it is absolutely the truth—when I was young, at home, I had four brothers and two sisters. Very often, our father obliged us to pull our pants down and slapped our bare bottom either with the open hand (a spanking, in French *la fessée*) or with a martinet, a sort of whip with many lashes of leather.

In France you can buy a martinet in many stores and it's well known that, every year, 300,000 martinets are sold to French families. In our family, we got the spanking from three to nine years, and when we were older, up to 16 or 18, the martinet, always on our father's knees and with bare buttocks.

Now I am a father and I do the same with my three boys. The elder is 15 and in case of serious misdeeds, I give him 20 to 60 strokes with the martinet. It has been a good punishment. Concerning pain and pleasure, it is true that when I was 17 and my father gave me a severe tanning, I got an erection. My father noticed it one day and stopped that sort of punishment. I will do the same when I will notice it with my boys.—*J-P.L. (name and address withheld), Paris, France.*

* * *

I was interested in the letters about corporal punishment in your recent issues and hope you will publish more on this subject, especially relating to disciplining teenagers. I favor severe spankings for girls up to the age of 18. A spanking consisting of 30-40 smart whacks with a ping-pong bat on the bare buttocks is much more effective than a lecture in correcting a girl of 15.—*C.J. (name and address withheld), Austin, Texas.*

* * *

I read with great interest your September Forum with the wife's descriptions of spanking her husband. However, after reading her letter I would not consider her spankings as punishments at all—in my opinion what they are doing is just a little bit of playful sex.

In our family spankings are for real and have been now for almost twenty years. My own husband has not only been a sorry recipient of countless spankings over the years but I have also made him suffer through quite severe whippings when I thought the situation warranted it.

At first we started with spankings with my husband lying across my lap. In the beginning I used my palm, then a hairbrush, and then a paddle. I have long ago discarded those childish toys for my just simply beautiful, 36" long, slender, and so flexible rawhide riding crop that has become a permanent fixture resting on the top of the bedroom dresser.

So when my husband does something inexcusably wrong I make him undress completely and then direct him into our den where he must position himself over a large leather-covered hassock with his hands taped together behind his back. Then I take my riding cane and begin to work over his bare taut buttocks watching him arch frantically in an effort to escape the falling smacks. I can tell very well his faked sobbing and pleading from the real thing—and when his buttocks are scalding and covered with stripes and I know his pleading is genuine I then really make him deeply sorry for what he has done.

By then he has his legs stretched wide open thus allowing the swishing cane to reach the tender inside of his thighs and now he has a hard-on like you have never seen in your life. When I think he has had enough, I order him to kneel on hard dry beans with his knees spread wide open, toes touching, leaving his hands taped behind his back to make sure he cannot masturbate himself. Then I take two spring clothespins and firmly place one pin on each of his breast nipples making sure the tips are pinched very hard. To see what this does to him is simply divine. His penis stands up erect ready to explode, almost of course, but not quite, and this, also is a part of his punishment.

When I deem it necessary I let him stay like that for two to three hours doing his penance and readjusting the clothespins every half hour or so. You would not believe it but when I open the clothespin and then release it fast on his nipple again, tears are not only rushing down his eyes, but also from his stiff cock. Then I usually snap a thick strong rubber band on his penis—just below the rim and I will stand over him with my legs wide open bringing my pussy to his mouth.

What he does to me then with his tongue and lips is completely out of this world.

Sometimes I stand there and let him do me three or four times as he gets better and better because I do not allow him to come.—*L.K., address withheld*

* * *

I have been reading recently in your magazine letters about pain and pleasure. As one who was caned frequently by my mother for disobedience and bad behavior in general during my teens, I can say most emphatically that I received much pain and absolutely no pleasure.

The cane used was the thin, pliant kind and hung by its handle behind the door of my mother's wardrobe Unless the offense was on a weekend, when retribution was immediate, I was punished before going to bed after I had finished my homework. I was then sent to my bedroom to await my mother's arrival with cane in hand. I was made to take off my blouse and pants and stand in my stockings (no tights in those days) and my brown knickers. Mother would then lecture me about the offense and I then had to take down my knickers to my knees, till my bottom was bare. I was then made to bend over a bedroom chair and hold on to the seat while at least six strokes of the cane were administered. No matter how much I pleaded, struggled, or cried the next stroke was not given until I was properly in position and still. I can painfully remember on more than one occasion a caning taking twenty minutes or more. To some it may be pleasure but to me it was agony and I had the marks to prove it for three or four days afterwards.—*E.J., Hants, England*

* * *

I am a newly married housewife thirty-two years of age and have just been reacquainted with the virtues of spanking.

My first husband died rather suddenly in a tragic accident and I had the good fortune to meet my present husband.

While we were dating he and I discussed many subjects, one being spanking. He wasted no time in making his views on this matter very plain. In fact, he went so far as to say he would spank his wife if she needed discipline. I thought he was just talking, but after we were married he showed me different.

One morning before leaving for work he told me to do a certain thing for him. My husband thought this was very important but I thought otherwise, so I did not do it. When he arrived home after work he asked me if I had done what he requested and I told him no. When he asked why not, I told him I didn't think it was very important.

When I told him this he said, "Is that so," and he grabbed me. He then told me he was going to blister my back side. I tried to help myself but he was too strong for me and he soon had me face down across his knee. He pulled my skirt up and then I felt him slip his finger into the waistband of my panties. I knew what this meant and I cried, "No please, not on the bare bottom." But he pulled my britches down to my knees and then raised his hand. As his hand connected to my posterior, I squirmed, kicked my legs, and sobbed like a baby. As his hand repeatedly connected to my fanny, I cried at the top of my voice, but he didn't stop.

Two dozen whacks, twelve on each cheek, made me realize that I must obey the bread winner of our family. When he let me up, I rushed to the bathroom and looked at my bottom in the mirror. It was a pinkish, reddish color and felt like a pepper box. As I tenderly rubbed the smarting cheeks, I made up my mind never to disobey my husband again.—*Name and address withheld*

* * *

There are three women in my life. My two teenaged daughters, aged fifteen and thirteen, and their dark-haired mother, who looks ten years younger than her age of thirty-four. Both of the girls are normal healthy teenagers whose behavior occasionally merits a spanking. I am not particularly strict with the girls, but they know how far they can go before they get punished.

Humiliation is part of the spanking and whenever either girl is to be punished she is sent up to her room to change into a pajama jacket which is specially kept for the purpose. She then has to report back to the living room and in the presence of the family is put across my lap to have her bare bottom spanked with the palm of my hand. It gives me no pleasure, but I must agree that I do feel a sense of power being the judge and executioner and also being able to order a big girl to undress and submit to my authority.

Unknown to the girls however, in the privacy of our bedroom, I do experience pleasure in watching their mother undress and humbly lie across the bed to have her delightfully bared bottom spread out to receive an appropriate number of strokes according to her behavior.

Very occasionally, when either of the girls has offended my wife, she will express a wish to carry out the punishment herself. Then I sit and watch the naughty girl cry with pain because my wife usually spanks them with a lot more force than I use.—*P.C., Lancaster, England*

* * *

I have always been fascinated and excited by spanking sessions, even as a child at school when I used to see boys half-stripped and caned by the master. To me the most exciting part of a woman's body is the buttocks, and I often imagine them rousing under strokes of the cane. I don't know why I feel like this. In my childhood I was only beaten twice but it is too far away to remember whether or not I got any sexual pleasure from the experiences. It may well be the lack of corporal punishment in my childhood that makes me so fascinated by the subject.

I often practice spanking or caning sessions by myself with leather straps and wooden rulers, but I have never met a girl with whom I could have a spanking or caning session. How could I find a girl who would be interested in these things?—*G.A., Paris, France*

11

Navels

Lately, with the new attitudes toward sex, I have seen mention of just about every orifice and protrusion of the human body used as an implement or receiver of sexual gratification. One area of the body, however, seems to have gone neglected: the navel. How soon we forget the little belly button that once connected us to our mother's womb!

Centrally located, attractive, and easy to clean, the navel is a virtual oasis of sexual pleasure. Whether you have an "in" navel or an "out," you will find that certain touches and probings stimulate nerve endings that lead all through the body.

Having a rather deep navel myself, I fill it with creamed corn or cheese whip and have my girl friend nibble it out. Not only is it tasty for her, but it's ecstasy for me.

The possibilities are endless: oral-navel, anal-navel, pedal-navel, penile-navel, and many, many more. I highly recommend exploration of this erogenous zone to all *Penthouse* readers and hope to see navel-oriented pictures and stories soon.—*W.G. (name withheld), Leonia, N.J.*

* * *

I really enjoyed Fred Darwin's View From The Top concerning navels. I have always been turned-on by navels, and have fondled them whenever possible! I especially like girls with protruding navels or "outies," and would like to see more "outies" in your mag.

I happen to have an "outie" myself that has been an erogenous zone since I was a small child. At that time my mother used to push my protruding navel in and tape it with adhesive tape, but the tape did no good, and now in my late thirties, my navel still protrudes.

I have turned my wife on to her navel as a very erotic spot, and sometimes she plays with it during the day when I am not home. She says it's very soothing and gives her a comfortable feeling.

Navels play a great part in our foreplay and intercourse. I lick and probe her navel, and she licks and sucks my umbilical lump.

I have often threatened to have my "outie" turned in by plastic surgery, but my wife insists she likes my protrusion. She loves to rub it for good luck!

I'd like to know if you have other female readers who get turned on by navels as my wife does.—*Name and address withheld*

* * *

I was pleased to see the article by Fred Darwin in the November 1973 issue of *Penthouse*. It is also good to see the readers of your fine publication recognize the fact that people do have navels (*Penthouse* Forum, January 1974). I have always felt a deep sexual attraction to navels of the opposite sex.

Much to my dismay, the new high-waisted look in fashions have robbed me and my fellow navel watchers of many a young navel. Living in a college town as I do, it is easy to see that nothing has yet been created to beat a halter top and hip-hugger pants. The slender mid-section of a beautiful young girl with her navel exposed for all to see is enough to drive any man into a frenzy.

My friends and I feel that the most pleasant way to enjoy this erogenous zone is by oral/navel contact. This not only excites the one doing the stimulating, but the recipient of this kind of attention as well. This is also one of the few practices that can be applied to either sex. I know of no homosexual activities in this area, but surely this practice is in existence.

Hopefully, this letter will serve a threefold purpose: to stimulate communication among your readers on this subject, to encourage you to uncover your models' navels, and lastly to lower the waistline of the women of America. Maybe now women will realize they have an erogenous zone that isn't restricted to being exposed by local laws.—*B.F., Norman, Okla.*

* * *

I was rather astonished to learn of the widespread lack of knowledge of the navel as an erogenous zone (View From the Top, November 1973).

These students are rediscovering something I knew about and enjoyed thirty-five years ago.

Let me illustrate the use of navel eroticism as I used it in my youth. Nothing gave me greater joy then or now than to perform cunnilingus on a girl who really turned me on.

I was about twenty-one years old when I met a lovely, black-haired girl, with a body that had to be seen to be believed. It was evident from the beginning that she really loved sex. On our frequent dates, we did just about everything except for one thing. No matter how aroused she became, if I attempted to go down on her, she turned off but fast. She insisted it was "dirty" or "perverted" to use one's mouth on the genitals. When I persisted on later dates, she finally told me that if I couldn't be satisfied with fucking and occasional anal intercourse, she would stop seeing me. I was really hung up on this girl, so I promised to stop.

A few weeks after this we were on a weekend trip to a resort about one hundred miles from home. After dinner and dancing on Saturday night, we went to our hotel room, ready for a long night of lovemaking. I proceeded in the usual manner of foreplay, tongue-kissing, breast fondling, and so on.

As I kissed her tummy, I came to her navel. I had done this many times before, but this time, instead of moving on to something else after a minute or so, I stayed there, gently probing with my tongue, and occasionally with my fingers, for about ten minutes or so. I felt her hand begin to stroke the back of my neck, harder and harder. At the same time, her tummy began to undulate, gently at first, then more rapidly. Suddenly, with a strangled scream, she grabbed my head with both hands, and pushed me lower. She was like a madwoman! She had an orgasm such as I had never seen. When I tried to come up for air, she grabbed me and kept me at it until she had at least four more orgasms, each one more violent than the previous one.

From then on, she was hooked! We went together for about a year after that, and most sexual activity had to be preceded by my "navel maneuvers," or no play.

One big bonus—she decided to try the same with me. Who said navel fondling was new?—*Name and address withheld*

* * *

12

Shaving Pubic Hair

I am writing this letter to let you know that my latest female companion has the distinction of being the "Girl With the Home Plate Pussy." She has shaved her pubic triangle in such a way as to form its shape in the exact proportional dimensions of the regulation size home plate according to the Official Rules of the Commissioner of Baseball. Needless to say, I have slid into home plate many times and have never been called out.—*Name and address withheld*

* * *

I just returned from a world tour where I met many girls. In the Far East, pubic hair is almost non-existent. Over there to be hairless is a sign of beauty. In France, Germany, England, Sweden, and all over Europe the trend is towards shaved pubic areas. A girl's mound is a beautiful thing, but when it's covered with hair it might as well be covered with a piece of cloth.

Here in Canada more and more girls are shaving off

their hair. There are still lots who have it, but they are also shaving off the lower patch so their lips are exposed. I'm a gynecologist and see women every day so what I say is the truth and not just a small sampling. With more and more girls shaving partially or fully you should naturally start showing girls of this sort.—*Name withheld, Calgary, Canada*

* * *

Mrs. F.H.: in reply to your letter (February), you should certainly not feel like freaks because you and your husband both prefer depilating your pubic hair. If you really enjoy cunnilingus and fellatio, it's the *only* way to go!

My husband and I have been shaving our pubic hair —every bit of it—for six or seven years, and we certainly don't feel that we are freaks. Not only do we enjoy cunnilingus and fellatio more, but we are convinced that the absence of hair is more conducive to sexual excitement. Certainly then those most intimate parts of our bodies are cleaner and more appetizing. We even receive a considerable amount of sexual arousal in the act of shaving ourselves or each other, and that should be an inducement for more people to try it.

* * *

The letter from my compatriot, J.M. (June) about completely shaven women caught my eye. When I met the girl who is now my wife, I had no idea she was hairless owing to an illness when she was 16. During our courtship, I found out she had no pubic hair, but I thought she had shaved it off. When I asked her to marry me, she told me of her illness and her hairless condition. Then she took off her wig and showed me her bald head. It was quite a shock, but I found it exciting.

On our honeymoon night, when she stripped completely, she looked so sexy standing there completely nude with not a hair anywhere on her body that I almost lost control. Sometimes at parties and other select gatherings my wife will slip off her wig and the guests go wild. The men can hardly keep their hands off her bald head!—*S.Y. (name and address withheld), Toronto, Canada.*

* * *

Within six months of the start of my marriage (I was 18, my husband 27) he talked me into shaving my pubic hair. That was eight years ago. I had many misgivings about it and we had some very hot arguments, but once I took the step and lived with it for a while there was no road back to my strawberry blonde triangle! Now I have a wonderful feeling of "freedom" and tremendous female vitality as well as a rising surge of what might vulgarly be termed "Pussy Power." Shortly after shedding my little beard, I also gave up wearing panties.

My husband and I are well matched sexually now, though when we first married his constant preoccupation with sex generally, and with my sexual parts specifically, caused me not a little worry. During our first three years of marriage, I underwent the transition from girl to woman, a very fortunate awakening for me, since we have met many couples where the wives have retained immature and girlish concepts, some of them even into their early 30s. I credit my nude little bunny with helping me to grow up sexually. Since I keep things under control daily—I shave while showering—I have grown used to, and familiar with, my own body. I really groove on the warm soapy massaging and the slick, clean feeling the razor leaves. I always cream and powder the shaved areas and I find the sensation most erotic. It is very sexy to feel the soft, satiny texture of that skin which formerly was hairy and not half so pretty.

Being naked brings to mind our first "trial" visit to a nudist park in Western Massachusetts. I discovered immediately that a pubic hair bush draws hardly one glance from nudists, but a defoliated crotch almost causes a riot. We were told later by some of the younger men that a confrontation with a shaved pussy is raw, blatant, gut sex which challenges virile and uncomplicated male feelings. Pubic hair aficionados remind me of horny little boys under a boardwalk getting turned on by "peeping" up the girls' skirts—lookers not doers, morbidly fascinated by what's concealed, yet afraid of what's there to be revealed! It takes a healthy man to make a strong and effective response to direct vaginal impact.

When we eventually became members of this nudist park, my hairless "li'l number" became a popular topic of conversation, especially among the women. Several said they would love to shave and their husbands had even urged it, but they lacked the courage to try. During the first summer, one of the younger and most attractive mothers required minor surgery and the usual prerequisite "tummy trim." When she returned to the park, I successfully encouraged her to pick up a razor and stay all bare. That was a beginning—now, three summers later, we have seven shavers going strong, and a bunch of potentials teetering on the brink as well.

I won't detail all the marvelous sensual and visual contributions total nudity brings to my sex life, but will close with the idea that if you are young, attractive and have a man who turns you on, shave and please him like he's never been pleased before. It's the most fascinating interest-arouser there is. Show him the total you.
—*Mrs. F.D.A. (name and address withheld), Two Rivers, Wisconsin.*

* * *

I, too, have joined the ranks of those liberated females who believe that shaving is the way to go. We have been married for almost ten years and my husband prefers me this way to the excessive hair I once had. I think he looks sexier without all the foliage and allows me to get right to the root of the matter.

I have briefly mentioned to a few close friends at work that I am shaved, knowing they would tell other people in the office, particularly the men. We now play a game with each other. With my miniskirt 11 inches above my knee and wearing only sheer-to-the-waist pantyhose (occasionally crotchless), I flash myself when they are looking, but making it appear they are not. Needless to say after eight hours of this in the office, I'm raring to go with my man the minute I get in the house.

We have found this an excellent way to keep our marriage alive and I advise all couples to try it. Shave each other to try it. Shave each other regularly (at least once a week), eat regularly (at least once a day) and don't stop until the meal is *completely* over. Protein never hurt anyone! Finally, always keep a plentiful supply of *lip* sticks (the nonindelible kind) in *two* different colors.

Keep up the good work, Penthouse and keep plugging the great pleasures that can be derived from the regular use of a razor.—*Mrs. A.P.M. (name and address withheld), Edgewater, Md.*

* * *

Congratulations should be extended to R.C. for advocating the shaving of male pubic hair, likewise to Mrs. E. D. M. (December) for explaining why she has shaved her pubic hair. My wife and I have kept our pubic areas bare for over 40 years, for twofold reasons. Firstly, female pubic hair is unhygienic, unesthetic and quite inedible; moreover, it conceals one of the most beautiful areas of the female anatomy. Secondly, as R.C. convincingly set forth in his letter, male pubic hair is unesthetic. With a typical lack of logic, most women shave under their arms but not between their legs, though for hygienic reasons alone it should be the other way round. I echo R.C.'s hope that pubic shaving will become not only "a general thing among women" but that "it may well catch on among men." Also, I wish (vain hope?) that your pictures of nude women will in future show *not* the pubic hair but that which it has hitherto concealed. No more fig leaves, please, figuratively or otherwise.—*G.C.P. (name and address withheld), St. Augustine, Fla.*

* * *

I take exception to R.C.'s letter; I don't agree that shaving enhances the natural and beautiful appearance of the genital area, displaying the penis and testicles to their best advantage.

To me, removing the pubic hair makes the skin look like from a plucked hen, which certainly loses all beauty. I've had the experience of being shaved in the genital area on three separate occasions—because of hemorrhoids, cystitis, and for a spinal operation. Personally, I found it very irritating.

There are reasons for pubic hair as nature has put it there for beauty, comfort and ease in the groin to avoid rubbing and rashes. Does R.C. realize that the hair acts as a static in intercourse? I wonder if all female partners would appreciate a prickly feeling and coarse surface in coitus.

Let's hear from women whether they'd really like to see their men without the added feature of pubic hair. Would they enjoy sexual foreplay, holding the penis during penetration and the prickly feel of the skin so much? I am sure that most men would agree that pubic hair adds to their masculinity and maturity.—*R.O. (name and address withheld), Milwaukee, Wis.*

* * *

In support of R.C.'s contention (May) that shaving away pubic hair is pleasing to men and women alike, I can offer the following in evidence:

At a relatively advanced age in life, I had to be circumcised and, of course, all my pubic area was shaved preparatory to the operation. In the months that followed, I continued to shave my penis and testicles. Eventually, my wife, who at first was noncommittal about my new look, was ready to admit that it had become a new titillatory experience for her and, after some coaxing, she permitted me to shave her pubic area.

But, because she has not continued to shave with the same regularity as I do, she complains that the stubble becomes uncomfortable. I can see that I have some more coaxing to do, but the only discomfort that a man might encounter is when sitting, especially with crossed legs, if he is not wearing some form of underwear which provides the necessary uplift. A fairly snug-fitting pair of underpants that keeps the scrotum up is essential if a man is to derive all the benefits of genital shaving. In conclusion, I must say that I certainly prefer our clean-shaven appearance to the shaggy, gray-haired look we both had before. However, the greatest benefit of genital shaving, one that R.C. didn't mention, is its effect on the sex act.—*M.C. (name and address withheld), Canada.*

* * *

I want to thank you for publishing the letter of Mrs. E.D.M. (December). Because of her statement that "full nakedness is the ultimate in sexiness" I picked up my razor and shaved off the golden fleece of my beaver three days before I married the greatest guy in the world.

Bill and I are not kids—he is in his early thirties and I am in the mid twenties. During our courtship we had sex—both straight and oral—but on our wedding night he was introduced to my new identity. And he loved it and he still loves it. But to a woman, shaving the pubic area is not really unusual. What may interest your readers is the fact that now Bill is fully naked in his pubic area. I did the barbering job on him two days after our marriage and you can be sure I was extremely careful. We do a touch-up job on each other about once a week and have become accustomed to the feeling of airiness that the lack of hair on the body gives.

We enjoyed sex before but now, with both of us completely naked, there is a feeling of togetherness which is difficult to describe. And girls—you don't really know how beautiful the male sex organs are until you have seen them free of that beard.—*Mrs. R.M. (name and address withheld), Chicago, Ill.*

* * *

Congratulations on your excellent April issue. Your interview with John Chancellor was excellent; William Iversen's satire on "Sox" was hilarious; and Mickey Spillane and Henry Morgan showed to their usual standards.

I have been following the letters from your readers re the shaving of the pubic area with a great deal of interest, as I prefer the soft sensation of labial skin to the coarseness of pubic hair. If any of your woman readers question the esthetics of "taking up her razor," I suggest she check your Pets of the Month in January and March. The neatly clipped pubes of Patricia "Cherokee" Barrett (pages 56 and 59—January) have it all over (no pun) shaggy Billie Deane who can't seem to keep her overgrowth in her panties (page 57—March). Apparently I wasn't the only one who noticed this—for in the centerspread, Miss Deane's inner thigh either has been shaved or retouched, and I can't believe the latter of Penthouse.

I believe most men share my preference for a shaved pussy, and I think I know why most women don't. In my bachelor days, I discussed this with a number of young—and not-so-young—women. It is not the "itching" because a periodic touch-up prevents itching, just as it does under the arms. It is the fact that most women have not seen their external organs since pre-puberty, and when they do, they don't like what they see. One of my pre-marriage girl friends put it just that way. Another said: "Pubic hair is cosmetic."

My wife originally felt that way, but we have worked out a mutually satisfactory solution which might be helpful to some of your readers. She had seen some of my erotic magazines and agreed that "I see why you like it better without hair." Knowing how she felt, I suggested that we leave the top inch or inch and a half of her rather considerable thatch intact, and shave only her lips from just above her clitoris back to just past her vagina. This way, I could see, fondle, enjoy, kiss, or whatever, soft skin. And she has the rest of her bush to filter her view of something she would rather not look at. It has worked out fine, especially the times that *we* do the shaving.—*J. D. (name and address withheld), Columbus, Ohio.*

* * *

I would like to state my point of view on the urgings of some of your readers that women shave their pubic area: first, I think that each woman will decide for herself. I prefer women who do *not* shave any part of their anatomy. That means no shaving of legs, armpits, pubic area or anywhere else. I would be immediately turned off by any woman, no matter how beautiful, if I discovered that her pubic area were bare. Of course I do prefer women who have soft, fine body hair rather than coarse masculine hair.

A revelation such as I have stated usually evokes the usual stupid cliché about going with a gorilla but I wish to point out that there are other standards of beauty throughout the world which do not agree with the Miss America standards that are constantly bombarding susceptible people. I don't think the razor advocates can improve on nature.—*K.R. (name and address withheld), Bronx, New York.*

* * *

As a man, I find a girl's shaved vaginal area has many disadvantages. Pubic hairs are erotic and stimulating to me and lack of them would enable one only to approximate a young girl's age (if 16 would get you 20, what might 13 get you?). Another advantage of pubic hairs is that they tell you the true color of the maiden's hair. This method is absolutely fool-proof.

In shaving my face everyday, I find I sometimes become lax in this and develop a heavy "five o'clock shadow." This irritates the tender skin of my girlfriend's breasts. My girlfriend might also become lax in pubic shaving and develop a heavy "five o'clock shadow" on her vaginal region. The results of this stubble on my lips and tongue would be catastrophic.—*H.L.P. (name and address withheld), Olean, New York.*

* * *

May a lady comment on the letters by Tony Robinson and S.E.R. in the August Penthouse? Mr. Robinson asks you to publish photos of female nudes with their pubic areas shaved, and urges girl readers to "pick up your razors" to be "beautiful" and therefore sexually "satisfied." S.E.R. also approves of complete nudity in photos and asks that vaginal lips be shown.

I am one who did "pick up her razor" more than three years ago when on the rebound from an unhappy marriage and I was trying to establish a new personal identity. Another divorcée suggested it to me, by the way, and since then I have discovered that this is by no means a rare practice. I now give myself a retouching job twice a week, and love the result, for several reasons. The first is a feeling of comfort and airy cleanliness. Now that I am used to the idea and the feeling I know I will never go back to my "beaver." I feel gorgeously free.

But more than that, as Mr. Robinson says, I do feel "beautiful" in the sense that I know my full nakedness is the ultimate in sexiness. So far the men who have been in my life have been delighted, without exception, and I am therefore "satisfied" in this respect, if not necessarily in sexual fulfillment provided by some of these gentlemen. Moreover, I have been pleased to find that not a single girlfriend has been at all negative or shocked at what I have done, and several have followed my example.

I am of course extremely circumspect about who I confide my "secret" to. Neither my middle-aged boss nor some of the nosy old witches at nearby desks know my "secret." On the other hand, there are times when I do want someone to know, and other times—such as certain social gatherings—when I do not care if someone finds out accidentally. Then there are definite rewards in the looks of amazement, or disbelief that can be stimulated on an unsuspecting face, either male or female, and in the typical male follow-up, which is naturally what has made me want that "someone" to know in the first place. Being all bare helps me to *enjoy* being a girl.

Having said so much, I suppose I should explain the practical aspects of my come-hither displays when I see a cute fellow across the room at a party, for instance. In brief, I am not only shaved, but for most social occasions, pantie-less. In this I feel I am less of a trendsetter than in shaving, though I have been so unencumbered a good deal of the time for the past eight years—since I was 19, in fact.

I am now so accustomed to full nudity that I feel no compunction whatever in purposely revealing my vaginal area to friends, or even total strangers in some circumstances. I don't think my displays are any more brazen than the constant display of breasts and nipples by the zillions of girls now going bra-less.

There is one final argument for shaving I have left until last. I will leave the psychology to someone else, but practically *every* girl thinks it would be vulgar or disgusting or inexcusably sloppy not to shave her armpits. Why do they hesitate, then, to shave everywhere? I predict that in five years everyone will be doing it, and maybe Penthouse readers will be ogling beautiful girls who are *completely* naked.—*Mrs. E.D.M. (name and address withheld), Washington, D.C.*

* * *

13

The World of Amputee Sex

P.D.'s letter headed "Art and Amputees" (February) stirred me deeply. Like his, my sexual interest is in amputee women—specifically leg amputees. In my case, I'm told this desire stems from (to use Desmond Morris' term) "malimprinting," during my early childhood. My mother was too busy to give me the love and attention I craved, but I found a "surrogate mother" in a one-legged woman neighbor who was a frequent visitor to our home.

Over the years, my interest in her—and, indeed, in all female amputees—was reinforced by my fantasies. Sketches of my handicapped dream girls, drawn and panted over in secret, heightened my frustrated desires until there was no longer room for any "normal" impulses. Meanwhile, my possessive and tyrannical mother managed to keep me captive at home long after my agemates had established their own families. At 25, I managed to find what I'd always yearned for—a one-legged girlfriend.

Doris, as she was called, delighted me physically,

spiritually, and intellectually. Eventually, of course, I had to tell my mother about her. Predictably, she greeted the news with tears, anger, and threats of suicide. I shrivelled with guilt and Mother soon convinced me that bringing such a girl into the family was no way to repay my debt for all that my parents had done for me.

Eventually the pain of our separation abated. I decided to abandon my search for a real, live amputee and seek solace in sheer fantasy. Then, at 35, I abruptly decided to marry a physically normal girl.

During the early years of marriage I was able to conceal my secret passion behind a smokescreen of sexual activity with my wife. About all that either of us got out of it, though, were several children. Despite my best efforts to build a sound affectionate and sexual relationship with her—and she's a warm, attractive woman—the unseen barrier between us—my inability to react normally to a normal female—has proved impregnable.

A few years ago, at my wife's urging (though she didn't know exactly what was wrong), I agreed to try psychotherapy. But, until recently, this was a waste of time and money because I couldn't bring myself to tell even my "shrink" what had me hung up. Several weeks ago I did tell him, after a particularly rough argument with my wife made me desperate to resolve my inner conflict. The psychiatrist advised me to "tell all" to my wife. That took more guts than I'd thought I had, but I told her quite bluntly what it takes to turn me on and why *she* couldn't do it.

I couldn't believe her reaction: no shock or revulsion; just relief, understanding, and sympathy. With my therapist's concurrence, she's now urging me actively to seek an extramarital relationship with an amputee woman. At the same time, by mutual arrangement, my wife will arrange an affair of her own with a man who's capable of fully satisfying her sexual needs. In all nonsexual matters, we'll continue our marriage as before.—*S.K.L., (name and address withheld), Ridgewood, N.J.*

* * *

Like another of your correspondents, I had my first sexual experience with a one-legged woman, but in far different circumstances. When I was 16 my parents were both working full-time in the family business, and the virtual parent of my younger sister, brother and myself was my mother's younger stepsister, who had come to live with us when I was 10 years old, following the death of her husband.

The business was a prosperous one, so that my "aunt," as we called her, was no poor-relation drudge, but well-paid, with servants to assist in running the place. She was a college graduate, widow of a professor whom she had married when still a student. At the time, she was 32, which then seemed very elderly to me. Attractive and lively, her most unusual characteristic was that she had only one leg, having lost the other as a child. She wore an artificial limb on formal occasions, but she could manage only an unnatural, stiff-legged walk with it, and normally walked with crutches, with astonishing grace and agility.

One night, when my parents were away, I came home in a state of frustration following an unsuccessful date. Aunt saw something was wrong and soon I had told her the whole story. She hugged me and said she thought the time had come to show me what it was about. I had begun to be aware of Aunt's physical attractiveness, and had had some fantasies and dreams in which she had figured, so it was with eagerness that I followed her to my room, where she told me to undress. She quickly dropped her gown and nightdress, and before I had more than my shoes and pants off she stood naked, balanced on her one shapely leg and foot. I had seen her in her rather modest one-piece knit swimming suit with attached skirt, which had legs long enough that she could conceal the small stump of her missing thigh by just sewing shut the leg of the suit. I had seen pictures of naked women, but even so was quite unprepared for the glory of Aunt's nudity, and stood gaping, my penis rapidly stiffening. I had not visualized the smooth whiteness of the skin, nor the delicate contours of belly and buttocks, nor the glorious breasts, not huge but elegantly formed, with upstanding nipples and large, brown areolae. The familiar face, with its big wide-spaced eyes and mobile mouth looked unfamiliar on this lovely body, and the familiar voice was a shock when it said: "You mustn't mind my ugly stump." I didn't mind; I was fascinated. I had wanted to see Aunt's stump. It was small and soft and white, and I wanted to feel it. "Gosh, Aunt," I said, "You're beautiful!"

She shot me a quick look, then a lovely smile, and hopped over to where I sat on my bed, her breasts bouncing excitingly. "You are a darling," she said, and kissed me as I had never been kissed, her tongue seeking, and finally getting, a response from mine. We went on from there. She taught me how to titillate both myself and her by lightly touching her body and stroking it in many places, and she did the same to me until I was trembling with excitement. I suckled her breasts, and could see that she was becoming excited too, but she restrained me, saying: "You must never hurry your love-making. The longer you take to make ready, the longer you will last when you get started, and that is the secret of being a real man." It was the most valuable lesson I ever learned, and I bless her for it. For a beginner, I did pretty well. Just after I had my emission, it felt so good that I kept moving, and she started to become excited, saying, "Oh, that feels good!" and humping and bucking. Finally I heard her gasp, "Oh, God!—its—zuh!—been—uh!—so long!" I was scared, thinking she had a fit, she gasped and gagged and trembled, but managed to signal me to keep going, and by the time she was finished, I was finished too. I have never been one of those superstuds that can keep coming back for more. I make a production of it, and that's all for at least a few hours.

We made love many times after that, and I learned to control my emission for as long as I liked. She didn't much like the idea of my feeling her stump at first, but I found it very exciting, especially when she made it move in my hands, and she learned that she could use it to turn me on like a roman candle whenever she chose.

When I was 18, about to go away to college, she married again and I never had her after that. After many years I married, and have been happy with the same wife ever since. Many years after, I propositioned Aunt, who remained lovely as ever. She turned me down with a twinkle, saying: "Not fair to our spouses." But she gave me a sexy kiss and stirred my passions of old by nudging me with her stump. I told my wife about Aunt, figuring she would guess I hadn't learned all I knew from reading books, and I'm sure Aunt told her husband, for he always seemed to be sharing a delicious secret with me. I have never since made love to a one-legged woman, but I never see one to this day without my heart flipping over.—*H.C., (name and address withheld), Garrett Park, Maryland.*

* * *

I would like to cast a vote in favor of showing women amputees in poses just the same as you presently do for girls without handicaps. A beautiful, well-stacked girl is no less appealing because she happens to have a stump of an arm or a leg, and I personally have spent memorable nights with female amputees who never let their handicaps diminish their sex appeal.

On a local campus recently I saw a gorgeous little blonde with only one leg showing from her miniskirt struggling to maneuver her crutches and carry a load of books at the same time. It was a natural move for me to help her out, and I was rewarded a few evenings later with an invite to a pool party. My blonde chick showed up in a striking bikini that had heads turning left and right. She had lost her leg a little way below her hip and had just barely enough of a stump remaining to keep up the left side of her bikini bottom. I tell you, I had never seen a sexier sight than this chick's little bit of a thigh joggling rapidly back and forth as she hopped around the edge of the pool, with everyone wondering if that bikini bottom would stay up. Since I had already scored previously with other one-legged chicks, this blonde's sexual performance in my car later that night was no surprise. She had her one-sided motion well rehearsed and also had perfect control over her stump, which some one-legged girls have a problem with.

I once dated a beautiful one-armed girl whose favorite passion-arouser was to do a one-armed striptease that ended with the girl coyly covering her breasts with her single arm and holding up one leg to conceal her crotch, while holding out the stump of her arm to be kissed. She would not relax until she had the stump of her left arm fondled and kissed to prove to herself that she was still appealing. (She had the arm shot off above the elbow during a holdup of the bank where she worked as a teller.)

In bed, there is something fascinating about a one-legged girl's invitation to sex that other girls can't match. Of course, there is the full leg on one side that is posed in any of the usual ways. No two girls with an above-the-knee amputation have the same size and shape stump, it seems, and every one of them has her own unique way of manipulating her stump around to make her invitation most seductive. And they all want to be reassured that their lover doesn't find their stump repulsive to look at, for the girls themselves are usually very self-conscious of it, at first, in bed.

There is really nothing a one-legged girl or a one-armed girl can't do that any other girl can do when it comes to basic bedroom performance. I find the animated action of the stump moving around especially fascinating when a one-legged girl is hopping around nude, as they often do when dressing or undressing. Showing nude girl amputees won't shock me for one.—*James J. Perreault, Miami, Fla.*

* * *

I am a happy convert to Penthouse (from the bunny book) for over a year now, and am still wondering if all those explicitly horny and kinky letters you print each month are genuine or just fantasies conjured up by your editorial staff to titillate your readers. In either case, here is a genuine letter from a genuine Penthouse reader about my own pet passion.

I must confess to being an ardent aficionado of girl amputees ever since I was exposed to my first one (and vice versa) at the tender age of 14. My older sister had a girlfriend, about 18 or 19, with an artificial leg and she invited her to spend a weekend with us. The one-legged girl slept in our upstairs guestroom which adjoined my bedroom with a locked door in between. But there was a slight crack in the door panel, so I watched breathlessly as our pretty guest undressed for bed. I finally saw her walking around stark naked except for her artificial leg which was held on by a belt around her waist. She was well-stacked and stood before the mirror for a while admiring herself and rubbing her breasts, unaware of her audience on the other side of the door. I strained to keep silent.

Suddenly she leaned against the bureau, unstrapped her waist belt, and off came the artificial leg. She then stood it in the corner and hopped on her one leg across the room with her breasts bouncing furiously and her stump swinging back and forth like a pendulum. I found the scene strangely exciting, but I was disappointed when the girl put on a robe and then hopped across the hall to the bathroom. I was left on the other side of the door with just memories and an erection. I had vivid dreams of my one-legged neighbor that night.

But the big event came a few weeks later, one Saturday night after my sister had had a big party at the house. When everyone had left and my sister and parents had gone to bed, I sneaked downstairs to sample the leftover candy and snacks. When I switched on the light, I was stunned to see my sister's one-legged friend sprawled on the sofa with a fellow on top of her, and both were stark naked. Her artificial leg was unstrapped and lying with her pile of clothes on the floor. She had her one leg wrapped round the fellow and her little thigh stump jutting out to the side waving round vigorously when the lights came on. The fellow panicked, grabbed his clothes, and disappeared out the front hall. But the girl merely sat up, with no attempt to cover herself, and whispered:

"Let's keep this our little secret, okay?" She then picked up her purse from the floor and started to take out a few bills, presumably as a bribe for my silence. But then she changed her mind and closed her purse.

She got up and stood in front of me balanced on her one leg with her hands on her hips, still totally naked, while she swung her stump up at an angle. Her bushy triangle was staring me in the face, fully exposed. "Ever touch a girl's thing?" she asked. "Go ahead, it won't bite you." I timidly touched two fingers on to her patch of very moist hair and suddenly she moved her stump down and trapped my hand between her thighs, laughing. She began to rub her stump up and down as I struggled futilely to free my hand. She then sat down on the sofa and suddenly pulled down my pyjama bottom, exposing my childish erection, and pulled me down on top of her. She spread her leg and stump wide and began to guide my penis into her. Before I knew it, she was rhythmically pushing herself up and down with one leg and holding me in position by nudging me with her stump. "Don't be afraid," she said. "It feels nice, doesn't it?" It was ecstatic!

Thus I was initiated into the art of intercourse—and by a one-legged girl. On future visits to our house, she would unlock our bedroom connecting doors and let me watch her undress. I was allowed to take off her artificial leg and often invited to massage her stump, which she enjoyed. She would let me lie down next to her in bed and she would arouse me by rubbing her stump against me, after which I would get further one-legged instruction in sex. It felt strangely pleasant to feel her single leg against me and to see her other artificial leg standing in the corner, still dressed in a low-heeled shoe and a nylon stocking held up by a thick rubber band.

I was awfully disappointed when she moved out of state several months later, though I began having interesting liaisons with two-legged girls. To me, one-legged girls have a unique charm in the bedroom, and I definitely plan to marry one when I decide to settle down. I consider a stump a pleasantly different appendage to a shapely feminine body. One lovely leg is ample to satisfy me!—*P. D. (name and address withheld), West Lynn, Mass.*

* * *

It was indeed an eye-opener to learn that a not unimpressive segment of the population are monopodomaniacs or apodomaniacs: I thought I was in a one-man minority. But we can all cheer in knowing we're not the first to be attracted by stumps, for Michel de Montaigne (1533-1592), in Chapter 11 of Book III of his *Essays*, entitled "On Cripples," has these good words to say:

"As a matter of fact or beside the point, it doesn't matter, it's said as a common proverb in Italy that the person who hasn't slept with a cripple doesn't know Venus in her perfect sweetness. Luck, or some particular accident, put this saying in the mouth of the people long ago; and it's said of males as well as of females. For the Queen of the Amazons replied to the Scythian who invited her for love: "the cripple does it best." In this female republic, in order to get away from male domination, they maimed ['amputated' or 'mangled'] during childhood, arms, legs, and other members which gave them an advantage over the women, and they used the men only for what we've used women in fact. I would have said that the swaying motion of the cripple might bring some new pleasure to the toil [of love] and some bit of sweetness to those why try it, but I've just learned that even ancient philosophy was decided in that; it says that since the legs and thighs of crippled women, because of their imperfection, don't get the nourishment that is due them, it follows that the genitals, which are right about them, are fuller, more nourished and more vigorous. Or that, this default prohibiting exercise, those who are tainted use less force and come more fully to the games of Venus."

The translation is my own, but Maurice Rat, who edited the edition I have of Montaigne's *Essays*, indicates that the passage from antiquity in question is Aristotle's *Problems*, X, 26.—*M.F. (address withheld).*

It's not only exciting to make love to an amputee girl: it's so convenient. We start our activities on the couch when she lies down and I can perform cunnilingus while sitting on the floor with no leg in the way. Later, in the bedroom, it's so much easier to change positions. It's much better, too, when we get to 69, because some women clamp my head with their legs. She can't!—*J.E. (name and address withheld), Duluth, Minn.*

* * *

I am a mod, hip young man of 28, who has been confined to a wheelchair all of my life with muscular dystrophy. The letters you've published from female amputees have set me wondering whether any of these girls would be interested in me. Even if not, I'd like to set the chicks straight. Most people who see someone like myself just pity up and don't realize that we're just as human as they are and that we also have sexual feelings. Just like any other stud, we need a little pussy once in a while to keep us going!—*R.K. (name and address withheld), Windsor Locks, Conn.*

* * *

I was unaware of the sexual significance of an amputated leg on a woman until my wife lost her right leg above the knee in an accident about a year after we married. That was three years ago, and our mutual sexual pleasure since then has far surpassed the relationship we enjoyed when my lovely wife was a normal two-legged woman.

When she first came home from the hospital with a stump of a thigh where her right leg had been, she was afraid I would find her repugnant and would no longer want to make love to her. But as soon as the doctor pronounced her stump fully healed, we resumed our lovemaking and were both amazed to find that she was just as good a sex partner as before, if not better. She quickly got the knack of maneuvering her body with just the one leg and found that her stump was very sensitive to physical contact, especially against my body. Her stump became almost like a third hand and even now, when she embraces me while standing up, she expresses her affection, if she is not wearing her artificial leg, by pressing her stump against me while we are standing close.

Of course, I was used to seeing my wife nude in the days when she still had both legs. But the first time I saw her hop across the room on one leg without a stitch on and that little thigh stump waving around in space next to her crotch, I almost blew a fuse! I quickly invited her to hop back to bed and lie down for a quickie before I went off to work. Whatever sexuality she possessed as a two-legged woman seemed to have at least tripled when I saw her hopping around nude with just one leg now. I don't understand the phenomenon, but I know every guy who has a one-legged wife or girlfriend that I've compared notes with feels the same way.

As for my wife, she signals her interest in having relations merely by giving me a couple of nudges gently with her stump against my hip or groin, if I haven't already taken the initiative. Without her uttering a word, I get the message. She has excellent muscular control over her stump and can move it to any position easily. She especially enjoys having me massage her stump after she has unstrapped her wooden leg and quite often when I start running my hand up and down her stump inside her skirt, I discover she has also removed her panties. I challenge any husband to resist a gold-plated invitation like that.

But don't get the idea that being married to an amputee is a sex-for-the-asking deal. On the rare occasions when she's not in the mood or it's the wrong time of the month, my wife merely swings her right thigh stump across her crotch and it's as good as a chastity belt.

My wife has got over her self-consciousness and last year she accompanied me to the beach in a bikini. She can still swim with her leg off if I help her in and out of the water. She was by far the prettiest girl on the beach and I could tell by the interest she was attracting that plenty of guys had bedroom eyes for my wife despite her stump. I let them eat their hearts out, for she is as faithful as any man could want.—*D.R.K. (name and address withheld), Fort Lauderdale, Fla.*

* * *

Being an amputee myself, I have been intrigued by the recent correspondence advocating one-legged pets and recounting what great sex objects we are. Actually, it's a lot less enthralling and more mundane to be without a leg than your correspondents would have us believe, particularly the one who spends her time gliding from one Boston bar to another on her aluminum crutches, picking up men by letting the end of her stump poke out a bit below her skirt. It's true that some guys are turned on by our dangling modifiers, but they are outnumbered by those who find the whole idea repulsive and would no more be seen with a one-legged girl than with a rosy-cheeked baboon. And given the American fetish for apparent perfection and success, it's understandable.

Our supposed sexual desirability is more myth than reality. If anything, the loss of a limb creates a barrier, making it harder to meet people in spite of whatever charms and talents we may otherwise possess. Too often, what at first appears interest in us proves to be nothing more than a search for novelty and cheap thrills. That is not to say that we are damned by our flaws to a life of celibacy—far from it—but it is an added burden that I would rather do without. It gets tedious being stared at and deferred to, not to mention having to rely on mechanical contrivances that won't go quite everywhere to get about.

To be perfectly honest, being minus much of my left leg is not exactly the greatest thing that ever happened to me, but after a while one comes to terms with it and learns to get by. It gives my husband something to play with—an ironic dividend. Not that that has much to do with us or why he married me. He would have preferred me complete, but neither of us had much choice in the matter.—*Mrs. S.F. (name and address withheld), Pittsburg, Pa.*

* * *

I am 27, and have been an amputee since I lost my left leg at midthigh when I was about eight. Probably because I've been an amputee for so long, I've never been shy about my lack of a leg. For the last four years I've been married to a man who, like many of your readers, is fascinated by the stump of a female amputee. As a result, I usually wear short skirts when I go out, allowing the end to show. When my husband is home, I wear short shorts so that my stump is fully exposed. I have never liked to use an artificial leg, and mostly I use a single crutch and, believe it or not, a good ol' peg leg.

When my husband and I go out socially I use a crutch. I have several painted different colors to match whatever outfit I wear. However since a crutch is somewhat cumbersome when doing the housework or grocery shopping, I strap on my peg leg for such occasions. Probably many people think a peg leg is not very feminine, but it's practical for me. Besides, I always wear clothes which show off my very feminine figure (39-23-35). Because very few amputees use peg legs any more I get a lot of stares when I wear it in public, but they don't bother me.

Sexually, I feel I can compete with any two-legged girl. Because my husband is so turned on by the sight of my stump, I usually begin our lovemaking by undressing slowly at the foot of the bed. Once I have my clothes off, I lift my stump so that it points toward my husband and I begin slowly to massage it. This excites my husband greatly, so he takes over and we go on from there. —*Ann B. (name and address withheld), Ft. Worth, Tex.*

* * *

The problems encountered by Jane of Mobile, Ala. (February), since her amputation struck a sympathetic chord with me. I married my first husband when I was 19 and he was 22. He had a tendency to overindulge in alcohol whenever we went to parties. We had been married only 10 months when, returning from one of his drinking bouts at a party, he ran a stop sign. Our car was hit broadside by another car on the passenger side where I was seated. The accident resulted in only minor injuries to my ex-husband. However, it was necessary for doctors to amputate my right leg above the knee, leaving only a five-inch stump. A week later, my right arm was amputated also, about two inches above the elbow. Thank heavens I am left-handed!

After my recovery, our first sexual encounter and those following were a disaster. He said the sight of my stumps sickened him and he could not get aroused. These were strange words! Our marriage didn't last too long after that.

Through a friend I obtained a job as a filing clerk, a job requiring only one arm. After three years I met a man who was able to accept my disfigurement and have since had five years of married happiness. Like so many of the men that write to you, he has a fetish for female amputees. When he returns from work, he prefers to find me not wearing my artificial leg. To please him, I wear hot pants and a sleeveless top, allowing full view of both stumps. The circular movement of the stumps when I hop from place to place usually ends up in the bedroom. So don't worry, Jane of Mobile, you may still find a man who'll appreciate you the way you are now.—*Mrs. S.P. (name and address withheld), Danville, Ill.*

* * *

I was interested to read the letter in your anniversary issue from the one-legged British war bride, Mrs. D.D., since my own mother was also an amputee war bride who had lost her right leg during the World War II bombing of London. She met my father at a seaside resort when he was on leave and was angry at first when she noticed him staring at her stump as she walked along with her crutches in her bathing suit. She always told us how fascinated he was with her stump of a thigh from that day and the fascination never diminished throughout the marriage.

Despite her amputated leg, mother bore six children and raised us all herself without any maids. I was the oldest, with two brothers and three sisters. She always wore a peg leg when working or shopping, but she was happiest when she could take it off to rest her stump. Her favourite way of getting around was with just one crutch and her single leg, and when she was busy in the kitchen, she would sometimes hop around on her one leg and swing her stump on a stool so she could stand erect without her crutch.

We children never thought it odd to see mother's stump of a thigh exposed every day. Father would always kid my mother about her stump and they had a secret understanding about it that wasn't shared with us children. When mother was walking around on her crutch, father would sometimes playfully tickle or pat the end of her stump inside her skirt, and she would scold, "Please, not in front of the children."

From my earliest days I can recall my parents frequently having discussions about their finances, which took place behind the locked door of their bedroom and lasted at least half an hour. We thought nothing of it as mother hopped off, balancing on her one leg and leaning on father's shoulder, into the bedroom without bothering to use the crutch. Later, when father came out, he would ask one of us to bring mother her crutch. Sometimes when I went into the bedroom, I wondered why mother had to take off her stocking to talk about money. It was only later that I realized the warm love that existed between my parents, and that my father wanted privacy with his one-legged wife and stump for other reasons than money.
—F.B.K. *(name and address withheld), Arlington, Mass.*

* * *

Following a car accident about 18 months ago, I lost both my legs. Unfortunately, my husband does not find my stumps exciting. Though we had a good sexual relationship before the accident, he has been impotent in all attempts since. He recently told me that the sight of my scarred stumps turns him off, and he did not think he could ever obtain an erection with me again.

Since I am only 26 and do not relish the thought of never having sex again, I am considering a divorce. Most men have thought me attractive in the past, and I still have a good figure.

I hope you will continue to publish letters from men who find amputees like me attractive. I know that reading such letters in your magazine has helped my morale.
—*Jane (name and address withheld), Mobile, Ala.*

* * *

While my wife, who is legless, does not hang from willow trees like the girl D.H.W. of Decatur, Ga., knew (October), she has proved to be an exciting lover. I met her three years ago when my company transferred me to a new regional office where she worked as a receptionist. It was over a week after meeting her at work that I found out she has no legs because she used a regular office chair and a desk concealed where her legs should have been. She says this helped her get dates since many guys would not bother to ask out a girl they saw seated in a wheelchair. Some of them backed out or dated her only once when they found out. But there were a few like me who were fascinated by her lack of legs. We married about six months after we started dating.

My wife's lack of legs is the result of a congenital deformity. She is 24 and, having been legless since birth, she has adapted well to her condition. Since her legs were not amputated, but just failed to form, her stumps, which protrude just a short way out of her panties, are not scarred. She has a rather elaborate prosthetic device which fits her lower body and allows her to walk.

After nearly three years of marriage, I'm still turned on by the way she handles her legless body. We enjoy bathing together. She has large breasts (40D) with big dark nipples and aureolae. It is very exciting to watch her swing her nude, legless body into the bathtub with her beautiful breasts bouncing. In keeping with the current trend she does not wear a bra.

We have a child of six months. Those of your readers who are turned on by female amputees would probably flip their lids at the sight of a pregnant one. As you can see, there's a lot to be said for being married to a legless woman.—*D.F. (name and address withheld), Florida*

* * *

H.C.'s sexual experience with his one-legged aunt (June) brought back fond memories to me. For my own first sexual intimacies were also a family affair with a woman amputee, my stepmother.

My real mother died when I was eight and a year later my father married his bookkeeper, who was a very beautiful 27-year-old spinster. Our new stepmother proved very kind and affectionate, and my two younger sisters and I soon learned to love her almost as much as we had our own mother.

My stepmother's left leg had been amputated a few inches above her knee, but she wore her artificial leg only part of the time, mostly when doing housework. More often, we saw her on crutches and sometimes she would hop around the kitchen or bedroom balanced on just the one leg. She never tried to hide the stump from us and would even joke about it at times. She gave birth to two daughters, but always treated her stepchildren and natural children as equals.

I was 17 when my father passed away and my stepmother began calling me the man of the house since I was the only male among six females. He left us well provided for, and we continued as the same tightknit family, with my stepmother supervising his business.

About six months after my father died, I knocked at my stepmother's door in my pajamas to tell her goodnight, as I always did. To my surprise, she invited me in and I found her sitting up on her bed, on top of the blanket, wearing only a sheer nightgown and reading a book. She was sitting up against the backboard with her one leg drawn up close to her and the book resting on her upraised knee. Her nightgown wasn't pulled down and, with her knee up high, it was formed into an open-ended tent through which I could see her stump resting on the blanket, plus the underside of her full upraised thigh. To my shock and embarrassment, I realized she had no panties under her nightgown, for I saw a bushy mass of light brown hair matching the color of the hair flowing onto her shoulders. I tried to avoid looking, but she seemed absorbed in her book, though I kept stealing glances up to the junction of her leg and stump.

She asked me to sit down beside her on the bed and, putting her arm around me, she began complimenting me on the way I had taken over my father's responsibilities since his death. She spoke softly and fondly of my father and started talking about "other responsibilities" of his that she hadn't yet mentioned. She whispered, "A woman needs a very special kind of love that only a man can give her," and hugged me tight. "Your father knew all about that, but now that he is gone, I think you should learn about it, too." Then she kissed me and added, "After all, you're the man of the house."

I sat in stunned silence as my stepmother suddenly stood up next to the bed, balanced herself on the one leg and, to my shock, pulled her nightgown up over her head and tossed it aside. I was afraid to look, but she said it was okay and I was "old enough to know the facts of life." She was twice my age, but still very slim and beautiful, despite having had two children. Her breasts sagged a little and she had big, dark brown nipples instead of the pink ones I thought all women had. With her hands on her hips, she balanced herself on her leg with her stump thigh twitching back and forth in space.

She smiled down at me, amused at the embarrassed way I was trying to conceal the bulging erection that was forming. "One-legged women look a little different, I know," she said, lifting her stump for a second. "But it's a difference your father appreciated and I hope you will, too. Watch."

My stepmother began to hop on one leg in a big circle round the bed from one side to the other, watching my reaction all the time. Her breasts flopped and bounced wildly with each hop and her stump was jerking around in a broad arc more than when I had seen it waving around when she played ball with us at the beach.

She approached my side of the bed a bit out of breath, snapped off the light and lay down next to me. I was in a cold sweat wondering what to expect next, and hoping none of my sisters would wake up and find out where I was. Soon, I was aware that my stepmother was pressing her body against my thigh and rhythmically rubbing the stump of her leg back and forth. She told me to slip my pajamas down and soon I could feel her hand gently on my penis guiding it into the fluffy, soft mass of hair I had gaped at moments before. We began rocking in unison till she whispered: "Remember, take it slow until you get used to my stump."

That evening was the start of a regular intimate relationship that lasted until I went off to college. I'd wanted to continue living at home, but she insisted it was time "I left the nest and flew on my own." I began to have affairs with girls on the campus, but found it a trifle less satisfying when my partner had two legs.

One weekend, my stepmother revealed she had started dating a widower who had just moved into town. So we decided to end our relationship. We kissed and embraced like mother and son, and I never again shared her bed.

But she knew I had developed a taste for amputees and gave me the phone number of a couple of girls my age who had each lost a leg. She had met them on visits to her artificial limb makers. She'd jotted down a brief description of each girl—left leg off below knee, right leg off at upper thigh, etc. Next to one girl's name was "no stump, but very cute."

A year ago I married a one-legged girl (though not one on my stepmother's list). I first saw her hopping past me at a swimming pool. She was wearing a bikini and a little five-inch stump was waving around where her left leg should have been. When I told my wife about the old relationship with my stepmother, she was very understanding, but laughingly promised, that if it ever started again, she would break her wooden leg over my head.—*G.P.R. (name and address withheld), Phoenix, Ariz.*

* * *

I feel sorry for those married women who lost a leg and then found they lost their husbands' love as well. But it was fortunate that some were able to remarry to men who appreciate the sexual significance of a one-legged woman's stump.

I was lucky enough to be married to such a man when, after only seven months of marriage, I had my right leg amputated in an auto accident. It's off near the knee.

After my stump healed I waited anxiously to learn if my husband would want to have intercourse with a wife who was now one-legged.

I didn't have long to wait, for the instant we got home from the doctor's office after my stump bandages were removed, my husband gently took away my crutches and carried me to the bedroom. In a flash he had my skirt up, my panties down, and my one remaining leg out to the side so he could enter me.

That was three years ago and our marriage is growing happier by the minute. My husband is utterly fascinated by the stump of my right leg and begs me to wear the shortest miniskirts so he can see my stump while I'm getting around the house on my crutches.

I wear an artificial leg for just my housework, and I make sure I am wearing it when he returns from work each evening. For his greatest pleasure is to unstrap the leg and slip it off my stump, leaving me balanced on one leg and leaning against the hall table.

Then he gives my stump a welcome massage, which I love, and helps me hop to the studio couch for a little before-dinner lovemaking.

My one leg is still shapely, especially with a nylon on, but my husband is intrigued by my stump. He fondles it at every chance and is thrilled when I rub my stump against him in bed.

Other men seem to get excited by seeing my stump showing below my skirt too. But I'm always faithful since I couldn't ask for a better husband.—*S.K. (name withheld), Boston, Mass.*

* * *

I was recently introduced to your magazine by my current boyfriend when he brought me a stack so I could read the letters you have published about men who prefer women amputees to those who still have their arms and legs. He happens to be one of those men and is frank and open about it. While I am attractive and have a good figure (39-26-36), he admitted that he was attracted to me primarily because I have no arms and only one leg. I was born without arms, but a car wreck eight years ago was responsible for my being one-legged.

For twenty years I managed very well without arms, using my feet as other people use hands. Never having had arms and hands, I didn't miss them, although as a child, I was subjected to the cruel tormenting that children inflict upon other children who are different. I soon learned to dress and feed myself, and learned to write in school by holding a pencil or pen with my toes. I was a curiosity at school for a while, but the other kids soon got used to seeing my feet up on my desk writing or holding a book. At one time I had a set of artificial arms, but I could do more things with my feet so I rarely wore them. When I outgrew the arms, they were not replaced. I learned to type in high school, hunting and pecking with my two big toes, and was good enough to get a typing job in a typing pool after graduation. Now, with only one foot, I do have problems doing things for myself, but not much more than someone who has had an arm amputated.

As I reached my early teens, I had resigned myself to not having a social life and was very surprised when I was approached for dates. I wouldn't have believed a boy would want to date a deformed girl. Happily, I was wrong and was asked out as often as any of the other girls. It was not long before I discovered that my lack of arms was one of my attractions. While going through the adolescent stage of necking and groping on the back seat of cars, I found that my dates devoted as much time to my empty, armless shoulders as they did to groping for my budding breasts. I enjoyed their attentions in both areas but couldn't understand why they liked to feel my shoulders so much.

The way I used my feet and legs was a unique experience for my dates, since I grew up in an era when girls wore full skirts that reached to mid-calf and effectively hid legs. Also, at that time a "nice" girl wouldn't let a boy touch her anywhere below the waist. I would have my date pull my skirt up over my hips to clear my legs and have him sit between them. Then I could hold him around the waist with one leg and reach my other foot up to hold him at his shoulder or neck. I always wore shorts over my panties to maintain some decorum, but in such a contorted position, he could not help touching my exposed thighs. Since I never objected, my legs were thoroughly stroked, examined and played with. I am sure I left many a young man extremely frustrated, as I was a virgin until I was twenty.

I celebrated my twenty-first birthday with a party, a car wreck and having my left leg amputated a little above mid-thigh. I was quite despondent and bitter for a while. Not having any arms in the first place, losing a leg was a little too much. I finally got over my self-pity and found that my friends were still my friends.

I know that any man who dates an amputee does so because he prefers amputees. From my experience, a man either likes a stump or he doesn't. I have never dated a man who didn't care one way or the other. I also know that most of the men I date do not care for my false leg because they like to see and hold my stump. However, since I can't use crutches and refuse to ride in a wheelchair, I have to wear it whenever I go out. If he wants, I will let my date take my leg off at the first opportunity. Once, I let a fellow take it off while we were in a movie. Unfortunately, we misjudged the time and he was attempting to strap it back on me when the picture ended and the lights came on. It was very embarrassing to be caught in a crowded theater with my skirt up around my waist and him fumbling with the straps. After that experience, I have made sure I kept my leg on until we were in a more private situation. If I am entertaining a date in my apartment, I don't wear the leg at all and just hop if I have to move around.

I guess the main reason for this letter is in response to the two legless girls who wrote you not long ago and are now very unhappy about their future prospects. My advice to both is—circulate! Don't be a recluse just because you don't have your legs anymore. Don't try to hide your stumps or pretend you still have legs. Go into any place where men hang out, usually a bar, and you will find many more men who will like your stumps than those who won't. I know from experience and I have amputee girl friends who agree with me. My roommate is one-legged and says her dates like her to wear a pegleg or crutches. When I lived in California several years ago, I knew a beautiful girl with no legs. Although she had artificial legs, she seldom wore them. Instead, she straddled a padded peg, strapped it to both her stumps, and walked with crutches. Her skirts were just short enough to allow the ends of her short stumps to show. She always had plenty of male attention. Another girl I once knew was, like me, born without arms. She got the attention of every man by walking up to a bar, ordering a drink in a stem glass and then standing there, balanced on her left leg, while she held her drink with the toes of her right foot. Of course, with her looks, figure and long shapely legs, she would not have had any trouble getting men in any case, but being armless didn't detract from her appeal at all.

Finally, one last thing for Jane of Mobile, whose leg-stumps turn off her husband. He can't help the way he feels about your stumps any more than the men who will like them. It is beyond their control. Get your divorce and get back into circulation. You won't have any trouble finding a man who will love you, scarred stumps and all.—*C. D. (name withheld), Columbus, Ohio*

* * *

Monopede Mania (March, 1973) has been read with considerable interest by our staff and board of directors, many of whom are female amputees.

There will undoubtedly be those, including amputees, who will object to our Association involving itself with what many people might consider a perversion or an unhealthy attitude.

To such people we respectfully point out that the loss of one or more limbs is an intense physical, spiritual and emotional experience. Amputation can affect the amputee's sex life and anything that concerns amputees is of vital interest to us—the American Amputee Association.

The physical attractiveness of amputees to some members of the opposite sex is not unknown to us. While certainly not common, it is not all that rare, as letters from your readers seem to indicate.

We have discussed this so-called mania with several female amputees and their consensus is that while they don't quite understand it, they consider it a plus for their side.

Our studies indicate that one of the more negative attitudes that can result from amputation is that the amputee will no longer be attractive to members of the opposite sex. This is not difficult to understand. Amputees, like everyone else, seldom see themselves as others see them. Consequently they are likely to focus their attention on their stump or stumps to an unwarranted degree. They fail to remember that sexual attraction is a combination of many factors and that a physical deformity can be, and often is, overlooked or diminished in the eyes of the beholder by reason of personality, character or simply by a beautiful smile or sexy eyes.

While we have in our files instances of marriages or romances that could not survive the trauma of amputation, in the majority of cases it has brought couples closer together. We also have histories where amputation led to suicide.

Since "monopede mania" definitely does exist, and since it involves amputees of both sexes, we asked several psychologists to give us their views. We share with you what they had to say.

Please understand that we made no sophisticated or well-organized study of this mania, nor do we know of any. The observations and comments are open for discussion and conjecture.

Our learned friends say monopede mania probably stems from one of three sexual factors and that in some individuals all three could bear on the libido and produce quite profound results.

First, each of us, when viewed physically by the opposite sex is, in a figurative way, an amputee. The primary outward appearance of the male and female depends on the absence or presence of the primary and secondary sex organs. The male has a penis and testicles; the female has nothing clearly visible in that area of her body.

Conversely, the female with her breasts is displaying to the male parts he does not have. This visual difference is well understood. But what might happen if this difference sharply increased by the absence of one or more limbs? Limbs, after all, account for a considerable amount of the human form. Well, in some cases this increased difference can increase the attractiveness, which in turn makes the amputee that much more appealing in the eyes of certain beholders. We submit that this is quite an interesting theory.

Second, many women and some men have a highly developed maternal instinct. Because an amputee has a certain amount of visible helplessness, his or her appeal to maternal people may be increased.

Third, there are those who have a serious interest in that sexual deviation called "bondage," in which the sex partner is tied up and rendered helpless. Since the amputee is already helpless to some degree, people who find this appealing will find the amputee more attractive.

There are undoubtedly many other theories concerning monopede mania, and this association would appreciate hearing about them.

Ours is a relatively new organization and still in its

formative stage. We are not, therefore, actively recruiting members at this time. However, if anyone is interested in learning more about our association, please make an inquiry, which will be kept in the strictest confidence.

We are busily engaged in the task of putting together the first issue of our periodical, *The American Amputee Quarterly*, which we hope to publish some time this summer. We are including in the first issue an article about monopede mania, and if the response warrants, we will make it the subject of a regular feature. We are, therefore, most anxious to hear from anyone who has had experience with it or would care to comment.

It is refreshing, at least to us, to find a publication that does not shy away from the subject of amputees, especially as it regards sex, which is as much an integral part of an amputee's life as it is anyone else's. We hope you will continue your interest.—*Carl E. Gullans, Pres., American Amputee Association, 852 Lafayette Road, Hampton, N.H.*

* * *

Let me begin by saying I'm a female amputee. Two years ago I had the misfortune (or so I thought) to lose my right foot and part of my right leg. For a year after my accident I avoided almost all social contacts. I considered my disfigurement total and could not face the rejection I was certain would accompany any male's realization of my condition.

A year ago I dated a man on the chance that he wouldn't notice my missing leg until he had gotten to know me. You can't imagine my surprise when he noticed it on the first date and wasn't bothered by it. This led to a sexually satisfying relationship, and as time went on it became apparent that he was actually *sexually excited* by my stump. Since then I've dated several other men. I have found in all of them some degree of sexual stimulation due to my amputated leg. I can't speak for all female amputees, only for myself, but I would have to say that 100% of the men I've known find some kind of intensified sexual pleasure with a girl with an amputated limb.

I would love to see a pictorial series of female amputees in your magazine. In fact, were it not for my family, I would love to be one of your subjects!—*Miss A.K. (name and address withheld), Cleveland, Ohio.*

* * *

About two years ago my husband brought home a copy of *Penthouse* and showed me the letters concerning "monopede mania." Every month since then I have read these letters with interest and amusement, and I have shared them with a half-dozen of my girl friends who are also "unipedettes." I reluctantly joined our exclusive sorority nine years ago when I was in a car accident the night of my high school senior prom. My biggest concern at the time was that my new gown was ruined with blood from what I believed to be a broken leg. However, as it turned out, my leg had been severely mangled, and you can imagine my shock when I discovered my right leg had been taken off a few inches below the hip.

As with the other unipedettes, I initially underwent periods of depression, bitterness, and frustration. I struggled through the agony of having an artificial limb, and, as with most other girls who have lost a leg above the knee, I discarded the limb when I realized that the price of appearing "normal" was continuous discomfort and pain, constant public attention to the plastic prosthesis, and most of all—a serious loss of freedom in movement and speed. I abandoned this mockery of normalcy and happily returned to crutches.

Nearly 2,000,000 girls and women in the U.S. are missing one or more limbs, and more than half of these have lost one leg. Amputee Louise Baker authored a humorous book entitled *Out on a Limb*, and in 1968, an article was printed in *Good Housekeeping* about amputated beauty queen Roberta Scott. There have been several famous women, including the late actresses Sarah Bernhardt and Susan Ball, who went through life "without a leg to stand on." They did not hop into a hole of self-pity, nor have I.

I find the old-fashioned underarm crutches give me the best support and service, and they make me stand up straight. When mini-skirts were in style, I wore some which were just long enough to cover the short stub of my right leg while I was standing. Panty hose came into being at that time, and by turning the right hose slightly inside out and tucking in my little stump, I was able to dress it properly just in case it showed itself when I sat down. (My two-legged girl friends still give me panty hose which have a run in one leg.) Since they removed almost my entire leg, I am able to sew in a patch of material and close up the leg hole of my bathing suits. (Incidentally, the working end of plumber's plungers in place of rubber crutch tips are excellent for walking on the beach.)

I had hardly set foot in public when I encountered my first "monopede maniacs." One day, after practicing my new style of walking, I was resting against a railing when I noticed a man standing beneath the railing and looking up my skirt. With his hand in his pocket, he was ogling my naked little stump! (Ever since that experience, although my little leg may be bare around the house, I always dress it in a stump sock or inside-out panty hose when I go out.) Often in public I am asked to pose for snapshots, obviously not because I have a pretty face or nice shape, and I have been offered (and declined) $100 if I would perform for home movies. I classify these peculiar men as the passive type, and found they are really quite harmless. They are no more strange than those who have a fetish for huge mammaries or crude pornographic movies.

The other type, the active aficionado, engages in physical contact. While standing in elevators, I first thought the hands that brushed against my half-thigh were there accidentally, then I realized those fingers rubbing the tip of my foreshortened limb weren't there by accident and were quite deliberately inquisitive. Rather than fondling my breasts, some of my dates preferred to fondle the rounded appendage hanging from my right hip, and some went not a step further! The boldest act I've experienced happened while I was asleep on a jet. Suddenly I was awakened by a hand beneath my dress massaging my tiny stub! To be truthful, I have enjoyed a few of these encounters and I have enjoyed the stammering explanations that followed, but some of my sorority sisters become quite upset when a stranger touches their amputation sites.

By no means is this unusual interest limited to legless ladies alone. I know a career girl who was amazed that her attraction to men *increased* after her right arm was chopped off above the elbow in a waterskiing accident. At first she tried to conceal her loss, but when she found men were intrigued by it, she gradually began to draw attention to it. The empty sleeve of her sweaters has been rewoven as a snug sock for her stump, and one sleeve of her shortsleeved dresses scarcely hides the tip of her short arm. She uses that short arm to touch and hold things, and to point and gesture while she talks. She, too, has had "feeling" encounters, most frequently in singles bars. She claims her sex life has doubled since her arm was taken off, but I doubt it. At any rate, this girl with something missing is now a girl with something extra!

Every one of my sorority sisters admits to being sexually aroused when the end and inside of their stumps are massaged. When my husband is standing and holding me in his arms, he wants me to raise my stub and massage his genitals with it. My husband and I also enjoy a super sex experience when I lie on my left side and he straddles my leg, inserting his penis into me sideways. There is an older woman I know with both legs off near the hips, who claims a double orgasm when she puts her trunk on the edge of the dining room table and lies back as her husband goes in deeply while standing at the edge of the table.

I have met many fascinating people and have had some different experiences since they took my leg off. Life as a unipedette has been interesting and does have some compensations, but I think my lifestyle could

be just as interesting if my lonely left leg still had its mate.
—*Name and address withheld*

* * *

I write to add my comments to the interesting correspondence in your columns headed *Monopede Mania*. I am a monopede and as a result have become a student of that abnormal sexual interest in amputees and cripples.

I am a one-legged woman. I come from a good family and hold a graduate degree. I have a good job, but make just about as much money working as an occasional prostitute. On the whole, I have found the experience to be interesting and enjoyable. Now in my late twenties, I am unmarried and, I fear, likely to remain so. Having been without my right leg since childhood, I have compensated well for the physical handicap; I am skillful at walking with one or two crutches, a peg leg or an artificial limb. But the psychological handicap is harder to deal with; a one-legged woman is unable to forget her mutilation or the painful difference between her and normal women.

I became involved in prostitution at the urging of a business acquaintance, who put it to me frankly that he would consider it a great favor if I would accommodate him on a purely business basis. He was obsessed by amputees and this frustration was beginning to have an adverse effect on his life. He loved his wife and family and wanted only to get the monkey off his back. I was no virgin, though my sex life had not been exactly crowded. I was in no sense promiscuous. This man was decent and attractive. He made no pretense about his intentions, so I consented.

It is a blow to a woman to find the most sensitive and painful fact of her life becoming the source of her attractiveness, so I can't say the experience turned me on. On the other hand, it was not unpleasant or humiliating. The man was considerate and there was a little part of me that enjoyed the attention. This man was the first of my steadies; soon there were more.

The effect on my first client of my "therapy" was

dramatic and he reported to me a Renaissance of his sex life at home. He comes back to me about once every six weeks. Others without families or with less commitment at home come oftener, and there are two who are very special to me, normal men who come to me as a woman rather than an amputee. Sad for me, they are both married. I never take more than two or three men in one week, never more than one in any twenty-four-hour period, never a man whom I dislike and never a "quickie." I feel a genuine affection for my steadies; they are nice people. Most of them are prosperous—I am expert in their needs and command high prices.

Recognizing that I am being well paid to be an amputee and a cripple, I have made a study of what appeals to the monopede maniac. Each man has his special tastes, of course, but what I learn from one helps to provide variety for the others. Much is made of prosthetic devices, and I have an understanding with each man that if he pays for some special device, I can use it with my other clients. Other than that I take great care never to give out any information concerning any of my clients, some of whom know each other but others of whom remain anonymous.

It was a problem for me to overcome my feeling of repugnance at exploiting the sexual appeal of my handicap, and once in a while it still overcomes me, but mostly I have adjusted to it well enough to often enjoy the love-making that goes with it. There is, of course, much foreplay, not much of which I can enjoy, but my men are good lovers, and I often enjoy real orgasms with them. They like to see me walk and of course they want me to hop so they can see my breasts jiggling up and down (they are reasonably large, but they don't "flop") and my stump swinging. I have learned that my lameness is sexually exciting and I have learned to exaggerate it in certain ways. Being in first-class physical shape I can do a fetching one-legged dance and also a crutch dance. This is usually in the nude, of course, unless the client wants me to wear some item of clothing that he finds exciting.

One client has paid for a special foot for my limb that

I can wear with four-and-a-half-inch heels. He loves to see me teetering around on them with long, black stockings and garter belt.

Prostheses interest my clients, the more so, I have noted, if they include some leather harness with formidable lacing. I have a pair of boots such as are worn by double amputees when they walk on their stumps. The left boot laces up tightly to hold my leg and foot folded back, so it appears I have a knee-length stump. My real stump being very short and small, I sometimes walk with this boot and a pair of short crutches, and other times with a boot that extends my stump to knee length. The left boot is painful and I do not wear it for long. That act fills me with horror, but some of my men love it.

One of these prosthetic devices actually turns me on. It is a special stump socket that one man thought up. He fastens it to his left thigh so I can put my stump in it, and then we walk three-legged together. This gives substance to my eternal fantasy of walking with two live legs, and I am walking around our vast estates with my loving husband. I have padded out the weight-bearing saddle on the stump socket and can masturbate myself with it while we walk. I love it dearly.

Most of my clients are passionately interested in my stump, the exceptions being my two normal men and one who concentrates on my one remaining leg and foot. (He is still classified as a monopede maniac, since he is uninterested when there are two legs and feet.) My stump is undersized, misshapen, scarred and ugly. I wince when I look at it and yearn for a leg in its place, but to them it must have a great charm—they want to caress, lick, bite or "massage" it. One man likes to hold it tightly while I struggle to move it, and all are delighted by any genital contact with it. I have found that my stump's sex appeal is heightened by something tied or laced around it; I have a tiny corset of black leather for that purpose, though I leave the stump's scarred and ugly tip to protrude.

In a limited way, a stump can be an asset in lovemaking. As I sit astride a man's right thigh, facing him with no leg to come between us, I can come very close to him and use my stump to caress his genitals. I enjoy this and can become excited by it.

But being one-legged is a great handicap in bed. I fantasize about locking my legs around a man's body while he fucks me long and hard. I also dream of sitting astride my partner and taking charge of the action from the superior position, but both of these actions are totally impossible without another leg.

I have my moments of depression and loneliness, and even repugnance for the acts that I perform for the sexual gratification of my clients, but these are becoming fewer, and my life is ordinarily pleasant and interesting. Without exception, my men treat me as a lady and not as a whore, and take trouble to let me know they find me attractive as a woman and as a person. It has done wonders for my ailing self-image and I love them for it. Nevertheless, my dream remains that of being a wife and mother, and having a loving husband who sees me as a woman and not as an adjunct to a hideous stump. I keep my hopes up and in fact, receive an occasional proposal of marriage.

My hope is that this letter will add something to the valuable documentation of this and other similar sexual aberrations that *Penthouse* has made possible. This service to science and mankind has revolutionized the lives of some people by making it plain that they are not unique, perverted or immoral. I have come to understand my clients and their problems and to take pride in the professionalism of the service I perform for them. I feel that there must be a good many others like me.—*Name and address withheld.*

* * *

Being an amputee myself, I detected a note of sour grapes from one-legged Mrs. S.F. who, in her [June] letter pooh-poohs the erotic appeal that many men find in a female amputee. She scoffs, too, at a one-legged woman who might exploit her stump to attract a man. Yet she grudgingly admits that her own stump is an "ironic dividend" that gives her husband "something to play with." I hope that's not her only concession to his sexual needs.

Obviously, no one enjoys losing a leg. But if fate has so decreed, why shouldn't a one-legged woman capitalize on the sexual advantage her unwanted stump gives her? When I lost my right leg at eighteen, it was almost the end of the world for me. But now, ten years later and a happily married wife and mother, I realize I could be lots worse off than having only one leg.

My husband is still just as spellbound by the six-inch stump of my right thigh as when he first saw me reluctantly take off my artificial leg on our wedding night five years ago. But now that I am no longer ashamed of my stump, I suffer the discomfort of my artificial leg only a few hours each morning, when I can do my housework with both hands free. Otherwise, I get around very nicely on my one leg and my trusty crutch, with my stump just hanging free and comfy under my skirt where I can massage it as often as I like—and where my husband can ogle it and fondle it as often as he likes.

Mrs. S.F. forgets that men see us differently and thank God for that! While I'm dressing in the morning, I personally feel like a lopsided freak as I hop around on the one leg with my homely little stump wagging so pathetically from the other side of my panties. But my husband devours my one leg with his eyes, and savors the view of my bare stump with no less relish than when he admires my breasts flopping above as I hop to the bureau for my bra. My little remnant of a thigh makes me an incomplete woman, but to my husband it makes me a more erotic sex object than I could ever be otherwise. Figure that!

After looking green with envy at your lovely Pets with their two lovely legs in those inviting poses, I feel so ludicrous when I lie back on the bed with my one long leg and my puny stump spread for my husband. But he doesn't complain, bless him, and says he loves the feel of my stump rubbing against him in bed, especially when I stroke it rhythmically up and down.

Since my stump is a bundle of interrupted nerves,

muscles and veins, it can be an irritating source of odd sensations brought on by weather, nervous tension, overexertion or pressure of my artificial leg. The only way I can relieve those sensations is to massage my stump. But no matter how well I do it myself, it always seems so much more soothing when my husband's fingers are rubbing my stump. Of course, the physical relief I experience when he rubs my stump is different from the erotic pleasure he gets from the act.

On a female amputee, a stump can also be bothersome just before her period, because of changes in body chemistry. That's when I especially welcome having my stump massaged vigorously by my husband. And since he realizes that I may be "closed for alterations" in a few days, I'm not too surprised to feel my panties being slipped down before my stump rubdown is over.

To be a one-legged woman and still be able to sexually arouse and satisfy the man I love is one of the greatest personal triumphs I'll ever enjoy. Every night that my husband caresses my stump with his fingers or asks to have it rubbed against him while we are embracing, I say a silent prayer of gratitude for having such a husband.—*(name and address withheld)*

* * *

I am an amputee, and it is Donald Carpenter's letter in your July issue that prompts my writing. My experience has been that I have had the pleasure of being inundated with willing gems since losing my leg.

Women who previously gave me the cold shoulder are now willing sex companions. The attraction is my thigh stump, for which most women seem to have a mania. Make it quite clear, I do not object and am not offended. I can't help but notice male curiosity about my stump on the rare occasions I go swimming.

I heartily agree with Mr. Carpenter that a pictorial featuring a beautiful amputee female would be welcomed by those of us who are handicapped, as well as those who are not.—*W.P. (name and address withheld), New York, N.Y.*

* * *

I must comment on correspondence concerning the possible display in Penthouse of an attractive female amputee, since I am one of those who find them sexually attractive. I am married to a lovely amputee who well understands the nature of her peculiar sexual attractiveness to me, as well as the effective use of it. She also understands that she is a lovely woman. Our marriage is no sexual flash in the pan, since we have been married many years and our love is deep and abiding. Our sex life is satisfying and ever fresh; we never permit it to become trivial or perfunctory. We are secure enough in our love that neither of us feels threatened when the other enjoys sexual relations with somebody else, so that over the years each of us has enjoyed a number of lovers.

Penthouse and other publications cover without embarrassment a wide variety of particular sexual appetites in a way that represents a great step forward in the dispelling of unhealthy taboos and hypocrisy, so that it seems perfectly reasonable to recognize this particular sexual appetite similarly. Simply publish a picture of an attractive amputee (just as pictures have been published of women with grotesquely large breasts, for example) to appeal to those who find such a thing sexually stimulating.

My wife says: "I would love to pose but, alas, I am no longer glamorous, and it would surely shock many of our more staid friends." I dissent from this in part. She is still glamorous, with a figure lovely as any girl's. But I do fear that no camera art could entirely conceal that she is a grandmother, albeit an uncommonly beautiful one.—*M.P. (name and address withheld), New Hampshire.*

* * *

Three cheers to Donald Carpenter (Forum, July) for his letter pertaining to female amputees. I have been reading numerous men's magazines for five years and all

I have seen are women with four limbs. This may be fine, but why not a little change of pace? I am certain that, somewhere in this world, is a beautiful female amputee willing to pose for your fine publication.

At present I am engaged to a young woman who was born with no right leg. She is not only beautiful and talented but also very graceful when on crutches. The one thing that bothers me is when we go out: people stare at her and many treat her as a helpless cripple. Too many people have this concept that all amputees are helpless and I feel that a pictorial featuring a beautiful female amputee would clear up that stupid idea.

When you do that article I am certain that it would be a first, but it would be done in the usual good taste that Penthouse is known for. Or are you just another magazine that does not have the nerve to be different?—*J.T. (name and address withheld), Cleveland, Ohio 44106*

* * *

One-legged Mr. W.P. may marvel at the way his stump stirs woman's passions (October), but his experiences are nothing compared to the way any reasonably attractive *girl* amputee can delight and arouse males to fever pitch by just the sight and feel of her thigh stump. I'm a girl who speaks from long experience, since I lost my left leg 5 inches above the knee when I was in high school and I am now 26.

I think the key is that a one-legged girl's stump becomes a sort of symbol of feminine weakness and vulnerability. And how men dig a supposedly helpless female! When I smartened up by leaving my artificial leg at home and started going out on just my remaining leg with a pair of those elbow-height metal crutches, I suddenly discovered that I had sex appeal that I never dreamed existed. I found myself being dated by guys who were scoring regularly with two-legged beauties, and even a few supposedly happy married men with supposedly sexy two-legged wives sharing their bed with them every night. I was astounded to discover that instead of being repelled by the thought of sleeping with a one-legged girl, as I had so wrongly assumed, the guys were actually intrigued. And they wasted no time in proving it! I still find it hard to believe that my funny looking little stump actually increases my desirability to many men, but it is true. Some guys play with my stump like it was a toy.

If a fellow is giving me a goodnight kiss in my hallway and I want to drop a hint that I'd like him to linger a while longer, I have only to slowly swing my stump up inside my skirt until it presses against his leg and he practically lights up. He can hardly wait for me to get my apartment door open. I can enter any cocktail lounge on my one leg and crutches, and within minutes I can have my choice of nearly any guy in the place if I want him. I dress smartly but not flashily, and wear my skirt just long enough to cover the end of my stump when I'm standing. But when I sit down or bend over, the end of my stump usually pokes out a bit (by design) and that's when male eyes start popping and hearts pounding with anticipation. Once I satisfy the inevitable question of "Gee, how did you lose that leg?" the conversation usually takes a romantic turn. And if I feel a friendly hand probing the end of my stump under the table I know I have scored a home run.

Why not give your readers a treat and show them what a one-legged girl has going for her that other girls don't have—the unique and even mysterious sex appeal of her stump.—*Diane S. (name and address withheld), Boston, Mass.*

* * *

I think the idea of a pictorial on women amputees is the best thing I've heard in a long time. I'm sure this hang-up about public display of women amputees is a uniquely American thing, for I don't think that Europeans, for example, think of a one-legged woman as a pitiful, repulsive creature to be hidden away until spinsterhood overtakes her. In the recent Spanish movie *Tristana*, the heroine was a lovely one-legged girl. And over the past few years I recall seeing a couple of foreign films that also had one-legged girls in them. One in particular had several nude scenes showing a henpecked executive seducing his one-legged secretary and later playfully chasing her while she hopped around the bedroom on her single leg. In the story, he later left his wife and married the amputee.

Since losing my left leg when I was 16 (it's off midway between my knee and hip, the result of an auto accident), I have found plenty of fellows who didn't think me repulsive, regardless of whether I was walking on my artificial leg or just on the one leg with my crutches. I've been married two years, and they've been the happiest two years of my life. Until my wedding night I used to be ashamed of my stump and kept it constantly covered in public. I dreaded having to undress in front of my husband that night. But before I knew it, he had unstrapped my artificial leg himself and slipped it off my stump within seconds of entering our hotel room. Next thing I knew his hand was gently stroking my stump of a thigh and moving it into the best position for our lovemaking. I learned that night, to my astonishment, that a one-legged woman can enjoy a normal sex life as easily as anyone else.

I have three married girl friends who are also one-legged, and their husbands are just as loving as mine is, they report. I read a statistic that there are approximately 75,000 one-legged women in the United States between the ages of 18 and 35, and probably even more one-armed women. If we assume that even half this number are married, just think of the number of happily married men who don't mind looking at a woman amputee's stump for the rest of their lives or sleeping with a woman who is able to return their love only with one arm or one leg. And daily even more women lose a limb through accident or disease. I, for one, would be very interested to see the American public shown that feminine pulchritude isn't limited to just two-armed and two-legged women. The famous actress Sarah Bernhardt was one-legged in her later years, but was no less an attraction. There used to be a Hollywood starlet named Suzan Ball who was also one-legged but appeared in pictures. And another one-legged girl named Roberta Scott has appeared on TV and, I believe, won a Miss Handicapped America contest competing with other amputee beauties.—*Mrs. J.F.M. (name and address withheld), Brockton, Mass.*

* * *

I have been reading your magazine now for the past several months, and I have noticed that many of your readers have a great interest in female amputees. Last summer, I met a beautiful girl who had lost her right leg above the knee, and we are going to get married this fall. I, like most men, thought that making love with an amputee would not be a very erotic experience. Well, I proved myself wrong and I would like to relate to your readers my first experience with her. One day last summer, I went to a less crowded area of a large Long Island beach and to my surprise I saw this girl, who was extremely beautiful with firm, full breasts and a perfectly proportioned figure, lying on a blanket in a very skimpy two-piece bathing suit. It wasn't until she sat up that I noticed that she didn't have a right leg. She had her stump fully exposed and when I saw this I got an immediate hard-on. She had noticed that I was staring at her and she also spotted my erection. I was terribly embarrassed but I built up enough nerve to go over to speak to her. For the next couple of hours, I found her to be an extremely warm, intelligent, and personable individual. I asked her out to dinner that evening but she suggested that we have dinner at her apartment instead. From the moment I left her on the beach all I could think about was her stump, which seemed to excite me no end. When I arrived at her place she was wearing a tight sweater without a bra (which is sufficient enough to excite me), but when I saw that she was wearing a mini-skirt with her stump exposed and wiggling about, well, that put me over the top. All through dinner I had the urge to go to bed with her, but I didn't know how to approach her. After dinner we were sitting on the sofa talking but she noticed that I was staring at her stump and that I had an erection that bulged through my pants. To my surprise, she placed her hand upon the bulge and then unfastened my pants. After caressing my penis for a while, she rearranged her position on the sofa so that she could rub my penis with her stump. Needless to say, I was ready. We went into her bedroom and for the next several hours I made love with a woman who knows what lovemaking is all about. I am not ashamed to say that when it comes to having sex, she is the only one who can fulfill my desires. As far as I'm concerned my fiancée can make love better than any two-legged woman and I am proud to know that she will be my wife.—*Name and address withheld*

* * *

As a regular reader of *Penthouse*, I have been puzzled by the letters printed in Forum concerning female amputees. I just couldn't understand how an amputated stump could be sexually stimulating to a man. Like most other single men approaching age thirty, I have had experiences with various young ladies while looking for the right one to settle down with. Some of them I have had the pleasure of taking to bed; some I have not. Several just haven't been the right girls for me for other reasons. Trying to understand this professed stump attraction, I thought of how I would react to each of the girls I have known if they had only one leg. I decided that it would turn me off in some cases, while if I really liked the girl I could overlook her amputation and still enjoy being with her. However, using my wildest imagination, I was unable to see how I could become aroused by her stump. Now, I still don't understand it, but have found that I am just as aroused and stimulated by the look and feel of the thigh stump as any of the others who have written you.

I met a fantastic young woman while I was visiting relatives in Florida. She lives with her parents next door and, having become good friends with my aunt, often comes over for coffee in the mornings. The first time I saw her, I was immediately aware of a strong desire to know her better. Not only is she very beautiful and well-built, but she has that quality of liking people and being very easy to talk to. I talked with her and my aunt for about an hour and, just before she left, I asked her for a date that evening. She accepted, then got up to leave. I was startled when she picked up a crutch and swung out on one very well-shaped leg. She had been sitting at the breakfast table when I came in and I had not seen the crutch or been aware of her having only one leg.

Watching her leave, I found I was becoming very aroused. She was wearing a short skirt and, while I couldn't see how much of her leg had been amputated, the sight of just one shapely leg extending from under her skirt was strangely erotic.

On our first date, we found that we enjoyed each other's company very much, although our relationship didn't progress beyond a casual good-night kiss. The second evening I took her out, however, was different. When I took her home, she informed me that her parents were gone for the night and invited me in. We were soon fooling around on the sofa and she made no protests as I caressed her ample breasts and stroked her one leg. When I slipped my hand up under her skirt and placed it on her little stump, which I had not yet seen, I thought I had blown it. She immediately stiffened up and I was afraid she was going to demand that I leave. But, as I gently massaged her stump, she gradually relaxed and soon was as excited as I was.

After we had thoroughly exhausted each other, we were lying on her bed talking and I learned that I was the first man she had been with since losing her leg almost a year before. She was very self-conscious about her stump and her reaction to my touching it had been caused by a fear that I would find it repulsive. Instead, she soon found that she was stimulated by my fondling it.

By the time I left Florida last week, she was no longer self-conscious and, instead, seemed to enjoy my playing with her stump as much as I did.

Now that we have been apart for a week, I am very

anxious to see her again as soon as possible. Trying to figure out just how much her being one-legged has affected our relationship, I have given it much thought and again played the mental game of imagining how I would feel about the girls I have known if they had only one leg.

My conclusions may be all wrong, but I believe that the stump of an amputated leg or arm can be sexually stimulating, but only when one is attracted to the amputee for some other reason. I don't think that a girl that I am not sexually attracted to would suddenly become a sexual object if she had a leg cut off. On the other hand, if I have had a good time in bed with a girl, I would enjoy her more if she should lose a leg. Anyway, I no longer think that those who have written you letters are a bunch of kooks.—*Name and address withheld*

* * *

After reading several of the letters sent to Forum about amputees, I have finally worked up enough nerve to tell you what happened to me. First off, I guess I should tell you that I too am an amputee, having had my leg cut off after an auto accident. But unlike the others, I am a man and do not feel hampered by the loss. Of course, I did not always feel this way—right after the accident I went into deep depression, feeling sorry for myself and acting as though the world had come to an end.

I moved to California and hoped for a new life. I found it. I got a job that is ideal for me. I work the graveyard shift for a hotel as night auditor. It was at work that my experience took place.

A girl about twenty-eight years old checked into our place at about midnight. I gave her a room and went about doing my books. At about 5 A.M. she called down to the desk and said she was looking for someone to talk to. I couldn't leave the desk alone, so she asked if she could join me. I said okay. We talked for a while and then I got up from my desk and I guess she noticed I was limping. She asked what I had done to my foot, and I explained what happened. When the day auditor came on, we both went for breakfast. We started talking about sex. She asked me if I was able to get it on, a thought I hadn't dwelled on until then. The doctors had assured me that I could perform but to tell the truth I didn't believe them. Anyway we did get it on and I had the wildest sex ever. After getting undressed she caressed my shortened leg and this turned both of us on. She went down on me and soon I couldn't hold back. I'm happy to say that this went on for three days.

This girl changed my outlook. For every girl turned off by the loss of a limb there are, I'm sure, the same number that are not.—*Name and address withheld*

* * *

Concerning H.K.'s letter in your November issue, I suppose I would qualify as one "turned on" by orthopedically handicapped girls, not specifically amputees.

This has not been a lifelong attraction for me, but rather one fostered as a result of my late wife's becoming handicapped. As a result of cancer surgery, she lost use of her right leg, although she retained the limb. The last several years of her life were spent mainly in a wheelchair, since she never became very adept with crutches.

These last years were the happiest of a very successful marriage. Part of this was due to the sharing and understanding between us necessary for her rehabilitation to a very full and active life. However, part was also due to a marvelous enrichment of our sexual experience. I never ceased to be thrilled when lifting her in or out of her chair. I did this, when we were alone, long after any physical necessity had passed. Her feet, soft and uncallused from disuse, became close to a fetish for me. Helping her undress before bed became for us the center of foreplay.

I have begun to date again and am convinced that any future meaningful relationship in my life must be with a handicapped girl. I always wondered whether the wiring diagram of my psyche was particularly unique in this respect—after reading several months of Monopede Mania, I rather doubt it. Therefore H.K., take heart, there are a few of us guys around.—*Name and address withheld*

* * *

I have followed your correspondence on one-legged girls with more than passing interest because I am what your column has chosen to call a monopede. I must say that I find some of the letters a trifle unreal and after ten years without my left leg I cannot agree with the woman who wrote that she does not consider her amputation a handicap. I was just eighteen when I had my leg removed and up till then had played hockey and tennis as well as enjoying ice-skating, all of which stopped overnight. Although I gradually came to terms with my one-leggedness and can now swim, water-ski and dance quite well I still miss the more active games.

It also seems odd to me that all the letters talk about girls going about on crutches all the time, which I do not think is the case if one looks around. While I would be the first one to agree that it is much easier to walk with crutches than with an artificial limb, the trouble is that when using crutches your arms and hands are not really free to do anything other than help you move around. Because I have a house and two young children to look after I simply have to wear the artificial limb. Because I have always found the modern artificial leg very difficult to handle, I only use it when I go out, so that I look more normal, while in the house I find it much more mobile to use a simple peg leg. I have had this specially made because I do find the standard peg leg with its ugly foot to be quite grotesque. Mine is a flesh-colored, tapered hollow tube with a cup foot which I can usually wear with tights or stockings. I often wear it at dances and functions when I can wear a long dress.

Another thing which none of your correspondents ever seem to mention is stump care. Unless I bathe, cream, and powder my stump three or four times a day I cannot continue to wear an artificial limb, and I also have to sleep with an elastic sock on my stump.

The letters are correct in their indication that there are a lot of men about who are unusually attracted to girls who have lost a leg, as I found out after I had got over the shock of the amputation. I found out most of them preferred me to use crutches when I went out with them and, of course, my husband is one of these. Even now after nearly eight years of marriage he is always telling me and showing me he is excited by my one-leggedness. He too prefers me not to wear an artificial limb and in the evening when the children are in bed and I know we are staying in I unstrap whichever of my legs I am wearing. When I do this I always wear tights which I have made to fit my stump and more often than not my husband sits beside me and caresses my nylon-clad stump which greatly excites him as well as being enjoyable for me.

He is always thinking up ways of enhancing my one-leggedness that draw attention to my stump, which is about nine inches long and therefore shows below most of my clothes. My own particular favorite is a pair of black bell-bottomed slacks with cuffs that I have altered by shortening the left leg and putting a matching cuff on it so that my stump, which I clad in a sheer black stump sock, just shows. His favorite, which I did not like at first, because I thought it rather sadistic, grew out of his desire to have me wear platform boots. I found I could not handle them while wearing my artificial leg, although I was fine with crutches, so he cut the foot off my left boot, sewed the end up and put an extra gusset in the leg part so that it could be zipped on my stump. He asked me to wear these with hot pants and although I was not too keen I tried it by myself one night while he was out. As I stood in front of the mirror in yellow hot pants with my stump tightly encased in brown leather to match the boot on the other leg I suddenly felt quite fruity. So much so that I stayed as I was and when my husband came home he gave me a night to remember.

We have often discussed why he should be so affected by my one-leggedness, and he says it arouses feelings of tenderness and affection for me. I think *Penthouse* has discovered an important area of sexual attraction which is much more widespread than anyone supposes and I hope you continue your good work.—*H.P., Stockport, Lancashire, England*

* * *

Having acquired several recent copies of *Penthouse* I was surprised and delighted to find what appears to be a long-established correspondence on female amputees.

I think my interest started when I used to see a rather plain girl wearing a black footless stump type of artificial leg on my school journey every morning when I was about fourteen. In spite of her plainness I found myself looking forward to seeing her each day and then, on one particular day, I caught her without her stump and wearing crutches. I felt a thrill go up my spine as she came into view and was excited about it for several days afterwards. Later she reverted to wearing the stump and my excitement was never the same again. I did not try to make her acquaintance for fear of ridicule from my schoolmates for trying to date a crippled girl.

Shortly after this incident with the crutches, on my homeward journey, I saw a really beautiful amputee girl standing at the bus stop. She had a single black enamel crutch and it appeared that her left leg had been amputated at the hip. She was immaculately dressed and made up and wore a shoe with a heel of about two and one half inches. I was wildly excited and nearly ejaculated, but never saw her again.

Since those early days I have seen many female amputees and have found that I am only mildly interested in those who wear artificial limbs, but as the crudeness of the prosthesis increases so does my excitement. I still find that a one-legged girl with crutches gives me the greatest sexual stimulation possible and a pair of crutches is slightly more arousing than a single crutch followed closely by a peg leg.

I have never had the opportunity of meeting one of these fascinating girls socially, and whenever I see one I usually have to go away and masturbate. I have tried to analyze what it is about one-legged girls but so far

I have been unsuccessful. Possibly it is curiosity about the site of the amputation which, unless the girl is using a prosthesis, is invariably about the skirt line.

As far as the girls themselves are concerned, while commiserating with them on their misfortune, can I appeal to them to write to *Penthouse* and give a good deal of sexual pleasure to men like myself?—*R.P., Twickenham, England*

* * *

Over a year ago my husband showed me the letters in *Penthouse* from and about female amputees, and since that time I have read them all faithfully with a mixture of feelings: gratitude to *Penthouse* for dragging us one-leggers and our sister one-armers out from the unmentionable class, and pleased surprise to learn that men find us especially sexy, even though I am sorry to realize that I do not qualify for the really sexy sisterhood because I have no stump. Except for that disastrous southwest pelvic area I am not otherwise unattractive.

I could perhaps qualify for associate membership in the sisterhood by virtue of my considerable virtuosity as a hopper—and my breasts *do* bounce nicely when I hop, even though I have no stump to wave enticingly. It all stems from my two-legged girlhood and my passion for dancing, which has carried over into my one-legged womanhood the ballerina's fierce devotion to physical discipline and her unquenchable need to dance. So I dance, with only my husband an occasional onlooker, and keep in superb physical condition, a true monopede.

Since an artificial limb is of little use without a stump to propel it, we stumpless one-leggers, if we wish to use our hands while we move about, must hop. I can carry two filled cups of coffee across the room without spilling and without rattling the lamps. When I use my crutches I become a three-legger, able to take four-foot strides, and I can outwalk any two-legger, male or female.

My amputation was a traumatic experience, of course, followed by deep depression, but after this reaction there was a swift change to a determination to compensate.

I have done this not only by mobilizing all of my physical and intellectual resources, but also by resolving to be the best sex partner my disabilities will allow. My husband, who never knew me as a two-legger, is a strong, understanding, and compassionate man, and with him I am what must be the world's happiest woman. I suspect I have my amputation to thank for finding myself and my true potential, and if I had the choice to trade any of this to be whole again, I certainly wouldn't.

I enjoy reading the letters and identifying with the one-legged heroines and their sexual adventures, even though none of them is stumpless like me, and I recognize that many of them must be fantasies themselves. I also appreciate what so many of your correspondents remark about the unusual sexuality of one-legged women. We have that drive to compensate for our sadly damaged self-images, and we try harder! I feel as though I should contribute a few sexual advantages of my own, but all I can perceive in the way of sexual advantage in being a stumpless one-legged woman is the ability to perform in a few positions impossible for any other female. This adds to variety, but I would cheerfully trade this small gain for a good leg or even a stump.

A little exhibitionism must be required for a one-legged woman to write about herself to a men's magazine. If I had a stump and if I were just a wee bit younger, I would try to overcome your addiction to those beautiful two-leggers, and send you my picture. I hope some nice one-legger does—a lot of us would cheer.—*Name and address withheld*

* * *

Thank you for *Penthouse* and the Forum letter section. Some of the views expressed have helped me greatly. Just allowing issues like Monopede Mania to be voiced is a help to a lot of people.

I feel that amputee women are *people* too. Although it's nice, a mere passion for a certain part of the anatomy (or lack of it) is a solitary thing. What I'm saying is that just because a man finds the type of woman he is attracted to, they don't necessarily have a relationship. I think many men are so preoccupied with finding the "right woman," that they don't stop to ask themselves, "What is she getting out of this?" I think this is why women feel that they are being treated as objects.

I am an open and sincere guy who likes women in general and amputee women in particular. I have many friends, but I always like to make new ones. I'm sure there are many other men who feel the same way. To any woman who feels she is lonely because of a handicap, such as H.K. in November Forum, I would say, "Don't lock yourself at home, come out and meet us."—*J.C. (name withheld), Los Angeles, Calif.*

* * *

Is Carol E. of Dallas, Texas (December), by any chance kidding when she asks if many men feel attracted to female amputees? Not only should she research the columns of Penthouse Forum for every month of 1972 —except July—to get an idea of the variety and intensity of men's interest in female amputees, but I can personally assure her there is an unknown but large number of us who feel that a woman's stump is a fascinating asset to her desirability, while possession of two stumps would, in algebraic parlance, raise the factor exponentially!

I have been married for years to a one-armed girl who still bewitches me. I have also had the pleasure of knowing intimately more than one stimulating stump, and I am not unaware of the charms of a double ration at the same helping. There are many eligible young men who would love the company of a legless chick not only in bed but in all activities. As I recollect, in the October issue you published a letter from a New Jersey group called Ampals formed to encourage social contact between amputees and non-amputees of the opposite sex. I am sure they would be able to help Carol feel reassured of her desirability as a woman, and at the same time gladden the hearts of many of their male members. At 26 years of age and with her stated combination of two stumps and 46-25-36 figure, Carol could have her choice of men, 18 to 80, rich or poor, he-man or bookworm and any size, shape or type she wanted.—*M.W.W. (name and address withheld), West 42nd St., New York, N.Y.*

* * *

Your reader Carol E. asks what we think of making it with a legless chick and if many men are attracted to female amputees. I cannot answer for many men, as I have not taken an extensive poll. But we have six male commercial artists in our studio, and here is the result of my own small survey.

One of my colleagues is only interested in perfectly-shaped girls. Another prefers very obese women, while my boss really digs girls with permanent tattoos. One man likes his girls to wear leg braces. Two of us have been involved with amputee girls. The other fellow had known a girl who'd lost a leg and another who'd lost an arm.

Since adolescence, I have had a preference for amputees. I have known, to varying degrees, a girl missing one arm above the elbow, a girl who lost both legs below the knees, a girl who lost both legs near the hips and a girl who is missing most of her fingers. Though I have a preference for amputees, I do not consider it a fetish in that I enjoy other women as well.

Carol shouldn't have too much difficulty meeting fellows at the beach or a singles bar if she wears some provocative outfits which show off her stumps. When you haven't got it, flaunt it, so to speak! I've seen two girl amputees in the same location at different times, one in slacks and wooden leg hiding all, the other in a mini-micro on crutches attracting lots of whistles. It depends on the girl. Good luck, Carol!—*R.L. (name and address withheld), New York, N.Y.*

* * *

Several weeks ago my roommate was given a copy of *Penthouse* magazine with readers' letters entitled Monopede Mania. Since we are both amputees she called and told me about it. I was able to acquire several back issues and was quite interested in your readers' comments on this subject. Then I decided to write about my own experiences.

I lost both feet in an accident some time ago and, as can be imagined, was terribly depressed; doubly so since I was a professional dancer. However, life must go on and mine did. I was fitted with artificial feet and went to work with a large insurance firm. I shared an apartment with a co-worker and gradually became very content with my new work. An advantage which a foot amputee has over other types of amputees is that we can walk on our stumps, and this I learned to do well.

I had formed the habit of removing my artificial feet when I got home from work if there were no visitors. One evening I was alone when the doorbell rang. I was wearing hot pants and an old shirt, so the man at the door, who was a salesman, couldn't help seeing my legs. When he noticed my bare stumps, he got an immediate and obvious erection. He became flustered and quickly left. I was perplexed by his behavior but didn't think too much about it until a similar incident occurred several weeks later.

During that time I had been dating a friend of my roommate's boyfriend and decided to see what his reaction to my stumps would be. Several days later we had dinner alone in the apartment. After the meal I mixed some drinks, excused myself, and went into the bedroom to change. I removed my feet and put on a very short skirt and sexy blouse, and then padded back into the living room on my stumps. His eyes bugged out when he saw me and he couldn't take them off my legs. I sat on the far end of the couch and stretched my legs out so that they touched his thigh. He began stroking my stumps and we both became very aroused. I reached over and unzipped his fly and gently massaged his penis with the tips of my stumps. This was more than he could stand, and he took me into the bedroom for a very passionate evening of lovemaking.

I have discussed this with other women amputees and

have found that sexual attraction for amputated limbs is almost universal. Most commonly, men say they are attracted to women for the usual reasons, but that a stump is extremely sexy, and being with a woman with an amputated leg heightens their sexual enjoyment. I am no longer sensitive about my feet and sometimes emphasize not having any. I had a pair of boots made that have small walking surfaces similar to flat ice-skate blades. When I wear these, it is certainly obvious that I don't have any feet. I also have a pair of boots that end in wide, round wooden pegs. And a man once gave me a pair of shoes with six-inch stiletto heels and I had special feet made so that I could wear them. I would not try to walk far in them but can get around well enough and men enjoy seeing me wear them.

We are hoping that *Penthouse* will begin printing photos of amputee girls. It would have great appeal to men, and would be a tremendous morale booster to amputee women everywhere who would learn that their amputations are a sexual advantage.—*K.A., Venice, Calif.*

* * *

As a lifelong devotee of above-the-knee amputees, I was surprised and delighted to read the many letters from and about female amputees.

I have a special interest in the subject because my wife is an amputee—her left leg is amputated at the hip. Since she lacks any semblance of a stump she is forced to use crutches for locomotion. She is an inveterate hopper and is able to perform most household chores on one leg, without crutches. When she has to carry things from place to play she sits on a high stool on which I have installed a set of casters; thus, the carrying problem is solved.

A one-legged woman, from the male viewpoint, is an erotic thing. As a male I am especially aroused by the sight of a female monopede wearing slacks or a pantsuit; the pinned-up empty leg really gets to me. As my wife knows of my peculiar desire, and because she herself prefers to wear her pant leg folded and pinned up at the waistband, I am in a state of perpetual ecstasy.

I wish to thank *Penthouse* for publishing the many letters regarding female amputees. It is surprising that so many people have an interest in the subject. I will say quite frankly that a two-legged woman no longer has any appeal for me whatsoever. If I had not the good fortune to meet and marry the one-legged girl of my dreams, I would be, to this day, an unhappy celibate.
—*W.S., Tewksbury, Mass.*

* * *

Living the past five years without legs, the result of a car wreck when I was eighteen, has not exactly been an enjoyable experience. On the other hand, it has not been the overwhelming tragedy I expected. With my wheelchair, a car equipped with full hand controls, and stump boots, I have retained my mobility.

The primary reason I have been able to be happy and content is that I am married to a wonderful man whom I met after becoming legless. He is, naturally, one of those men who are fascinated by female amputees and gets a great deal of pleasure from my two short stumps. I say naturally because, considering the importance of a woman's physical attractiveness to a man, I can't imagine a man voluntarily dating and marrying a legless women unless he has a thing about her stumps. I know that my husband was initially attracted to me because of my lack of legs but, as time passed, a much more substantial basis for our relationship has developed. Now we truly love each other and my being without legs is only a physical characteristic that is sexually useful.

My attitude toward my husband's liking my stumps has also changed with time. At first, before we were married, I was repelled by his wanting to fondle and hold them. To me my stumps represented a painful and traumatic episode in my life that I didn't care to have emphasized, and the idea that they were sexually stimulating to a man was distasteful to me. Besides, I had the other more conventional female parts that he was more than welcome to explore and fondle all he wanted. Gradually, I got over my reluctance to his use of my stumps for his own pleasure. When we make love, I hold him tightly with my arms, grip his hips with my stumps, and am truly grateful that some men do prefer a woman without legs.—*Name and address withheld*

* * *

Several years ago I had the pleasure of dating a girl who had lost both her left arm and her left leg. We met in the fall, and dated throughout the winter, but I never saw her wearing anything but slacks and long sleeves. She always wore an artificial arm and leg and I was not allowed to see or touch either. In fact, I never got much farther than a good-night kiss.

When warm weather came, I wanted to go to the beach, but she, being shy and self-conscious about her appearance, would not even think of it. Finally, toward the end of the summer, she agreed to go, but only on the condition that we go to a beach she knew of where we could be completely alone. Of course I agreed.

When I picked her up, she was wearing a long-sleeved bare-midriff blouse and hip-hugger blue jeans. She was not wearing her artificial arm, and the sight of her empty sleeve excited me as much as the sight of the end of the peg leg which showed from the end of the leg of her jeans. It looked like a piece of pipe with a crutch tip on the end.

She directed me to a pier at the lake, where there was a speedboat tied up. It was her father's, and I helped her into the driver's seat on the right. After we were well away from the shore, she asked me to hold the wheel, and she went to the stern of the boat and asked me not to turn around. In a few minutes she took the wheel again, but was no longer wearing the peg leg.

The empty sleeve was exciting enough, but the empty pant leg almost drove me wild. I hoped she wouldn't notice my condition, for I was sure she'd be offended.

When we reached the beach, which was inaccessible except by boat, she held the boat in position in shallow water while I tied it up to a small tree just past the beach. Then I spread a blanket and went back to help her out of the boat. She refused to be carried, so I helped her hop slowly through the shallows to the blanket.

Once there, she sat for some time, not talking, just staring out at the water. Then she asked me to close my eyes and lie back. I did, and after a few minutes she was lying across my chest—without the blouse! She was wearing a knit bikini top which barely contained her large breasts. When she began rubbing my chest with her arm stump, I though I'd go crazy!

Later, I suggested we go into the water. She looked reluctant, but finally agreed, and asked me to help her stand. While I held her up, she let the blue jeans drop, and asked me to lift her up so she could get her foot free. The bikini bottom was little more than a G-string, and her short leg stump was beautiful!

I helped her hop down to the water, where we splashed around for a while. Then, coming out of the water, her bikini started to fall off! It seems it was meant for sunning, not swimming, and soaked up too much water. By this time she must have been pretty horny too, because she seemed unconcerned, and when we reached the blanket she took it off! As I had suspected, the bottom of it only fit because she had shaved. Wow!

After the fun and games, she asked me to get her peg leg from the boat. It turned out to be a stump socket with a perforated metal tube attached. I strapped in on for her, and we went for a long walk in the nude.

Needless to say, we spent many days at that beach. But the following winter, she moved to the other end of the country, and I never saw her again.—*Name and address withheld*

* * *

In your readers' discussions about their sexual preference for one-legged women, nothing has been said of the fact that this preference is something that one is either born with or not born with. It is not something that one acquires later in life as a developing preference. According to some psychiatrist friends of mine, the preference may remain dormant for years until awakened by visual exposure to a one-legged woman.

In my own case, the "awakening" occurred when I was about thirteen or fourteen. One of the customers on my paper route was an attractive young housewife who had lost her left leg. When I made my weekly collections she would greet me at the door standing on her one leg and leaning on a single crutch. I found it strangely fascinating to see just one leg below her knee-length dress and I looked forward to my stop at her house. But I was especially intrigued by the way she propped up her purse with her stump while she paid me.

One day when I called at her house for my weekly paper money she didn't come to the door, but called to me to come in and wait a moment in the living room while she finished a telephone conversation.

Just then a car pulled up in the driveway and the one-legged housewife ended her phone conversation with the announcement that her husband had arrived. She grabbed her crutch and limped to the door to greet him. I sat watching from the living room, completely ignored.

The instant he closed the door, her husband dropped his attaché case and embraced his wife tightly in a hug which she returned with equal passion. As they embraced they murmured all sorts of endearing phrases about how much they missed each other, and kissed each other repeatedly. I felt embarrassed watching all this, but they evidently thought they were alone and didn't even glance into the living room.

After about five minutes of this, the husband slipped his wife's crutch out from under her arm and leaned her crutch against the hall table so he could embrace her even more tightly without her crutch getting in the way. Their tight embrace kept the wife from losing her balance on just one leg, and she took little hops on her foot to keep up with her husband as they swayed around in their hugging and kissing session.

As they stood there, the husband's hands began to roam down his wife's back to around her hips. I watched dumbfounded as he slowly started to slide her dress up until he had it bunched up above her hips. Suddenly I saw the back of her white panties and, of still greater interest to me, her stump. Her left leg had been amputated midway between her knee and hip, leaving her with half a thigh as her stump. As I watched her bare stump, she swung it up and began rubbing it against her husband's pant leg. He responded by fondling his wife's stump with one hand while he clutched her tightly with his other hand. I was afraid to breathe lest they discover I was watching.

Suddenly the husband slipped down his wife's panties and let them drop around her one foot. She giggled as her husband lifted her momentarily to free her foot from the panties. Then, with her dress still above her hips, she hopped around and faced me for the first time. She stiffened and screamed, "My God! The paper boy is still here! He saw everything!" It was my first front-view look.

For a few seconds I gaped like an idiot at her exposed patch of pubic hair until she recovered her senses and swung her stump up to cover the patch. She frantically pushed her dress down and hopped out of sight as fast as her one leg could carry her. Her husband paid me and gave me a $5.00 tip with the observation that he was sure I wasn't the kind of kid to go blabbing things all over the neighborhood. The wife was too embarrassed to ever face me again. But she had awakened me to the strange sexual power that a one-legged woman could exert over me.

I found sex with a two-legged girl enjoyable but always wondered how much more pleasurably different it might be if my mate had a stump on one side of her body. Eventually I found out, and I was not disappointed. More power to you, *Penthouse*, in lighting some of the enshadowed areas of our sexual world.—*Name and address withheld*

* * *

Count me another aficionado of female amputees. My

interest dates back as far as I can remember. My fascinations and fantasies coincide with those of many of your correspondents. However, I have a thought to add, which I have never seen in print to this date.

When I finally had my first affair with an amputee, I discovered a virility in myself which I never suspected I possessed. I also discovered that the purely physical gratification I experienced was because the one-legged lady could assume positions no two-legged woman could. Because of the particular way in which I am built, I had not been able to find a perfect fit in copulation which produced the ecstasies which the one-legged lady was able to provide.

I wonder, therefore, if the desire for amputees isn't preprogrammed into the psyche to coincide with the physical structure of the individual? Nature can be awesomely sophisticated, as well as too often misunderstood. Perhaps other so-called deviant desires can be analogously explained.—*Name and address withheld*

* * *

The series in the Forum about amuptees is of much interest to me; I have never met anyone who is turned on by an amputee the way I am, so I am surprised to find out that there are so many of us. I think that a number of escapades in these letters occurred only in the mind of the letter writer, but I can recognize the true interest that is shown.

Most of the writers haven't mentioned any real early interest in amputees, so I thought that I would tell you that my interest goes back as far as I can remember. Even though I am heterosexual, the sight of a one-legged man on crutches will give me an erection, and this was true even when I was a small child. Long before I reached puberty, my mother would take me downtown shopping with her, and occasionally we would see a one-legged man. This would give me an erection as I walked along the sidewalk, and I didn't know why (actually, I still don't know why). Once, I saw a legless man with some sort of leather boots strapped to his thigh stumps walking along the sidewalk on his stumps. This, too, gave me a powerful erection. Considering my age at the time, the sight of a naked woman would probably have had no effect on me.

Once I reached puberty, the thought of a female leg amputee entered my mind, and this would seem to be about the greatest sex object that a person such as myself could have. Unfortunately, I have never met one and have only seen two or three, but the sight of one is enough to make me breathe hard and break out in a sweat.

If a one-legged female thinks that she is not quite sexy enough on crutches, (for sexual effect, artificial legs should be avoided like the plague) she should learn to walk using only *one* crutch. This would leave one hand free for carrying things and opening doors, and would make her even more attractive than a two-crutched woman.—*J.S. (name withheld), Kansas City, Mo.*

* * *

Having seen some of your articles on female amputees I felt that I should write of my own experiences. I would like to preface that portion of my life with some added information. Before my husband and I were married he asked me to wear what I considered to be rather unusual underwear. For him I began to wear long, black seamed stockings and garter belts; also corselettes, half bras, girdles, and other articles of this nature. At first I thought his requests were very strange, yet I came to enjoy wearing these garments to please him. It added an extra element to our sex life and I continue to do it now that we are married.

Last year, I lost my leg above the knee in an automobile accident. I suffered the same fear that most amputees experience, that their sexual appeal is diminished or destroyed. However, my husband was wonderful at this time, a constant source of encouragement and inspiration in my deep depression. When I returned home my fears sometimes plagued me as my stump healed. Nevertheless, I began to wear a nylon on my good leg and dressed as I always had. To my great surprise and pleasure my husband became even more sexually excited than in the past when he saw me dressed this way. He even asked me to wear a stocking on the short stump of my thigh. He further requested that I wear my artificial limb only when he is not home. I can hardly satisfy his desires now and while the discomfort and awkwardness of being an amputee are almost unbearable, I am fortunate that I have my husband to turn to for the reassurance I need.

I now move about the house on my crutches dressed in a miniskirt and seamed stocking with my stump just visible to continually please my husband in any way I can. I thought that other women in my situation would be cheered by the news that they will be appealing to men and may even capitalize on their handicap by doing as I do. Thank you for being so open in your choice of articles and allowing me the chance to write.—*Name and address withheld*

* * *

For a long while I've been reading articles about love and women amputees. When are you going to print an article dealing with love and men amputees?

When I returned from Vietnam minus two legs, I thought it was the end of the world, much less my sex life. The girl I had been engaged to before leaving for Nam a year and a half earlier Dear-Johned me when she heard the news. I was down and out. While confined to a V.A. hospital back in the States, I couldn't see why I should continue living. I thought no one would ever consider dating me, much less living with me.

One afternoon, when I thought no one else was around, I indulged in some self-pity. My nurse, an attractive blond in her early twenties, happened to be checking out my medication at the time. She inquired what was wrong: I told her that that day was the day I was supposed to be married. She displayed a great deal of compassion. I never suspected that it could have been anything more serious, for who could love a man without legs?

The next day the nurse removed the bandages from my stumps. Was it my imagination? Was she just removing my bandages, or was she actually caressing my stumps? I glanced at her—she smiled. As she continued to feel up my stumps I developed an intense erection. I knew then that I wanted to make love to her—not so much with my penis, as with my stumps.

Our love developed quickly. She bathed my stumps daily—it gave her an excellent excuse to finger them. When our relationship developed further, she gave me what I consider to be the climactic experience of my sex career. She sucked my stumps, gently plying each bump with her soft, sensuous tongue. She loved to rub her crotch on my stumps, and occasionally bite them! Needless to say, we were soon married, and have since made out very well.

I am not ashamed of my stumps. They have helped me win the woman of my dreams.—*Name and address withheld*

* * *

As a handicapped girl, I would like to comment on the many male letters extolling the sexuality of amputee girls that have appeared in Forum in recent months. Like the girls they have written about, I too am handicapped, but in a very different way. I had polio as a child and as a result, I wear two long leg braces and use crutches to walk—and without them I am helpless. With so many men apparently "turned on" by legless girls and by their stumps, I wonder if there are other men who are similarly excited by girls wearing braces or using crutches? After all, we have legs!

As a young girl, in my twenties, attractive, well-built (36-24-36), who, thus far, has been completely unapproached by the male sex (due, I feel, to the braces and crutches) I am extremely interested. If there are, I'm sure there are many handicapped girls in braces and crutches, who would like to know! I would for one!—*H. K. (name withheld), Brooklyn, N.Y.*

* * *

I only started reading *Penthouse*, and have been interested to see the letters concerning female amputees. I am a thirty-two-year-old college graduate, and one of those men who find women amputees especially attractive. It was a relief to learn that this feeling is apparently much more common than I had supposed.

I date regularly and my taste in women varies considerably, but I would prefer an amputee. I have often hoped to meet an amputee socially, but have thus far not been so fortunate. If I found I had little in common with a woman, I would certainly not want to continue the relationship just because she was an amputee. But if we did prove to be otherwise compatible, the fact that she was an amputee would certainly represent a very delightful extra.

The knowledge that many men share this "mania" eliminates the nagging feeling that there was somehow something abnormal or wrong about it. Your magazine is to be commended for bringing such subjects out into the open.—*J.B., Washington, D.C.*

* * *

14

Autofellatio

I would disagree with J.B.W. of Washington, who in describing his performance of autofellation (October) claims that the act would be difficult unless the performer was "slim with a longish upper body."

When I was a student at Bennington College, Vt. a pudgy boy from Dartmouth used to perform autofellatio at our dorm parties. He sat cross-legged in yoga fashion and simply bent forward and sucked himself.—*Mrs. N.M.K. (name and address withheld), Boston, Pa.*

* * *

Your correspondent, B.D.B. (July) doubts the possibility of autofellatio: I have been a performer for the last 40 years. I agree that it is not physically possible for all men, as you need to be slim with a longish upper body. I started the habit when I was about 14 because I was scared of girls.

I found that after a hot bath I could sit on a chair, bend forward and wrap my arms under my thighs and pull. Then my penis would rise up right into my mouth.

Now I'm over 50, it gets a little more difficult. First, I need a hot bath to relax the back muscles, then I lie on the bed with my head toward the pillow, throw my legs over till they hit the wall, and then wrap my arms round my thighs and pull. To accomplish this feat may require two-three weeks of practice, because the back muscles won't relax sufficiently at first, but persistence pays off in the end.—*J.B.W. (name and address withheld), Washington, D.C.*

* * *

15

Potpourri

* * *

Have you ever tried Alka Seltzer sex? It is really great! After my girl friend's vagina is moist, she inserts an Alka Seltzer tablet and when the juices begin to flow, the tablet begins to foam. The heat and tingling sensation is very pleasurable for both of us.

Another girl friend also likes the sensation we get from the Alka Seltzer but she prefers to quarter the tablet before insertion.

After a stroke or two the tablet is pushed aside so the only thing felt is the very nice sensation.—*F.W., Dallas, Texas*

* * *

I am very interested in the *Penthouse* letters dealing with fetishim and the liking for disabled girls.

I have always been attracted to women who wear very strong glasses, and I have known quite a number over the years. The bane of my life is contact lenses and I often wish I could have lived before they were invented.

This fascination is so strong and deep-rooted that I find it useless to try and ignore it. Some time ago I had some glasses made with tremendously thick lenses and I masturbate while putting these round magazine covers showing seductive-looking girls. The effect is terrific and after considerable foreplay I achieve a fabulous orgasm and go into deep sleep for about an hour.

However, with contact lenses making thick glasses increasingly rare, I have become interested in girls with braces, surgical boots, or who have had a leg amputated. The sensation of stroking a girl's thigh while she is wearing a leg brace is fantastic and I love the contrast between the soft warm flesh and the cold hard metal.—*F. G., London, England*

* * *

I just discovered the most far-out turn-on that anybody has heard of. Actually, *it* discovered me when I broke up with my first girl. She was the only chick I'd ever known, and getting to meet and pick up other girls was a problem. About the only thing I could do for my sex life was jerk off. I tried it every way I knew of, or my buddies recommended, but it was still the same old thing.

One day I was getting a tan in my backyard and a fly landed on the inside of my thigh. It took a few steps —and those were little steps—and I had a hard-on to bust my gut. I twitched my leg to get the fly off, but moving my muscles made me hornier. I started thinking about Debbie, my ex-girl, and I had to go indoors and jerk off. After I relieved myself I went back outside and it happened again. But instead of giving myself a hand-job, I lay there thinking about Debbie. The fly crawled up and down my leg, and as the sun beat down on me, I slowly came inside my shorts.

That night I had a fantastic wet dream about some fuzzy thing huge, muscular (like Debbie's pussy), covering me and rubbing me to a climax. I had a terrific explosion.

When I woke up an idea hit me like a bullet: catch a

jar of flies, turn them loose in a locked room, and let them itch me to my cock's content. I collected about fifty big, hairy buggers and took them to my bathroom. I shut the door and windows, took off my clothes, rubbed my cock with honey, stretched out on the floor, and set the flies free. They crawled and hopped and danced all over my appetizing cock. I discovered I had more sensuous skin than I thought. I came three times that afternoon, and it was almost better than sinking into a wet quim. I only wished that some chick would've sucked and licked me off afterwards. When I do pick up a new woman, I hope she'll want to do the flies with me.—*J.P., address withheld*

* * *

After reading your magazine for many years, I've decided to write in and tell you of my new experience. Recently my wife and I discovered a new sensation. I find it very exciting to position myself over our acquarium so that my genitals dangle in the water.

If I hold quite still, the fish come up to them and start nibbling. It is quite a sensuous feeling and very arousing. If there are any others who have done this, I would like them to write in and tell what they think about this new adventure.—*B.P., Colorado Springs, Colo.*

* * *

I'll bet not many people can top this for weirdness— I have a sneezing fetish. For as long as I can remember, sneezing and watching other people sneeze has turned me on.

As a young adolescent and teenager I spent hours in my room (under the pretense of doing homework) tickling the inside of my nose to make myself sneeze, watching myself in the mirror, and then masturbating —reaching a climax maybe five times in a twenty-minute period.

I've been married for seven years now and have a

very conventional and satisfying sex life. I've never told my husband (or anyone) about my fetish. Often while having sexual intercourse I fantasize about a man sneezing. It always brings me to a more intense climax when I'm in the mood for sex, or gets me in the mood when I'm not. Somewhere in my mind, I must have the violent discharge of a sneeze mixed up with the male ejaculation. My favorite fantasy is that of a man masturbating and having to sneeze just as he's ejaculating.

In conjunction with this fetish, things like handkerchiefs and the size of people's noses have a special erotic significance to me. Whenever my husband has a head cold, I'm in a state of sexual excitement until he gets well. He's probably mystified by my unexplained ardor.

I would be curious to hear about anyone else who has a similar fetish—am I really all alone in the world? Or maybe someone has a theory on how such a fetish might develop.—*S. B. (address withheld).*

* * *

After reading your magazine for many months, I just had to write and tell the world that *Penthouse* can improve a person's self-esteem much more than months of costly, weekly sessions with a psychiatrist. Your understanding attitude towards readers who are excited by amputees, spankings, enemas, etc., has made me realize that my own sexual behavior, while perhaps unusual, is not wrong—and certainly not "perverted and sick" (as even my closest of friends thought when I confided in them).

My wife and I fell in love in high school, but due to the extreme diminutiveness of my penis (she still lovingly refers to it as "her little pencil eraser") we were never able to make love in the conventional manner. I was apprehensive about oral sex as my wife wore braces at the time, and although I didn't have much to lose, I was afraid it would feel like trying to ball a hole in a screen door. Then, the week before our wedding night, in the heat of passion, I suggested that I put my organ in her ear. This was the start of years of ecstasy for both of us. She says it makes her feel closer to me than I could ever imagine possible, and even after she had her braces removed she still preferred the old *auditory coitus*. And I must confess, so do I. Naturally, I am extremely gentle and careful, for as you've probably heard, "Nothing should be put into the ear that is smaller than your elbow." Our technique has the added advantage of eliminating the need for contraceptives, although my wife says she thinks she may be pregnant, so I'm not absolutely sure on this point.—*Name withheld, Austin, Texas*

* * *

I have never written to a magazine, but your recent pictorial *Mirage* (September 1974) has moved me to do so.

I am a nineteen-year-old coed here, and I was introduced to the glories of female love by an older friend when we were sixteen. We still get together occasionally, but she is married now with two small children so our relationship has cooled considerably over the past few years.

When I first came to school (I am from the Chicago area) I was very apprehensive about a lot of things: grades, friends, guys, but most of all—my lesbian love life. I was afraid that I wouldn't be able to find any willing partners for myself. How wrong I was.

I moved into a dorm during New Student Week. I was all moved in by the afternoon, however, my roommate had not shown up. Then, there was a knock on the door and there stood the most beautiful blond I had ever seen in my life. (I had better mention right here that for obvious reasons I cannot use my real name. Other students can sometimes be very cruel.) She said, "Hi! You must be Jan." I said, "That's right." She told me her name was Lynn, and I helped her move her things in.

I couldn't keep my eyes off of her. She was gorgeous! She was wearing the shortest cut-offs I had ever seen, and they served to accent her perfectly formed legs, which she kept slightly separated during our conversation. My eyes kept wandering to the "V" of her crotch. She was also wearing a tiny pink halter-top, which barely contained the fullness of her breasts. Her nipples showed plainly through the material. We finally decided to go out for some dinner, but I couldn't wait for nightfall to come, so I could have Lynn alone again.

By the time we arrived back in our room, it was getting to be pretty late, and I was getting hot! Every time Lynn took a step, her tanned breasts jiggled in the tiny top. I told her I was going to take a shower and get ready for bed. I hurried through it as quickly as I could and returned to the room in my robe. I found that Lynn had also undressed, and was wrapped in a towel that barely reached below her pubic area.

I must say that I consider myself a good-looking girl. I was a high school cheerleader, and I have a good figure with full breasts and shapely legs. I noticed that she seemed as interested in looking at me as I was in her. I sat on my bed and started to apply baby powder to my shoulders. Suddenly, Lynn came over and took the bottle out of my hand. She said, "Here, let me do that for you. Why don't you slip your robe down?" I slipped the robe from my shoulders and lay on my stomach on the bed. She started to smooth the baby powder into my back. My heart was racing from the soft touch of her delicate fingers. Slowly, she pulled the robe completely away to reveal my smooth buttocks. She delicately squeezed them between her fingers. She ran her fingers down the insides of my legs and I thought a flood was going to pour from my pussy.

"Turn over," she whispered, and I did. She gasped as she saw for the first time my beautiful breasts. First she massaged them. Then, in a flash, her mouth was all over them kissing, sucking, licking, biting. She slid out of her towel—and it was my turn to gasp. Her creamy-skinned breasts were tipped by two rosy nipples that stood out like little pebbles just waiting to be sucked. I nearly lost my breath when I saw her silky-blond pubic hair. Her hands sank to my thighs and she gently separated them. She plunged her sleek middle finger into me, and I grabbed for her breasts with all the passion in me. Finally, she lowered her head to my vaginal lips, and her licking drove me into ecstasy. I knew I wanted to do the same for her, and I pulled her crotch to my face. We made passionate love throughout the night and we have been tight ever since.

The point is that I am gratified to see a man's magazine appreciate the tender relationship that two women can have with each other. I have read your letters from other women saying that they were turned-on by the thought of making it with another gorgeous girl, and I also think that secretly most men would enjoy viewing two beautiful women making it. So here's a vote of confidence from someone who thinks you're the greatest.—*J.N., address withheld*

* * *

My girl friend and I have read several of your letters regarding different types of male chastity devices and believe that we have found an almost foolproof device. My girl believes that no man can be trusted, and that all men require restraints to force themselves to remain true to a single woman. When we first met I promised that I would remain true, and I kept this promise for a full year during which I had the most fantastic sex life imaginable. However, when I did stray, I was given the ultimatum that something had to be done to prevent my ever attempting to stray again. I didn't know what she had in mind but I immediately agreed to her terms. I would have done anything to prevent losing her. I was not to have any sex until she was satisfied that I had been true to her for a month.

As I am not circumcised, it was decided to make use of this foreskin by piercing it and placing a ring through it. The healing was complete and permanent holes formed within a week. During this week my girl observed that I was able to masturbate, which was never to be allowed again either.

Design and construction started with a four-inch by one-inch conical shaped chastity device with the small end having an opening to permit urination. The entire device inside and out was coated with a coarse sand mixed with an epoxy cement thus preventing the wearer from giving or receiving any sexual pleasure while wearing it.

The next problem of attachment proved to be quite simple. The foreskin was threaded with a wire that went through matching holes in the device and was then securely attached to my penis. As this wire could be removed and replaced at ease we had still not arrived at a positive system. Then I remembered the lead seals that are used to seal electrical meters to prevent tampering. The ends of the wires are threaded through the lead seal and then locked in place by a pliers-type tool. We purchased a special tool with her initials in the seal which can't be duplicated. This she keeps in her purse with her at all times.

Finally to her satisfaction, I had a foolproof chastity device. I passed my thirty-day probation, and have been wearing it since which is now more than a year. My girl is very happy with the results and is thoroughly enjoying controlling my sex life. I am a very strong, active, virile male who has to be totally submissive to her or suffer the consequences. She has invented several games where I am forced to perform to her complete satisfaction in order for her to remove what has come to be known as my "Iron Maiden."

I am often forced to disrobe in front of her friends to model the "Iron Maiden" while they attempt to excite me. These girls have been so impressed that their lovers will soon be wearing "Iron Maidens" too.—*T.L., Ottawa, Canada*

* * *

There is one sexual experience I wish to share with my fellow *Penthouse* readers. It was World War II and I was on liberty around Alexandria, Egypa. I believe I must have been up and down all the brothel stairs they had in that city. There was one house in particular I had visited many times because they really had some very attractive bints there. After being with three or four girls there many times, one girl asked me if I would like to try something very different: First, I had to promise not to tell any of my friends, and second, I was told it would cost more money than I had been paying. It sounded really exciting and I agreed.

First she took me to another section of the house that I didn't even know existed. Then she led me through a dark room, and, at her request, a door was opened. This room was brightly lit and quite colorful. Six other girls of all shades and colors rushed to greet me; they proceeded to undress me, all giggling and squealing; finally after they had all my clothes off, they laid me down on some pillows, and all six started kissing me all over my body. I was tremendously hard, and ready for their special surprise. As I was lying down I noticed a basket-type chair tied to the very high ceiling—then the girl who had taken me into the room started maneuvering a cloth rope on a pully and thereby freeing the basket chair to slowly come down. As the chair got close to me, she asked me which girl I would like to sit in this unusual chair which had no bottom on it. I pointed to the girl I liked the most and as she sat in this chair all except one of the other girls went to work the rope. Now there I was laying on my back on top of a bunch of cushions with one girl making sure (lips and tongue) that I had a bone-type hard-on. Then they lowered the girl down in the basket chair. It was designed so that her nice round rear and juicy box was protruding quite far—then, after a few teases, they lowered her down and the girl on the floor guided my joy stick so that it was just entering that magic box. Then they pulled the pully up and down ever so slightly, continuing to tease me. After a few seconds they let her all the way down until my cock was deep inside her.

Now one of the girls spun the girl in the basket chair around, around, and around with almost all of me inside her juicy cunt. When I came I thought I had squirted my belly button, balls and everything else, right through the end of my peter. Anyhow they kept this up until I had come three times. It was so wonderful that as I am writing this I can almost relive it again.—*K.S., Talpa, Mexico*

* * *

I am a professor of Classics at an eastern university and I have never written a letter to *Penthouse* or any similar magazine. Recently I had the opportunity to read through the letters column of one of your magazines and I was struck by two things. I was rather pleasantly impressed by the literary quality of *some* of the letters, and I was rather taken by the striking similarities between some of the sexual revelries that some of your readers partake in, and the rather eclectic sexual romps that abounded in Imperial Rome.

Certainly I am not suggesting that the literary quality of the *Penthouse* letters column is equal to that of the *PMLA*, but I am suggesting that pornography can be literary. When Suetonius tells us about the Emperor Tiberius's "minnows"—little boys who swam naked in the emperor's pools and pinched the emperor's testicles—or about certain rather perverse and sexually cruel punishments that the emperor inflicted on some of his less welcome guests—like tying a cord tightly around a guest's penis and scrotum in order to prevent the victim from relieving himself—we are apt to be more than a little surprised at finding such overtly sexual renditions of events in the works of an honored historian. On the other hand Suetonius may only be an honored historian because of his obviously voyeuristic view of the private lives of the emperors.

Certainly many of your readers can understand not only Tiberius's affinity for his "minnows," but also Suetonius's verve when he tells the story. At another juncture Suetonius refers to Nero as "that little pervert" because Nero enjoyed being flagellated and eating peeled plums from his stepmother's vagina. Upon reflection, it might appear that perhaps Suetonius was being a little hard on Nero; and, if we can give credence to such letters as *Naughty nurses* or *Tantalizing toes* in past issues of *Penthouse*, then history bears us out, not Suetonius.

As to whether these actions, both past and present, are immoral, I can only say immorality is a horribly evasive term which should perhaps be left to rest among the cobwebs of classical ethics. Although many of your readers might not understand the moral significance of Caligula naming his horse the head Consul of the Roman Senate, Caligula might well not understand a *Penthouse* reader's desire to dress up in black-lace panties and high heels, and stand in front of a mirror masturbating. But for Caligula, boredom was rampant. His only true friend, his horse, was reputed to be damned dull, and Caligula, like the rest of us had to find his diversions.

It seems that contemporary man considers himself quite a "sexpert"—that he feels he has tasted of all the forbidden fruits and, perhaps, even discovered some new ones himself. But how mistaken he is. Your *Penthouse* section titled *Monopede mania* may to some seem quite grotesque, but historians have preserved some rather unusual and provocative accounts of Roman soldiers finding themselves peculiarly attracted to one-legged women in villages they had plundered. The positions that some of these Teutonic fräuleins could attain almost borders on the sublime.

Sexual freedom, orgies, spankings—the domain of the modern *Penthouse* reader? Hardly. History tends to reemphasize old patterns of human behavior—and human behavior, in periods of *high civilization*, has always shown a tendency towards the sexually innovative. Why should we presume to greater heights of eroticism than a culture steeped in a decadence that is almost inconceivable?

On the other hand I don't mean to imply that our current twentieth century is sexually a wasteland—on the contrary even my own experience suggests the opposite. Oftentimes in a tutorial with some young vital coed our conversations quickly move from talk of Romulus and Remus or the Gracchi brothers to the more interesting "diversions" of the emperors of Imperial Rome. It seems that many of these young ladies have found the classics more interesting than they had anticipated—all in all they seem to be quite pleasantly pleased that these early records of civilization are replete with some rather titillating episodes. One such coed wanted to act out the rape of the Sabine women with me in my office. Although quite intrigued by the idea, I hesitatingly demurred.—*B.W., address withheld*

* * *

An often debated question is that of the etymology of the word fuck. In your recent issue you commented on the possibility of its derivation from the acronym "For Unlawful Carnal Knowledge." I disagree with this notion on the basis of professional expertise.

A few years ago while I was an undergraduate at Arizona State University majoring in English I took a course in modern grammar, and during this course of study I prepared a paper dealing with the etymology, pronunciation, and definition of the words fuck and shit. Shit is well covered in the *Oxford English Dictionary*, but I could find nothing concerning fuck, not even in Webster's Third International Dictionary, which is today's most authoritative index to the English language as used now.

Having read a number of articles which dealt with the *Webster's Third*, most of them very critical of the editors' practices, I discovered that the word fuck was the only common obscene-slang term left out because of fears that libraries and schools, who are the principal buyers of unabridged dictionaries, would not purchase the dictionary if fuck appeared within. Therefore, I wrote to Mr. H. B. Woolf, editorial director of *Webster's Third*.

The following is quoted from Mr. Woolf's letter (November 1971): "The decision to omit the word from *Webster's Third New International Dictionary* was made in the late 1950's, and we believe that the same decision would not be made today. The acronymic theory of its origin is without foundation. Our etymologists have prepared the following on the basis of our present knowledge:

"perh. of Scand origin; akin to Norw dial. *fukka* to copulate, Sw dial. *focka* to copulate, strike,

    push, *fock* penis; perh. akin to L *pugnus* fist,
    pungere to prick, string Gk *pygme* fist

"The earliest use of the word that has come to our attention is in the writings of the Scottish poet William Dunbar (1460?-?1520). In this connection see Craigie's *Dictionary of the Older Scottish Tongue* s.v. fuk."

So there you have it, about as authoritative as I think you will find for now. And to think that fuck apparently was a poetic word, acceptable in the finest form of literature. Maybe it's on its way back to respectability.
—*Patrick Ivers, Tempe, Ariz.*

* * *

I would like to preface my experience by saying that I am dying to hear other girls' comments, but I'm too embarrassed to inquire among my own friends.

I think I have a rather unusual hang-up and would like to know if other women can relate to me. I have an absolutely uncontrollable appetite for male semen. My boss is a twenty-seven-year-old corporate executive who I can't thank enough for introducing me to oral sex. Here's how it all began.

One rainy afternoon my boss took me to a late lunch, a few drinks, etc., and we decided to take the rest of the afternoon off to go to see *Deep Throat*. While watching Linda Lovelace I got so turned on that I could hardly wait to get him to my car. By the time the show ended I was going crazy with excitement, imagination, hard nipples, sticky panties, etc. Prior to this particular afternoon the only experience I had was giving my boyfriend's cock a little lip service.

When my boss and I got to my car I gave him the keys and told him to drive. We just left the parking lot when I could no longer resist the temptation to suck him. As I unzipped his pants I unveiled the most gorgeous erection I had ever imagined. His flat stomach and thin legs made it look like a skyscraper. After he instructed me to give his cock a tongue bath I began to ease it into my mouth. When he came I was startled until I realized that this was what it was all about. I found myself in a world of ecstasy as the texture and taste of his sperm was the most sensational thing I had ever experienced.

Ever since that beautiful afternoon I have craved the taste of semen. I now give him head at least once a day in his private office. One thing I noticed since taking on a steady diet of semen is that my breasts have enlarged. Is this my imagination?—*Name withheld, Newport Beach, Calif.*

* * *

I recently discovered my oldest boy having very adult, sophisticated sex with a cute neighbor girl who is only eleven-and-a-half. He is twelve years and four months. When I questioned him, he said he had been enjoying intercourse with her for nearly a year and also has had relations with seven other girls. The girl I found him in bed with seduced him—if that is the word for it (at least they both agree she made the first overtures). He accepts sex as part of the new lifestyle, saying sex is what kids do, so he does it.

He is very well developed for his age, in fact has always had a long penis compared to the tight, little ones most boys have. When he started having intercourse he didn't produce any semen but he has been ejaculating for the past four or five months. His father and I know he has been masturbating since he was six or seven years old, and we deliberately haven't discouraged him. His voice hasn't changed yet, his testicles are still small and boyish, and he has only a very little pubic hair which grew quite recently. But apparently he is a real man in bed.

The girl had her first period at ten-and-a-half and still has girlish hips. She has quite noticeable breasts and a thicker pubic patch than our son's. She is proud of her body and her ten other bedpartners (some as old as sixteen). She carries condoms in her purse, including red, green, black, and other colored ones, and makes the boys use them—most of the time—but says, in dead seriousness, that her mother's gynecologist will put her on the Pill soon. The mother more or less confirms this.

None of us really disapproves of our children's sex habits. My husband had sex when he was twelve, but only about once every three months at first, and I had my first intercourse at thirteen-and-a-half. The girl's parents say they started "quite young," so what our kids are doing is just what we did, only one or two years younger. The difference is the regularity and complete acceptance of sex as normal recreation at their age, and their adult approach to stripping down and hopping into bed when the mood strikes. They even do it in broad daylight with any friend of the opposite sex—not as a "date" or someone they have a special liking for, but simply because they enjoy sex. They both expect to keep having sex with new partners the rest of their lives, and can't seem to understand why promiscuity of this kind might be considered bad. Our son just told me, "Aw, Ma, all the kids do it and I like it. What's the big deal about a little fun?"

I'm not asking for advice, since we are adjusting to the kids' lifestyle the only way we can, in effect telling them to go ahead with our blessing. But I do wonder how typical this is elsewhere, or if it is just done in our suburb. Everyone now thinks masturbation is okay, in fact a good things for kids, especially girls. Think what a change this is. My mother would have died a thousand deaths and punished me the worst possible way she could if she had known I masturbated, at any age. I wasn't supposed to know how people had intercourse, let alone do it before I was married.

I think I have indicated we aren't shocked, or disapproving fuddy-duddies. I suppose we are secretly proud of our boy's adjustment and having achieved adult sex status, and a little envious of his full acceptance of sex as normal fun. We would have thought there was something wrong with our son if he hadn't shown a little awkward effort to begin screwing by the time he was thirteen or at the least fourteen, the trend of the times being what it is. The girl's parents say they were prepared to say farewell to her virginity by thirteen, or even twelve, considering her early periods. So neither family feels there is any problem with their uncomplicated sex life, or that any of us should be ashamed of their acquiring sexual expertise and enjoying the wonderful pleasure of sex as early as they have. We really wish we might have done so as easily and as young as they. We all agree on that. There used to be a joke that a girl is "old enough if she's big enough," which of course has a lot of truth in it. But aren't kids also "big enough" if they are "old enough" in the sense of being mentally, socially, and physically prepared by the world they live in? I wonder. For me this is a confusing point.—*Name withheld, Baltimore, Md.*

What do Americans love almost as much as sex? Talking about it. Here, as told in their own, uninhibited words, is the state of the union between men and women today, in all its inventive, eccentric, energetic variety. The sex is unbelievable ... and every word is true!

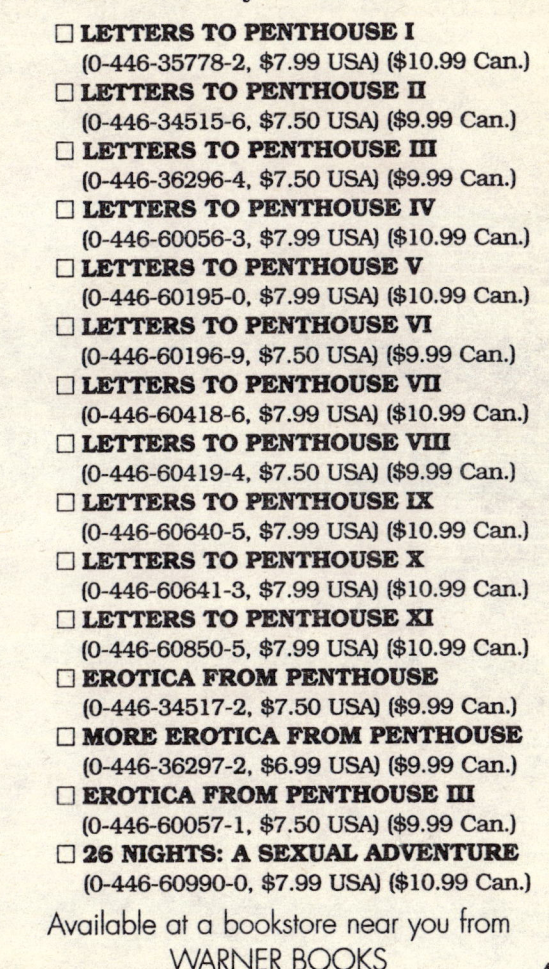

☐ **LETTERS TO PENTHOUSE I**
(0-446-35778-2, $7.99 USA) ($10.99 Can.)

☐ **LETTERS TO PENTHOUSE II**
(0-446-34515-6, $7.50 USA) ($9.99 Can.)

☐ **LETTERS TO PENTHOUSE III**
(0-446-36296-4, $7.50 USA) ($9.99 Can.)

☐ **LETTERS TO PENTHOUSE IV**
(0-446-60056-3, $7.99 USA) ($10.99 Can.)

☐ **LETTERS TO PENTHOUSE V**
(0-446-60195-0, $7.99 USA) ($10.99 Can.)

☐ **LETTERS TO PENTHOUSE VI**
(0-446-60196-9, $7.50 USA) ($9.99 Can.)

☐ **LETTERS TO PENTHOUSE VII**
(0-446-60418-6, $7.99 USA) ($10.99 Can.)

☐ **LETTERS TO PENTHOUSE VIII**
(0-446-60419-4, $7.50 USA) ($9.99 Can.)

☐ **LETTERS TO PENTHOUSE IX**
(0-446-60640-5, $7.99 USA) ($10.99 Can.)

☐ **LETTERS TO PENTHOUSE X**
(0-446-60641-3, $7.99 USA) ($10.99 Can.)

☐ **LETTERS TO PENTHOUSE XI**
(0-446-60850-5, $7.99 USA) ($10.99 Can.)

☐ **EROTICA FROM PENTHOUSE**
(0-446-34517-2, $7.50 USA) ($9.99 Can.)

☐ **MORE EROTICA FROM PENTHOUSE**
(0-446-36297-2, $6.99 USA) ($9.99 Can.)

☐ **EROTICA FROM PENTHOUSE III**
(0-446-60057-1, $7.50 USA) ($9.99 Can.)

☐ **26 NIGHTS: A SEXUAL ADVENTURE**
(0-446-60990-0, $7.99 USA) ($10.99 Can.)

Available at a bookstore near you from
WARNER BOOKS